## Sentinel Rising · Book 2

Crystal Frost

# Praise For Crystal Frost

"I literally could not put the book down and was hooked from page one right till the end. I felt like I was transported into the Sentinel Clan world and was so sad when it ended. My exact thoughts were, okay where is book three."

Anel G. - Moon & Ruin

"Frost had so many twists and turns that I could hardly put Moon & Ruin down. The writing was absolutely captivating! This exciting book included lots of adventure, and even slow moving and clean romance! It was truly a pleasure to read."

- Debbie Barry, NASM Master Trainer - Moon & Ruin

"Very engaging. I couldn't put it down and cannot wait for book no. 2! It transported me to another world. Very descriptive!"

Juli M. - Sun & Blood

"Step into a world of wolven clans where there are rivalries, secrets, personal conflict and triumph, struggle to fit in, and deep relationships. Frost can weave a story for sure!"

Angel C. - Sun & Blood

"There is action, there is romance, there are rivalries, sleepovers, and cookies.An absolute page-turner!"
Janesa Watson - Sun & Blood

"Sun & Blood is a book that will entangle you in the intertwining webs of its story, and will leave you with a burning desire to know what happens next. The adventure I did not expect became an adventure worth experience again and again."
OhMyMuffins (Mikey) - Sun & Blood

"I laughed. I cried. I cheered. I wanted to grab my boxing gloves. I was yanked into this world and fell in love with the characters from the first chapter. I'm excited to see what comes next."
Erin K., Amazon Reviewer - Sun & Blood

# Also by Crystal Frost

Sentinel Rising Trilogy

Sun & Blood

Sentinel Rising · Book 2

Crystal Frost

Moon & Ruin



Printed in the United States of America.



Summary: ***Blood Moon pack grows more aggressive, secrets must be unveiled, and Violet Draven is caught in the middle of it all while trying to figure out what her new abilities mean.***

For information contact :

**http://frostcrystal.com**

Cover and Interior by Crystal Frost

Hardcover ISBN: 978-1-957051-03-1

Softcover ISBN: 978-1-957051-04-8

Ebook ISBN: 978-1-957051-05-5

First Hardcover Edition: May 2023

10 9 8 7 6 5 4 3 2 1

To my Warrior Mom,
This book would not have happened without your encouragement to keep writing through your fight.
You inspire me every day.

# Chapter 1

## Violet

***The rhythmic thump of paws was a*** *battery of bass drums against Violet Draven's ears.* She was grateful to Lexie's family for letting her run with their dog, but sleepless nights had a way of making her head throb and her hearing extra sensitive. Concrete didn't give the same way the ground and underbrush of the forest did, but running was the only training she'd been able to do while staying with Lexie in her sleepy hometown for the last three weeks.

Violet veered into an old playground as the inky night sky gave way to the light blue of a new day, clicking at her canine companion to follow her lead. The Aussiedoodle never had a problem following Violet's commands—Thor would have followed her even without a command or even a leash—but Lexie complained about the dog having trouble staying on task. Violet guessed the animal sensed whatever wolven blood she possessed but to respect the training Lexie's family had been working on with Thor, Violet followed their rules.

Her phone buzzed in the pocket of her lime green leggings, and she pulled it out just in time to see the "shutting down" notification. With a shake of her head, she slid the device back into her pocket. She'd forgotten to charge her phone the night before but had hoped it would last through her run. Guess not. But, with just over a mile remaining, she'd be back at

Lexie's house in no time.

Violet closed her eyes briefly when she stepped off the concrete path and the soft earth beneath the dewy grass gave under her feet. The brisk morning air filled her lungs when she drew in a deep breath, and she scrunched her nose. Spring was right around the corner, but instead of fresh sprigs and blossoming flowers to assault her nose, the heavy perfume scent of humans clung to everything and their garbage was everywhere.

She missed the smell of the forest, even if this time of year brought wolven-sized allergies.

Her heart sank.

There were a lot of things she missed.

She missed the familiar routine of life on the wolven base.

She missed her bed.

She missed her mom, Jax, Mya, Aiden, and Patrick.

She did *not* miss her father, Alpha Draven, or the looks her clanmates had given her when word about her witch abilities had spread.

After Vikter's horrific murder of Patrick's neighbors, Jax followed orders and debriefed their father on everything he knew... including her dream. Or vision. Or premonition. Or whatever it was. No one had an exact name for it, but they knew it wasn't *wolven.*

When her twin had finished explaining everything he could, Alpha Draven turned on Violet.

"No daughter of mine would have witch abilities."

"I'm not a witch!" Violet had insisted as betrayal etched into her heart.

Alpha Draven's startling ombre-blue eyes had narrowed to slits and he'd thrust a finger in her direction. "No wolven can do what you've been doing!"

"But I am wolven." The words felt like acid on her tongue. It wasn't the truth, but it wasn't a lie either. "I have the genetic markers."

Dr. Penmann had run test after test, and drew vial after vial of Violet's blood, to figure out why Violet didn't have a wolf spirit and how she'd survived. In the wolven community, only the stronger twin lived. The other always passed away shortly after birth.

Alpha Draven snorted and his lips curled back in disgust. "That's not the only thing in your blood. Whatever you are, whatever you have become, you are not my daughter."

His words haunted her and his actions toward her grew more aggressive.

With the help of Violet's mom, Luna of the clan, a plan had been made and Violet left for Lexie's house under the guise that the two girls would be scouting colleges.

Violet hoped the distance would help.

It didn't.

Nightmares plagued her every attempt to sleep, and the fight with her father ran through her brain during the quiet hours of the day when she was alone. Which was often. Lexie still had school and her parents had work.

After three weeks, Violet was still at a loss for answers regarding her new ability. Doc had no more information to give, but promised to keep searching. She'd tried to pry information from her mom, but Evalyn Draven grew suspiciously quiet, or would change the topic, and Violet found herself growing angrier and angrier at the unknowns.

She knew she wouldn't find answers in the human world, but other than reporting to Jax when she had another nightmare-vision-thing, she also didn't have any expectations hovering over her. No one knew what she was, except Lexie. No one knew she was the alpha's daughter and should have some pretty impressive abilities. She fit in with humans. After all, aside from her heightened senses and weird prophetic power, she basically was one.

A rustling in the nearby trees extracted Violet from her thoughts at the same time her fluffy, gray-marbled canine companion turned his head. The sun ascending over the horizon, combined with the street lights ahead, made her vision clear as midday, but she still couldn't see through the bushes.

"What is it, Thor?" Violet quietly asked, while keeping her feet moving.

Talking to the animal had become an odd comfort for Violet. Even though she couldn't actually communicate with Thor, it felt good to voice her troubles. She wasn't expecting the dog to growl in response.

Thor's hackles lifted, and he licked his lips, which had curled back to bare his teeth—clear warning signs.

A spike of nerves shot through Violet and she picked up their pace. A minute or so later, they were back on the sidewalk racing past houses on the last mile to Lexie's house.

Another thing she missed—being able to run at her wolven speed. To be able to push her lungs and legs to the limit as she raced through the trees. And even though she rarely saw another person during her runs, she didn't want to risk the unwanted attention that exposure would bring. Lexie had let Violet borrow her fitness watch to track her pace to make sure she was running at an acceptable speed, but it only took a couple of runs for her to get into a rhythm and find a pace Thor could sustain.

They crossed a street and Violet startled when another runner came into view. Over the last three weeks, she hadn't seen a single runner along their path. He was headed down the crossroad so they wouldn't be going the same direction, but after being spooked in the park, Violet's metaphorical hackles were raised.

Keeping the runner in the corner of her eye, Violet pushed Thor to run a little faster to drive more distance between them and the new guy.

"Not much longer, pup." Violet patted the dog's head mid-stride. "Almost home."

She turned to check that the guy had indeed crossed the street, then nearly jumped into Thor.

He was behind her with less than twenty feet separating them.

She could see no discernible features beneath his long-sleeved black athletic shirt, black joggers, black neck gator, and black beanie. Even his hands were covered by black gloves. What was with this guy and black clothing? Especially while running at night!

Violet looked at the sky. Sure, the stars were slipping out of sight as the sun conquered the darkness, but it had been dark only a couple of minutes ago.

Turning her head again, she sucked in a sharp breath, throwing off her breathing pattern. The guy had gained a few feet on them and the tension through his body radiated ill will.

Offering a silent prayer that Thor would be okay, Violet darted down the next street at the last second and increased her speed. Her long, rich-brown ponytail flung over her shoulder when she looked behind to see if the guy had followed.

His dark form skidded through the turn and a frantic breath filled her lungs.

There was no pretending now.

He was chasing her.

Without her clan, without her brother to call on, and her phone acting as a useless weight in her pocket—she was completely on her own. She couldn't return to Lexie's with a stalker on her trail, but Thor was beginning to drag at her current pace. Thankfully Lexie's family had taught him to "go home", but she had to get him to an area they'd worked on.

She turned down another road, taking a roundabout path to get closer to Lexie's without telling the guy where her friend lived. Garbage cans lined the street, full and ready to be picked up. Another look over her shoulder told her the guy had gained another couple of feet on her and Thor couldn't run any faster. As she passed the next garbage can, she snagged the handle and flung the hunk of plastic behind her.

The whisper of a curse sounded over the thundering of her heart.

She flung another garbage can behind her, but the trick didn't work a second time. Her stalker had fallen far enough behind with the first trash can that he flew over the next obstacle like he was a star track athlete and it was just another hurdle.

Violet turned down another street into the zone Lexie's family had worked on with Thor and tossed the leash away. "Go home, Thor!"

The Aussiedoodle darted to the right and fell out of sight, disappearing behind a row of tall junipers. Without her canine friend to slow her down, Violet leaned into her wolven speed. It was dangerous to expose her abilities in an area full of humans, but most were still asleep.

And the stalker was still after her.

She ran for a street that she knew would take her into the small town's center. Hopefully, she would be able to lose the guy in an alleyway.

Thankfully, running was one gift she seemed to retain from her wolven genetics. She was fast. Really fast. In fact, she was one of the first to arrive at the Natural Bridges when Patrick, Aiden, and she had worked to bring down Vikter Stravek—the former future alpha of Stanislaus Clan.

Unfortunately, this guy was fast, too.

The small housing complex fell away to a single road lined by trees, and Violet stepped off the road in favor of the coverage the trees could offer. Hopefully, if any cars drove by, they wouldn't notice the two people running at breakneck speeds. The human government already knew of the existence of wolven, and while they allowed the clans to operate on their own, they'd painted a very clear picture of what would happen if the rest of the world became aware of them. The experimental and/or extinction event was not worth the risk of being seen.

Every move Violet made, Stalker Guy countered or mimicked.

She dodged a tree. So did he.

She threw a branch behind her. He avoided it.

When she made a beeline for the back alley of the quiet main street, the guy cut the corner, gaining a few feet as he did so.

Darting into the small space between two buildings, Violet flinched against the heavy stench of coffee in the air. Its potent smell was enough to overpower the trash can she used as a stepping stone to ascend a dumpster, and then leap for the fire escape. If she could get up and then pull the ladder out of his reach, maybe she could lose him.

Cold metal met her hand and she curled her fingers around the rung to pull herself up.

A heavy weight slammed into her torso, knocking the air from her lungs as her hand was ripped away from her salvation. The momentum from the added weight accelerated her descent, and she wondered briefly if she'd survive being smushed into the ground by the anvil wrapped around her body. She never had the chance to find out. Moments before she hit the asphalt, her attacker twisted his body to take the brunt of the fall.

Stalker Guy groaned when they landed in a heap in the middle of the darkened alleyway. Gravel dug into Violet's exposed flesh, but her lungs seized on impact and the need for air made her head throb.

Her lungs released and a flood of oxygen filled her in one large breath. Her head and nearly half her body had landed atop the guy, but the areas that had hit the ground cried out when she turned in Stalker Guy's arm. She pushed off his sternum, making him groan a second time, and rose out of his hold and returned to her feet.

She tried to catch his scent to identify where he was from, but the coffee odor was all-consuming.

"Who are you?" Violet asked, curling her hands into fists and ignoring the complaint of tender flesh from one of her hands. "What do you want?"

Slowly rolling into a seated position, Stalker Guy grabbed the back of his head.

Had he hurt himself when he'd twisted to take the impact of the fall? Violet was torn between roundhouse kicking his head or letting him stand. "Why didn't you just squish me?"

When he moved into a crouch without answering, she wished she'd just kicked him.

It was too late now. He was back on his feet, easily standing a foot taller than her, and it was obvious his head wasn't hurting him badly enough to stop him.

Violet cursed herself for standing around and turned to bolt, but gloved fingers snatched her shirt.

She wasn't going to get away. She wasn't going to outrun him.

It was time to draw attention and fight back.

She screamed. High and loud.

It tore at her throat until his other hand clamped over her mouth. He shoved her back against the nearest wall.

Breathing deep through her nose, Violet steadied herself and then grabbed his wrist near her mouth. She ducked under his arm, spinning away from the hand holding her shirt, came around full circle, and drove her fist into his side. He grunted, dropped his elbows so his sides were protected, then stepped toward her.

She darted around him, but his arm struck out, glancing a cross punch over the front of her shoulder. Off-centered, Violet staggered and took a few steps back. Movement from the end of the alley made her freeze, but Stalker Guy kept coming. He snagged her arm, making her suck in a sharp breath when his fingers grazed over a painful spot, then grabbed her waist and tried to corner her once more.

"Hey! Leave her alone!" yelled a man from the end of the alley.

Stalker Guy hesitated and a triumphant grin flicked across Violet's lips despite her pounding heart.

He wasn't about to risk exposing them.

A low growl rolled off him when the man started rushing toward them and Stalker Guy released her to back away. Maintaining the secret of wolven and lycan existence was one of the primary rules. He could have easily taken the human man out, but an unexplained death this close to the clan, in a quiet small town would lead to too many questions.

The man was almost upon them. "I'm calling the cops!"

And cops would lead to even more questions and an investigation.

Stalker Guy rushed out of the alley, back the way they'd come, without another glance at her.

Weathered copper skin complimented the warm brown of her rescuer's eyes as he approached her with caution. "Are you all right, miss?" he asked. "Did he hurt you?"

Violet slumped against the wall, forcing herself to breathe deeper than she needed to keep up appearances. She lowered her chin and shook her head. "No, no. I'm okay. Thanks to you." She sucked in a sharp breath and then looked at her savior. "I don't know what would've happened if you hadn't heard me."

The truth of that statement shot a bolt of fear through her body.

If Stalker Guy hadn't softened her fall, if he'd attacked her instead of trying to capture her, if he'd killed this kind man instead of running away... there was so much that could have gone differently. Given his speed and strength, and the fact that she was alone, it could have ended very badly.

"I'm glad I did." The man's words pulled her out of her spiraling thoughts, and it took her a second to realize what he was talking about.

Yes, he had heard her. None of those things had happened. He had heard her. Her hands started trembling and a chill settled over her.

Concern flickered across the man's gaze. "Don't worry. You're safe." He looked toward the back of the alley where Stalker Guy had disappeared. "What are you doing out here this early anyway? Shouldn't you be at home getting ready for school?"

Violet shrugged a weary shoulder. Her adrenaline was beginning to wear off. "I was out for a run with my dog when that guy came out of nowhere and started chasing me. I came down the back of the alley to..." she eyed the dumpster and fire escape and shook her head at the crazy plan she'd thought up. He'd never believe it. "I was trying to get to the main street, but he tackled me," she partially lied. A deep sting drew her gaze to her arm and she turned it to see a four-inch-long road rash glaring back at her; red, angry, and bleeding. No wonder it had hurt when Stalker Guy had grabbed her there.

"Oof, that's gonna hurt to clean out. Come on, I'm sure the coffee shop has a first aid kit." He looked over his shoulder, gesturing with his thumb, and the light of the morning caught in his lightly-peppered brown hair. "Looks like you took quite the tumble. We can get you cleaned up while we wait for the cops."

Violet looked down at herself. Dirt covered her clothes and there was a tear in her leggings by her knee, exposing more angry skin. The pinky side of her hand had gravel and dirt darkening her red road rash.

Shaking her head, she looked at the man. "There's no need to call the cops. I'm mostly okay and wouldn't have anything to tell them anyway. The guy was big and tall, but was covered from head to toe." She headed toward the main street with the guy following closely beside her. "I'd better find my dog, though."

"What happened to it?"

"I let go of his leash to try and run faster. He was afraid of the guy."

"I think you need a new dog to run with."

There was no point in telling him that any dog would have been afraid of her stalker. Dogs usually had one of two reactions toward wolven; Feel threatened and attack, or submit and become a loyal lap dog.

They exited the darkened alleyway and he squinted against the morning sun. "Are you sure you don't want me to call the cops?"

Violet shook her head. "No, it's okay. Thank you, though."

"Can I at least get you a cup of coffee for your nerves?"

She couldn't stop herself. Her face scrunched with disgust and she visibly shuddered.

He lifted a questioning brow.

"Sorry," she muttered. "I can't stand coffee. The smell is way too strong; I can't imagine what it would taste like."

"I'm guessing that means you don't want to venture inside to get the first aid kit either?"

Raising one shoulder, Violet took a step in the direction she needed to be going. "I don't live far from here. I'll clean up as soon as I get home."

"If you're sure?" Her affirming nod brought a soft smile to the man's face. "All right, why don't I give you my number just in case you need help finding that dog of yours?"

She breathed through her teeth and pulled her phone from her pocket. As if being dead hadn't been enough, spiderweb cracks now riddled the screen. Of course, it'd been on the side of her body that hit the ground.

"Um..."

The man whistled. "I'm guessing that happened when he tackled you?"

Violet sighed. "My dad's gonna kill me."

"I bet he'll just be happy that you're okay." He unlocked his phone. "Do you want to call him?"

She blinked at him. "I don't have his number memorized." Truly, she'd never had her father's cell number, but she'd never bothered to memorize her mom's either. It was on her phone. She'd never thought to remember it.

He eyed her as if she'd lost it. "I suggest you memorize a few contacts so you can call people even when your cell is dead."

"Yeah, I'll make sure to do that." She tightened her ponytail and offered a small smile. "Thanks again for coming to my rescue."

He waved her off as she ran onto the street, maintaining a normal, human pace.

By the time Lexie's hunter-green family home came into view, Violet was pretty sure she'd run close to ten miles. She'd wanted to run straight to Lexie's, but making sure no one was following her was important, too. Once she was certain it was safe, she'd found the familiar home and let out a giant relieved sigh.

The leaves on the hip-height hedges were soft against the back of her hand as she dragged her feet across the stepping stones lining the right side of the driveway. Her legs were jello, and for the first time in nearly a week, she thought she could actually sleep.

But sleep was going to have to wait. The second Violet stepped onto the driveway; Lexie burst out of the house. Still in her pink llama pajamas with her white-blonde hair falling out of a messy bun, her best friend nearly tackled her.

"Oh my gosh, are you okay?" Lexie panicked, throwing her arms around Violet's neck in a quick hug. "When Thor started pawing at the door to be let inside, I was so scared something bad had happened to you."

"Well," Violet drew out the word then bit her lip when Lexie stepped back to look her over from head to toe. Her friend lingered at the road rash on her arm until Violet waved her off. "I'm okay, but I was followed and attacked."

"What?" Lexie shrieked.

"Shh." Violet turned her head to see if anyone on the small residential street was outside, but they were the only two people as far as she could see. With her attention back on Lexie, she held her palms up in a settling gesture. "It's okay. I'm okay. But it was weird. I don't think he was actually trying to hurt me."

Lexie planted her fists on her hips—a move Violet noticed Lexie's mother did as well. "He chased you down, attacked you, and you feel like he wasn't trying to hurt you?"

Violet shrugged. "If he wanted to hurt me there would have been more of a fight. It was more like he was trying to grab me. The one punch he threw landed, but it was pulled back and glanced off my shoulder."

"He punched you?" Lexie's shoulders pulled back and she stomped into Violet's space, towering over her at a staggering height of 5'10". "Did you recognize him? Smell him? Can we track this sucker down and sic Jax and Patrick on him?"

"Whoa!" Violet planted her hands on her friend's heaving shoulders and gently directed her toward the house. "I think we need to lower our voices and talk about this inside."

Lexie threw her arms out against the door frame, keeping them from going inside. “Okay, but Mom hasn’t left yet so—”

“Then this conversation will have to wait, won’t it?” Violet shoved her friend through the door before following her.

Thor greeted Violet with happy yips and a frantically wagging back end the moment she walked in and shut the door. “Hey, boy. I’m glad you made it home. That was smart for your humans to teach you that. Yes, it was.”

“Stop talking to him like that,” Lexie grumbled, watching Violet’s display of affection to Thor, who was now on his back getting a nice belly scratch. “Seriously, why doesn’t he love me like that? Is it a dog thing?”

Violet shot Lexie an exasperated look. “I’m not a dog. He just knows I’m the alpha here.”

“Do all dogs treat you like this? You could be the next Dog Whisperer.”

“That would be a bad idea,” Violet explained while patting Thor’s belly. “Some dogs would attack the moment I made eye contact with them.”

“That doesn’t make—”

“Violet!” Lexie’s mom hurried toward them with a stack of papers in her arms. Unlike her daughter, Mrs. Davis was about Violet’s same height. She did, however, have the same platinum blond hair as Lexie and stunning cheekbones. Even though she didn’t have the model height, the older woman seemed to have legs for days and the fact that she always wore heels made that illusion even greater. “I’m so glad you made it home safe. Lexie said you must have lost Thor at one point, and she was so worried. Do you really have to run so early in the morning?”

Violet accepted Mrs. Davis’ one-armed hug before answering. “It’s nice to be up before everyone else, but I can run later in the day if it worries you that much. Thor just got too excited and took off without me.” Another lie. There’d been too many lately, but she couldn’t tell Lexie’s family the truth. It was bad enough that Lexie knew. Violet looked at Thor who had happily planted himself at her feet. “I’m glad he ran home. And thanks again for the running clothes. I’ll make sure to pay you back.”

“I already told you that isn’t necessary. You couldn’t run in the dark with your usual workout gear.” Mrs. Davis smiled and then shifted her weight to one side and propped her papers on her hip. “I’m glad you’re home safe.

You girls have a busy day ahead of you touring the college. This is your last one, right?"

Both girls nodded.

"That's exciting. I'm not trying to sway your opinion, but I think this is the best one."

Lexie snorted. "That's because it's the closest one."

Mrs. Davis winked at her daughter. "I'm allowed to want my baby girl close to home. I can't wait to hear all about it when I get home tonight."

Violet eyed the stack of papers in the woman's arms, then glanced at the sunburst clock on the wall. It was barely 7 am. "Are you off to work?"

"Yup. Harold already left for the office and, unfortunately, this stack of papers won't grade themselves. I work better in my classroom, and you two need to get going soon anyway." She rose on her toes and kissed Lexie on the cheek. "Good luck today, girls. Be safe and keep in touch."

Both Violet and Lexie answered, "Okay."

With a little wave, Mrs. Davis walked out the garage door.

"Seriously, how early did you get up today?" Lexie asked.

Violet held a finger to her lips and listened to Mrs. Davis's heels click to the car as the garage opened. Once the car was gone and the garage closed, she nodded for Lexie to continue. Her friend repeated the question and Violet sighed. She rubbed her eye, then looked disgusted at the dirt on her fingers. "I'm not really sure. I only know I slept because of the reoccurring nightmare and then another dream... or vision... I had."

"Another one?" Lexie followed her into the kitchen and leaned her hip against the counter while Violet washed her hands. "Did you tell Jax?"

Violet nodded. "As soon as I woke up. He told me I was being paranoid and that it was unlikely an attack would happen again so soon after the last one."

"That jerk," Lexie grumbled. "Seriously, the next time I see him—"

"He's just doing his job, Lexie." Violet shook her head while she dried her hands. "He still reported to Alpha Draven, and I'm sure they will be extra defensive, but it's not like these visions are precise or anything."

"Really? They sure seem that way to me. You had one the night Vikter killed those two guys. Every time you have a vision, it usually comes true within a day."

Violet's brows pulled together. "I didn't realize you were keeping such close tabs on my new weird ability."

"Someone has to," Lexie answered softly. "I know you say it's okay to be out on your own, but I've seen the toll it's taking on you. At least in the base, you'd be safe and be able to rest when you got tired."

Sorrow dragged Violet's shoulders down. "My lack of sleep has nothing to do with whether I feel safe here or not. I know it's a risk being away from the clan, but both my mom and I felt a little space would be good." She sighed and smiled sadly. "And I know I'm putting your family in more danger the longer I stay."

Lexie opened her mouth, but Violet held up a hand to stop her.

"Whether you say it's okay or not doesn't change that. I am. I'm going back to the base tonight." She started toward Lexie's room and her friend was hot on her heels. There hadn't been much of a threat other than Violet staying there, but now there was someone after her.

"Do you think the guy that chased you would come here?" Lexie asked after easily catching up with her extra-long legs.

Violet turned into the hallway bathroom and ducked down to pull the first aid kit from under the sink. "Since he found me on my running route, I'm sure he has an idea of where I'm staying, but I always make sure I'm not followed back here. I can't guarantee he doesn't know, though, which is why I need to leave. If I'm not here, he should leave you alone, and your safety is more important than my fight with my dad."

"Is that why you haven't been sleeping?" Lexie asked as she stood in the bathroom doorway. "Because you're worried about my safety?"

Taking a moment to gather her thoughts, Violet pulled what she needed from the kit. At least the road rash on her hand had healed to pink. It was a minor scrape, so it would heal quickly. Her knee probably still needed some attention, and her arm definitely did.

A quick look out of the corner of her eye told her that Lexie was growing impatient waiting for an answer, but how could she tell her friend that she was terrified to sleep? When she'd first arrived, Violet had been worried about being found out, and when she wasn't awake because of that, she was having nightmares of Vikter's attack or visions of Sentinel Clan being attacked. But as time went on, and the possibility of threat lessened, she'd started to feel safe. She even felt like she was fitting in with the humans. If it weren't for the nightmares, she probably would have started sleeping better, but the intensity of her premonitions had grown and the images that flashed through her mind were horrific. This morning had proven all of her worries true.

"You know you kinda stopped talking to me about stuff, right?" Lexie's gentle voice broke through Violet's thoughts and the taller girl stepped into the bathroom. She took the cleaning spray and some gauze and eyed Violet's arm. "You used to tell me everything."

Violet flinched as the spray burned her arm and Lexie dragged the gauze across the road rash. "I'm always worried about your safety, but if I've learned one thing about you, it's that I can't stop you from doing anything. We tried to deter you from learning about the existence of wolven when you started getting suspicious of me in middle school, but the more we pushed the harder you pushed back."

The reflection of Lexie's smirk in the mirror made Violet shake her head. Of course, her friend would be proud of that.

"You made a whole clan give you special clearance because you poking your nose around would have been more dangerous than just telling you and trying to protect you," Violet continued. "You break rules every day by being my friend. You snuck into one of the Clan Games and practically taunted a Blood Moon pack member. If me not telling you things can increase your safety even by a fraction, then that's what I'll do."

Lexie glared at her through the mirror and then aggressively sprayed Violet's arm again. "That's dumb. You just listed a bunch of reasons why my safety is screwed, and I still don't care. And not telling me makes me worry."

"Not telling you leaves you with deniability," Violet countered. She growled when Lexie made another swipe across her arm, but then she pushed Violet's elbow out to the side so she could help wrap up her injury. "If you were ever captured, they would be able to tell if you were telling the truth. Wolven make some of the best lie detectors because if they concentrate, they can hear your pulse, which always gives away a liar."

Lexie snorted as she finished wrapping Violet's arm then crossed her arms over her chest. "Your idea of deniability really sucks, you know that? As you *just* said, I already know way more than I should, and I already know you have some witchy-prophetic visions."

The word *witch* made Violet flinch.

"Sorry," Lexie whispered.

Violet shook her head and set about cleaning up her knee. She set her foot on the closed toilet and ripped the hole in her leggings even more to make room. "I should probably get over being called a witch. It's not normal for wolven to be able to do what I can do."

"Maybe, but your dad—"

"Isn't here," Violet interrupted, then slapped a large band-aid over her knee. She clenched her jaw shut to keep from snapping at Lexie. The anger Violet felt toward Alpha Draven had nothing to do with Lexie. Violet forced herself to take deep breaths and closed her eyes for a moment. She refused to take her emotional turmoil out on her best friend.

When she opened her eyes, Lexie was staring at her with one brow raised. Silently, the two girls worked together to put the first aid kit away and then walked to Lexie's room.

A twin-sized air mattress had been set up for Violet alongside Lexie's bed. They'd pushed the two together the first night and there it had stayed. As always, Violet's bed was made tidily. Lexie was like Jax who left the blankets looking like a tornado blew through them, but her room was clean. The comparison to her twin brought an ache into Violet's heart that she promptly pushed away. She'd see him tonight.

With a sigh, Violet sank onto her air mattress. Lexie's picture mural over her desk stared back at her. It was one of Violet's favorite parts of her friend's room. So many of the pictures were times they'd shared, but there were others with Lexie's human friends as well. It was fun to see some of their memories captured and displayed. When they first became friends, Violet wouldn't allow pictures. Any flash photography made wolven eyes luminescent and not only could that be dangerous for exposure purposes, but it often ruined the picture. It wasn't until a couple of years ago that

Lexie convinced Violet she could still take a good photo without a flash. Now there were pictures of them together everywhere in Lexie's home.

The hurricane of emotions that had been rising settled at the visual evidence of her friend's love. "You're right, you know way more than you should," Violet gently told her friend as she turned to look up at Lexie's gorgeous porcelain complexion. "And not telling you things may not help at all, but it's all I can do. You would break down the clan gates if I tried to stop being your friend—"

"Darn right," Lexie snorted.

A small smile tugged at the corners of Violet's mouth. "And, even though you know I'm having premonitions, you don't totally know what they are about. Or why I have them."

Lexie crossed her arms. "Neither do you."

Violet nodded. "You're right, but when I find out, I don't know if I'm going to tell you. I'm already the weird twin that survived. These visions are just another thing to put a target on my back. Finding out why could make that target even bigger. Not knowing could keep you safe and alive, and that's more important to me than even our friendship."

The tension between Lexie's pinched brows relaxed and after a moment she sank onto the foot of her bed and sighed, "I don't agree with you, but I think I understand. I also don't want to fight because I'm really excited about touring the college today and I want to have fun." She snagged the brochure off her desk and wiggled it in front of her. "So, are you ready for this college?"

Violet would forever be amazed at how Lexie could set aside one matter and cling to another. It was a unique talent. One she desperately needed to feed off of. When Lexie started jumping up and down with excitement, Violet's lips tipped up into a smile.

Her friend's energy was practically oozing out of her.

Violet chuckled. "Yeah. I think this college might be the one."

"Close to home, but not too close. Business degree. On *or* off-campus housing." Lexie clapped enthusiastically, wrinkling the college brochure. "I think we saved the best for last. Hurry up and get ready so we can go. You can fill me in on everything else while we drive."

Lexie snagged an armful of clothes from her drawer and rushed toward the bathroom, closing the bedroom door behind her. As soon as the door clicked shut, Violet's smile slipped from her face. No matter how much Lexie said she understood, Violet knew her friend would keep pushing for information... and not telling her was going to hurt Lexie sooner or later.

# Chapter 2

## Violet

***The smell of the college** campus reminded Violet of coffee.*

Probably because nearly every person they passed was holding some sort of coffee mug, cup, flask, thermos, and so on.

"Midterms. Lexie clicked her tongue. "It's gotta be that time."

Violet tipped her head to the side. "Why?"

"That lingering smell of coffee everywhere we go doesn't clue you in?" Lexie teased as she skipped ahead and walked backward for a few steps.

Violet tugged her messenger bag over her head to the other shoulder as she stared at the large main building. "Are you forgetting I've been home-schooled the last couple of years and was very sheltered before that?"

"Pssh." Lexie fell back into step beside Violet as they passed under a large oak tree. "Compared to a lot of people, you've seen a whole lot more."

"Let's not get into that right now while we are surrounded by people who don't know me."

"Fair enough." Lexie called out to a coffee cart vendor as he rolled toward his next stop. He happily waited and moved into position to take his next order. "I'll have a caramel frap, please, heavy on the whip." She looked back at Violet whose eyes bugged.

"What are you looking at me for? I have no idea what to order. Coffee doesn't mix well with..." Violet pinched her lips together. "Uh... my family."

Lexie laughed and shook her head. "How about a hot chocolate?"

Hot chocolate was usually reserved for talks with her mom... who hadn't spoken to her much lately. Her stomach turned, but she found herself saying, "Sure."

Violet turned her back on the vendor to look up at the giant building once again. She wondered what it would be like to permanently live in the dorms or somewhere close by off-campus. Visiting Lexie had given her an idea, but she was only visiting. It would be different if she actually lived here.

She would make it a priority to visit her family on the base at least every two weeks. And calls with her mom wouldn't be so short and tense. Maybe Jax would send her more than the occasional quick mind-link message with more topics than just her visions. She and Mya could plan girl's nights instead of relying on only a handful of calls and messages. And Patrick... Anything would be better than what she had now. Which was nothing. Violet hadn't heard from him at all.

Jax told her she was missed.

Mya told her she was missed.

Mom told her she was missed and loved.

Despite all their words, Violet felt neither missed nor loved.

Wolven often talked about an emptiness that settled in their gut if they were ever without their clan too long or on their own. They were pack animals. Kinship drove nearly everything they did. Which was why many lone wolven eventually lost their minds.

Violet understood the protection of the clan, and had missed it when Stalker Guy attacked her, but she didn't have the connection other members of the clan had. She didn't have a wolf spirit, she didn't have the clan-link—only the twin-mind-link-thing—she missed the people she saw every day, but according to Lexie, that was normal even for humans. The only gaping hole she felt was the one Patrick had left her with, but that was heartbreak, not the loss of a clan.

It both relieved and unsettled her to realize she didn't feel what other wolven had experienced. It was one more thing to prove she wasn't wolven, and that list did *not* need to get any longer.

Sighing, Violet drew in a deep breath, but instead of settling her unraveling emotions, the intense coffee odor made her nose scrunch. She'd have to get used to that if she was going to live away from the clan.

"Here ya go." Lexie passed Violet a steaming cup, interrupting her thought process, then tucked her wallet back into her purse. "You're buying lunch."

Violet laughed. "When was breakfast?"

"Mmm." Lexie sipped her drink. "For a college student, this is breakfast."

"Yeah, well. I'm gonna have to grab something else." Violet grinned at Lexie and followed her down the sidewalk. "Gotta keep this stomach from growling like an animal."

Lexie snorted, then held her nose. "Ow! Ow. Drink. In. Nose."

Violet winced. "Sorry! Uh..." She looked around for the vendor, but the coffee guy had wandered off and she didn't see another one in sight. How'd he move so fast?

"I need a napkin," Lexie's feet did a quick little stomp dance and Violet could only imagine how uncomfortable her friend was.

"Uh..." Violet took a few more steps down the sidewalk, still looking.

"Heard someone needed a napkin?"

A hand landed on Violet's shoulder. She spun around, grabbing the guy's wrist.

"Woah! Easy, fighter!" The stranger laughed and broke through her grip—a little too easily. She may not be wolven strong, but she was definitely stronger than any human. His green eyes sparked with amusement before he lifted his other hand. "I have an extra napkin."

Tension filled Violet's neck as she breathed a little heavily. "Right." She hurriedly apologized, snagged the napkin, and rushed to give it to Lexie, who then shooed Violet away so she could blow her nose in peace.

"Is she okay?" the stranger asked, looking over Violet's head.

His height was easy to guess, considering it matched a lot of guys in the clan. He was probably 6'4" -ish, which made Violet have to crane her neck back just a touch less than she had to with Patrick. A sharp sting hit her heart and she shoved all thoughts of her twin brother's best friend away.

"Yeah, she just... I mean, I..." Violet blew out a breath, making some of her hair fly into the air before it fell back into her face. "I said something that made her snort coffee."

He winced and grabbed the strap of his messenger bag. "Ah, well that does happen sometimes." A familiar spark of gold lit the center of his eyes when he looked back at her.

Patrick's eyes had gold in the center, too.

Violet looked away when longing punched her in the gut. She cleared the knot of emotions from her throat and said, "Thanks for coming to the rescue and all that." Forcing a polite smile to her face, she lifted her gaze to his once again. "I'm sure Lexie will appreciate her napkin hero once her nose stops burning."

His face lit up and a small laugh escaped him. "Yeah, it's no problem."

He started to walk away, but Violet stepped toward him, realizing he also might be able to solve her food problem. "Hey, um..."

He looked back at her with a raised brow.

"Sorry, I'm sure you have somewhere else to be, but we're new on campus and don't know where anything is. Do you know somewhere I could get some real food?" She shook her drink, which she hadn't even sipped. "I'm sure this is good and all, but I eat a lot of food and this isn't going to cut it."

Warm, rich laughter left him as he shook his head. "Most girls wouldn't admit that."

"Crap." Realizing her mistake, Violet laughed, and a flush of warmth filled her cheeks. "You're right! I am definitely not like most girls."

His mirth subsided and he eyed the surrounding area before stepping toward her, dipping his chin. "No, you sure aren't." Without warning, silver swallowed his green eyes.

Violet gasped and jumped back. She clamped her hand over her mouth while she blinked at him.

He grinned as his eyes shifted back.

"How did you know?" she whispered, closing the distance between them until they were nearly toe to toe. "I could have been human."

"People like us tend to carry ourselves a little differently."

"Really?" She tilted her head to one side as she thought about that. "Huh, I've never noticed."

He mimicked her head tilt. "How many times have you ventured away from home?"

"Admittedly, not many." Violet shrugged. "We're just checking out the campus to see if I… uh… we want to go here or not."

"Interesting." His gaze rose over Violet's head and she turned to see what he was looking at. Lexie was sitting on a bench with her phone to her ear while she rubbed her nose with the napkin. "Initially I thought she was one of us too, but… she's human."

It wasn't a question and held no inflection of offense or disgust… which bothered her. Every wolven reacted to her friendship with Lexie. Most were negative reactions.

She tried to keep the glare off her face but felt her eyes pinching ever so slightly. "How do you know that? And why does that matter?"

He shrugged and gave her a blank stare with one raised eyebrow. "Because relationships between our kind and theirs are a bit tricky. And, to be blunt, humans stink."

Violet snorted. "That's not nice."

"You haven't noticed?" His other brow lifted to match the first one while he stared at her like she was an enigma he wanted to solve.

"Well, I mean…" Truthfully, she *had* noticed. It just wasn't polite to say. Humans always smelled like super heavy perfume. Then when they actually *wore* perfume or cologne, it stung her eyes, nose, and throat. Feeling a little guilty, Violet ducked her head as she smiled sheepishly. "That doesn't mean it's nice."

"See?" He laughed.

"You could really tell just by the way I carry myself?" Violet narrowed her gaze.

He shook his head and then adjusted the strap on his bag. "No. I have to admit, you're the shortest wolven I've ever seen."

Violet let out a dramatic sigh. "Such is the curse of my existence. So how did you know?"

He shrugged again. "Your scent gave you away, just like it did with your friend."

"My scent? Is it really that different from my friend's?"

His face bunched. "Why wouldn't it be?"

"Oh, no it's just—" Violet huffed a laugh. "I've been hanging out with her a lot lately, so I didn't know if it changed anything." She made a mental note to be more careful about giving away information about herself and her abilities—or lack thereof. "I'm just curious."

His eyes narrowed ever so slightly with suspicion, but he shifted the strap of his backpack and said, "Every clan is different, but usually they carry the scent of a tree they live by, mixed with something else." His gaze warmed her face. "You, for example, smell like cedar and rain."

"Hm." Violet nodded. She'd noticed most of her clan had a hint of cedar behind their scents, but hadn't really paid attention to other clans. She'd never spent enough time around them. "Well, at least it's a pleasant smell."

"What about me?" he asked, stretching his hands to the sides.

"You want me to smell you?" Violet laughed again. "That's a little weird."

He grinned. "You haven't already?"

Violet's tongue pressed against the inside of her back teeth and she let out an embarrassed chuckle. "Actually, no. All I can smell is coffee."

Amusement sparked in his eyes. "You'll get used to that and then you'll be able to pick up other things as well. It's annoying at first, but it helps develop your sense of smell, among other things." He held her gaze a little longer, then cleared his throat and looked down the sidewalk. "To answer your original question, there's a stand at the end of this building with a delicious breakfast assortment. Or, if you're in the mood for some slightly greasy—but absolutely mouth-watering tacos—that'll be on the other side. They're always out there, no matter the day, weather, or time."

Violet looked in the directions he'd pointed, then turned back to him. "Thank you."

"You're welcome."

He didn't leave.

"So... you know why I'm here." Violet raised her shoulders. "What's your excuse?"

He drew in a deep breath and scuffed his shoe against the ground. "Oh, you know. Just wandering around looking for damsels in distress, so I can swoop in with my napkin and save the day."

"I hope you use a clean one every time."

He made a face. "Of course. I take great pride in my work."

Surprised laughter shook her shoulders and he grinned. She hadn't had a good playful volley of words in a while, and he hadn't missed a beat.

"I've been going to school here for the last semester," he finally answered, "but I've bounced around a lot. You know, trying to find my own place."

Ah, code for: I wanted to leave the clan my parents were in and find my own.

"Have you been on your own this whole time?" Violet worried.

He shook his head. "I have people looking out for me, but it's not where I want to stay."

Violet nodded. "Well... maybe while you're here you should check out the trails." She raised her brows and his smile grew. He was catching on to her subtle hints. "There are some pretty amazing ones with waterfalls. If you're an avid hiker, that is."

"I've been known to trek through the woods from time to time," he answered, clinging to her every word.

A slow grin spread across Violet's face. When was the last time she'd had a clandestine conversation with someone? She didn't know, but it was fun. "That's great." She lowered her voice and added, "You should check out Sentinel Fall. There are some excellent trails and a secluded campground, too."

"Where exactly is that?"

Violet held out her hand. "I can show you on a map if you give me your phone."

With a knowing smile, he pulled out his phone, entered the map app, and placed the device in her hand. "Be gentle. It's brand new."

"I'll try, but I tend to be rough on electronics. Especially my laptops and I broke my phone this morning."

"Maybe I should take that back then," he teased, but instead of taking the phone, he stepped closer to see what she was doing.

She zoomed in on the map and pointed out the location of the clan base. "Here. Tell them you're looking for Alpha Draven."

He took his phone back, pinned the location, and then pocketed the small device. "Thank you."

"You're welcome." Violet beamed.

Looking at his watch, he sucked in a breath through his teeth. "I'm sorry, I have to go. I still have to get a good grade in order to actually pass this class, and the teacher is a nightmare when it comes to attendance."

"Oh, yeah, no, uh... Go." Violet jumbled her words and he chuckled before hurrying away.

He turned back after a few steps and called, "I didn't catch your name!"

"Guess you'll have to check out that trail, then!" Violet called back, making him laugh again before jogging off to class.

Lexie appeared beside her and melted against Violet's side. "Yum. Hello, handsome. Can you introduce me?"

Violet gave an apologetic grin. "Sorry, Lexie. He's not really your type."

"Um, he is definitely my type," Lexie countered. "Taller than me. Rich, chocolaty hair—oh, you mean he's like you, don't you?" Lexie made a face and looked down at Violet.

"Yeah, sorry."

Lexie sighed. "I have got to find a way to change that. Or stop hanging out with you so much. All the guys I start crushing on are... unavailable."

Violet headed toward the breakfast stand Lexie's napkin hero had mentioned and lowered her voice. "Even though I know it's a lost cause, I'll help you look for a way to become wolven. I don't know what I'd do if you stopped hanging out with me."

"Probably die of boredom."

A burst of laughter left Violet and she shook her head.

"So, what do you think?" Lexie asked after taking a sip of her coffee.

"About what?"

"The guy, obviously."

Violet groaned. "Lex..."

"Ew! Hey, no! Don't *Jax* me." Lexie glared and pointed at her around the coffee cup. "Only he calls me that, and you know I hate it."

Shaking her head, Violet mumbled a halfhearted apology. "Napkin Hero was fine. He was fun to banter with, and I think we could be friends. There, is that better?"

"Napkin Hero?" Lexie bunched her lips together, then a soft snort left her as she shook her head. "You and your nicknames. I like it though. You know, he doesn't come with a crap ton of baggage, either."

Violet narrowed her eyes. "I know you're talking about Patrick."

"Well, I'm not wrong." Lexie raised her hands, and coffee cup, in surrender. "I'm just trying to get you to see there are other guys. More considerate guys... you know... ones that would actually check in on you."

"Thanks for that reminder," Violet grumbled, then turned down another walkway.

"Okay, okay." Lexie hurried to catch up, then slowed her stride, so Violet's shorter legs could keep up. "I'm sorry. Kind of."

Violet narrowed her eyes.

Lexie chuckled. "What about this campus? I know you liked the one from last week. How does this one compare?"

Taking the chance to change the topic, Violet dove into an explanation, "I did like that one. It seems like a good school, the campus was pretty straightforward, and I liked the classes they offered. That one was my favorite."

A spark of interest lit Lexie's eyes and one of her brows lifted. "Was?"

"It's not because of the guy!" Violet shot down the thought Lexie wasn't saying, and her friend gave a faux pout. "I like the layout of this campus. Plus, it's close to the clan, but not so close that I'd be worried about people dropping by."

"Wait." Lexie grabbed her arm, pulling her to a stop. "You're seriously thinking of living outside the clan?" Her eyes bulged. "Like, permanently?"

Violet waved a hand. "We can talk about that another time. The school still has a business degree and some other classes that look—"

"But you would live outside the clan," Lexie interrupted, not letting the topic go. "I thought you said that was dangerous for wolven. Isn't that why you're going home tonight?"

"I'm going home tonight because of the risk to *you.*" Violet gave her friend a pointed look. "Besides, it's not uncommon for wolven to attend college. We learn to blend in and are still part of our clan. It's the ones that renounce their clans that are in the biggest danger. As long as I don't have a target on my back, I will be fine." She shrugged. "It's more dangerous for future alphas, anyway, and at the rate I'm going, I won't ever have a rank. I'd be like any other college student. I'm even surprised that Napkin Hero was able to tell what I am."

Lexie's brows pinched together. "But he *was* able to, and you *were* targeted this morning."

"I know," Violet admitted. "There are some things that would need to be sorted out, but this time away has shown me that it's possible. It would give me the freedom to hunt down any clue I found about what I am, too."

"Whatever that is." Lexie joked, and then shifted her weight to the other leg. "Wow. I thought you were just playing along with me whenever I mentioned living on campus." A wide grin spread across her face. "So, the plan is to apply to the same colleges and hope we both get into the same one, right? It would be amazing to room together if you're up for it."

Violet laughed. "Of course, I am."

A high-pitched squeak left Lexie, and she threw her arms around Violet. When they split, Lexie was practically shaking with excitement.

"I've literally never lived alone before," Violet reminded her. "I think that would be a bit too much for me. Besides, these last three weeks have been fun."

"They have." Lexie agreed. "I can't wait to start packing and planning out our dorm together!"

"We have to be accepted first." Violet's laughter doubled and she shook her head. "And before that..." Her stomach growled loud enough to make both girls pause. "I need to get something to eat. And we shouldn't stay too much longer. I need to pack my things to head home."

"What? Seriously?" Lexie asked, her smile fading.

"Lexie, you knew that was the plan."

"Yeah, I just thought it would be later tonight. Or that I'd maybe be able to convince you to stay one more day."

"You know I can't risk that." Violet looked around the campus as she continued, "Besides, I've been gone a long time. Mom likes it when I help with the solstice celebrations—" She cut her thought short when a young woman passed by and gave them a strange look. Violet offered a toothy grin to the girl, who then hurried away. "Plus, my birthday is a week after that. She would kill me if I wasn't home for that preparation."

"Oh." Lexie tipped her head to the side as disappointment gave way to understanding. "That's true. This isn't exactly a normal birthday for you, is it?"

Violet shook her head. "Definitely not."

Sadness filled Lexie's eyes and her shoulders drooped. "It's gonna be weird without you at home. I've gotten used to it. Well, except for the ridiculously early morning interruptions."

"Nah, you know you'll miss those too," Violet teased and started toward the breakfast vendor again.

"Not even a little bit, but—" Lexie skipped ahead and then spun around to face her as she walked backward. "I want to make sure you know you'll be missed. So, let's make sure you get a proper breakfast!" She turned and hurried the last few feet to the breakfast stand, leaving Violet chuckling to herself.

Gratitude for her friend bubbled up inside Violet. She didn't know how she'd gotten so lucky, and she didn't know what she would do without Lexie. Those simple words filled a hole in her heart that she'd had since leaving the clan. She wasn't sure if she was truly missed there, but she knew without a doubt that Lexie would miss her.

# Chapter 3
## Patrick

***"Hey, what are you doing** out here again?"*

The familiar voice of his friend drew Patrick's attention over his shoulder as Aiden jogged to catch up with him. His sandy-brown hair was in need of a cut, and he tossed his head to the side to throw the front of his hair out of his face, then patted Patrick's shoulder.

"What are *you* doing out here? I thought you had the night off to spend with Mya." Patrick reminded him, hoping his light-hearted friend hadn't accidentally blown off his new mate.

Aiden's birthday had been the night the Blood Moon attacked and effectively shut down the Clan Games Tournament. It worked out pretty well for him, though. He spent the night in a recovery tent with his brand-new mate, who'd been waiting for his birthday so he would recognize her as such.

They'd been nearly inseparable since.

"I did, but Levi had a thing and then the cafe asked if Mya could come in tonight, so here I am." He shrugged and they stepped around a boulder together. "I thought you liked having me out on patrols with you."

Patrick allowed one corner of his mouth to tilt into a slight smile. He did. He enjoyed having Aiden around. Things were easy between them, and Aiden always helped ease the tension of any situation. Plus, he looked out for Violet without being asked, and that earned him a lot of respect in Patrick's book.

"We haven't had much time to chat with all the patrols you've been on. What is this? The third in a row? When do you sleep?"

Patrick glanced at his friend who raised a brow, then looked off into the forest around them. "I don't."

Aiden chuckled, believing it was a joke. "Well, you should. I can't imagine keeping that other half of yours at bay is easy when you're tired."

*"He has no idea."* Answered Patrick's darker half in his mind, and he imagined a steel door slamming shut on the reckless wolf. *"Rude."* Alistair's voice faded into the background.

"No, he's not very cooperative even on a good day." That didn't stop Patrick from staying awake and patrolling as much as he could. This clan was his home. They took him in when no one else would. He would protect them with every breath and minute he had.

Aiden didn't know Patrick's wolf had red eyes—only a handful of people did—but his friend knew Patrick struggled with Alistair.

"All right, well why are you on patrol tonight, Future-Beta?" Aiden asked, hopping up onto a small boulder and leaping across to three others.

"You know I stepped down from that role, Aiden," Patrick reminded him as he made another sweep around the area. Something felt off tonight, but there wasn't a sight, sound, or smell of anything amiss.

Aiden landed softly beside him and shrugged. "You're beta until they find someone else, and Jax will wait until the very last minute to replace you. You know that." He elbowed Patrick, drawing his attention. "So?"

With a sigh, Patrick shrugged a shoulder. "My new neighbor, Lucas, has been pulling double shifts for almost two weeks. He needed sleep and we just had an attack so—"

"Don't feed me the nonsense that everyone else is. I don't care if we had an attack this morning, they could do another on the same day if they wanted to."

"Glad someone recognizes that," Patrick grumbled, then bent to brush some leaves off a track in the ground.

Aiden peered over his shoulder. "Mountain lion, right?"

Patrick nodded his approval. "You've been working on your tracking knowledge."

"Learning from the best." He gave a toothy grin, which pulled a small chuckle from Patrick.

Aiden was learning from Patrick. Patrick was only the best in the Sentinel Clan. He knew others who were better.

"If you're so aware of the imminent threat, how are you so carefree right now?"

Aiden gave him a weird, bunched expression, and then mocked hurt. "Do you not know me at all? Carefree is how I thrive."

"Yes, but how are you paying attention to your surroundings?" Patrick nodded to the area around them as they continued on their path.

Shrugging, Aiden stepped onto a fallen log and walked its length. "My madness does have a reason. To everyone else, it looks like I'm not paying attention at all. I've had several people get mad at me while on patrol. In reality, I use every jump, every goofy thing, every moment of lingering in mid-air to extend my line of sight." He jumped from the log onto a low-hanging branch, making it shudder beneath his weight. "I may not be as tall as the rest of you, or strong, or fast, but I make up for it in other ways."

"You discredit yourself." Patrick froze at movement in the far trees.

Unlike Aiden, Patrick was the best at pretty much everything. And that wasn't bragging, it was just fact and genetics. For example, most wolven had to concentrate to hear another's heartbeat. Patrick had to concentrate on *not* hearing everyone's heartbeat. A gift and a curse - one that often left him with headaches if he wasn't careful.

"You can't say that and then go quiet. I'm not fishing for compliments here, but you gotta give me something after that."

Patrick signaled him to be quiet and Aiden crouched low on his branch, following Patrick's gaze.

*"I don't see anything."* Aiden's voice slipped through their clan-link. *"I don't hear anything either."*

*"I didn't get a good look, either,"* Patrick answered truthfully. *"I think it was a deer. There are a lot of them out at dusk."*

*"Are we good then?"* Aiden asked.

Patrick gave the all-clear and Aiden jumped down from the tree. He landed in a crouch, barely making a sound.

"Whew. That got my heart going a bit." He brushed his hair out of his face and gave a goofy smile. "Mya would kill me if she found out I got in a fight tonight."

Patrick didn't return his playfulness. Even with Aiden's calm facade, he hadn't been joking about his heart. It was racing. "Aiden, are you sure you should be out here? I know that last patrol you were on didn't end well."

Aiden's smile slipped. "We all have to make sacrifices, right? Our clan needs us, and I was available."

"Okay, but you—" A second pulse caught Patrick's attention. His ear twitched and he turned his head ever so slightly to hear the sound better.

The heartbeat raced even faster than Aiden's and it was gaining speed. Foliage crunched in the distance.

Patrick turned his attention back to his friend to warn him of the incoming threat.

Copper fur launched over Patrick's head and Aiden's wolf form collided with that of a gray wolf.

Patrick sounded the alarm to their patrol party through their clan-link, then raced toward the two grappling wolves.

He never made it.

Hot breath blazed across Patrick's skin and he dove to the side, narrowly avoiding the snap of the new wolf's teeth.

While he had just told Aiden that Blood Moon pack could attack at any time, they had never attacked during the day. The sky was only just beginning to change from light blue to navy. Yet, here he was, face to face with a second gray wolf sporting two blood-red eyes, gleaming in the fading light like rubies.

The wolf, who had stupidly decided to square off with Patrick alone, paced around a tree and then darted toward him. Patrick hunkered down, unaffected by the zigzag run the wolf was attempting. Many wolven may have been intimidated by the jagged movements, but Patrick had trained for this. His father had made sure he'd trained for every scenario.

He huffed a laugh at the obvious pattern, clenched his fists, and ducked under the wolf's lunge.

His opponent yelped when Patrick drove an uppercut into his stomach. The wolf landed unevenly, legs crumpling beneath his weight.

*"Let me out!"* Alistair yelled, clawing at the mental cage Patrick had created for him when Patrick had won control during his trial. Sometimes that wall slipped, like earlier, but he had a vice-tight grip on his wolf's leash right now.

*"I don't need you,"* Patrick growled as a couple of Sentinel warriors came into view.

One launched into the air as a human and then landed in wolf form atop a Blood Moon member. Her teeth clamped around the guy's head and his scream was cut short a moment later. The other remained in human form, fighting off anyone who came near.

The beast Patrick was fighting was back on its feet. It telegraphed its next attack, leaning to the right, then shot toward Patrick. With a last-second sidestep, Patrick wrapped his arm around the large wolf's neck and threw it over his shoulder.

The wolf's big furry head bounced off the ground when his body landed like a sack of potatoes.

There was no time to rest. The warrior who had chosen to stay in human form was being driven backward toward a cliff by two wolves. His torso was covered in blood dripping from a nasty tear stretching nearly from shoulder to shoulder. Patrick embedded himself between his clan mate and the Blood Moon wolven, drawing their attention immediately.

He knew it would.

They were after him, of course.

Unfortunately for them, they went down just as easily as the last one had, and his clan mate thanked him for the rescue.

"Stay alive." Patrick nodded to him and then ran back to where he'd last seen Aiden.

*"Patrick!"* Jax's cry for help rang through Patrick's skull drawing him to a skidding halt.

There wasn't another fight happening in his vicinity, so he opened his senses—Alistair pacing in his locked cage, yelling that he could do more—and shut out all sounds that didn't belong to his best friend. It took a moment, but Jax's battle cry of rage pinpointed his location and Patrick bolted for the cliff.

He knew the area well. A straight jump wouldn't be comfortable when he landed, but he'd be fine.

Pushing off the last inch of ground, Patrick soared into the air. From there he found his future alpha pinned against the cliff base. A large gray wolf pressed in on him while two men held either side. Jax's golden eyes warned them off, but the Blood Moon pack members didn't back away. Jax was hurt, and they knew it. The smell of blood was everywhere, and a large portion of it was Patrick's best friend's.

The wolf bared its teeth, licking his curled lips as it moved closer to its target.

Two more steps and Patrick would have fallen onto the beast. Instead, he landed with one knee down and his opposite palm hitting the ground only a foot from the wolf.

Violet would have made fun of him for trying to look like a superhero—that thought made him smirk—but it was just a convenient way to land and absorb *some* impact. It still rattled his bones and his knee was going to hurt for a bit.

Patrick twisted his smirk to look sinister as he lifted his gaze to the gray wolf who blinked at him before baring his teeth again.

"Surprise," Patrick muttered.

The wolf launched at him.

The leg that took the brunt of Patrick's landing refused to move. Raising his arm at the last second, the wolf's teeth clamped over his forearm, driving as deep as they could.

Patrick snarled. His fist beat against the wolf's skull until it blinked and fell away, stumbling and shaking its head. Using his position, Patrick sent himself running forward like a sprinter coming out of the starting blocks. He didn't slow down as he ran into the gray beast, driving it into a tree. The snap of ribs made the wolf cry out and its body shuddered.

"You have two options," Patrick told the wolf, lowering his voice to sound more menacing. He crouched over the large beast. "You can stay and fight and I'll break more ribs—you may even lose your life—or you can leave and go tell whomever you work for that Sentinel Clan is under my protection."

The wolf barked a laugh, then winced. When it growled and tried to stand, Patrick grabbed its throat. The wolf snarled; mouth open, threatening to bite. With Patrick's current hold, that was all it was going to be able to do.

"I wouldn't recommend shifting until your ribs are healed. It'll be excruciating if you try it right now."

The wolf thrashed in his hold. The crunch of leaves told him that his time was up. Another Blood Moon member had joined the fight.

"Wrong choice." Patrick smashed his elbow against the wolf's head and its eyes closed. The only indicator that the creature was still living was the rise and fall of its large chest.

The next fight took longer. The guy clearly hadn't been fighting long, because his moves were all still fresh. He was also well-trained, bigger, and stronger than the others Patrick had gone up against. And he didn't shift.

Patrick was grateful for that. If he had, Patrick may have been forced to do the same... which he tried to avoid doing. The possibility of someone seeing his red eyes or Alistair being closer to the surface and taking over was too great a risk.

A couple of deep, painful breaths helped calm his heart and his stomach when he turned away from his opponent who lay still with his eyes staring blankly at the rapidly darkening sky. Alistair told him it was a necessary death... Patrick's logical side understood that it was. That the man had no intention of taking Patrick alive. It didn't change the stomach-rolling disgust Patrick felt for himself as he stared down at his bloodied hands.

The guy had managed to get a few very well-placed hits and Patrick's ribs screamed with each breath. No doubt he had broken a few, but they would heal quickly. Just as the wolf bites along his arm had—they were nearly closed.

A cry of startled pain drew Patrick out of his thoughts and he darted toward Jax. His best friend who had already been bleeding, now held his side, eyes blazing gold while blood seeped through his fingers.

The last ribbons of daylight glinted off a bloodied knife wielded in the Blood Moon pack member's hand and the girl smirked.

"Since when did Blood Moon pack start carrying weapons?" Patrick asked, stalking straight up to her.

A few feet away, a body lay face down in the dirt—Jax's other attacker. With all the heartbeats around, Patrick couldn't tell immediately if the guy was alive or dead, but he wasn't Patrick's concern right now.

The girl shrugged. "A girl's gotta protect herself somehow."

"Cause your wolven abilities aren't enough?" Patrick eyed the knife in her hands. Crimson smeared the entire blade and he briefly worried about how deep Jax's wound went.

She pointed the tip of her weapon at Patrick's chest. "Not against you."

Patrick growled and could feel the shift as his eyes turned red. Alistair pressed against his cage, ready to be released at any moment.

"If you know about me, then you know a knife isn't going to save you."

She chuckled darkly. "Maybe not, but your future alpha won't last long after a cut from this bad boy." She clicked her tongue. "Not to mention that other poor boy I stabbed in the chest."

Patrick's senses exploded. He breathed deep, drawing in the acrid stench of wolfsbane, and cursed. His hearing picked up heavy, labored breathing somewhere behind him.

"Jax, rally the patrol. Find out who she's talking about. I'll handle her quickly."

Patrick listened to the crunch of his friend's footsteps, making sure he made it a safe distance while he watched the female in front of him cockily flip her dagger around.

Alistair pressed against his mind. *"How fast do you want to kill her?"*

*"I don't want to kill her."*

*"We'll see."* Alistair shrunk back.

"You know how easily that knife could be turned around on you?" Patrick asked, tilting his head to the side.

Her blonde hair swayed as she shook her head. "Not likely. I'm pretty good with a bla—"

Before she could finish her sentence, Patrick rushed her. He forced his way into Alistair's power, making his wolf half scream in rage, and pulled for added speed. She didn't even have time to draw a breath before he snapped the weapon from her hand and brought it to her throat.

"You overestimate your abilities." Patrick breathed heavily as his control over Alistair waned.

His voice tipped lower and a gravely tone took over as his darker half added, "And you underestimate mine."

Terror rushed through Patrick's veins when a thin line of blood appeared beneath the blade.

"NO!" Patrick's strength returned, surging through him at lightning speed. He threw the knife into the soft dirt before taking the girl by surprise with a hook across her jaw. She nearly spun in a full circle before crumbling to lay beside her weapon.

Alistair's dark laugh echoed in his mind. *"That was a close one, Boy Scout. I almost had you."*

*"How did you do that?"* Patrick asked as he threw up his mental barrier.

*"Tsk. Tsk. Tsk. I can't tell you all my secrets."*

*"You know all mine,"* Patrick grumbled as he pulled a pair of cuffs from his back pocket and then knelt over the girl to clamp them around her wrists, behind her back.

With all the attacks from Blood Moon pack, they'd needed something stronger than zip-ties. Supposedly, these cuffs were made from a special alloy that no wolven could break out of. Every patrol member carried three to five on them while on duty. Which was a good thing, because Patrick had a few more to cuff.

*"Knowing your secrets comes with my territory. I'm in your head. So are all your thoughts and secrets... and dark desires."*

Patrick wished he could glare at Alistair. *"I don't have dark desires. Those belong to you."*

*"On the contrary, lusting after your best friend's sister is pretty—"*

*"I don't* lust *after Violet,"* Patrick snapped as he clamped his last set of cuffs.

Alistair laughed. *"Who are you trying to convince?"*

"Patrick!" shouted one of the female warriors as she hurried over to him. "Something's wrong with Aiden. We can't get his wound to stop bleeding… and Jax…"

He was running before she finished explaining. Reaching through the mind-link, Patrick felt Jax's presence and yelled, *"Don't you dare be dead!"* He dodged a tree and kept going. *"Violet will kill me and then bring you back from the dead to kill you!"*

*"I'm not dead!"* Jax shouted back. *"Not yet anyway."*

Patrick skidded to a stop beside a pale Jax, who was hovering over an ashen-skinned Aiden. His breathing was labored and blood spread across the ground beneath him.

"Aiden, did you get stabbed by a knife?" Patrick pulled his shirt over his head and pressed it against the wound.

Aiden cried out against the pressure, arching his back off the ground.

"I'm sorry." Patrick grimaced. This was bad.

With his face pinched, Aiden nodded. "Yeah, it was a knife. I didn't…" He wheezed in a breath. "Why a knife?"

Patrick shouted orders to get some help carrying Aiden and Jax back to Doc.

"I'm fine," Jax insisted, but the gash on his side was still bleeding and the pale color of his skin didn't bode well.

"The blade was coated with wolfsbane. You've already been infected," Patrick grumbled as a couple of patrol members came over. "We don't need it spreading through your blood any more than it already has. Keeping your pulse lower by having you carried is the only way we are doing this."

"Wolfsbane?" Aiden lifted his head but dropped it again with a thud. "Dang… no wonder I feel like death."

"You're going to be fine," Patrick insisted.

Jax wrapped an arm around one of the other warriors and the guy lifted him into the air. "We will never speak of this again."

"Understood," mumbled the warrior, though the grin on his face announced his humor.

Aiden moaned, drawing Patrick's attention. Blue-black lines peeked over his collar, stretching up his neck.

A curse flew from Patrick's mouth and he scooped Aiden into his arms. "I'll take him myself."

The warrior who'd come to help, gaped open-mouthed as Patrick took off running.

Aiden's body was getting colder, but Patrick couldn't keep pressure on his wound while carrying him.

*"If there was ever a time to help me, now would be it!"* Patrick shouted at Alistair.

*"To help the weakling pup? No, thanks."*

*"Alistair!"* Patrick yelled at his darker half. *"He's my friend!"*

Patrick could feel Alistair's resolve waning, but the wolf didn't give in.

*"You're always begging to be let loose,"* Patrick offered.

*"Not to be locked up immediately after."*

*"Please! I'll..."*

*"You'll what?"* Alistair's presence magnified, pressing closer to the surface, as his interest peaked. *"Say it, Boy Scout."*

*"I'll owe you a favor."*

*"To be called in whenever I want? For whatever I want?"*

Patrick looked down at Aiden. His breathing was shallow. The blue-black veins had spread, nearly reaching his jaw. He needed help **now**. He needed Alistair's speed.

*"Anything you want,"* Patrick agreed, feeling like he had just signed his death warrant. His mouth ran dry, but the trees began to pass him in a blur. His eyesight cleared. Darkness had no effect on his senses, now.

*"Enjoy your run,"* Alistair nearly purred.

# Chapter 4

## Patrick

***With the full power of his wolf,*** *Patrick lurched forward with Aiden in his arms.* There was no fear of smashing into a tree or missing a turn. Things he had missed before became clear. The fresh scent of rain hung in the air, telling of a coming storm, and deer dashed away in the distance.

Soon, the medical clinic came into view, but Patrick didn't pull back until he saw someone exit the building.

Alistair retreated into Patrick's mind, taking the red from Patrick's eyes with him. *"Remember, Boy Scout,"* Alistair said as he drifted back. *"You owe me."*

"Move!" Patrick yelled as he kicked open the front door of the clinic.

A female wolven in the corner shrieked, but the nurse jumped to his feet. He took one look at Aiden, launched himself over the desk, and pressed down on Patrick's wadded-up, bloodied shirt.

Aiden groaned, but it was quiet and he didn't even flinch.

"What happened?" The nurse asked, moving with Patrick into an exam room.

"Blood Moon attacked and one of them had a knife dipped in—"

"Wolfsbane," Doctor Penmann's raspy voice cut him off as she flew into the room. "I can smell it."

She dug through a couple of drawers, cursed, then threw open a cupboard. "I haven't had to use wolfsbane antidote in a long time. I hope it's not expired."

Withdrawing from the cupboard with three vials of light purple fluid, she looked over each of them. The horizontal lines across her throat shifted when she swallowed hard. With a nod, she lunged across the room and injected one syringe into his neck while the other was emptied into his shoulder. "I'm giving him two just to be safe."

"How expired was it?" Patrick asked quietly.

Her lips pressing into a thin line was enough of an answer.

Jax stumbled into the door frame, sweat lining his forehead. "How is he?"

"We'll know momentarily," Doc answered without taking her gaze off Aiden.

"Doc, we need more of that antidote." Patrick caught her eye and then nodded at Jax.

Without warning, she attacked Jax with the remaining vial.

"Ow!" He flinched back, holding his neck while his eyes flared gold.

Doc fled across the room. "I'm giving you one more." She grabbed another syringe. "Where were you stabbed?"

Jax didn't need to answer. Blood covered his right side, seeping down his pant leg.

Once again, Doc lunged for Jax, but this time he braced for it. She drove the syringe into his stomach and he doubled over with a groan.

"That looked like it hurt," Aiden's whisper-quiet voice filled the small room.

Nodding, Jax straightened his back and stiffly walked to Aiden's side. "You had us worried for a minute there."

"You?" Aiden coughed a laugh. "I thought I was about to meet the goddess."

"Not today." Patrick patted his friend's leg. "Does Mya know?"

Aiden swallowed. "She was working, but she's coming. She's gonna be so mad."

His limbs started quivering.

"Doc, I can't feel my feet." Aiden's eyes fell half shut. "Or... my hands."

Patrick grabbed his arm when it shook off the exam bed. "Aiden, look at me."

Convulsions overtook Aiden's body. His eyes remained partially open, but were void of color.

"He's seizing!" She growled and grabbed one of his arms. "Help me roll him over."

Patrick lifted Aiden's shoulder and Dr. Penmann held his head.

Jax's face had gone sheet white. He stepped away from the bed, knocking a tray off the counter. It clattered to the floor.

"Why is he seizing?" Patrick asked, his gaze darting between his two friends in the room. Would Jax be next? "What's going on?"

Doc's brows drew together and she lifted her gaze to Patrick's as Aiden's trembling stopped.

Along with his heart.

A gut-wrenching scream filled the clinic.

Patrick's ears rang as he turned to see Jax wrap Mya Thomas, one of Violet's best friends, in a bear hug. She melted to the floor, clutching her chest. Jax sank with her—jaw clenched and tears moistening his eyes.

The nurse reached for her, but Mya shoved him off. She buried her face into Jax's arm and sobbed Aiden's name.

No attempt was made to reach Aiden.

She knew better than anyone that her mate was gone.

Dr. Penmann knelt on the floor beside Mya and Jax, offering soothing words and the lightest of touches across the brokenhearted girl's back.

Minutes passed in paralyzing sorrow.

Patrick knew he would remember the combined sounds of Mya's sobbing and the doc's strangely soothing, raspy voice for years to come. His bloodstained hands clenched into fists at his sides and rage flooded his veins. He burned from the inside out.

*"Easy, Boy Scout. You're losing control."*

*"Leave me alone."*

*"I can't do that. See, if I let you lose it right now, you may not hold up our end of the deal. So, get your act together and cool it."*

He hated that his wolf half was right. He hated that Alistair was somehow able to balance his emotions so he wasn't on the verge of punching a hole through the wall. He hated that there was nothing he could do to fix this. Mya had lost her mate because of him. If he had never come here, they never would have been targets.

"I know it doesn't feel like it right now, but you're going to make it through this," Dr. Penmann nodded to the nurse and he gently pried Jax's shirt out of Mya's hands. "Take her into the other room. I'll be there shortly. You know what to do."

The nurse nodded, wrapped his arms around Mya's middle, and gently lifted her off the floor.

Jax stayed there, on his knees. His hands trembled.

Patrick took a step toward him. "Jax?"

Shaking his head, Jax slowly lifted his gaze. "How did this happen?"

"Jax, you're shaking."

Alarmed, Dr. Penmann stared at Jax who was now looking at his hands.

"My fingers are tingly," the future alpha admitted. "I hadn't noticed until now."

"Can you feel everything else?" Doc asked.

Jax shook his head. Then nodded. "Sorry. Pain. I feel... so much pain."

Understanding softened the doctor's eyes and she sat back slightly.

"Ah, one of the burdens of an alpha."

Jax's connection with Aiden had been strong. Aiden would have been one of his closest companions when Jax was ready to take over as alpha. He'd even spoken about making him his second in command.

The gaping hole in Patrick's chest suddenly made sense. He'd never felt anything like it before. A vast emptiness that devoured all happiness, like a black hole enveloping all light. Actually, there was one time he had felt it before—the night his eyes turned red.

Patrick turned his hazel gaze to the lifeless form of his friend. Someone he had kept further than arms-length until recently... and now wished he'd taken the chance to be friends with much sooner.

"Doc, do you have something I can cover him with?" Patrick asked, his voice sounding hollow.

Dr. Penmann pointed to the bottom cupboards. "There are some sheets on the right side."

With stiff legs, Patrick followed her directions.

"Jax, can you stand and come into the room?" Doc asked. "I'd like to take a closer look at you."

Patrick rolled Aiden onto his back, fixed his hands over his stomach, and draped the sheet over his body.

Slowly, Jax entered the room.

Closing the door behind them, Doc looked over Jax and asked a few more questions.

"I don't feel any worse," Jax answered at one point. "Some of my fingers are tingly. Some of them are numb. Everything else just feels tired."

"Good." Doc nodded. "I'd like to keep you here a bit longer, just to keep an eye on you. But, based on how quickly we lost Aiden..." Her voice faded away and she shook her head before continuing. "I think you're out of the woods."

"Why me?" Jax asked. "Why not him?"

Later when Patrick lay mulling over the day, he would remember the things Dr. Penmann had said... that timing, location, and depth of the wound were critical when it came to wolfsbane.

An hour passed in numbing sorrow.

Patrick was summoned to Alpha House while Jax remained behind. He hadn't wanted to sit in the room with Aiden's body, so when Patrick left the clinic, Jax was attempting to help with Mya—who had lashed out attempting to hurt the nurse and herself—and then gone catatonic.

She wasn't speaking.

She wasn't moving.

Tears silently rolled down her cheeks.

Staring at the red Alpha House, Patrick's only thoughts were of her and the pain he had caused. Another clan member had died... because of him.

And Jax could have been next.

Patrick raised his hand to knock, only to have the door swing open.

Alpha Draven's wide shoulders filled the doorway before he stepped out onto the porch, driving Patrick down the steps until he was back on the stone walkway. The alpha remained at the top of the steps, making it easy for Patrick to keep his gaze slightly lowered—an act of respect for the man's title and rank. Anyone else in the clan would have been compelled to do so, but the alpha's aura had no effect on him.

*"If I called in my favor now, would you look this sorry excuse for an alpha in the eye?"* Alistair growled.

Patrick closed his eyes momentarily, making sure his mental barriers were intact. *"I... We owe this man a lot. A little respect is the least we can do to show our gratitude."*

*"For what? Taking us in after you killed three teenagers?"*

Patrick flinched.

"Alistair," Alpha Draven grumbled. "I'd appreciate it if you'd let Patrick and I speak uninterrupted."

Alistair snorted. *"Not likely."*

Clearing his throat, Patrick nodded. "He'll try, sir."

Alpha Draven tucked his hands behind his back and looked off to the side. "What report am I getting today, Patrick?"

"Why do you ask when you already know the answer?" Patrick kept his voice level and quiet.

Alpha Draven would have known what was going on the moment it happened. Maybe not to whom it had happened, but he would've felt the severed connection from one of his clan members. The other clan members would have filled him in on the rest.

"It's important to report your side of the story, so rumors and half-truths can be silenced."

Patrick's hands curled into fists and he shoved them into his pockets. "We were ambushed on our patrol. They outnumbered us. One of them had a knife coated in wolfsbane and landed attacks on both Aiden and Jax. We lost Aiden."

Alpha Draven's blue-ombre eyes melted to gold.

"Jax will be fine." Patrick continued. "We caught it in time. Doc says he should have full feeling back in his hands in a day or two. We'll double the number of warriors on patrol and encourage more wolven to train."

"Why didn't you do more?"

Patrick hesitated. A deep growl rumbled around him, coming from his alpha. Anger poured off the older man and Patrick's body tensed in response. "Sir," he started slowly. "I helped every patrol member I could. I killed one of the Blood Moon members. I raced Aiden here as fast as I could, risking exposure—"

"To hell with exposure!" Alpha Draven yelled and Patrick backed up a step as the man stalked down the porch steps. "You are stronger than anyone here. You could have taken them all out if you'd tapped into that power. Aiden could still be alive!"

*"He's not wrong."* Alistair growled, *"But he needs to get out of our face."*

"And risk Alistair killing everyone," Patrick tried to calmly remind the alpha, but his voice held a threatening tone—a warning Alpha Draven didn't ignore. The older man took a step back and drew in a deep breath, allowing Patrick to continue, "Alistair cares for no one. If I unleash him, he will destroy anyone in his path."

Alpha Draven's molten gold eyes narrowed. "We made a mistake letting you into our clan."

Terror ran down Patrick's spine and a cold sweat lingered on the back of his neck. He'd lived every day worrying when they would realize that. It had taken longer than he thought it would. It still hurt. He swallowed the lump in his throat while Alistair growled in the background. "I know," he said weakly. "I'm doing what I can to protect you all, now."

Alpha Draven drew in a deep, slow breath through his nose. The anger rippling off him simmered as he continued with barely contained rage. "We welcomed you here. You've been an asset to the clan. A friend to Jax. You take your duties seriously." His jaw clenched. "But I will not endanger my clan for one wolf."

Patrick lowered his chin and stared at the rocks. His hands shook inside his pockets as a vortex of emotions threatened to overwhelm him. "I understand," he answered quietly.

When they'd captured Vikter Stravek a few weeks ago, he revealed that he'd been tasked to deliver a message after murdering Patrick's neighbors.

His words haunted Patrick's dreams and waking thoughts; *"We know what you are. We know where you are. We know what you did... We're coming for you."*

Maybe it wasn't Blood Moon pack's sole reason for attacking Sentinel Clan, but it was a big motivator.

"You're dismissed." Alpha Draven turned away and his footsteps thudded against the porch steps.

Before dominance by combat was outlawed, an alpha turning his back would have been an invitation to attack. Thankfully, wolven had grown more civilized and alpha bloodlines were more prominent. That didn't stop Alistair from pacing in his mind like an animal in a cage, but Patrick didn't need to prove he was stronger than his alpha. They both knew he was.

The door slammed shut.

Sprinkling raindrops shifted into a steady downpour as Patrick stood on the walkway to Alpha House long after the alpha had gone inside.

The last thing he wanted was to endanger those he cared for.

He cared deeply for this clan.

Slowly, his feet carried him away from the house filled with people who had taken him in years before. They were the only family he had.

The thought of saying goodbye was agony.

He knew when he arrived three years ago that he probably wouldn't be able to stay, but as time passed, he began to hope it would be forever.

Forever was a luxury he couldn't afford.

It would take some time to figure out where he was going and to finalize everything. In the meantime, he would continue patrolling and doing his part to defend the clan.

Twenty feet up the road, Patrick tilted his head back, allowing the raindrops to run down his face. The smell of rain was one of the first things Patrick had fallen in love with when he'd moved here. Home had a similar smell, but with different trees. Familiar and new all at once.

Another smell overcame the rain. One that melted his convictions and sent his heart racing. Lowering his chin, Patrick breathed in the sweet scent of vanilla and cinnamon that reminded him of Christmas cookies. Slowly, he turned to find the origin of both his dreams and nightmares. Standing in the t-shirt he'd given her during his trials, soaked through from the rain.

Water droplets fell from Violet's nose, chin, and the ends of her hair. Her gorgeous amethyst eyes slowly traveled the length of his body before she breathed a greeting, "Hi."

Memories of her warm breath against his skin, her voice begging him to come back to her, made Patrick feel feverish. Heat welled in his lower abdomen and made his palms go clammy. What he would give to welcome her home with a long embrace... but that wasn't possible.

"I didn't know you were coming back today." The roughness in his voice from speaking with Alpha Draven helped him play his part. It was more important than ever that he kept her at arm's distance. He was leaving. It would be easier if she didn't like him.

"I didn't either," Violet admitted, raising a shoulder. The oversized collar of his old shirt slipped off her shoulder.

Patrick swallowed hard, looked away from her, and rubbed the back of his neck.

"I just felt it was time," she continued. "I would've been here sooner, but Lexie was distracting me. I was finishing packing when Jax said I needed to come home."

He froze. Mya's scream ripped through his mind. The hole he had in his chest ached. "Did he tell you why?"

She shook her head. "Are you..." The concern in Violet's tone tugged at his will, and he found himself gazing at her once again. "Are you okay?"

Confusion tugged Patrick's brows together until he remembered he was still covered in blood. "It's not mine." Patrick sighed. "Well, not all of it. A lot has happened since you left."

Nodding, Violet dragged her lower lip through her teeth, and warmth pooled in Patrick's abdomen. She had no clue how alluring that was.

"Yeah, I guess it has." The sorrow in her words made that warmth vanish.

"Violet, something happened tonight." He slowly made his way toward her as he recounted the night's events. When he told her about the attack, and Aiden, her bag splattered in the mud, painting both their legs when she covered her mouth with her hand. His brows pulled together when he neared the end. "We thought he was recovering. He sounded like he was recovering. And then he just..."

Violet shook her head, her eyes filling with salty tears. "No," she begged, but something in his face must have driven it home because her tears finally fell, mixing with the rain on her face.

The pain in her eyes radiated through him, matching his own. Even if Patrick had tried to stop himself, his arms still would have found their way around her waist. Alistair stirred from the depths of his mind and reached for her, as well. Patrick almost pulled away. He never wanted Alistair near Violet. But for once, his darker half had no lustful or sinister plans.

Together, Patrick and Alistair held her in an effort to comfort her breaking heart.

Her tiny hands clung to his shirt, curling the fabric in her fists. "He's gone?" she cried. "Aiden's really gone?"

Patrick pressed his lips to the top of her head. His own tears threatened to fall, but he held them back, now wasn't the time to fall apart. "I'm sorry, Vi."

A shuddery sob dropped her shoulders, but then her head kicked back and she stared at him with wide eyes. "Where's Mya?"

His brows drew together as he listened to her racing heart and wild eyes. "Mya is resting at Doc's."

"I have to see her!" Violet tried to shove away from him, but he held her tight. "Let go! She needs me!"

"Violet, stop. Look at me."

A few large breaths later, she finally turned her narrowed gaze on him.

"No one is allowed to see her right now. She's not ready."

"What are you talking about? She just lost her mate. Being with people she loves is exactly what she needs."

"She turned violent," Patrick blurted, but there wasn't a nice way to say what needed to be said. "She attacked the nurse and tried to hurt herself. She's been sedated. But Doc says she has a better chance than some of the others because of how new their bond was."

Losing a mate was the worst pain a wolven could experience. People described it as feeling like half their heart was ripped from their chest. Like half of themselves was gone. The mating bond was so much more than just physical. It ran deep within their emotions and thoughts. Sadly, it was pretty common for the surviving half to end their life... or at least try.

Patrick slid his fingers into her hair and cupped her cheek. His thumb gently swept through the rain that soaked her cheek. "I'll let you know when you can visit her."

"Okay." Violet nodded. "Thank you."

Slowly, she pushed away from him and grabbed her bag out of the mud. On her way passed him toward Alpha House, she brushed her fingers against his and he almost pulled her back to him. He curled his hands into fists and shoved them deep into his pockets to resist the overwhelming desire to do so.

*"Patrick, she—"*

*"Let her go, Alistair,"* Patrick growled in the confines of his mind.

*"You hate that idea just as much as I do."*

*"It doesn't matter. We can't have her. It would only end in misery."*

The front door of Alpha House closed without a backward glance from Violet, and two minutes later the smell of hot chocolate wafted into the air.

*"She doesn't need us."* Patrick insisted to himself and his darker half. *"Luna is there. She'll take care of her."*

*"Not like we could."*

Patrick expected some sort of snark or lustfulness from Alistair, but all he felt was genuine concern. The desire to simply hold her and help. And that made it all the harder. It was the first time Patrick found himself agreeing with the part of himself that he hated.

# Chapter 5

## Violet

***After staying up halfway through** the night with her mom and crying until her tears ran dry,* Violet was not happy to have Jax burst into her room at six o'clock in the morning.

"Get out!" Violet yelled at him, throwing one of her many pillows in his general direction.

"Come on, I haven't seen you in weeks." Jax picked up her pillow and set it at the foot of her bed, out of her reach. "You show up unannounced last night and didn't even say hi."

Violet groaned her protest and buried her head under her pillow. Her face was puffy. Especially her eyes. Crying was awful.

"I bet you need to get back into training and I need some twin time." Jax ran a finger down her foot and she lashed out like a startled horse, her heel connecting with his rib.

He yelped in pain and she shot off the bed. "I'm so sorry! Are you okay? Please, tell me I didn't hit your—"

"Whoa, whoa!" Jax held up the hand not holding his side. "Who told you?"

Violet bit her lip and then shrugged. "It doesn't matter." Rage poured through her veins a moment later. "And why wouldn't someone tell me!" She socked his arm, making him cry out in surprise. She hadn't hit him hard enough to do any damage. He was hurt enough as it was. "You're my twin! Why didn't *you* tell me?"

"I was going to, but I thought it would be better to wait until after you had something to eat, so you didn't try to bite my head off!" He yelled back at her, then winced and gently prodded his side.

"Training's off the table, Jax." Violet glared at him, taking a seat on her bed and pulling the covers into her lap.

Jax growled but nodded. "Doc would probably approve of that."

Rolling her eyes, Violet threw herself back into her pillows. "If you're just going to be annoying then you're obviously fine so let me get back to sleep."

The image of him poking at her popped into her mind as his voice filled her thoughts. *"You know I can just pester you like this so you can't sleep."*

"Watch me," Violet snapped out loud and pulled the covers over her face.

"I may not be able to train, but you can."

Her bed shifted when he got up.

"So, get your butt off this bed and downstairs in five, or I'm coming back up here."

"No. Jaaaaax!" Violet wanted to throw something again, but he was closing the door already.

"Five minutes!"

She was downstairs in three with an oversized shirt slipping off her shoulder and an epic glare on her face that didn't even faze her twin. In fact, Jax happily threw a toasted waffle in her face.

"Eat. I'll talk on the way."

"I'd rather you didn't."

Jax chuckled and then held the front door open for her.

It would never be said out loud, but Violet knew her twin was right. She did need to get back into training. That didn't mean she needed to start that day!

"Jax, I don't want to train," she complained but continued following him down the road. "I stayed up way too late and I want to go see Mya and cry into a pint of ice cream with her." Her tired brain jumped tracks of thought and she blurted, "Did you know Lexie's family rarely has dessert in the house? I need sugar!"

He ignored her sugar demands. "Mya is not allowed to have any visitors right now besides Doc, Mom, and Dad. When she is, I'm betting her parents will be first."

"She's one of my best friends..."

"You'll get to see her soon, but she's not ready yet, Violet."

She stopped walking and Jax tipped his head back in a groan as he slowly turned toward her.

"That's bull." Tears built in her eyes and a heaviness settled over her chest. "We all lost Aiden. She should be with those who loved him and her. She needs to be able to grieve with everyone."

Jax's face softened and he hesitantly rested a hand on her shoulder. "I know better than most how Mya is feeling right now. I didn't realize how much dad felt on a day-to-day basis until I started feeling it. He's connected to the clan in a way no one else is. I *felt* Aiden's heart stop. I *felt* Mya's pain rip through me like lightning, as if it were my own. Trust me when I say that right now, Mya needs time, and the clan needs to train more than ever, so we don't have to lose anyone else."

"Me." Violet looked down at the road. "You mean me."

"No." Jax shook his head. "I mean anyone. You being home just means we need to be even more vigilant."

Violet glared. "I'm not helpless, Jax. I can fight. I've taken down Blood Moon members before."

"You've surprised them; it's not the same thing as a head-to-head fight."

Anger pulsed through her, and she threw her uneaten waffle at his face before heading back toward Alpha House. "I'll see you later."

"No, wait." Jax caught up to her, waffle in hand. "Look you don't understand..."

"I understand, Jax!" Violet yelled as she rounded on him. "I get it. I'm the clan girl who can't connect with her wolf. So clearly, I can't handle anything, and everyone has to protect me because I'm fragile!"

Jax stepped back a step, surprised by her outburst.

She shook her head. "I didn't come back here to be treated like a child." She bit her lip and looked off to the side. She turned to leave, but Jax's voice stopped her.

"Our patrols have been attacked seven times since you left. We've lost four clan members, countless others were badly wounded, and Mya is being heavily sedated so we won't lose her too."

Violet's chest rose and fell heavily as she calculated the number of attacks to the number of her premonitions. Slowly, she looked at her twin with disbelief.

He nodded. "Yes, every time you contacted me about a vision, we were attacked. Sometimes the attacks happened as you were telling me, other times it took a day or two, but it happened exactly as you described."

"Then I really do have..." Violet's voice shook and her words faded away. She didn't know why it was such a shock. She already knew, but having it confirmed was something else entirely.

Jax stepped toward her. "I don't know why or how, but you have magic, Violet."

Panic filled her. She'd been trying to ignore the fact that she'd had a premonition about Vikter. Jax hadn't told her if her dreams had ever come true or not, so she figured everything was fine. "Why didn't you tell me? All you said was that it was unlikely an attack would happen so soon after the last one. I had no idea there had been so many. Why didn't you tell me?" She repeated the question.

"You haven't felt any sort of loss while you've been gone?" Jax's brows pulled together. "The clan-mates we've lost... you didn't notice?"

Violet wrapped her arms around herself, feeling the need to hold on to whatever connection she had with her clan. When she spoke, her voice was nearly a whisper, "No. I didn't."

"And you didn't feel anything when I was poisoned?"

She shook her head. "But we don't always notice when each other is hurt."

"True." He watched her for a moment and then added, "I was surprised when you didn't ask what was going on. I guess I know why now."

"Just add it to the list of things I can't do," she said sadly. "I wish I could feel it."

He fiddled with the waffle in his hands and then let out a huff of air. "I just wanted a nice morning with you, Violet. I wanted to skip all this and move on to the good stuff. We have some great things coming up, and..."

"You can't skip over the hard or difficult things, Jax," Violet interrupted. "That doesn't fix anything. You can't skip the death of our clan mates..." Hot, angry tears gathered in her eyes, threatening to fall. "Aiden died," her voice broke against the emotions building inside her. She gestured between the two of them. "Our *friend* died!"

"I know that! *I* was the one with him when his heart stopped. *I* was the one who caught Mya when she collapsed. *You* weren't here!" Jax's eyes widened as soon as the words left his mouth and regret filtered through their twin connection. "I shouldn't have said that. I didn't mean—"

"Yes, you did. You may not have meant to say it, but you meant every word." Violet's voice was quiet, and hurt spread from her heart to her fingers and toes. "And you're right. I wasn't here. I didn't know how bad things were. Otherwise, I would have been."

Jax turned away, hands on his hips, and kicked at a rock in the dirt road. "You just got back. I haven't seen you in almost a month. I just... didn't want to talk about this."

Sighing, Violet looked at the dirt road. "That's just it," she paused, nibbling on her lower lip. "You don't talk to me about things that matter anymore."

He opened his mouth but closed it again when nothing came out.

She nodded and huffed a sad laugh. "I get it. You're the future alpha of Sentinel Clan, and I couldn't be prouder of you. But I'm just a clan girl with magic I shouldn't have and no wolf."

Her twin's brows furrowed, but he remained silent.

"You should know, I'm considering living on campus for college."

Confusion danced in his eyes, but she interrupted him before he could say anything.

"I don't think I belong here anymore," she added quietly, and sorrow pulsed through their bond. "I'm gonna go train. You should rest."

He didn't try to stop her as she walked away, and a strange mixture of sadness and anger rolled around inside her chest, making it burn.

After a sweaty half hour of punching the stuffing out of a creepy human-shaped dummy, Violet stopped to catch her breath and grab a drink. She yanked off her oversized shirt and used it to wipe down her face before taking a long drink. The cool air was a welcome change against the flushed skin of her stomach.

"If I didn't know better, I'd think you were trying to take this guy's head off," Robin sauntered into Violet's training space and landed a soft, mock jab to the dummy's jaw.

Violet swished some water around in her mouth before swallowing. "If you knew better, you'd avoid me this morning."

"Ooh." Robin made a face and wrapped an arm around the dummy.

Violet had no idea what Robin's natural hair color was. She dyed it so often that it was impossible to keep track of it. Currently, it was a light brown with a mix of high and low lights, and she must have gotten extensions because even in a high ponytail, the tips brushed her waist.

She and Violet had hung out quite a bit when Robin and her dad had moved into Sentinel Clan. But, as time went on, and Violet had grown closer with Mya, and then Lexie, Robin drifted away. They were very different people, so it never really bothered Violet, until recently when the vain girl started being more of a frenemy. They hadn't talked much since the night Blood Moon ended the Clan Games, and the fact that she'd openly chased after Patrick didn't help Violet's feelings toward Robin improve.

Robin turned her attention to Violet and frowned. "Bad morning?"

"Bad last twelve hours," corrected Violet as she tossed her shirt onto her gym bag, opting to stay in her cropped tank, and walked back to the dummy.

The frown on Robin's face gave way to sorrow. "I guess you heard about what's been happening, huh?"

"If I hadn't, would you have told me?" Violet's level stare made Robin's gaze drop and she backed away a step. "Yeah. I didn't think so."

"Wow, I don't think I've seen you this upset since... well... Ever." Robin ducked away when Violet slammed a high kick into the side of the dummy's head.

Ignoring the trembling she felt in her hands, Violet grumbled, "I don't think I've ever felt like this before."

She threw a quick combo of punches and Robin let out a low whistle.

"If it helps, you're definitely not lacking in speed. Those were fast even to me."

That actually did make Violet feel a little better, but she didn't want to admit that. It still wasn't fast enough.

Robin walked past Violet and grabbed some sparring pads. "You'll get better practice with moving targets."

"You want me to hit you?" Violet asked, hoping she didn't sound too enthusiastic.

Robin huffed a laugh. "Definitely not. Especially with how angry you are right now. That's why I'm wearing these." She slapped her now padded hands and forearms together. "Strike!"

Violet shook her head. "That's too easy. Call out a combo or something."

"Just move your butt, Draven," Robin snapped, but the grin on her face betrayed her harsh tone.

While Robin shifted around the mat, making Violet move more and be more accurate with her attacks, she talked about things that had happened over the period Violet had been gone.

"I don't know if I envy or pity you," Robin said when Violet told her she hadn't felt the loss for the clan when the other members had been killed.

Glaring, Violet slammed her fist into one of the pads and Robin shook her hand after the impact. "Don't pity me."

"Got it." Robin lifted the pads again, allowing Violet to continue attacking. "I do have some fun news though."

Violet grunted as Robin raised her hand too high to hit or kick. She leaped off the mat to deliver her attack then landed in a slight crouch.

"Nice delivery," Robin complimented her with a smile.

"Thanks. What news?" Violet asked, walking away to grab a drink.

"Patrick and I have been on a few dates."

Violet nearly choked on her water. "That's..." she coughed. "That's... really?"

"I mean, we've been flirting for months, so it shouldn't be that big of a surprise."

Not from what Violet remembered. Robin was the one doing the flirting, Patrick usually just tolerated it. Although that time in the diner had been different. It had seemed like he was enjoying her attention, for once.

"So, dates, huh?" Violet wandered toward her again, feeling a new surge through her limbs.

"Yeah," Robin grunted when her arm was knocked to the side by a kick. "Although, I've had to ask him every time and he still won't kiss me. How long did it take before you two kissed?"

Violet froze. "We never..."

"Oh." Robin blinked. "Oh, really? Sorry, I just assumed with how much you liked him and how much time you spent together..."

"He's my bodyguard, Robin."

"Right." Robin raised the pads again. "Well, anyway, he's never said no to a date and seems like he enjoys himself."

Violet's jab, cross, jab knocked Robin back a step.

"Ow." Robin shook her hand out. "I probably should have asked this before, but you are over him, aren't you? Are you okay with all that?"

"All what?" Violet asked as she whipped around for another kick, but Robin ducked instead of allowing Violet to hit the pad.

"Me dating Patrick."

"Why wouldn't I be? I'm not his keeper."

Robin deftly blocked a few more attacks. "Okay, but..."

"It's fine. It's not like he ever returned those feelings, or sought me out, or tried to call or at least send a text while I've been gone." Violet threw a wicked combo and Robin shook out her padded hand.

"Ow!" Robin hesitantly returned to position with a guarded expression. "Are you sure, 'cause..."

"It's fine, Robin," Violet insisted, jabbing the pads a few times.

"It doesn't seem like you're fine, Viol—"

"I said I'm fine!" Violet's fist plowed into Robin's pad, knocking her back a couple of feet.

"Woah!" Robin threw the pads on the ground and held her hands in the air. "I'm out!"

Violet's chest heaved. Her mind was cloudy and forming a full thought was difficult. "I-I'm sorry..." She shook her head, trying to clear away the confusion. "I didn't mean to—"

"Your eyes!" Robin squealed, running toward her and smooshing Violet's cheeks with her hands. "Violet! What do you feel right now?"

Violet blinked a couple of times. The haze disappeared. "I feel... fine, I guess."

"What? Were you angry? Sad? Did you feel like someone was sharing your space or maybe like someone was watching through your eyes?"

One of Violet's brows dragged down while the other lifted. "What?"

Robin grabbed her shoulders. "Your eyes changed color, Violet! You hit me so hard my hand is still tingling and you sent me flying!"

"They did?" Surprise surged through Violet, building to excitement. "What color were they?"

Robin did a small jump while she smiled. "I don't know."

Violet's excitement vanished. "What do you mean you don't know?"

"I mean, I don't know." Robin's shoulders raised, but she was still grinning like a fool.

"Hey!" Patrick's voice called from behind Violet.

Violet closed her eyes once Robin had left her eyesight and drew in a deep breath before turning around.

"Hey yourself." Robin lifted onto her toes and kissed Patrick's cheek. Other than clenching his jaw, he did nothing. She ran her hand up Patrick's chest, but he captured her fingers before they grazed the skin above his workout tank.

Violet shifted her weight uncomfortably, and looked at the mats beneath her feet.

"Hey, guess what?" Robin let out a little squeal. "Violet's eyes just changed color."

Shock snapped Violet's head back up and she stared wide-eyed at Robin.

"Really?" Patrick's gaze moved to Violet as she pinched her lips together. "Congratulations. What color were they?"

Violet crossed her arms and stared at Robin. "I'd like to know that, too."

Groaning, Robin crossed her arms. "I told you; I don't know."

"How do you not know?" Patrick asked, making Robin roll her eyes.

"They were all swirly." Robin rolled one of her hands in the air. "Not really any defined color, kinda like Luna's, but not totally. They definitely weren't your annoyingly captivating purple."

Violet stared just above Robin's head, right into Patrick's hazel eyes. A thoughtful look had fallen over his features as he watched her.

"What was happening when her eyes changed?" Patrick asked. "Maybe we can repeat it."

"Oh, sure!" Robin grinned and bent to gather the pads she'd dropped. "I was asking Violet if she had a problem with—"

"Nothing!" Violet hurried to gather her things before any more information left Robin's mouth.

Robin followed after her. "Violet, I'm sure we can get the same results."

Violet tugged her sweaty oversized shirt back on and glared at Robin. "I don't want to repeat that conversation." She narrowly avoided crashing into the girl's shoulder as she moved around her and stepped off the mats. "I have to get back to my mom anyway. She still needs a lot of help with decorating and planning, and she won't appreciate it if I'm a sweaty mess."

Without offering a goodbye, Violet headed for the doors and didn't look back. She breathed in the brisk morning air, welcoming it against the heat that had settled over her skin.

Spring was right around the corner, but winter still held the mornings firmly in its grasp. By the time she made it up the Alpha House stairs, her skin had cooled and her breathing had evened out, the tension rising inside her had settled enough that she could focus on her next tasks.

Shower.

Eat.

Spring Solstice Preparations.

Nodding to herself, she opened the front door and nearly dropped her bag.

"Mom?"

Evalyn Draven's gaze snapped to her, her eyes a swirling vortex of gold and silver with hints of bronze. She lowered her hand from her temple and relaxed her white-knuckled grip on the back of her desk chair, as a gentle smile lifted the corners of her mouth. "Oh, there's my little miracle."

Slowly, her mother's eyes melted back to a light gray and she stepped away from her desk to meet Violet halfway across the room.

"Are you okay?" Violet asked, worry flooding her senses as she took in her mom's appearance. She had lost a little weight since Violet left, and darkness blotted the skin around her eyes.

Evalyn's brows creased. She smiled, grabbed Violet's free hand, and shook her head. "I'm fine, honey. Why are you so worried?"

"You would tell me, right mom?" Violet stared into her mom's eyes and gently squeezed her hand. "If something was wrong, you'd tell me?"

With a sigh, Evalyn released her hand and briefly touched her head. "It's just a headache. You need to go get cleaned up, so we can get started on decorations for the solstice."

"Mom—"

"Don't *mom* me, get your butt upstairs and in the shower." Evalyn waved her hand to dismiss Violet and pointed to the stairs. "Go."

No one could say Violet wasn't her mother's child. Their eyes were different, but their hair was a nearly identical dark chocolate brown. Violet was like a mini version of her mom. Even down to the stubbornness that pulsed through both of them.

A brief stare-down that resulted in Violet losing took place before she trudged up the stairs. She cast a backward glance at Evalyn who raised a brow, planted one fist on her hip, and pointed to the stairs again.

She wasn't budging, but Violet had a nagging feeling that something was very wrong with her mother.

# Chapter 6
## Violet

***"I want to wear a** green tie with my suit."*

Violet groaned as Jax's voice entered her thoughts, interrupting the order she was giving to a young wolven helping hang sheer pastel fabric from the ceiling.

"Are you okay?" He lifted a brow, watching her with concern.

Shaking her head, Violet grumbled. "I'm fine. Jax is being annoying."

He smothered a smile and then nodded his understanding.

"You're doing a great job making sure the different pieces meet together at the ceiling, but your angle is starting to be a diagonal instead of a curve." Violet pointed to the ceiling to indicate where the fabric needed to be. "Do you see that curve in the beam?"

"Ah man," he grumbled.

"You don't need to fix it." Violet lifted her clipboard and made a note about leaving the fabric and telling her mom to leave it as well. "We don't have time for that, and I doubt anyone other than myself and Luna will notice."

His face paled.

"Luna's not going to care," Violet assured him. "She just appreciates the help. Continue what you're doing and try to angle it back to where it needs to be to meet up in the center with the other side."

"Yes, ma'am."

Violet cringed at being called ma'am, but he had already rushed away, and was halfway up the ladder with the next sheet of fabric before she could address it.

*"I don't care what color your tie is,"* Violet answered Jax through their twin-link. He hadn't spoken to her since this morning, so the sudden topic of their birthday attire was more than a little annoying.

*"Mom wants us to match."* Jax quickly shot back.

Throwing her head back, Violet closed her eyes and let out a long breath through her nose. It wasn't very often that their mom asked them to match because she knew they despised it.

*"Green is fine,"* She could practically hear her sigh in her mind, *"but remember it's spring so make it a sage green, at least."*

*"Copy that."*

Violet shook her head at her twin's weirdness, then grabbed a faux feathered lantern and ascended a nearby ladder.

Turning the clan house, which was normally used for meals and the occasional clan meeting, into an elegant gathering spot took some work. A few tables were left out near the kitchen so members of the clan could still get a free, warm meal, but space was limited. Many took their food to go or ate in their own homes while celebration preparations were underway.

A man, human by the overwhelming smell of cologne that poorly masked his body odor, in a dark blue jumpsuit stepped toward her. His name tag read **Bob** and he offered her a clipboard. "I need you to sign off on this delivery."

"What delivery?" Violet asked as a young woman held out pastel blue and summer orange tablecloths for her to choose from. She gave the girl an incredulous look and then pointed to the pastel blue. "This is spring, not summer."

Bob-the-delivery-guy snorted, "A crap-ton of twinkle lights, that's what." He glanced around the chaos. "What do you guys have going on in this cute little community?"

Violet raised a brow. This was why they always had wolves deliver things. He was showing interest and that could be dangerous. Who let a human into the clan territory anyway?

*"Jax, I need you to ask mom if she ordered a boatload of twinkle lights."* Violet waved another clan member with a box of utensils toward a corner near the kitchen while trying to act as normal as possible as she telepathically spoke with her twin.

*"What? Why?"*

*"A human is here trying to get me to sign for a delivery and he's expressing curiosity."*

There was a momentary pause and Violet answered a couple of questions from other wolves while she waited.

*"Yes, she ordered them."* Jax finally answered, then sent, *"I'll look into the human."*

Violet smiled at the delivery guy, quickly signed her name to accept the delivery, and shrugged a shoulder. "Just a spring dance, that's all. Teenagers love it." She gently shoved the clipboard against the man's chest, drawing his attention away from the chaos around him. "Bryce!" Violet called one of the guys helping bring in a large statue of two wolves with three pups at their paws.

He, and the other guy helping him, set the statue down before he hurried over to her. "What do you need?"

With a sweet, but tense smile, Violet gestured to the human in front of her. "Please, make sure Bob here doesn't get lost on his way back to the gate."

Bryce did not hide his reaction very well when he caught on to Bob's human scent. His nose scrunched before he turned his head to fake a cough, then directed Bob out the door.

"One crazy thing down, a thousand more to go."

Hours passed in the hurried chaos of solstice preparations, and by the time the chefs started preparing dinner, Violet's feet were killing her. Once the food was done, she announced to the room that they would pick up again in the morning. A mix of gratitude and groaning filled the room, but she ignored it all.

After grabbing a bunch of food to go, Violet headed out the door to eat in the solitude of her room.

"Violet!"

Groaning, Violet picked up her pace, pretending she hadn't heard Zander calling to her. Unfortunately, he was not so easily swayed and caught up to her in a matter of ten steps.

"Violet, I've called you a couple of times." He skidded to a stop in front of her. "Why didn't you stop?"

Violet shook her head. "I've had people calling my name all day long."

"Right, yeah, I saw the work you're putting in to help Luna Draven." Zander shoved his hands in his pockets and looked uneasy as he glanced down the road. The sun cast a gentle glow over his head, making his light-brown hair appear blonder. "You're doing a fantastic job."

Confusion pulled Violet's brows down. Why was he being so sweet? "Thank... you?"

Zander's boyish smile lit up his face. It was the smile of a long-lost friend that Violet missed from time to time, but Zander wasn't that sweet boy anymore. He hadn't been since his trial. When he'd returned, he was obsessive and more than a little unhinged.

"I don't know what game you're playing at, Zander," Violet gently said, not wanting to disrupt whatever peace he had going on in his head, "but I don't want anything to do with it."

Shaking his head, Zander lifted his hands in surrender. "No games, I promise. I'm just trying to be the friend you once knew."

Violet shifted her food in her arms so the nachos on top wouldn't fall and scatter across the dirt road. "So... you aren't about to tell me how we belong together and how I'm your mate?"

Some dark emotion clouded Zander's blue eyes. His jaw clenched, but then he smiled again and it vanished. "Not if you don't want to hear it."

Violet started toward Alpha House again, side-stepping around him. "Good. Cause that is the last thing I want to hear right now."

"Really, the last thing?" Zander asked when he fell into step beside her, but the glare she gave him made him raise his hands again. "Okay, I get it."

Violet sighed. "What do you want, Zander?"

"I want to be your friend again."

"I don't believe you," Violet admitted matter-of-factly as they neared

Alpha House. "All you've done is hound me for a year and a half now. That doesn't change overnight."

Zander shot her a sideways glance. "This hasn't been overnight. I've been working really hard at this for weeks."

"Okay, fine. Talk." Violet stopped abruptly just before the pathway to Alpha House. "How's work? You're still working at the lumberyard, aren't you?"

His playful smirk used to make her laugh, but it only meant trouble now and her body tensed in response.

"Keeping tabs on me?" When she didn't answer he chuckled and shook his head. He blew out a long breath before continuing, "Yeah, I just got promoted actually. I'm making some good money and learning a whole lot more."

"That's great."

"Yeah, I mean—" Zander shrugged. "—the guy who had the position before me died… which kinda sucks… but I'm happy to take over."

Violet blinked. "Oh. That's… awful."

His smile slipped.

"I'm happy for you. It's just sad about the other guy." Her stomach rumbled and she looked longingly at her nachos that were getting cold and then at Alpha House. "I'm gonna go, 'kay?"

Hard fingers snagged her upper arm when she turned to leave. "That's it?"

"Let go of me, Zander," Violet growled, and surprisingly he did.

Shaking his head, he backed up a step. "Sorry." He bunched his mouth to the side and looked away. "I get it. I'll talk to you later."

"Zander," Violet groaned, drawing his attention again. He looked like a kid who had his favorite stuffed animal taken away. "Look, I am happy for you, I really am. And, I'm trying to be friendly, but you caught me after I've been on my feet all day long. I'm hungry. I'm tired. I just want to go home and sit down."

He eyed her suspiciously like he used to when they were kids and she was trying to get away with lying. He'd always known when she was lying. Thankfully, she wasn't right then. "I'm sorry to keep you. Have a good night, Violet."

The farther he walked down the road, the more guilty Violet felt. "Are you..." she mentally kicked herself for calling him back, but it was too late. He'd already stopped. "Are you going to attend the celebration tomorrow night?"

Zander grinned as he turned toward her. "Pretty sure Luna would murder me in my sleep if I didn't."

"She isn't the murdering type." A genuine smile lifted a corner of her mouth. "You could end up with a month of kitchen duty, though. I'm sure she remembers how much you love dishes and mopping."

Mock terror chased away Zander's grin. "That would be awful."

A small chuckle rolled through Violet and she shook her head remembering this kind of banter before his trials. Violet hadn't realized how much she missed it.

"If you don't have a date, do you want to go with me?"

And there went the happy feeling.

Violet frowned. "You're pretty brave to ask that in front of my house."

"Jax and Patrick aren't here."

A sliver of unease raced down Violet's spine. How did he know that? Even with her weird twin connection to Jax, she couldn't tell if he was in the house or not. And the confidence he'd said it with. He knew, and that's why he sought her out. He wouldn't have dared if there was a chance her brother or bodyguard were around. He wasn't even supposed to be talking to her.

"So, do you have a date?" Zander asked, walking closer to her.

Violet took a step toward the house. "No, but I don't want one."

"Why not?"

"Because..." She searched for a reason to give him without lying. He was only a couple of feet away from her now. "I'm going to be way too busy at the celebration to entertain a date."

"I'd be very understanding about your duties to your mom." Zander offered, holding his hands slightly out to the sides in invitation.

Only those who Luna Draven had permitted to could call her anything besides Luna. Zander's disrespect for her mom turned Violet's veins to ice.

"*Luna Draven*," Violet corrected him. "I'm not going with anyone, Zander. That includes you. Besides, my brother and Patrick would never allow that to happen."

The lines in Zander's face deepened and a slight spark of silver in his eyes told Violet she'd hit a nerve. "They can't stop everything, Violet."

A hint of threat wove through his words and the hairs on the back of her neck stood on end. Without turning her back to him, Violet moved toward Alpha House. "I'll see you at the celebration," she said when the side of her foot hit the lowest step.

He didn't answer and she hurried into the house. She shut the door, leaned back against the wooden barrier, closed her eyes, and breathed in the familiar calming scent of her home.

"Violet?"

Alpha Draven's voice made her jerk back to a standing position. "Sorry, I didn't—" She stared open-mouthed at the guy standing beside her father.

Napkin Hero's lips tilted up into a wide grin.

Shaking her head, Violet cleared her throat. "I didn't realize you had company."

"Just finished up an interview with a possible new member of our clan." Alpha Draven looked away from her to shake Napkin Hero's hand. "Again, thank you for stopping by. I'll be in touch."

Napkin Hero bowed his head respectfully. "I look forward to it."

Turning to head out the back door, Alpha Draven called over his shoulder. "Violet, see him out and tell him about the celebration tomorrow night."

He stepped out of the house and the air in the room grew significantly thicker.

"Violet, huh?" Napkin Hero turned back to her with a giant smile brightening his face.

She smiled back. She couldn't help it, his smile was contagious and a welcome change from the guy she'd left standing outside. "You sure didn't waste time finding the place," she said, moving through the room to drop her stuff on the kitchen counter and snag a nacho.

"And I see you found some food."

Violet nodded. "Oh yes, they keep me very well-fed here."

A low chuckle rolled out of Napkin Hero and then he glanced at the door. "Should I go?"

"Well," she said around a mouthful of nachos. Not wanting to be rude, she swallowed before continuing, "Alpha Draven did tell me to see you out, but I'm practically starving so, if you can wait a minute, you're welcome to hang out for a bit."

"I can definitely wait a minute."

She sucked the cheese from her thumb, then froze, realizing he was watching her and looked on the verge of laughing. Suddenly self-conscious, she pulled her thumb from her mouth and grabbed a nearby napkin. "Cool," she mumbled as she snagged a fork from a nearby drawer before plopping down on one of the couches. "Don't tell my mom I had nacho cheese on the couch."

"Mom?" Napkin Hero asked, then gestured toward the armchair across from her.

With a dismissive wave from Violet, he took the seat and waited for her to answer.

"Yeah... I'm kinda the alpha's daughter," she slowly let that information set in. To stop herself from saying more, she popped another nacho into her mouth, completely ignoring the fork she had.

Napkin Hero's brows shot toward the ceiling. "You are?"

"Much to his dislike, yeah, I am."

"That would make you the future alpha."

Violet shook her head. "That would be my brother, Jax. You'll see him at the celebration tomorrow night if you come."

He snorted. "That was subtle."

"I try."

He smiled, then sat back in the chair and thought for a moment. "Tomorrow, huh? Unfortunately, I have something else going on."

"That is unfortunate. Luna loves these celebrations and goes all out. I've been decorating the clan house all day."

Lifting his arms, he shrugged. "I mean, it would be a shame to miss that."

"It really would."

A huff of laughter left him and he leaned forward again. "Would you be sad if I didn't come?"

"I barely know you."

"Yeah, but I make you laugh."

A slow grin spread across her face. "I think *you* would be sad if you didn't come. Besides, Lexie will be there and she is one of the best people to have at parties." She tipped her head side to side. "At least for me."

Napkin Hero blinked. "The human? She's allowed here?"

"That *human* has sleepovers here. Lots of them."

"Wow." He nodded and took a moment to absorb the information. "That's definitely different."

Violet swallowed another chip and then shrugged. "She's the only one allowed and that's only because she is relentless, wouldn't take no for an answer, and refused to let our friendship go."

A gentle smile tugged at his mouth. "Sounds like a friend for life."

"Yeah," Violet agreed, then ate another cheese and meat-smothered chip.

Napkin Hero patted his knees. "Well, I can't promise I'll make it, but I can say that I'll try."

"Sounds great." She ignored his chuckle as she licked the cheese from her fingers because it was just too good. "I guess I should see you to the door, then, so you can be on your way."

They both stood and walked to the door and with his hand resting on the knob, Napkin Hero turned to gaze at her. "Violet..." he mulled her name over like it was a great riddle to solve. "I like it. It suits you."

With that he walked out the door, gently closing it behind him.

# Chapter 7
## Patrick

***"Why are we doing this** again?" Patrick grumbled as he and* Jax walked down the boulder-lined path toward Lockup.

Jax sighed. "Dad wants the transition between alphas to go as smoothly as possible—whenever that time comes. He wants me to be prepared. Which means, taking on more and more of his duties."

Shaking his head, Patrick cast his friend a glance. "I get that. Why are we skulking toward Lockup when you should be at practice for the tourney game tomorrow?"

Clearing his throat, Jax looked off to the side of the road. "Because I'm not going."

Patrick's eyes widened. "What are you talking about? You live for the Clan Games."

"Yeah, but not anymore." Jax shook his head and waved a dismissive arm. "It doesn't matter. I've got too much on my shoulders, and I'm about to turn eighteen, which—"

"Isn't tomorrow," Patrick interrupted. "You should be allowed one last game before you're kicked off the league and replaced by the next rookie standing on the sidelines."

Jax grinned. "Someone sounds a bit bitter that he can't play anymore."

Patrick groaned. "Maybe."

With a shrug, his best friend said, "I'll think about it."

The concrete complex of Lockup emerged from behind the boulders and trees, a harsh contrast to the lush greenery that surrounded them. Two clan members guarded the door; one stood at attention, her eyes glowing silver, while the other sat in his gray and tawny wolf form. The wolf's muzzle turned toward them and his ears swiveled atop his head.

"Jax," the woman greeted, lowering her chin respectfully while the wolf followed suit. "We weren't expecting you."

"Alpha Draven sent me in his place." Jax's voice dropped a level when he was in authoritative situations. The tone he adopted, even without any malice behind it, would make many lower-ranking clan members lower their gaze.

These two guards were no exception.

The woman now stared at Jax's chin... or throat... it was hard for Patrick to tell, while the wolf stared at his stomach.

"And him?"

Patrick clenched his jaw when her brown eyes dared to meet his.

The snarl that pulled Jax's lips back startled her into lowering her gaze to his knees. "Patrick is my beta. You have no right to question either of us."

Her braid bobbed as she nodded. "My apologies. I'd heard that was no longer the case."

Jax opened his mouth to speak, but Patrick beat him to it. "My position will not be dissolved until Jax has appointed a new beta."

"Which I haven't," Jax added.

The two guards eyed one another before opening the doors to Lockup.

Once the doors closed behind them, Jax puffed out his cheeks with a large breath. "People are taking you stepping down pretty seriously, aren't they?"

"It *is* serious," Patrick grumbled, moving past his friend toward the hall that lead to the cells.

"I already told you I wouldn't accept that." Jax caught up to him and almost matched his stride, but Patrick still had a couple of inches on him, so that made it difficult.

He sighed. "And I told you, you don't have a say in the matter."

"I'm your future alpha. I'm the only one who should have a say."

Patrick was ready to argue his point, but Jax tapped his knuckles off the wall beside a cell.

"Hey, wake up," he called to the cell's occupant.

Unease made Patrick's arm hair stand on end as the Blood Moon wolf behind the bars rolled into a sitting position to stare at them through her long hair. Ruby eyes bored into Patrick's soul. Dread filled him as he gazed into his future if he ever lost control of Alistair.

*"Give me some credit, Boy Scout. I'd make sure we looked much better than that."*

Patrick groaned internally. *"That isn't comforting."*

Alistair's chuckle faded into the back of his mind as the crimson-eyed prisoner spoke, "Like anyone could sleep on this rock of a bed."

"You're lucky to have that rock after killing a member of our clan." Jax glared through the bars at the prisoner who was smiling demonically back at him. "Is there anything..." he cleared his throat and tried again. "Is there anything we can help you with?"

"Sure." The prisoner slumped off the cot and dragged her feet toward the cell.

Patrick put a hand on Jax's shoulder, ready to pull him away at the first sign of trouble. And that's all the Blood Moon pack was... trouble.

The prisoner stopped mere inches from the bars, wary of the electricity running through them. "You can open this cell, hand over Patrick, and let me go."

"Why?" The question flew from both Patrick and Jax at the same time, but it was Patrick who continued, "I'm nothing special."

The prisoner clicked her tongue. "Don't take me for a fool. I know so much about you, including what you did to those three teenagers."

Tension rippled across Patrick's shoulders.

"I even know their names," she whispered.

Patrick growled, "How?"

The prisoner's crimson eyes faded to reveal a dark blue. Her voice took on a desperate tone and she spoke rapidly, "Teach me how to tame this monster in my head and I'll tell you ev—" Her hands clamped around her head and a shriek echoed in her cell. She breathed heavily for a moment, then lowered her hands back to her sides. A cocky smile slipped over her cracked lips. Her greasy hair fell into her face when she tipped her head to the side and stared back at them through narrowed blood-red eyes. "We're done here." She sauntered back toward the cot with a laugh. "Unless you want to discuss the details of your murder."

Disgust contorted Patrick's face. "Pass."

With a shrug, the prisoner returned to her previous position on the cot without another word.

"That was strange," Jax muttered as they walked toward the next prisoner.

Patrick looked over his shoulder, catching one last glimpse of the Blood Moon member reclining nonchalantly on the cot. Strange was a good word for it. For a moment, it was as if the wolven within was trying to break free.

But that wasn't possible. No one had ever gained control over their blood-lusting self after they'd taken an innocent life.

No one... Except Patrick.

His brows pinched together.

He thought he had gotten lucky and was only able to keep Alistair in check because he never let his darker half gain full control. But maybe... if others could come back from that void of helplessness... then he wasn't doomed after all.

"You all right?" Jax asked as they neared the next occupied cell.

Patrick nodded. Until he had more to tell, he'd keep that ribbon of hope to himself. Jax was already delusional about keeping Patrick as his beta. He didn't need his friend to get his hopes up even more.

It took a lot out of him to check in on the ten Blood Moon pack members currently in Lockup. Each one showed him different versions of himself if Alistair ever took over. And only the female had exhibited that strange sense of awareness.

Patrick walked away from the last cell before Jax, who had stopped standing so close to the bars when one of them eventually did try to snag him. He knew Jax wouldn't try that again, so he felt safe in taking a few steps away. He leaned heavily against the wall, resting his head back against the cement.

The female's other half seemingly trying to regain control wasn't the only thing bothering him. Patrick thought he had been so careful keeping his past a secret. After this visit, he knew someone had betrayed his trust. Every single Blood Moon member knew him by name. They knew his wolf had red eyes. They knew how he'd obtained them.

Not one of them mentioned it was an accident.

Jax sighed, drawing Patrick's attention as his friend walked toward him. "One more."

"You might have to take this last one by yourself." Patrick pushed off the wall to fall into step beside his future alpha. "I'm sick of seeing them."

"Who? The Blood Moon pack?"

Ice raced down Patrick's spine and he barely contained a shiver. "The ghosts of my future."

A snort burst out of Jax. "Are you serious, right now?" He looked up and his smirk faded when he saw the glare hardening Patrick's face. "Oh, you are serious." Jax cleared his throat, then shook his head. "You've conquered Alistair time and time again. You've got nothing to worry about. That point of no return that they've all crossed isn't anywhere close to the path you're on."

"It's closer than you think, Jax."

Jax snagged Patrick's shoulder, pulling him to a stop. "You don't have to believe me if you don't want to, but I know what I see in you every day. You never stop fighting. On top of that, you walked out of that trial ring. The magic behind those trial rings is so old it puts our ancestors to shame."

Patrick huffed a laugh.

"You wouldn't have been able to leave that ring if there was even a threat of you being unstable."

"What if it's only in that moment? We don't fully understand how the rings work. What if they aren't taking the future into account? Look at Zander. How the heck did he make it out of the ring?"

Jax's mouth opened but closed again when no words came out. After a moment, he shook his head. "I don't know how Zander came back from the ring. But you're not him. You are none of them. And, you are more powerful than all of them combined. I know that. You know that. Everyone who knows you, knows that."

"That's a lot of power you seem to think I have." Patrick smirked, trying to lighten the situation so they could move on.

Shaking his head, Jax let out a short laugh. "Don't let it get to your head. You're still my beta."

Patrick's mirth died. "I don't want to be alpha, Jax. You know that."

"Doesn't mean you couldn't take it from me, or Alpha Draven, if you ever wanted to."

"I wouldn't."

"But you could."

Patrick never wanted to be an alpha. It was one of the things he hated about his family's clan. They had expected it... before the accident.

Regardless, whatever power he did have offered him very little reassurance. Whatever he had, Alistair did too. Something could happen later on in life and ruin his ability to keep Alistair at bay. There were too many unknowns.

*"What's the fun in being old and decrepit? I would gladly return to the confines of your mind in our withering old age."*

*"Don't lie."* Patrick chided his darker half. *"We both know you would never give up that control."*

Alistair's dark chuckle echoed through his body, making his muscles tense. *"It might be hard after such a long time. There may not be enough of you left."*

*"So, it's true then? Blood Moon wolves lose their former selves?"*

*"Do you really expect me to have all the answers when you keep me tethered on a very short leash?"*

*"You have to know something."*

*"Even if I knew that there was a way for them to break the control of their blood-thirsty side, do you truly believe I would tell you?"*

Patrick growled.

Jax shot him a worried look. "Everything all right in that crowded brain of yours?"

"Alistair is being difficult."

*"I thought you'd be used to that by now, Boy Scout."* Alistair laughed at the same time Jax asked, "Isn't he always?"

Patrick didn't answer either of them. They walked in silence for a minute, reaching the top floor of the compound before Patrick realized the quality of the cells had changed.

Full mattresses and fluffy-looking bedding filled the larger space. A half wall in the back corner allowed some privacy for the toilet. A few of the cells even had a small window and a small armchair. Plexiglass replaced the bars and helped give the cell a more apartment-like feel.

"Jax, who is our last stop?" Patrick asked in a hushed tone.

A heavy sigh pulled his friend's shoulders down. "I didn't want to tell you in case you backed out, but my dad asked that we check in on Mya."

Patrick stopped. He hadn't seen Mya in days. Not since she collapsed in Jax's arms from the worst kind of pain any of their kind could ever experience. They'd all lost Aiden, but she had lost her mate—her other half.

Without looking back, Jax continued on to the next cell and gently knocked his knuckles against the plexiglass wall. "Hey Mya," his tone was more gentle than Patrick had ever heard before. "Alpha Draven and Dr. Penmann wanted us to check in on you. How are you doing?"

There was no reply.

Slowly, Patrick made his way to Jax's side. He peered into the cell and clenched his jaw. In the farthest corner of the room sat the full-sized bed with no bedding. Atop it, with her knees tucked up against her chest, sat the shell of a girl he'd once hesitated to call a friend. It was dangerous to get too close to people, but now he wished he had told her how much her kindness meant to him. How much her friendship with Violet meant to him.

"Mya?" Jax called a little louder.

Her mane of coiled chestnut hair looked like it hadn't been washed, or brushed, and it was possible some type of creature had taken residence on one side.

The quietest whisper reached them, "Go away."

"I can't do that, Mya," Jax answered, no longer attempting to be gentle with her. "Dr. Penmann allowed you to move into this cell because she felt that with the right sedative, you would be able to be on your own. Don't make me call that woman a liar. She can be very scary."

Mya turned her face toward them and Patrick sucked in a sharp breath. Agony-filled green eyes set within dark rings were evidence she hadn't been sleeping. It had only been a few days, but her cheeks looked slightly sunken in, making Patrick wonder when the last time she'd eaten.

"You have to prove her right," Jax told her, sounding more like an order than a comforting friend.

Opening his mind, Patrick reached through the clan-link to Jax. *"What are you trying to do?"*

*"I'm supposed to make sure Mya is doing okay on the sedative. It's a large enough dose that doc isn't worried about her attempting to join Aiden and by what I see, I don't think she will either."*

Patrick snorted. *"You're an idiot."*

*"What?"* Jax glared. *"I'm doing what I was told."*

*"You have the worst bedside manner I've ever seen."* Patrick moved toward the cell door. "Open it for me."

"What?" Jax repeated, out loud. "I don't think that's a good idea."

"You were just telling me how powerful I am, do you really think this is dangerous?"

Jax's glare narrowed even further before he punched a code into the keypad beside the cell. Part of the plexiglass slowly swung open in response.

Patrick had only taken two steps inside when Mya flinched. She pulled herself into a tighter ball and looked toward the window.

After closing the door behind him, he lowered into a crouch with his palms facing her. "Mya, do you recognize me?"

No response.

"I'm going to come a little closer, okay?" He told her gently as if he was speaking to a frightened, wounded animal. And in a way, he was.

Her gaze dragged back to him when he'd taken a couple more steps. Fear and pain radiated out of her, but there was a haze in her eyes—like she wasn't fully there.

Patrick held his ground when her fingers curled into fists.

"It's okay," he reassured her. Her response was slow, but her shoulders relaxed a little. "Can you understand me?"

It took a second, but Mya finally gave a single nod.

Not wanting to risk setting her off, Patrick lowered one knee to the floor and rested his elbows on the other. He wasn't about to push her boundaries right now. "Jax just told you why we're here, do you remember?"

Mya eyed him, then looked at Jax. Her gaze returned to Patrick and she slowly blinked.

"Mya?" He asked, trying to find some awareness in her gaze. "Do you know who I am?"

An incredulous stare contorted her face. Her voice was rough and quiet as she slowly slurred, "Everyone knows who you are, Patrick."

A small, amused smile lifted one corner of Patrick's mouth. "That's good. Do you know why Jax and I are here?"

A moment passed and Patrick was beginning to think he wouldn't get an answer out of her. He shot a look at Jax as he sent, *"I think her dosage is too high. We need Dr. Penmann to reevaluate the situation."*

Jax nodded, then looked away, concentrating on a different internal conversation. While Jax could connect with nearly everyone in the clan now, he'd told Patrick there were some members that required more effort. Dr. Penmann must be one of them.

"Mya?" Patrick tried again. "Do you know why we're here?"

She shook her head.

"Do you know why *you're* here?"

Tears filled her eyes and she squeezed her knees against her chest. "Yes," she whispered. "Aiden..." She dropped her forehead to her knees and let out a heavy sob. "H-he's gone. I t-tried to hurt myself... and o-others."

Patrick's heart ached for her. Mya was such a sweet girl. He'd watched her tag along with Violet for years, being one of the only true friends Violet had. She didn't care about Violet's rank or lineage. She didn't care that Violet didn't have a wolf. She was wary but accepting of Patrick. He always felt like she knew more than she actually did about him, but was happy to be friends with him anyway.

Aiden had been a friend to everyone, but when she and Aiden started growing closer, his friendship with them grew fast and fierce. He was the missing piece in their group. He brought light and laughter to every situation, but protected others with everything he had. Even defending Violet against a future alpha from another clan, knowing he would lose.

Patrick missed him.

He regretted not being friends with him sooner. Not letting him close enough to be friends.

He could use some of Aiden's playful antics right now.

Drawing in a deep breath, Patrick asked, "Did you want to hurt anyone?"

Tears dribbled down her cheeks, filling the air with a hint of salt. "No." Her words were slow, but there was a surety behind them. "I never... I don't want to hurt anyone."

A tap on the glass drew both of their attention and Jax announced, "Doc's on her way."

With a relieved sigh, Patrick looked back at Mya. "I think you'll feel a little better once Doc takes a look at you. I know it's going to take time for you to feel ready for anything, bu—"

"How could you know that?" Mya snapped, surprising him with the fire in her tone and fierceness in her once-vacant eyes. A dull silver began to swirl within the green, but it faded almost immediately. "You don't even have a mate."

Patrick glanced at Jax who was watching them with concern pulling his brows together. Patrick moved forward, staying as low and small as he could, but Mya still eyed him like he was a snake. When he was only a couple feet from her, he whispered as quietly as he could, hoping she would hear him, but Jax wouldn't, "Actually, I do."

For a split second, the old Mya was back. Her eyes brightened and happiness pulled a small smile across her mouth, but then it was like someone had turned off her joy and she sank back against the wall.

"See..." Patrick wet his lips, not believing he was admitting this out loud. "I've been pushing her away because the thought of losing her kills me." He lowered his head as emotion clouded his voice. "Being with me would put a target on her. I won't do that. And I'm..." He swallowed the knot that had built in his throat. "I'm so sorry for the part I played in Aiden's death. I should have left before any of this happened."

He lifted his gaze to find Mya watching him. It was disturbing to find no emotion on her face. She blinked at him. Slowly her eyebrows pulled down. "You didn't kill him, Patrick."

Patrick clenched his jaw. "Not directly." The truth behind his words was a knife to his heart. "Don't forget, Mya, we knew Aiden, too. I know you lost your mate and you're going to feel that deeper and longer than anyone else, but we are all hurting from losing our friend."

Mya moaned and buried her face in her knees once again. Her shoulders trembled as a hint of salt filled the air once again. Taking a chance, Patrick rose from the floor and closed the gap between them. The mattress sank under his weight, causing her to fall into his side. He wrapped an arm around her shoulders and gave a small squeeze.

"When you're ready, there are people who want to see you. Violet wants to see you."

Shaking her head, Mya answered between her sobs. "I don't... want... to see her... Or anyone... He's everywhere."

Patrick rubbed her arm and she turned her face into his chest, clinging to his shirt. "I know. Aiden helped a lot of people. He protected Violet when I wasn't there. He gave selflessly, and protected others with everything he had. He was a true Sentinel. I think seeing those he helped, could help you. He's not completely gone, Mya. He's in everything around us."

"That's what makes it so painful," she cried. "He's everywhere."

He clenched his jaw as the faces of the teens he'd killed flashed through his mind. "I know." And he did. He understood better than she knew. He saw them in the teens around him. He saw them whenever he climbed into the driver's seat of his truck. He saw them every day.

*"And you'll never forget them, Boy Scout."*

*"You misunderstood that thought."* Patrick huffed a laugh internally to his other half. *"I never want to forget them. They help me remain in control. They are my reminder to never be so careless again."*

"Patrick." The doc's soothing, raspy voice entered the cell and he looked up into the warmth of her gentle smile. "I'll take it from here."

Together they removed his shirt from Mya's grasp and laid the despairing girl on her side. The doc sat on the edge where Patrick had been moments before and set her hand on Mya's shoulder.

"Did you need something else?" Doc blinked at him.

"No, ma'am." Patrick backed away, bowing respectfully, but when he got to the door he turned back. "Can I check on her again tomorrow?"

Dr. Penmann's smile brightened her face. "I think that would be all right. Thank you for voicing your concerns."

Patrick nodded, then slipped out the door and down the hall. He passed Jax without a word who quickly fell into step beside him.

"What was that?" Jax asked once they were in the stairwell. His words echoed and Patrick clenched his jaw against the volume while they descended the stairs.

"What do you mean?" Patrick asked at a much lower volume, hoping his friend would copy it.

He didn't.

"You're suddenly mister sensitive? I've never seen you comfort any girl besides Violet."

Patrick rounded on Jax, nearly making his friend crash into him. "And you're not sensitive enough!" His snapped tone echoed louder than Jax's and they both winced before he continued a bit quieter. "You've been connected to your twin sister's brain and thoughts since the moment you were born, but somehow you still don't understand how to talk to, or be there for a girl when she needs you."

Jax snorted, crossing his arms. It was such a Violet thing to do when she was frustrated with Patrick. "And you do?"

"I have a little sister, Jax."

His friend's eyes bugged and his jaw fell a fraction. "What?"

Sighing, Patrick ran a hand through his hair. "I haven't seen her or talked to her since I left. My parents didn't want me to." He glanced at the stairs beneath his feet, uncomfortable sharing anything about his precious sister. Most of the time he even tried to avoid thinking about her. "She followed me around everywhere. She's only two years younger than me, but there were times when it felt like much more. She was such a pain, but we were very close. I got pretty good at comforting her. It's not that hard."

Jax's surprised expression pinched back into a glare.

"She was thirteen when..." Patrick swallowed hard and shook his head. "My parents didn't let me say goodbye."

The look Jax was giving him told him he wanted to say something, but didn't know what. Or maybe it was the how that was difficult.

"Look, all I'm saying is that for someone who's been literally linked to his sister, sometimes you act like you know nothing about her. Or any girl for that matter." Patrick turned and started down the stairs, not bothering to wait.

"You're not the only one who has had to hide things, Patrick."

Confusion pulled Patrick's brows together and he turned to stare up at his friend. "Really?"

"Mine isn't as drastic as yours, but you've said yourself you didn't understand why I was treating Violet the way I have been. You were ordered to leave. I've been ordered to sever any ties with Violet—as much as possible anyway."

"What?" Patrick growled and Alistair rose in the back of his mind.

Jax lifted a hand earning him a small amount of time before Patrick stormed off to find Alpha Draven. "And it's an order that I can suddenly defy."

The tension in Patrick's shoulders relaxed.

"I tried to start repairing our relationship the morning after she came back." Jax huffed a sad laugh. "Let's just say it's not going well."

"Ya think?" Patrick grumbled. He drew in a deep breath and sighed. "Glad to hear Dalim is helping you come into your power."

Jax smirked. "Oh, he's more than ready."

Patrick smiled back. "Good. We need some positive news around here."

With Jax gaining power, it wouldn't be long before the title of alpha was passed down. Jax was young and had a lot to learn, but Patrick had no doubt in his mind that his best friend would make a fantastic leader.

# Chapter 8

## Violet

***Violet groaned after hitting the mat*** *for the twentieth time that morning.* Her body ached from the abuse it'd taken yesterday after training for the first time in weeks. Muscles screamed with each movement, and even the cushioned mats couldn't protect her from the sting of impact against her sore body.

Patrick had taken his duty as her trainer pretty seriously before Violet's extended stay with Lexie had happened, but he'd kicked it into overdrive.

That morning he'd burst into her bedroom at the crack of dawn like some boot camp officer. When she didn't jump out of bed rearing to go, he flipped her mattress over and sent her sprawling across the floor in her shorts and sports bra.

A sound lashing of words from her drove him quickly out of the room and she'd taken her sweet time getting dressed. She was paying for that now.

Violet's muscles cried when she rolled onto her hands and knees, "I have a question."

"Ask later. Right now, we're training," Patrick reminded her, waiting for her to rise.

Shaking her head, Violet drew in a heavy breath. "I'm tired." She wasn't really. She was mad at him and didn't want to train with him.

"Being tired won't stop the Blood Moon Pack from killing you,"

Patrick's voice strained as he leaped toward her.

Violet rolled to the side and found her way to her feet. "Do you really think anything would stop them if they were targeting me?"

Her question caught him off guard and she thrust a front kick against his stomach. He caught her foot and twisted. Using the momentum he generated, Violet jumped and spun, smashing her other foot against the side of his head.

She crashed to the ground while he shook out his head.

"Impressive. Where'd you pick that up?"

Violet groaned as she rose onto her elbows. "Answer the question, Patrick."

He'd been avoiding her questions all morning, and she'd had enough.

Patrick shrugged. "I don't know."

Rolling to her feet, she shook out her right arm. "So, does it really matter how much I train or how hard you beat me into the mats?"

"Yes, it does." Patrick beckoned her forward.

"Bull."

Violet thrust forward and he stepped into her space, deflecting her attack. His leg locked behind hers. Driving his arm across her chest, Patrick tripped her before throwing her into the mat... again.

She rolled away and made her way to her feet with a groan.

"Do you have any clue how out of practice you are?" Patrick growled, storming toward her. "Didn't you do any training while you were gone?"

"You caught me off guard," Violet grumbled.

Patrick snorted. "You wish. It hasn't been that long since we trained together, yet I'm wiping the floor with you."

Frustration surged through her. "It's been three weeks."

"That's not the point, Vi."

"Don't call me that." Violet snapped, she was sick of hearing his breathy, warm tone and having her knees go weak.

Confusion froze Patrick momentarily. "I've always called you that."

"Yeah, well..." Violet waved a dismissive arm as she headed for her water. "Don't."

With speed she couldn't track, Patrick was suddenly beside her, sweeping her legs out from under her. Her back hit the mat—again—but this time her lungs seized. She curled in on herself until she could gasp for air, then lay flat out on the mat.

He bent over her and narrowed his gaze. His tone was harsh when he said, "You should have been able to jump over that attack, at the very least."

"Do you realize you move a lot faster since your trials?"

"Do you realize you're moving a lot slower since you left?"

"Am I?" Violet growled while making her way to her feet once again. "Or does it just seem that way because you're now connected to Alistair? How is he enjoying this, by the way? He did say he always liked a good sparring match with me."

Patrick's eyes flashed red and he dropped his chin so no one else would see. When he looked back at her, anger scorched his gaze, but the ruby tint was gone.

"Oh, now you're mad?" Violet huffed a laugh and stepped into his space, keeping her voice low. "Guess how I've been feeling since I had stitches put in my back after helping *you* only to have you ignore me!"

Tension pulsed in his jaw. "I haven't been ignoring you."

Violet scoffed. "Yes, you have."

She moved toward her water bottle again and Patrick attacked. If he hadn't been holding back, Violet may not have had time to dive out of the way. She rolled across the ground and then popped up to her feet.

"You keep trying to leave, but we're not done training."

"Who put you in charge?" Violet grumbled, ducking under another swing.

A low rumble of laughter left Patrick. "You did," he reminded her, feinting to one side when she threw another punch. "Almost a year and a half ago."

"I rescind that."

"Rescind what?" Patrick grunted when Violet snuck a sideways kick against his ribs. "You asked me to help you get stronger. So, I did."

Fury powered a series of kicks and throws while Violet advanced on Patrick, slowly forcing him back even though he blocked each one. His wrists crossed to block a kick before catching her foot. She'd been in this position before, many times, and it never ended well for her, but instead of showing her one of the countless ways he could take her down... he released her.

Violet stepped back, breathing heavily. "I will never be as strong as you. Or anyone in this clan. No amount of training will change that."

"You don't need to be strong to defeat someone. We've been over that. You are smart enough to—"

"I don't want to hear it, Patrick!" Violet yelled, briefly earning the attention of the few clan members also training. "Maybe before your trials you were content to be my brother's lapdog and my bodyguard or trainer or whatever this is, but I wasn't. Then, after everything that happened that night, I was naive enough to think things might change. They changed, but instead of getting better, they got worse!"

Patrick's breathing was heavier than usual and his normally cool hazel eyes filled with fire.

"Jax is being nicer, but it's awkward and weird, and he's so busy with alpha duties that we don't have much time together anyway. You and I connected during your trials, and were open and warm toward each other, but now you're with Robin more than not, and that..." Violet bit her lip.

She wasn't the kind of girl to break up a relationship. She wouldn't do it. No matter how much it killed her to see them together. No matter how much she disliked Robin.

Shaking her head, Violet stepped back. "I can't do this."

Patrick dropped into a spin and knocked her legs out from under her. Violet landed hard on her back, grunting from the impact. Tears stung her eyes as he leaned over her, and she kicked his legs in anger.

He tried to jump out of the way, but he had already been leaning forward and the sudden movement off-centered him. Violet realized very quickly that she had made a mistake when he came plummeting toward her.

Closing her eyes, she waited to be crushed, but a thud rattled the floor beneath her and something barely skimmed her chest.

Violet peeked one eye open, and then the other. Patrick held himself above her—resting on his right elbow and knee while his left hand acted as a pillar beside her. His chest brushed hers with each breath he drew.

The last time they'd been this close was during his trial. Memories scorched her mind, and heat swirled within her belly. With how angry she currently was, she hated that his close proximity had such an intense effect on her.

"You can't leave a training session like that, Vi." Patrick's hushed tone sent a ripple of excitement down her spine that she cursed herself for. "You can't walk away after saying all of that without giving me a chance to speak."

Those tears that had been threatening began to flood her vision. She shook her head, not knowing if she could trust her voice. It might help, but talking was the last thing she wanted to do. Her emotions were out of control, and she didn't know what she might say.

"I haven't been ignoring you. Avoiding, yes..." He shook his head and slid his left hand across the ground to cradle her waist. "I could never ignore you. You terrify me with your reckless bravery and unwavering love. You are everywhere I look, in everything I do. It has been an honor to train and guard you. If that's all I have the chance to do in this life, it would be enough."

Breathing became difficult as they stared at one another, the fire in his gaze seared her to the core. War raged within her, battling loyalty against longing.

She'd made a promise to Jax. Maybe she was over it, but she didn't want to hurt her brother. And Robin... how could she betray—.

Patrick's gaze fell to her lips. He lowered his head until the tips of his wavy hair met hers and she sucked in a breath when his nose grazed hers. Tension built in her neck and shoulders. She should have turned away. She should have told him to stop. He was giving her plenty of time to, but...

His lips feathered across hers.

The strain in her muscles melted away and she closed her eyes.

The whisper of a kiss was met with her answer, tipping her chin to deepen—

He was gone.

The air above her went cold.

Violet lurched into a sitting position. Her cheeks burned like living flames.

Patrick had his hands in his hair. He shook his head, pacing back and forth a few steps. "I shouldn't have... That was..."

Violet's heart sank when Patrick looked at her with his jaw locked and hard eyes.

"I'm sorry," he said. "That was a mistake."

"Patrick," Violet's voice came out a whisper when he started to grab his things.

His movements slowed, but then continued faster than before. "I'll assign someone else to take over your training."

"What?" Lightning struck her and she was on her feet. "No. You're my trainer. You're the best..."

"I can't train you properly."

"You said I'm out of practice. If I've regressed as much as you're suggesting then I need training."

"Exactly." He turned on her, and she flinched back at the sudden movement. "And I can't do that if I'm distracted by..." His words cut off when his attention dipped to her mouth. Driving his gaze back to hers he swallowed hard. "I can't train you."

He snatched his gear and walked away.

# Chapter 9
## Violet

***Mistake.***

*That's what he'd said.*

The word tore at Violet's heart.

Mistake.

It could have described a lot of things about her. Even her very existence. Twins didn't exist amongst wolven.

After Patrick had walked away Violet had left the training facility too, hoping no one had seen what'd happened. She cleaned herself up and checked on the last remaining preparations for the solstice celebration, which thankfully took the majority of the day.

She was about to head home, when her mom's voice filled the Clan House.

"You've outdone yourself!"

Violet spun in time to catch her mom in a crushing hug. "Thanks. I learned from the best."

Evalyn stepped out of their embrace to look around the room. "You've really done an incredible job. I couldn't have done it better myself." Her gaze halted on the ceiling and a corner of her mouth quirked upward.

Tracking her mom's gaze, Violet found the off-course sheer fabric draping from the ceiling. "The poor guy nearly had a heart attack when I told him you were going to notice. He did a great job correcting the rest of the line though."

Evalyn chuckled. "Even after all these years, people still think I'm capable of biting someone's head off."

"I've seen you angry. They have reason to fear that."

Her mom sent a teasing glare her way before heading toward a counter-height table against one of the walls. A large, sparkly box sat begging for attention. To her surprise, and glee, Evalyn lifted the box and carried it toward her.

"This is for you." Her mom set the box on the nearest table to Violet and then gestured for her to open it. The moment Violet's fingers began to lift the lid, Evalyn continued, "I know you've been very busy with decorations and haven't had a moment to yourself, so I bought this as a thank you. I hope you like it."

Pastel-purple fabric lay folded delicately in the sparkly tissue-lined box.

*Like* wasn't an appropriate word. Violet *loved* it!

Her fingers ran over the material which was light and flowy with tons of sparkles everywhere. When she lifted it from the box, it looked to be close to tea-length. It really was the perfect Spring Solstice dress... but when Evalyn dismissed her to get ready, Violet had placed the box on her desk and hadn't touched it again.

After a while, Evalyn dropped by her room to see if she was ready at one, and Violet told her she'd be there soon.

Instead of donning the dress and running off to the dance, Violet folded her clean clothes and put them away. Celebrating while one of her friends was in Lockup under heavy sedation and another had just been killed felt wrong. It felt so wrong to be happy while Mya was in agony. It felt wrong to laugh when Aiden would never laugh again.

"Knock knock!" Lexie's voice called through her bedroom door and Violet spun around as her friend entered the room. "Can I come... whoa." Two steps in, Lexie froze while her eyes bugged. "What demon possessed you?"

"What are you talking about?" Violet asked as she hung a shirt in the closet. She closed the door to find her friend staring at the spotless floor of her room. "I'm not possessed, Lexie."

"I've known you for years and I don't think I've ever seen your room this clean." Her blue eyes narrowed and then snapped to Violet. "What did he do to you?"

Confusion pinched Violet's face. "Who?"

Tension rolled off her friend as the tall blond stalked toward her. "I swear if he hurt you... I don't care how massive the guy is, I will find a way to take him down and make him regret it."

"Woah! Down girl!" Violet held out both hands to stop Lexie from walking straight into her. "What are you talking about?"

Lexie swung an arm indicating the room. "There is only one guy I know that can affect you this much, so now would be a great time to exact revenge."

Understanding dawned on Violet and she shook her head. "Revenge does not need to be... exacted..." she felt stupid for saying that, but she continued anyway, "Even if I knew where he was, I wouldn't tell you."

"It wouldn't be that hard to find out." Lexie started for the door.

Panic settled into her limbs and Violet grabbed her friend's arm. "Lexie—"

Lexie rounded on her and pointed at the clean floor. "This freaks me out. Where are your clothes?"

"They're in the drawer," Violet mumbled. "And hanging up in the closet."

Lexie froze with her jaw hanging open then pointed at Violet. "See? That. That's freaky. When was the last time you actually put your clothes away?"

Violet looked around her abnormally clean room. It was a little freaky.

Fury returned to Lexie's eyes. "What happened?"

There was an inner strength in Lexie that made her stand out from the rest of the humans Violet had met. She cared deeply for others, wanted happy endings for everyone, and had a fiercely protective nature that, while endearing, was also a little terrifying at times.

The cushy mattress of her bed met Violet with the promise of comfort when she sat down. But the comforter couldn't protect her against Lexie's ravenous curiosity. She would hunt for the answers until they revealed themselves to her.

Violet opened her mouth to argue that nothing had happened, but found herself saying, "Patrick kissed me."

"What?" Lexie shrieked, then sank into the desk chair. "When?"

"This morning."

Lexie's pale brows pinched together. "And his kisses are so magical they made your room clean?"

The monotone voice her friend used would have made Violet laugh under other circumstances, but instead, it just made Violet groan.

"No." She bit her lip, but Lexie watched her expectantly. When it was clear Lexie wasn't going to give in, Violet sighed. "He said it was a mistake."

For a moment, Lexie sat perfectly still, but then a large breath expanded her chest and she ran her tongue over her teeth. Tension pulled at every feature, turning her into an avenging angel. The eerie calm that had settled over Lexie leaked into her voice.

"I'm going to kill him."

"No, you will not," Violet ordered. "He had a reason."

Lexie blinked. "Say that again, and I'm gonna slap you."

"You don't understand." She twisted her sleeves around her hands. "We were in the middle of training. Close proximity, you know? And everyone's emotions have been running high since—"

"*Everyone* didn't kiss you and then say it was a mistake."

"Lexie."

"Violet!" Her friend snapped and threw her arms wide. "Stop defending him when he makes a jerk move, and start standing up for *your* feelings!"

Violet's face bunched. "It sounds horrible when you say it like that."

"That's because it *is* horrible!" Lexie leaned back in the chair and spun around in a circle. When she stopped, she said, "You should just date the napkin dude. He's a lot less complicated."

"Then you date him."

"I'd love to, but he's not interested in me. Plus, I'm human, remember?"

Violet grabbed a fuzzy forest green throw pillow and mashed it against her face as she fell back. "I don't like him like that," she muttered into the mass of fluff.

The mattress shifted before the pillow on her face lifted into the air. Lexie stared at her with her lips bunched to the side. "What if he's your mate?"

"Ugh! I'm so sick of hearing about mates!" Violet bolted upright, making Lexie sit back, and kept rambling. "What if someone is completely in love with someone and then finds their mate? What if they realize the person they've loved for years isn't their mate? What if their mate is a crazy person? What then?"

Lexie tilted her head to the side. "Been thinking about that much?"

Feeling self-conscious, Violet stole the pillow back and hugged it against her chest. "Maybe a little. It doesn't help that Zander keeps hounding me."

It was Lexie's turn to groan. Then she slapped her leg, stood up, and grabbed her discarded garment draped over the footboard. "That's it. Get up and put on that gorgeous dress your mom bought you."

"Um... okay?" Violet stared at her in confusion.

Lexie dragged the garment bag's zipper down. "Consider me your fairy godmother, without the wand or the dress."

Violet grinned.

"I'm going to do your hair and makeup, and we will attend the ball with you looking absolutely irresistible."

Her grin slipped. "What? Why can't I just go with my hair like this?"

Lexie's hand froze halfway through pulling a black dress out of the garment bag. "You're kidding, right?"

Suddenly self-conscious, Violet patted her hair. She honestly had no clue what she looked like.

"Right." Lexie nodded, opening the door more. "You're going to make Patrick realize what a fool he is for calling your kiss a mistake. So, are you going to wear that gorgeous number your mom splurged on, or are you just gonna stare at it all night?"

Pinching her lips together, Violet let out a heavy breath through her nose. She shook her head. "Not going would hurt Mom's feelings. But after Aiden and Mya, and everything else going on with Blood Moon and now Pa..."

"That's exactly why you should go."

Confusion pulled Violet's brows together, but she waited for her friend to explain.

"The clan needs this. And, they need you." Lexie lowered the black dress she'd now fully withdrawn from the bag and walked around the bed to wrap her arms around Violet's shoulders. "You've all been through so much. I didn't know Aiden super well, but even I'm hurting from the loss. I know he was a good friend to you and also Mya's mate. The clan needs a moment to reconnect and have a little fun. They need to have a moment to let go. And like it or not, they need to see that their leader's spirits are not burned out—that you are all still going strong."

"I'm not a leader, Lexie." Violet's voice was muffled against her friend's shoulder.

Lexie pulled back and looked at her with one eyebrow raised. "You are one of the best leaders I know. Even if you don't feel like you are. You are consistently running into danger and putting others before yourself. You're a member of the Alpha family, and you need to be there for your clan."

Violet sighed. Her friend had a point.

"Besides, you have a date who has been trying to crash one of these wolven-only parties for years." Lexie smiled and pointed to herself. "I even did my makeup."

A soft chuckle rolled out of Violet. It was true. Lexie rarely wore makeup, but tonight she'd gone all out with a smoky eye that made the blue stand out and a slightly more vivid than nude lipstick color.

Pretending to be annoyed, Violet let out a dramatic sigh. "I hate it when you're right." The smile that stretched across her face betrayed her true emotions.

Lexie practically squealed, and then she hurried to grab the black dress again. "When I get back, you better be dressed!"

A half-hour later, the two girls walked side by side toward the clan house. Violet was already cursing the heels her mom had bought to go with the dress and vowed to burn them the first chance she got. Lexie on the other hand thought that was a ridiculous statement considering how nice the shoes were.

"I don't care how nice they are," Violet grumbled as they reached the doors. "They pinch my toes, they are uncomfortable on every level, my calves feel like they have a rock permanently lodged in them, and I just know I'm going to fall on my face at some point tonight."

Lexie laughed. "It's amazing how you've gone this long without ever wearing heels."

Violet glared. "I've worn them! It's just not very common." She grabbed the door handle. "I can't run or fight in these. They are completely impractical."

"A lot of action films would disagree with you on that." Lexie chuckled. "Are you planning any fights tonight?"

"No," Violet grumbled again.

"Then I think you're safe." Lexie winked at her and then stepped through the door Violet opened. Two steps in and Lexie stopped walking. Her jaw dropped as she gazed at the fake ceiling of pastel-colored fabric, tulle, and twinkle lights. "Are you sure we are in the clan house?"

Violet laughed. "I'm positive. I was in charge of this mess."

"Mess?" Lexie shot her a look and Violet grabbed her arm to pull her out of the entryway. "This is gorgeous. Is every celebration like this?"

Shaking her head, Violet led Lexie to an empty tall table tucked against the wall. "All of the solstices and the Christmas party, but anything else has little to no decorations."

Lexie waved flirtatiously at a guy who was watching her from across the room.

"Don't you dare," Violet complained. "You said you would stay by me all night."

Groaning, Lexie turned her attention back to Violet. "I can't even have a couple of dances with a cute guy, if they ask? You hate dancing."

"I really don't think that's a good idea."

"Why?" When Violet didn't answer, Lexie nodded. "Because I'm human."

"That's one reason, yes. There isn't a future for you with any of the guys here. Having a fated mate with a human is almost as rare as having twins. And he—" Violet turned to point at the guy who was still staring at Lexie like she was a snack. "—knows that. Which means there is only one thing on his mind."

"Wow." Lexie snorted. "So, where did your trust in me go?"

Violet sighed and shook her head. "That has nothing to do with this. It's *him* I don't trust. Usually, when you're around we keep to ourselves or the boys are with us. I don't want you getting into any trouble."

"Violet, I'm fine!" Lexie snapped. "Sentinel Clan is one of the safest places for me to be because no one here is going to let me get hurt. They all know I have attachments to the alpha family." She waved a hand and looked toward the refreshment table. "I'm going to get a drink."

While she walked away, Violet tapped her fingers along the table. This was not her day.

Her eyes scanned the room, looking for Jax and Patrick. Sadness weighed heavily on her heart when she saw a couple who, from a distance in a dark room, could have passed for Aiden and Mya. Tears stung her eyes. She clenched her jaw and looked the other direction.

Right into silver-ringed blue eyes.

She sucked in a slow, steadying breath when Zander raised a brow and smirked. He started toward her, making Violet tense. The shake of her head stopped him in his tracks, but the ring of silver in his eyes flared to fill his irises.

After the last time they spoke, she knew he would only be so bold if he was sure Jax and Patrick weren't around. So, where were they?

A chorus of whoops, hollers, and clapping interrupted their stare-down. Alpha Draven led Luna Draven through a nearby door. While he was dressed in a typical suit with a pastel-blue tie and flower to match, her mom was dressed to kill. Her silver-streaked hair had been elegantly pulled back into a french-twist and her sparkly, floor-length dress matched the pastel-blue accents in her husband's attire. A slit that reached a couple of inches above the knee showed off Luna Draven's glorious leg with every stride.

It was the first time in a while that her mom's skin was clear and her eyes bright. Her smile lit the room. She was the ever-strong and gorgeous Luna.

"Dang, your mom looks amazing," Lexie commented around a bite of something and Violet turned toward her to agree, but Lexie held up a hand to stop her. "You were right, by the way. That guy was a jerk."

Violet took the drink Lexie held out for her. "I'm sorry. I didn't mean to sound like I didn't trust you. There's just been so much danger lately, and I don't want anything to happen to you. I know how bad you want to be a wolf..."

"I don't think you do." Lexie interrupted.

"You've brought it up more than a couple times," Violet chuckled, but her humor died quickly. "There just isn't a safe way to do that."

Lexie nodded, then tipped her glass back to take a long drink. When she set it down, she'd drained the contents completely. After a heavy sigh, she said, "Even if I can't be a wolf, I can still dance with one, right?"

A new song with a good beat came on and Lexie started bouncing in her heels.

"Lexie..."

"Come on!" her friend begged, pouting her lower lip and making her chin quiver.

Violet shook her head. "I can barely walk in these things and you want me to dance?"

"No!" Lexie's eyes went wide. "I've seen you dance. You could use some instruction. You just sit back and watch," Lexie teased. "I promise to stay in your line of sight."

She was dancing away before Violet could protest, making her way toward the mob of people.

Violet breathed a sigh of relief when she saw the group make room for Lexie, but allowed her to stay on the outskirts where Violet could see her.

Even though her shoes were killing her feet and the music was on the verge of being too loud, Violet found herself smiling as she watched her friend have the time of her life on the dance floor.

A few songs later, Violet's parents made their way up to the second level, and the crowd quieted down. After a quick glance at Lexie, who lifted an enthusiastic thumbs up, Violet made her way toward the stand as well to be the dutiful daughter.

Her eyes darted around, but the future alpha was still nowhere to be seen. *"Jax, where are you?"* Violet snapped through their link. *"Mom's about to speak!"*

Luna Draven took one step ahead of her husband and opened her arms wide to welcome everyone to the celebration just as Jax materialized out of the shadows to the right.

"Ah, there you are." Luna offered a tight smile as she addressed the future alpha, whose shirt was a little rumpled.

His date joined him, patting down her hair, and Luna's smile slipped. The girl had the good sense to look embarrassed and more than a little nervous. She fidgeted with the ends of her hair, and took the slightest step behind Jax.

"Thank you for gracing us with your presence." Luna kept a professional tone to her voice, but Violet could hear the mom threat behind her words.

Jax was going to get an earful tonight.

Violet tried to keep the grin off her face as she ascended half the staircase, then paused to stare up at her mom who returned her luminescent gaze to the rest of the clan. Even from here, Violet could see the swirling vortex in her mother's eyes. It was such a rare trait. Violet didn't think she'd seen another wolven with eyes like that.

"Thank you all for gathering here tonight to welcome this new season with us," Luna Draven called over the crowd. "I know things have been especially difficult as of late. We mourn for those we have lost in recent events..."

Violet swallowed the knot that built in her throat and turned to look out at the crowd while trying to keep a pleasant expression on her face. Apparently, she was doing a bad job because Lexie gestured for her to smile.

"... let us not forget the beautiful impact they made in our lives, but let us live each day for them. Let us cherish the times we had together. Let us speak about the happy and funny times. And let us never forget what they gave their lives protecting." Luna paused and slowly turned her head to look out across the expanse of the room. "You," she said quietly. "Our clan."

Tears built in Violet's eyes. She bowed her head, closed her eyes, and clenched her jaw, willing the tears to stop before they fell.

"Let this new season bring growth and an abundance of happiness to Sentinel Clan!"

Violet clapped while the clan exploded, similar to when Alpha and Luna Draven had first arrived, but even louder. She lifted her watery gaze to see Alpha Draven step forward and press a light kiss to her mom's cheek before they headed toward the stairs Violet was occupying. She descended as quickly as she dared with the death traps strapped to her feet, then released a sigh of relief when she reached the bottom.

"I'm so happy the dress fits!" Evalyn nearly squealed as she wrapped her arms around Violet from behind. "You're gorgeous, my little miracle."

A large smile spread across Violet's face as she turned in her mom's embrace. "And you were born to be luna, Mom." She tightened their hug briefly before stepping back. "You always seem to know what to say. That was a beautiful speech."

Luna Draven's smile was soft and humble. "Thank you. It's taken a lot of practice, and the words are never enough, but it's something. Words can help heal a wounded heart. They help encourage the clan to keep going."

Her words reflected what Lexie had said earlier, sending a blast of shock and awe through Violet's veins. How had her friend realized that before Violet?

Evalyn looked over Violet's shoulder. Amusement sparkled in her eyes as she said, "I see Lexie is enjoying herself."

"That makes one of us." Violet admitted, following her mother's gaze to find Lexie dancing with one of the warriors Violet recognized. "If Lexie's okay with it, and if you can keep an eye on her, I'm thinking about turning in early."

When she looked back at her mom, worry creased Evalyn's forehead. "Are you okay?"

Violet shrugged a shoulder. "I'm just not in the mood to celebrate anything right now."

A heavy sigh left her mom. "I was hoping Lexie being here would help with that."

"She *is* over the moon to be here. And seeing her so happy does help. Thanks for inviting her." Violet chuckled as she watched her friend having the time of her life. "I'll stay a little longer for her."

Evalyn smiled, then turned her head to watch Jax descend the stairs. "So, your brother has a date."

Pink tinged Jax's ears, revealing he'd heard her. His date looked mortified and to Violet's surprise, she actually pulled her hand from Jax's grasp.

"I think her name is Jess," Violet offered as the embarrassed couple came to stand beside them.

"You're correct," Jess announced in a soft, respectful tone, and then turned toward Luna with her gaze on the floor. "I can't apologize enough for my behavior. We..." She looked sideways at Jax, but he wouldn't look at her. "We got carried away."

Luna nodded slowly, but didn't speak.

That made it worse.

Jess' shoulders curled inward and she backed away a step. "My apologies. It will never happen again."

Luna's gaze swirled luminous as she turned to her son. "See that it doesn't."

Curling her lips inward to lightly bite them together, Violet's eyes widened and she shifted ever-so-slightly away from her mom.

"Looks like Patrick finally arrived." Luna changed topics, nodding toward one of the doors while simultaneously giving leave to Jess who scurried away under Jax's frustrated gaze.

Violet followed her mom's gaze to find Patrick lowering his head slightly to hear whatever Robin was trying to tell him. His mouth lifted into a half grin and Robin slipped her arm through his.

Pain pierced Violet's chest, constricting her lungs. Her chest collapsed with a heavy breath. She'd never been stabbed by a dagger, but she imagined it might feel something like this. It hurt to breathe. Her throat tightened, and the back of her eyes began to burn, warning of tears to come. "I didn't know Patrick had a date."

"He didn't," Jax growled.

The furiousity behind his words surprised Violet.

Her mom's sigh drove the dagger deeper into her chest. "What is he doing?" Evalyn touched Violet's shoulder, but Violet pulled away. "If I'd known..."

"Thank you for allowing Lexie to come tonight," she interrupted her mom, then cleared her throat. "It means a lot to her. And to me."

Worry pulled at her mom's brows, drawing them together in the center. "Of course."

Jax didn't say anything as Violet walked away. He didn't even look at her. The pinched expression on his face confused her more than anything. Since when did he care who Patrick spent time with?

"Looks like your bodyguard has another girl to look after." Zander's voice shot pins and needles down her spine. "I'd be happy to be your company for the night."

She clenched her jaw and kept moving. He was already behind her, so continuing to walk away wouldn't change anything. "Leave me alone."

"Or we can just talk," Zander offered, but his voice dipped into an angry tone, making her spin around to face him.

He was so close she brought up her hands and pushed off his chest so he wouldn't run her over. "Back off."

He held out his arms for her. "Come on, Vi."

The heat of rage welled up inside her. "You don't get to call me that!" she snapped. Her hands started shaking and her breathing grew uneven. "I told you to back off."

An animal-like growl echoed through her words. The clarity of the room sharpened.

Zander's eyes widened and he took a step back.

Glass shattered somewhere in the distance.

A few gasps filled her ears and a thick haze fell over her mind.

"Hey, girlfriend!" Lexie's bright voice cut through the fog right before she hip-bumped Violet... which nearly planted her well-shaped hip into Violet's side. "Come dance with me."

"I really don't want to dance right now," Violet grumbled, shooting a glare at Zander whose shock seemed to have worn off because he was shooting hateful daggers at her best friend.

Lexie looped her arm through Violet's and shrugged. "Too bad. You're coming with me anyway." She gave a sickly-sweet smile to Zander and waved a few fingers at him. "Goodbye." They were two steps away when she leaned down to whisper, "Tell Jax that Zander's here."

Nodding, Violet sent a quick message through their twin mind-link.

Jax answered immediately. *"I'll take care of it."*

Violet relayed the message while rubbing an ache out of her jaw and Lexie grinned.

"Good. Now," she grabbed Violet's hand and spun her, nearly sending her tripping over her heels. "When were you going to tell me that you'd made contact with your wolf?"

Once steady on her feet again, she blinked. "What wolf? I don't have a wolf."

Lexie snorted. "Girl, I just saw your eyes turn all colorful. They looked almost exactly like your mom's."

"What?" Violet asked, her heart thumping wildly in her chest. "You saw them?"

"So, this has happened before?"

"Once, it was a fluke! I was mad at Robin, but she couldn't tell me what color they were."

A laugh burst out of Lexie. "That's because they aren't *a* color. They are lots of colors. I'd say primarily, they kinda look like an opal? But then there are the other three colors swirling around in there; bronze, silver, and gold."

A slow grin pulled at Violet's lips. "I have wolf eyes."

"You have wolf eyes!" Lexie hopped up and down and then threw her arms around Violet's neck. "You *have* to dance with me now!"

Violet laughed. "Oh no, I'm going back to the table before I break an ankle. Come and find me when your legs give out."

Lexie smirked and waved her away.

# Chapter 10

## Violet

***Making her way back to*** *the table was hazardous.* People celebrating did not pay attention to where they were going, or how hard they slammed their butts and hips around while dancing. Violet shoved against a guy who lost his balance and nearly fell on top of her.

He apologized, at least, before going back to his crowd of people.

The hint of coffee lingered in the air, and Violet wondered which of the clan members had dared touch it. It messed with their senses, which could potentially lead to someone's death.

Violet made a mental note to check that out when she wasn't being tossed about.

She was almost out of the swarm, when someone rammed against her side. Fumbling to regain her balance, Violet waved her arms, but she had no hope when another person bumped into her. She was going to fall flat on her butt in front of everyone.

Instead of hitting the floor, Violet collided with another person who wrapped their hands around her arms to steady her. "I'm so sorry..." Her words trailed off as the smell of coffee and almonds hit her. She knew that smell.

"Don't apologize. You're so small, if you hadn't crashed into me, I'm not sure I ever would have found you." Once she was stable on her feet again, Violet looked up into Napkin Hero's green eyes with golden-flecked centers as he continued, "I'm not sure how I missed you, though."

With a laugh, Violet shook her head. "Is that supposed to be a compliment?"

He tossed his head back and forth slightly as his jaw jutted to the side, "It was, but apparently it wasn't a very good one. I must be out of practice. Has anyone told you how amazing you look tonight?"

"Actually, no." Violet shrugged. "Unless you count Lexie."

"Right, your human friend is here." His gaze darted around before he frowned. "Am I blind?"

A small chuckle rolled out of Violet. "No, she blends in better than I do here."

He smiled. "Blending in is overrated."

"Not when you're me." Violet waved a dismissive hand when he gave her a questioning look and then pointed to where Lexie was dancing. "She's having the time of her life."

He nodded. "Looks like it."

"You know," Violet said, drawing his attention once more. "it's not every day I crash into and get complimented by a complete stranger," Violet teased.

Napkin Hero laughed. "How am I still a stranger?"

"I still don't know your name." Violet shrugged a shoulder. "You heard my dad say mine, which is cheating by the way, but never told me yours."

"You never asked."

She lifted a brow. "If you don't want to tell me..." she faked like she was walking away and he laughed again before softly grabbing her arm—which he immediately released when he realized she wasn't actually going anywhere.

Amusement burned bright in his eyes, "I'm Cas."

"Cas, huh?" Violet lifted both brows this time.

Cas' smile grew. "Yeah, short for Caspian."

"Wait... like Prince Casp..."

"Yeah..." Cas interrupted before Violet could finish making the connection between his name and *The Chronicles of Narnia* character, "... spelled the same way just without the title."

Violet sucked a breath through her teeth. "Darn, I was really hoping you were a prince."

A burst of laughter escaped Cas and he shook his head. "You are something else."

The ridiculousness of that statement made her chuckle. "You have no idea."

"Maybe I can find out."

Violet's stomach clenched and rolled a little. It wasn't a completely unpleasant feeling, but it wasn't pleasant either. "Maybe."

Maybe was the best answer she could give. Maybe it was the intense way Cas was watching her. Maybe it was the fact he had no problem openly flirting with her even though she was trying to just be friendly. Maybe it was the fact that he hadn't taken his eyes off her from the moment they crashed into one another. Or maybe... she really didn't know.

Cas' smile widened. "Would it be too bold of me to ask for a dance?"

Dismay pulled Violet's jaw down before she laughed.

Cas' joyful expression faded as he lifted a brow.

"I'm sorry. Any other time I would have immediately said yes, but I can barely walk in these shoes. They are killing my feet."

Dropping his gaze to her feet, Cas' smile returned and he nodded, "Another time then." His gaze shifted just slightly over her shoulder. "In-coming."

It wasn't enough warning.

A curly mass of hair flew over Violet's shoulder and smacked her in the face. Long arms wrapped around her waist as Robin's happy tone nearly shattered her eardrum. "Hi!"

Jealousy ribboned with anger and Violet drew in a deep steadying breath so she didn't throw her head back into the girl's face. Instead, she spoke through clenched teeth, "Hi, Robin."

Robin withdrew from Violet, completely oblivious to the dark emotions she'd just caused. "You did such a good job with this place, I can hardly believe we are in the clan house."

Violet turned to face the overly excited girl and found Patrick walking toward them, his gaze locked with hers and the world froze for a moment.

"Thank you," she breathed when she finally broke Patrick's stare.

A slightly more animal version of Patrick's voice echoed in her mind like a song on the wind. *"She looks amazing."*

It was so soft, Violet wasn't sure if she'd actually heard Alistair or if she was imagining things. She stared at him, lips slightly parted before she decided to test something. Even if she wasn't the biggest fan of Patrick's darker half, a compliment deserved recognition. *"Thank you."*

Patrick jerked back ever so slightly, but it was enough. He stared at her with an emotionless expression, but she could see the surprise in his eyes and the cracks in his perfectly sculpted facade.

"Yeah, Violet did a great job with the clan house." Cas inserted himself into the conversation, drawing everyone's attention, but Violet peeked back at Patrick. His surprised expression slowly narrowed as he took in Cas' appearance and presence.

"Eeeee!" Robin jumped up and down. "Violet, you didn't tell me you had a date!"

Violet frowned. "I didn't." The look on Patrick's face told her he wasn't convinced. She shook her head. "I don't."

"She crashed into me just a minute ago." Cas lightly bumped into her arm and smiled. "Literally. But, I'm pretty sure she made my night."

Heat blossomed in Violet's cheeks. As flattering as that was, it was also embarrassing. She wasn't trying to flirt with Cas, but he didn't seem to notice that line.

Robin slapped her arm and Violet clenched her hands to keep herself from smacking the girl's hands away. "This is why you said you were okay with Patrick and me!"

She beamed up at Patrick who looked like someone had just poured a bottle of hot sauce in his veins and he was trying to play the tough guy. Every part of his body was tensed, hard as a statue. His hands were shoved deep inside his pockets which Violet had learned was his way of stopping himself from doing something. Usually something Alistair wanted him to do.

"Was this the conversation that—" Patrick's gaze darted to Cas who raised a brow. "When you surprised Robin?"

Violet's mouth was left hanging open when Robin jumped in to answer for her.

"Yes! It was right before her surprise. Isn't that great?"

No one answered.

Violet's breathing quickened.

Patrick was smart, but he didn't have the full story. What kind of crazy story would he put together with what he knew?

"Are you thirsty, Violet?" Cas asked, turning his full attention on her.

The song changed.

"I love this song! Talk later!" Robin yanked Patrick away to dance.

Violet stared after them, but Patrick didn't look back at her.

"So, she would go on the "cons" side of the list." Cas' voice pulled her away from her thoughts.

She looked at him questioningly. "Are you putting people on a pros and cons list?"

Shaking his head, he offered his arm to her which she took with only a small amount of hesitation.

"I try to avoid placing people on any sort of list, but I've broken that rule twice in the last couple days." He led them toward the refreshments table in the corner. "I have a pros and cons list for every clan I've looked into. I want to make sure I'm making the right decision."

"That's understandable," Violet agreed while squishing into his side to avoid being a casualty to someone's dancing. When they were safely away from the throng of people she tugged on his arm to pull him to a stop. "I hope you're not thinking of joining just because of me."

"You being here is a really big pro on my list, but not the only one." Cas drew in a deep breath and looked around the room. "I love the energy your clan has. That small town, family vibe."

Smiling, Violet tilted her head to the side. "That's one of my favorite things about the clan."

"Are you sure you don't want to dance?" Cas asked with a grin. "I promise not to let you fall."

"I thought you wanted a drink."

"No, I was trying to help get you out of an awkward situation."

"Was it that obvious?"

Cas grimaced. "It's not going to help if I lie and say no."

Violet sighed.

"So, do you want to dance?"

She chuckled and shook her head. "I guess I can try."

Joy lit Cas' face before he took her hand and led her to the very edge of the commotion as the song changed into a slow, romantic melody. One hand slipped along her waist to the small of her back while the other held her hand out to the side.

"Where'd you learn how to dance?" Violet asked, laughing at his stiff posture.

Cas laughed and his shoulders relaxed a little. "My mom. She was a competitive ballroom dancer."

Impressed, Violet nodded her head. "Wow. I... don't know anything about that."

Another laugh escaped him. "And I probably know too much." Cas' gaze found hers again and his smile slipped.

"What's wrong?"

His face scrunched before he let out a loud sigh. "I probably should have asked this before, but seeing how I met you on a college campus I didn't really think about it. How old are you?"

"Are you asking to genuinely find out or are you wondering if I have a mate?" Violet asked, feeling a wall begin to build.

Raising a brow, he dipped his head toward her. "The first one, but the second one was going to be a follow-up until I realized you probably wouldn't be dancing with me if you did."

Violet nodded. "Which means you don't either."

One side of Cas' mouth tilted upward, but it didn't reach his eyes.

With a sigh, she looked out at the crowd around them. "You should probably know I'm not eighteen, yet."

"Oh, well then..." Cas extended his arms out so there was a great distance between their bodies, surprising her into a laugh.

"My birthday is next week."

The teasing glint in his eyes faded. "Happy early birthday." Then, he gently pulled her closer again. "I'm twenty, in case you were wondering."

She smiled. "It may have come up later if you hadn't offered the information."

"So, what do we do now?" Cas led her through a slow turn and the stiletto of her heel slipped. She landed hard against his chest with his arms wrapped around her waist.

Violet huffed a laugh. "I think we're attempting to dance."

He snickered quietly as he helped her regain her balance. "I meant what do we do with the fact that I've been flirting with you?"

Another laugh left her, this one warmer than the last. "Oh, is that what you've been doing?"

"You wound me!" Cas placed a mocking hand over his heart, making Violet laugh again. He returned his hand to the small of her back and drew her a little closer. "But seriously, I haven't been able to take my eyes off you."

Pressure filled her chest. She looked to the side, catching a brief glimpse of Lexie who was having the time of her life, and then to the other side... but there was no Patrick. Her brows pinched together as she looked back at her dance partner. "Cas, I should tell..."

Brilliant white light blinded her. She clamped her hands over her ears and cried out at the concussive blast that sounded in her ears. Her knees hit the ground. Severe throbbing pulsed across her skull. Her stomach lurched, threatening to expose her dinner of Oreos. Something hit her side and then stabbing pain filled her arm.

Gentle hands wrapped around her shoulders. The pressure against her arm made it burn and she clenched her teeth, shying away from the touch, but whoever they were, they didn't let go. Muffled cries began to filter through the wringing in her ears. She tried to look around, but her vision was hazy and warped, tipping her stomach toward tossing once again.

She closed her eyes against the nightmare unfolding before her. From what she could tell, the flickering orange light and heat radiating off her skin meant there was a fire. The smoke in the air was a good indicator too. Violet coughed after a deep breath trying to brace against the pain in her arm.

"Violet!" It was murky, but Cas' voice called to her amongst the din. His long fingers replaced the soft ones and she jerked away only to have the world tip over on her. She fell to the side into soft arms.

"Violet, can you hear us?" Lexie's worried tone cut through the noise, drawing Violet's attention across the planes of pain.

Two very blurry Lexies gazed back at her with worried, pinched expressions. Her face was smeared with dirt and tiny abrasions marred her perfect porcelain skin. The metallic scent of blood flooded Violet's senses. She doubled over and heaved, but it must have been long enough because no evidence of cookies was exposed.

Once her stomach stopped trying to leave her body, Violet looked back at Lexie and froze. It was no wonder why the scent of blood was so strong, the skirt of Lexie's dress was stained with it.

"We need to get her out of here," Cas said.

Violet tried to nod, but it amplified everything, so she froze. "Yes! Lexie needs to be safe!"

Was she yelling? She couldn't tell.

"He's talking about you," Lexie muttered at her. "Can't you see I'm fine?"

She pointed at Lexie's skirt, but smacked her friend's leg instead, making Lexie suck in a sharp breath. "Sorry," Violet pulled her hand away. "I didn't realize how close you were."

"I think the flashbang hurt her more than everyone else," Cas' voice held an edge of worry as he looked from Lexie to Violet.

"You seem fine." Lexie sounded annoyed.

"Only because I've experienced one before, and we were too far away from the explosion."

Smoke was continuing to fill the air, and the flickering firelight along the walls was growing.

Cas ignored Violet's cry of pain as he firmly shoved his hands under her arms. "I'm getting her out of here."

"We should find Alpha and Luna. Jax and Patrick need to know, too."

Violet stumbled in her heels, trying to keep up with Cas, who was pretty much dragging her. "I can get her out of here faster on my own."

One of her heels slipped off Violet's foot. She happily kicked the other off as Lexie stepped in front of Cas.

"Everyone else is coming out of their haze and once she's out, she's gonna be ticked you left with her. Help me find—"

"Violet!" Patrick's worried tone cut Lexie off.

Cas pushed around Lexie and kept moving, but Violet pulled against him.

"I'm trying to help you," Cas growled, then swooped her legs out from under her.

They'd only taken a few more steps when Patrick's mountain of a body stepped in front of them.

"What are you doing?" Cas snapped, stopping mid-step. Rage widened his eyes and contorted his usually smiling face into a grimace.

"Put her down," Patrick ordered. His eyes narrowed as he held the newcomer's gaze.

"I'm taking her outside. It's not safe in here."

"Whoever set this up could be outside waiting!" Patrick growled, sounding more animal than human.

Violet reached for Patrick, who readily stepped into her range and pushed a hand between her body and Cas'.

"Patrick is Violet's bodyguard. If he thinks outside isn't safe, he's not going to let her go anywhere," Lexie explained to Cas, whose shoulders rose as his tension built."

Violet's gaze was focusing more and more by the second, and she gasped when she noticed the blood trickling from her friend's ear. "Lexie, your ear."

Her friend rolled her eyes as she looked back at Violet. "It's bleeding. I know. I'm pretty sure it ruptured. It's ringing, but there isn't much pain anymore." She looked at the boys. "So, what are we doing? I agree that there could be Blood Moon members outside, but that fire is spreading."

Violet turned her attention to the clan house and a heavy weight pressed in on her chest. Walls were blown out, bits of the roof on the far side had already collapsed, and the fire was devouring the structure at an alarming rate, but there were still people inside. Many weren't moving.

"Staying in here isn't acceptable," Cas defended, refusing to hand her over to Patrick. "Violet needs..."

"To throw up," Violet interrupted, kicking her legs out of Cas' arm. He steadied her around the waist, while Patrick wrapped his hands around her elbows, both attempting to slow her fall as she knelt on the ground and heaved. Once again, nothing came up. "Sorry."

Someone crashed past Lexie, and she snagged the young woman's arm. "You! Violet needs water, now."

The girl took one look at Violet and darted away toward the kitchen.

Her human friend turned her attention toward the room.

"Lexie?"

"It's chaos in here. Someone needs to step up."

Patrick tensed, but said, "I can."

Lexie shook her head. "Take care of Violet. I've got this." She pointed at another couple of people. "You two! Reach out to the alpha, luna, and Jax. We need to make sure they are taken care of."

Violet stared in awe at her best friend. A human, unafraid to stand up to creatures who could kill her in a heartbeat. They nodded, used to following orders, and bowed their heads in concentration.

*"Violet,"* Jax's voice in her head made her flinch, but she grabbed Patrick's arm and told him Jax was talking to her. *"Where are you?"*

*"With Patrick, Lexie, and Cas."*

*"Who's Ca... Nevermind. Where in the Clan House? Is Lexie okay?"*

The first young woman reported back, "The kitchen has been blocked by one of the beams that fell. I can't get her any water from here."

"Is there anyone trapped inside the kitchen?" Lexie asked, and the girl paled. "Go check!"

*"Opposite side of the kitchen. Lexie's fine. Where are you?"* Violet wondered through their twin-link.

*"I'm here. I'm checking the perimeter."*

*"You're outside?"* Violet looked at Patrick with wide eyes and he tilted his head to the side.

*"I was taking Zander to his apartment when the explosion happened. I'm*

*using it to my advantage."*

"I can't get in touch with Jax," reported one of the clan members.

Violet raised her hand. "That's because I'm talking to him."

Worry creased Lexie's forehead. "Is he okay?"

Violet nodded, and relayed what Jax had told her just before he started speaking again.

*"I don't see anyone. There are people already leaving the clan house. No one is getting attacked. I think it's safe to get people out."*

Violet explained to the group around her, and Lexie turned back to the other clan members who had gathered.

"You," she pointed at a group who looked a little battered, but otherwise okay. "Help Doc get to the clinic along with any patients she's already gathered. Find others to help you along the way."

They nodded and turned to run as Lexie gave orders to the next group, pointing as she spoke about getting the fires out.

*"Is that Lexie?"* Jax asked.

Violet smiled. *"Yeah. She's ordering everyone around like* she's *luna. Where are you now?"*

"Here." Jax jogged into view and nodded at Patrick. He eyed Cas suspiciously then knelt in front of Violet. "How are you?"

"I'll be okay." Violet held out her arm and sucked a breath through her teeth. A shard of wood protruded from her skin, just below her shoulder.

Patrick pulled on his tie as he knelt beside her. "I can remove it, but I didn't want to add to everything else you were going through." He cut a look at Cas, then slipped his tie beneath her arm. "I don't think it's super deep or touching anything vital."

Violet nodded. "Get it out."

Cas' fingers dug into her waist and she pressed against him to keep from flinching away from Patrick as he pulled the oversized splinter from her arm. Her breathing was deep, but quick, making her a little lightheaded while Patrick tied his tie over her wound.

The three young men let her breathe for a few seconds then helped her to her feet. Once she was settled, Jax stepped between Cas and her, holding her steady.

"While I appreciate your help with her, who are you?" Jax asked, eying Cas once again.

Cas thrust his hand toward Jax. "I'm Cas. Alpha Draven interviewed me as a possible new member of the clan, and personally invited me to this event."

Jax grunted. "Funny, he didn't mention you."

"Why would he?"

Violet leaned into Jax's side. "Jax is my twin and the future alpha."

The gruff demeanor Cas had adopted shifted instantly and he lowered his chin. "My apologies, I didn't..." His gaze cut to Violet's. "Wait, did you say twin?"

Jax shook his head. "We don't have time to get into that right now." He looked over his shoulder at Lexie who was still ordering people around. "We need to get everyone out of here." The roof groaned, drawing all of their gazes. "Quickly."

He shoved Violet toward Patrick, who caught her in a bear hug against his chest, then moved toward Lexie. He stepped up to the brave human girl and whispered in her ear. Lexie rolled her eyes at him but gestured for him to continue. Together, they got people moving quickly, and with more structure, toward the doors.

"What about the fire?" Asked one of the people carrying a water bucket.

Lexie answered. "We'll fight it from outside and make sure it doesn't spread to the other buildings."

"The kitchen is still blocked, and there are people inside."

Jax looked at Patrick. "We need you."

Patrick's gaze fell on Violet.

She smiled. "I'm okay. Go."

After a moment of hesitation, he nodded and took off at a run for the kitchen.

"Can I trust you to keep her safe?"

It took a second for Violet to realize Jax was talking to Cas.

Determination set Cas' jaw. "With my life."

"Good." He pointed toward the door. "Get her out of here."

"What? No!" Violet shrieked, but Jax had already turned away from her.

Cas grunted when her elbow connected with his stomach. "Violet, come on." He pushed her toward the door.

"I'm not leaving my brother or my best friend!" Violet snapped, shoving back against him.

He threw his head back in frustration. "Are you always like this?"

"Yes!"

Surprised, he froze. Clearly, he wasn't expecting that answer, but he recovered quickly. "I'm just following orders. If he really is the future alpha, I need him to approve of me, too."

"I never follow his orders. It won't surprise him." She tried to get around him again, but Cas ducked and threw her over his shoulder. "Hey!"

She drove her elbow into his back and he groaned. "Glad to know you can still put up a fight, even when disoriented."

"I'm fine." Violet yelped when Cas jumped through the door which was encircled by fire. "Seriously, put me down!"

Her feet thudded against the ground and her knees buckled. Her butt crashed into the dirt and she seethed through her teeth.

"There, you're down." Cas snapped, glaring down at her. "I've never met someone so determined to get herself hurt."

"I'm not trying to get hurt." Violet made her way back to her feet. "I'm trying to help the people I love."

Cas snorted. "That's very honorable of you, but putting yourself in harm's way to do so, doesn't help anything." He looked her over. "You seem fine, though. Other than your brother wanting to make sure you're safe, I can't see why you need a bodyguard."

"You can't read the whole story by just looking at the cover."

He shrugged and shook his head. "You're the daughter of an alpha. No one would touch you. And you have an alpha bloodline, which means you're stronger th—"

"Violet!" Tucker's frantic voice drew her widened gaze. The closer he got, the stronger the tangy smell of blood became. Dark red smeared the side of his face and covered his hands. It was hard to tell in the dim lighting, but it looked like it was even around his mouth. "Alpha-is-busy-with-Luna and Jax-is-helping-with-the clan house. No one is listening to me!"

"Tucker!" Violet yelled at him, shocking the guy who'd once tried to use her affection to win a bet. "I'm listening. Take a breath and slow down."

He shook his head, but did as he was told. Licking his lips, he grimaced and went to wipe his sleeve across his mouth, but flinched back at the last second.

"How much of that blood is yours?"

Cas sent her a concerned look.

Her clan mate swallowed hard. "Hardly any, but I'm covered in it."

"Explain," Violet ordered as she squared off with Tucker.

He nodded. "I was working Lockup tonight. Dad's been having me do more and more, and wanted me to take over for him tonight, so he could finally have a holiday off." He shook his head, and the salty scent of tears filled her nose. "Violet, I can't reach him."

Anguish clenched her stomach as she thought about the people who hadn't been moving in the clan house. "We'll find him, but right now I need you to focus."

"They hit Lockup. This was just a distraction."

Chills raced down Violet's spine. "Mya."

# Chapter 11

## Violet

***Tiny, dagger-like pebbles dug*** *into Violet's bare feet as she sprinted* toward Lockup with Tucker hot on her heels. She pulled the skirt of her dress to her knees, wishing she was in pants.

"Violet, stop!" Cas called after her, and then gave chase, but one thing Violet had always been able to do was outrun others.

He never caught her.

Tucker even began to fall away.

She winced when she slowed to a stop behind the giant boulders obscuring her view of Lockup. Flares of pain and heat lanced through the soles of her feet as she pressed herself against the chilled rock and inched sideways to get a look at—

Long, strong fingers snagged her shoulders, whipping her around until her back thudded against the boulders. "What is wrong with you?" Cas quietly hissed, his eyes wide with a mix of fury and concern. "You were completely disoriented a few minutes ago and had a shard of wood sticking out of your arm."

Tucker eyed them both as he came to a stop beside them, but remained silent.

"Something you should know about me. I don't stop until the people I love are safe." She pushed at his hands, but he held her firmly against the boulders. "Get off me."

"I'd listen to her, dude. If her boyfriend—"

"He's not my boyfriend!" Violet quietly snapped.

Tucker snorted. "Whatever. If Patrick finds out what you're doing, you might as well exile yourself from the clan."

Cas growled at Tucker but didn't take his eyes off Violet. "I don't know who you are, but her brother charged me with her safety."

"He charged Patrick with it, too." Tucker shrugged. "She still finds ways to end up in danger. Or hurt. Sometimes both."

Violet narrowed her eyes at the stupid blond beside them, but he just shrugged again.

"Just saying."

Sighing, Cas shook his head. "You can't run into a building that could still have threats inside it by yourself, without shoes, and in a dress."

She scoffed. "I can fight in a dress."

"Really?" Cas snagged a handful of her skirts. She let out a sharp, surprised yelp when he used it to spin her around. And then, he was pressing against her back, pinning her to the stupid rock that she had hoped to use as a protector. "Because I only see it as being in the way."

"Hey, that's enough." Tucker's voice dropped a fraction, veering toward his wolf half.

Surprised, Violet found his gaze, which was gleaming silver in the moonlight.

Ever so slowly, Cas moved away from her and held up his hands. "I was just making a point."

Tucker stepped closer to Violet, nearly putting himself between her and Cas. "Next time make it without laying your hands on her. She and I may not be on the best of terms, but she is the alpha's daughter. You'd be smart to remember that."

Rolling her eyes, Violet moved back to where she was before Cas had rudely interrupted her.

"They're gone," Tucker announced, walking past her with bleak confidence. "Everyone either left or is dead."

"What if they came back?"

Cas growled beside her. "They didn't."

Violet followed after Tucker and grabbed her skirts. She tied them into the best knot she could then cast a curious look at Cas.

"I don't hear anything," he answered her silent question.

"I don't either," Tucker added as they neared the doors.

Violet tried to ignore the overwhelming sweet, metallic scent of blood and the bodies strewn across the ground. One warrior was leaning against the wall beside the door. He wasn't the victim of a claw or bite. A clean slice had been made across his chest and black veins had spread over his skin.

"Poison." Cas cursed, then looked down at Violet's bare feet. "You're not going any farther unless we get something to cover your feet."

"Here." Tucker jogged over to another body, a female guard, and stole her shoes. "I don't know if they'll fit, but I figured she isn't using them anymore."

Violet muttered thanks and tried not to feel horrible about stealing a dead person's belongings. The shoes had some blood on them, but the inside was clean, so she slipped her feet in. Or rather shoved them in. Her feet were bigger than the guards, but they'd work for now.

She took a step and gasped.

"What?" Tucker groaned at the same time Cas asked, "Are you okay?"

Cas rested a hand on her back, gently rubbing his thumb back and forth. It gave her time to take a deep breath and let the stab of agony dull to a throb in her feet.

"I'm fine," Violet confirmed. "Just adjusting from dirt to shoes."

"You're an idiot." Tucker snorted. "Why aren't you wearing any shoes in the first place?"

Cas growled.

"Hey!" Violet snapped. "You're the one who came to find *me*, remember?"

Tension pulsed in Tucker's jaw, and he looked toward the entrance of Lockup.

"Besides, I was in heels, and that wasn't helping at all."

An amused smirk rose to Tucker's lips. "I would have loved to see that."

"Are we doing this or not?" Cas interrupted and walked through the doors. "Don't touch anything."

Violet nodded. "Wasn't planning on it."

It didn't take long for them to reach the top floor, but the amount of blood and fur made Violet queasy from time to time.

"We fought as hard as we could," Tucker whispered in reverence. "We weren't a match for them. Especially once they got the lycan out."

Cas' brows pulled low in confusion. "They have lycan in their pack now?"

Tucker nodded, "More than one, I think." He led the way around another body and into the hallway where Mya was being held.

"If you come through that I will kill you!" Mya's shrieking voice reached their ears spurring all three of them to run. "Stop!"

Bones cracked behind Violet and a roaring growl filled the hall.

"Look out!" Cas grabbed Violet's shoulders and shoved her against a wall while a mass of gray fur with red undertones brushed past them.

"Tucker?" Violet called, but the giant wolf's snarl drowned out her words and echoed in her ears.

Wolven didn't shift until the full moon following their eighteenth birthday, and Tucker's birthday wasn't for a few more months.

A small, sharp yelp sounded, followed by the final crunch of a macabre symphony.

Wolf Tucker tried to turn his head, but his body was far too large for the Lockup halls. He grunted when his nose struck the wall then shook his massive head. His fur started to disappear and at the first snap of bone, Violet shoved away from Cas and ran for Mya's cell.

The plexiglass was marred with scratches—all different shapes, sizes, and lengths—and a hole barely big enough for Violet to slip through had been created in the lower center. The sharp edges were not an appealing fight for her, so she opted to punch in the code she'd stolen from Jax, and the door slid open.

Mya screamed, her eyes red and swollen with tears until recognition relaxed her muscles. "Violet?"

Nodding frantically, Violet darted across the room and threw her arms around her friend. "I'm here. No one is going to hurt you."

"Okay, but who's protecting you?" Mya asked, tears instantly wetting Violet's shoulder. "What are you doing here?"

"I told her what happened," Tucker's disgruntled voice filled the cell and Mya sucked in a startled breath.

Violet turned to stare at Tucker who had fresh blood around his mouth. "I guess I don't need to ask how you got blood on your face."

He turned away from them to spit. "Using your teeth to rip someone's throat out, or snap their neck is effective, but gross."

"How did you shift?" Violet asked when he looked at them again. She wasn't sure where he got the sweatpants that sat low on his hips, but she was grateful for them.

Tucker shrugged. "People were dying. My wolf just..." His face bunched and he blew out a puff of air. "I don't know how to describe it. He kinda rushed forward to help, and I wanted to, too so..." He lifted his shoulders again. "I shifted."

"Are you okay?" Violet asked, thinking of Zander. "Any... complications?"

Shaking his head, Tucker crossed his arms. "No, but Dov said it will be really painful until our full moon, since we haven't come into our full abilities yet."

Mya shuddered. "That's why I don't. Even with Pena and I having gone through the trials, it's too painful for me. She prefers to stay in the background, anyway."

After giving Tucker one last worried look, Violet turned to Mya. Her coiled chestnut hair had been neatly braided so it fell over one shoulder. Dark circles clung around her green eyes, which were full of alarm, but alert and aware. The subtle collapse in her cheeks and the brittle feel of her arms were evidence of drastic weight loss, but she seemed otherwise... okay.

"Why didn't you come sooner?" Mya asked softly, lightly smacking Violet's injured arm.

She sucked in a sharp breath through her teeth, and Mya apologized. "It's fine. It's not that bad."

"No one knew Lockup had been hit," Tucker answered for her. "I only left when no one was answering our clan calls." Darkness settled over his face. "Some of those guards downstairs were still fighting when I left. I didn't get back fast enough."

"Don't do that, Tucker." Violet chided softly and his hard blue gaze crashed against hers. "You went for help."

"Yeah, and I found you."

"Hey!" Mya snapped, but Violet held up a hand to stop her.

"By what you've described, I don't think it would have mattered if you had come back with an army."

Tucker's eyes flared silver. "Then I should have stayed and fought!"

"All that would have done was added one more body to the count." Jax's calm voice called from down the hall. Relief sagged Violet's shoulders when her twin stepped into view. Two warriors walked past him to continue down the hall while Jax stepped into the cell and nodded at Mya. "Make that two because they would have made it to Mya without you here to stop them."

"These cells are clear," announced one of the warriors.

Tucker left Mya's cell and pointed to what Violet assumed was the Blood Moon member he'd stopped. "He was the last one stupid enough to stay."

Mya tapped Violet's good arm. "I meant why didn't you come *visit me* earlier?"

"I wanted to, but I was told not to." Violet looked around her friend's cell. "You can't stay here. Why don't you come stay the night with me?"

Fear tightened Mya's eyes and she wrapped her arms around her middle. "No. I can't leave."

"Everyone here is dead, Mya." She apologized when her friend flinched at her harsh words. "Please, let me take you away from here. Just for the night, until we can get another room set up for you."

Mya shook her head.

"Mya—"

"We'll help get you settled into a new cell tonight." Jax interrupted and the pressure building inside Violet's chest eased. "Doc said you probably wouldn't want to leave."

Violet turned to her brother and then froze as she took him in.

Soot covered nearly every inch of his body. Blood covered whatever was left. His white dress shirt would be forever ruined—it would probably need to be burned, and his hair was tousled haphazardly. The sorrow pulsing between their twin-link was written across the hard planes of his face.

The three remaining warriors stood outside Mya's cell looking ready for a fight, and Violet admitted to herself that Jax was smarter than her. He'd at least brought backup. Of course, he was usually the more levelheaded about these sorts of things.

"Where's Cas?" Violet wondered, realizing she'd forgotten about him in the midst of worrying about Mya.

"He headed out with a couple of the warriors when he heard us come in," Jax answered, then stepped toward her. "Why didn't you tell me you were heading here? I would have helped."

Violet shrugged a shoulder. "I didn't think about it. You were busy. Tucker said he'd already tried..."

"And he kept trying until he got through to me. It finally worked when he said you were here."

Tucker leaned against the cell wall a few feet away. "Figured someone of authority needed to be here. Alpha said he was busy, and that you could handle it."

"Yes," Jax grunted. "He had an important issue to take care of, and Luna needed his help."

"Is she okay?" Violet asked.

"She'll be fine."

"What about Patrick and Lexie?" Violet continued. and Mya visibly stiffened from her place on the floor.

Jax sighed. "They got everyone who was still alive out of the clan house. They were working on getting the bodies out when I left to come here. I sent Cas back to help them."

"Good to know," Violet said softly, then knelt beside her friend. "Wanna help us move you over?" She looked around the room and smiled to see it was at least a little homey. The full-sized bed had a purple ruffled comforter and a few fluffy-looking pillows. A large bookcase filled to the brim with books sat in one corner, and a desk was nearby. A cozy-looking chair sat on the other side, and Violet imagined her friend curled up with a book there for hours on end. "Looks like you've got quite a bit of stuff in here."

Mya's gaze shifted to Jax. "You're not making me leave?"

Shaking his head, Jax squatted down to be on her level and repeated what he'd said before. "Doc says you're not leaving until you feel ready to. Are you ready for that?"

Her braid swung back and forth as she shook her head in response.

"I didn't think so. Let's get you moved, and we'll have people stationed nearby until we get this mess cleaned up."

"Thank you," Mya softly smiled and Violet's heart pinched.

If this was her friend now, Violet couldn't imagine how she had been before. The old Mya was in there somewhere, but it was going to take a long time for her to come back... if she ever did.

Over the course of the next hour, the three of them worked together to move Mya into a different cell. She fluttered about making sure everything was just right, and fussed when one of the warriors got dirt on her mattress.

Violet smiled as the guy apologized and ducked quickly out of the room.

"I don't even have anything to clean this with," Mya grumbled, then frowned at the stain.

It wasn't much bigger than her fist, but when the rest of the bed was unmarred, it seemed much larger.

"I'll have someone come clean it in the morning if that's okay?" Jax asked.

Mya nodded before sinking onto her bed. "I'm exhausted."

"Try to rest. And eat." Violet ordered, earning a familiar glare from her friend. "Don't test me."

"Yes, ma'am." Mya shook her head and a hint of a smile tipped the corners of her lips skyward.

Knowing she was settled and the warriors would stay with her, Jax and Violet slipped out of the cell and headed for Alpha House.

"This is going to be a long night," Jax sighed and ran a soot-covered hand down the side of his face. "Debriefs, clean up, attendance, condolences..."

Violet interrupted, remembering that Jax could feel the deaths of his clan members. "How are you holding up?"

"I'm fine, I..." Her twin stopped walking and eyed her. His jaw and gaze softened the longer he looked at her. "Actually, no. I'm not fine. I ache everywhere, my chest feels like someone placed an anvil on it, and my sister ran off into danger without telling anyone."

Surprised by that last part, Violet leaned back. "Me?"

"Do I have another sister?"

"Jax, I was worried about Mya."

"And I was worried about you!"

Violet blinked at him. It'd been a very long time since he'd expressed this level of concern, and she wasn't quite sure what to do about it.

"The next time you're feeling overly heroic or idiotic, at least take Patrick with you."

She was surprised he hadn't told her not to do it, but his plan was still flawed. "Patrick was helping move a beam, and you told Cas to haul me out of the clan house."

Throwing his arms in the air, he looked at her like she was crazy. "A message then, at the very least."

She nodded. "I'll try to remember that."

"Thank you." Jax sighed, still staring at her. He started shaking his head and then his arms were around her shoulders in a giant hug that she stood awkwardly for with her arms at her sides for far too long. "Just hug me back."

Laughter burst from her and she threw her arms around her brother's waist. She closed her eyes and a part of her that hadn't relaxed in a very long time, let go and tears flooded her eyes.

"Are you crying?" Jax asked, sounding annoyed.

"No." She wiped her tears against his dirty shirt. "You are."

A huff of amusement made her head bounce. "Yeah, okay." He rubbed the top of her head like he used to a few years ago, and she batted his hand away. "Come on, let's get the rest of this night over with."

# Chapter 12

## Violet

***Days passed in a haze of duties*** *after Blood Moon's attack during spring solstice.* The night had been long and the body count steadily rose as more people were found.

Eight.

They had lost eight clan members.

Tucker's dad was counted among the dead.

Sorrow plagued the clan, and crying was often heard. Children weren't running across the dirt roads anymore, and all off base schooling had been suspended. Parents feared another attack, which spurred them into keeping their children indoors even with the warriors working double shifts. And, the clan gates were barred to all except Cas and Lexie.

Cas was given clearance since he was petitioning to join the clan. Some found his dedication to join during one of the hardest times Sentinel Clan had ever faced admirable. Others, like Patrick, found it suspicious and unsettling.

Violet didn't side with either opinion.

Truly, she wasn't sure what she felt. His reasons were understandable; wanting to help, already feeling a connection to the clan, etc. Honorable and noble causes, all of them. It was the lack of hesitation that made her stumble on her own opinion. Most would at least hesitate joining a clan that was heavily under attack by bloodthirsty rogues... right?

Lexie on the other hand was making waves throughout the clan. She'd come by every day after her school ended. Her bravery earned her respect from most, if not all of the clan members, and they welcomed her as one of their own. She'd been helping with the clean up of the clan house and lending an ear to those who needed comfort. She even stayed to help the chef's prepare and serve food from folding tables stationed in front of what was left of their gathering hall.

Violet had never been prouder to call Lexie her best friend.

A fist drove into Violet's gut, knocking her out of her thoughts.

Another thing that had changed; the training facility was packed every day with worried wolven. Desperation and fear clung to the air as clan members tried to make up for time they'd spent *not* training.

That also meant that there were plenty of people willing to spar with her under Patrick's glaring eye.

"I thought you weren't going to train me anymore," Violet wheezed while holding her stomach. Her gaze darted to Patrick who stood outside the sparring ring, arms folded as he analyzed the fight.

The guy dancing around her lunged into another strike, thinking she was distracted. Violet dove to avoid getting hit then rolled over her shoulder and popped to her feet. She lifted her leg and delivered a well-executed sidekick to the man's back. He stumbled over his feet and groaned.

She felt for the guy, really. He'd come in here to quietly box on his own, but Patrick had recruited him to fill in. He was short for a wolven male, but still had a good six inches on her. The muscles rippling his arms told her he worked out, but sparring didn't seem to be his thing. The only reason he'd managed to hit her in the stomach was because she'd completely looked away from him and had gotten lost in thought.

"This isn't doing anything," Violet dropped her arms to her sides and strode for her water. "Either he's not a fighter or he's really going easy on me."

"I hit you a moment ago," the guy disputed.

Violet huffed a laugh and bent to pick up her water. "You hit me because I zoned out."

An aggravated moan from Patrick drew her attention while she took a deep drink. "What I meant when I said I couldn't train you anymore was that I can't spar with you, but you're right." He leveled the man with narrowed eyes. "If your sparring partner isn't trying hard enough, then it's pointless."

She tossed her bottle back into her bag. "Then I guess we're done."

The man shrugged and went on his way to box on his own with a dummy.

"Violet," Patrick's chiding voice made her keep her gaze lowered. "I need you to take this seriously."

"It's hard to take anything seriously when others don't do the same."

Chocolate peppermint drifted over her, and she tilted her head back to gaze into Patrick's eyes. He'd closed the distance between them, finally stepping onto the mats. "I take this very seriously. I need to know you can protect yourself."

Feigning resignation, Violet drew in a deep breath and let her shoulders fall. Her eyes lowered to the ground before she swept her leg beneath Patrick's. Large hands gripped her arms and she was falling too. Her tiny body crashed gracelessly atop Patrick's.

He groaned when she pushed off his chest to stand near his head.

"It seems that as long as I can distract my opponent, I do pretty well." Amused smugness quirked the corner of her mouth. "It's worked fantastically."

Quick as lightning, Patrick's hands snagged her ankle. He pulled her footing out from under her as he curled his body to wrap his legs around her leg. An imanari roll. She never could figure that one out. Execution or defense. Her back hit the floor with a thud and one of Patrick's feet was against her chin while the other snaked under her leg to twist over her hip.

The first, second, third, fourth, fifth, and so on time he showed this move to her he'd told her in a real fight he would have tucked his feet safely away and broken her ankle in a nasty foothold with a twist.

But this was training. He'd never break any of her bones. The fact that he didn't put her in that hold, though, made her anger burn. She yanked on her leg, but his hands held her ankle firm.

"You've been lucky." Patrick tightened his hold when she tried to flip out of it again. "Luck runs out eventually."

"Isn't there a rule against pummeling a beautiful woman into the ground?" Cas' smooth voice slid over the tension surrounding them.

Patrick's hands disappeared from her leg, and he launched to his feet.

Feeling like a discarded dishtowel, Violet's assent was much slower. "No one's pummeling anyone. Patrick's been training me for years, and due to rece..."

Words failed her.

A muscle in Patrick's jaw ticked as Cas shifted his weight at the edge of the mat, shirt removed and tucked into the band of his sweatpants.

Most wolven were well-built due to shifting alone. The toll it took on the body made for some pretty impressive natural physiques. But you could still pick out those who trained. And then there were the few who stood out amongst the many. Members of the clan who trained beyond the basic needs and Cas was one of them. He stood in all his glistening glory, bare-chested with a post-workout swell adding to his already corded muscles.

The last guy to steal her words and thoughts like that was Patrick, but he so very rarely took off his shirt... it was unfortunate because she could look at him all day long. During Patrick's trial, Alistair had tormented her for hours, sauntering around without a shirt. Unfortunately, Patrick was pretty modest, and was careful to stay completely covered.

A slow, smoky grin spread across Cas' face.

Fire seared her cheeks. She dropped her gaze and cleared her throat. "After semi-recent events, it was pointed out..." She glared at Patrick. "Rather painfully, I might add... that my groundwork needs some attention."

"I can help with that." The thump of Cas' bag drew her attention. He slipped off his shoes and bounced onto the mat. "I've been undefeated in my clan for years."

"That will quickly change here." Patrick stepped into Cas's path. Whether his words were a promise or a threat, she wasn't sure, but she had no doubt Patrick would beat Cas in any fight. "Violet is *my* student."

She opened her mouth to say that if Patrick didn't want to spar with her,

Cas would, but then Cas' grin turned into a condescending smirk.

"Last one standing gets to train her?"

"Get over yourselves," Violet grumbled as she marched directly through the two of them to get to her bag. "I'm going home."

Patrick moved to her side as she lifted her bag onto her shoulder. "We need to finish this."

"Finish what? That's the first time you've stepped onto the mats today, and I don't have time for you to figure out how to train me without actually training *with* me." She held his gaze, hoping he'd say something.

Fire blazed in his eyes, but his mouth remained closed.

Shaking her head, Violet started to leave.

"Violet—"

"She said she's done," Cas interrupted.

She turned to find Cas' hand secured on Patrick's shoulder.

"A good trainer knows when his charge has reached their limit."

Tension rolled through Patrick, raising his shoulders. "I do know her, and she hasn't."

He was right.

Sweat sparsely dotted her forehead and not a single muscle ached or burned. The two of them together, though, was too much for her to handle. Patrick had her heart but said their kiss was a mistake. Cas was just a friend but acted like he wanted more.

Shaking her head, Violet said, "I can't do anymore today."

Patrick's face softened. "Okay," he relented, then rolled his shoulder out from under Cas' hand. "Don't touch me again."

"Patrick!" Robin's voice sang into the tension, shattering the ice the three of them had been walking on. She jogged up to Patrick and circled her hands around his bicep. "Jess was just telling me how excited she is for our double date tonight."

Patrick closed his eyes and drew in a long breath through his nose before gazing down at her. "Robin, about tonight—"

Bluish-black hair swung from Robin's ponytail as she bounced on her toes. "I know! I'm excited too! And I know the perfect place. You can make up for our last date."

Violet shouldn't have been surprised. They were at solstice together, after all... right after Patrick had kissed Violet. Shaking her head, Violet started for the door. It wasn't a real kiss, she told herself. It could hardly be considered a kiss, really.

Plus, he'd said it was a mistake.

"You okay?" Cas' appeared beside her, pulling her from her thoughts.

She planted a small smile on her lips. "Yeah, I'm fine. I'm just feeling a little drained." Wiping a hand down her face, she sighed. "When I was checking out campuses with Lexie, I was staying at her place. There was no training other than an early morning run while she made her way out of bed with the speed of a sloth."

A soft chuckle rolled out of Cas.

"Patrick's just trying to get me back to where I was before I left."

Curiosity tilted Cas' head to the side. "How long were you gone?"

"A few weeks," Violet admitted. "And in that time, a lot of stuff happened here. Sentinel Clan isn't at its best right now, which you've now seen first-hand." She lifted the strap of her bag higher onto her shoulder. "I think that's why he's pushing me so hard."

"Still..." Cas grumbled. "I didn't like seeing him all over you like that."

Violet opened her mouth to explain the hold Patrick had put her in, but was interrupted by Robin yelling them over.

"I just had a fantastic idea!" She squealed when they stopped in front of her. "What if we turn tonight's double date into a triple?" Robin clapped her hands excitedly.

Violet's jaw dropped.

"Sounds wonderful!" Cas answered, smiling wildly.

Her jaw dropped even further.

Patrick's attention darted between Cas and Violet, and his gaze turned to ice. "Robin, I don't think—"

"It'll be great!" Robin interrupted and draped her hand on Patrick's arm. "You guys are going to come, right?"

No one answered.

Violet's heart hammered against her chest. Watching the guy she liked with a girl she barely tolerated did not sound like a fun time. But... maybe she'd been holding on to old emotions for too long. Maybe Patrick and her had missed their moment. Maybe their sort-of-but-not-really kiss really had been a mistake.

Sorrow clenched her chest, making it hard to breathe. She looked at Patrick who was staring at the ground, the muscle in his jaw clenching every so often. Then, she turned her head to find Cas, a grin stretched from ear to ear across his face as he watched her expectantly.

Maybe... it was time to give Cas a chance.

She opened her mouth to give a confident answer, but it came out as a whisper, "Let's do it."

# Chapter 13

## Violet

***This was a bad idea.***

*Violet stared out the window* as Jax turned into the parking lot of a BBQ joint. The sun had set, casting the world in shadow, but the lights around the restaurant offered a welcoming glow. A few members of their clan worked there. It was the closest restaurant to the base that wasn't fast food.

The thought of food twisted Violet's stomach in knots. Why did she agree to a triple date?

Carpooling with Jax and his date, Jess, hadn't been too bad. She counted it a blessing that she didn't have to share a car with Patrick and Robin. As awkward as Jax's flirting was, it was also mildly entertaining to watch Jess laugh at him for being a fool. She wasn't the kind of girl Violet thought he would go for, but emotions made people do crazy things.

Cas smiled a lot during the drive and asked a few questions, but Violet's nerves kept her from holding a conversation for very long. Her answers were short and clipped, giving little to no room for additional questions.

Things weren't going very well.

Jax pulled into a parking spot, and Violet stepped out of the car, then fiddled with the bottom of her shirt. At least they were at a casual BBQ joint, and not some fancy, romantic restaurant. She may have tried to hide in the trunk if that had been the case.

"Hey," Cas' smooth tone rolled over her, but she still startled when he brushed his hand down her arm. "Everything alright?"

Violet pulled her bottom lip through her teeth. "I have a confession to make..."

Curious, Cas arched a brow, "Oh? And what confession might that be?"

Her mouth hung open—the words stuck in her throat. Was she really about to tell him this was a mistake? She knew how much those words stung. A shudder rolled down her spine. "I've... never been on a date."

Cas blinked, then riotous laughter kicked his head back. He finally managed an, "Uh huh." But, when he realized she wasn't joking, his eyes widened in surprise, and he sobered quickly. "You're serious. How is that even possible?"

"That would be my fault," Jax came around the car after opening Jess' door. He extended a friendly hand toward Cas. "I kind of made it a personal mission to make sure no boy got their hands on my sister."

Jax's hand didn't look so friendly anymore, but Cas took it anyway. "Nothing wrong with being protective."

"Agreed." Jax shook Cas' hand. "My dad likes you, and I think you could be a good addition to the clan." His knuckles turned white and he yanked Cas toward him to whisper in his ear. "Don't ruin that."

"Wouldn't dream of it," Cas answered in a level voice. He kept his gaze slightly cast down when Jax released him.

Her twin clamped a hand over Cas' back. "Then things should go swimmingly!"

Violet's eyes narrowed. Since when did Jax use words like *swimmingly*?

Once Jax returned his attention to his date, Cas stretched out his hand at his side. He leaned sideways toward her and whispered, "Is he going to kill me?"

A huff of laughter burst from Violet. "Only if you hurt me."

"I don't plan on it." Cas flashed a toothy grin her way. "So, I should be safe."

Violet returned his grin with a tight-lipped one of her own.

"Apparently, Patrick and Robin started without us," Jax announced, drawing their attention. He beckoned them to follow. "They're inside and already have a table."

"At least there won't be a wait." Cass held out an arm, motioning for Violet to take the lead, then followed closely behind her.

Jax led them right to the half-round, corner booth Patrick and Robin were occupying then let Jess slide in first. She scooted around the back until she was nearly shoulder-to-shoulder with Robin who gave her a tight side squeeze. Jax followed after her and Cas slipped in next, leaving the edge seat for Violet.

Right across from Patrick.

Jax shrugged out of his jacket. "So, what is this place?"

"It's the closest restaurant to base, that's what it is." Robin sneered, but Patrick's frown drew a quick smile to her mouth. "I mean, it supposedly has great food, and there's an open mic night tonight which means free entertainment." Her smile slipped. "Of the nails on a chalkboard variety."

Violet wiggled in her seat, trying to settle in as Patrick countered, "The waitress said some of the songs move you to tears."

Robin snorted. "Tears of regret."

Violet flinched at her harsh assessment.

Their waitress arrived, and the meal was underway shortly after with mostly polite conversation. Unfortunately, a few musical numbers grated on their sensitive wolven ears, which only added fuel to Robin's complaints, but Jax and Patrick were quick to change the subject.

"I mean, honestly, if you can't sing then you shouldn't be performing."

"You know what, Robin," Violet snapped, but bit her tongue when the whole table turned to look at her. She didn't want to cause a scene. "Never mind."

Cas snorted quietly beside her, then bumped his shoulder against hers after Jax turned the conversation toward his full moon training. "What's up? You seem on edge."

After quirking a brow, Violet leaned toward him and whispered so softly she practically breathed against his ear. "You know everyone at this table can hear you, right?"

He turned his face so his cheek was resting against hers while he answered just as softly. "That's unlikely."

His hot breath against her ear almost made her pull away, but she clenched her muscles and ordered herself to sit still.

"Speaking on a breath with this beat thumping through the atmosphere..." He clicked his tongue and she startled at the sudden noise, making him chuckle quietly. "I'd be willing to bet that even Jax can't hear me right now."

Violet's gaze rose over Cas' shoulder and sure enough, Jax was preoccupied with his date.

"I could say anything to you right now and not get punched for it."

No amount of restraint could have stopped her body from lurching away. Flames licked her cheeks as she stared at Cas with wide eyes.

He simply grinned at her, then picked up a bread roll and held it out for her. "You haven't eaten anything. Are you hungry?"

"So quick to smile." Patrick's deeper timbre called to Violet, calming her nerves... until she saw the seething rage barely contained behind his hazel eyes. "Do you ever take anything seriously?"

Robin elbowed him. "Patrick."

"No, it's alright." Cas turned his easy smile on Robin who blushed and nibbled on a piece of her own roll. "Patrick's right. I do smile a lot, but that doesn't mean I can't be serious."

"You sure about that?" Patrick challenged.

Cas's mouth slipped into a wicked smirk. "Just ask Violet how serious I was after the incident during solstice."

Tension rippled through Patrick. His jaw clenched, and his breathing evened out, long and slow. Violet wondered how hard he was concentrating to keep Alistair at bay.

Her lips parted ever so slightly, and a bated breath rushed out.

Patrick caught the subtle drop of her shoulders, breaking his concentration on Cas.

"So, Cas!" Jax called, louder than necessary. "Where are you from?"

Cas relaxed back against the seat and draped an arm across the back cushion behind Violet, making her lean forward. She gently shoved her plate of untouched food away, so she could press her elbows against the wood.

"Up north a ways," her exceptionally confident date answered.

Patrick's steady breathing hitched, but only Violet seemed to notice.

"I've been slowly making my way through a different college each semester and checking out the surrounding clans. My parents are a little..." Cas sucked in a breath through his teeth. "... controlling? They have a girl they picked out for me to marry and everything."

Curious, Jax's head tilted to the side. "Like an arranged marriage? I thought those died out among the clans due to complications with couples finding their mates later on."

Cas nodded, then took a long drink. "They have, for the most part." He set his glass down. "Unfortunately, not all clans, or all families for that matter, have accepted the current way of doing things. My parents' marriage was arranged, and neither of them have ever run into their mates, so I think they believe it's good enough."

Fingers trailed along Violet's back from one shoulder to the other and she closed her eyes, reminding herself that she wanted to give Cas a chance. He wasn't doing anything wrong. His touch wasn't unpleasant. He didn't have dry, cracking hands, or a rough approach. But everything was so new, from the breathy whispers to the constant touching. Being affectionate in public made it feel even more strange.

"I would like to find my other half on my own."

Violet's eyes ripped open. Did he think she was his other half? If she thought the fire along her cheeks before was warm, it was nothing compared to the blazing heat that cascaded down her neck and reached for the tips of her ears.

Patrick's brows ticked toward each other as his gaze flickered between them.

She ducked her chin while Cas leaned toward her and quietly chuckled against her ear. "You're really cute when you blush."

Cas' lips brushed Violet's ear, and she squirmed away. "Can you..." She turned her head toward Cas, and nearly bumped her nose against his.

"Yes?" His gaze flickered to her lips, before finding her eyes once again.

She clamped her teeth together and put a few inches between them. "I need you to slow down," she whispered. Hurt crashed through the playful glint in his eyes, so she continued quickly, "I told you I'm new to this."

The fingers on her back disappeared. He nodded respectfully, "If I have to wait, I will."

A relieved sigh deflated her shoulders.

"It may kill me, but I can," he teased.

Her stomach twisted. That was it. That was the problem. Her amethyst eyes collided with pained hazel ones, then she bowed her head as tears threatened to build.

This wasn't a game.

Cas had real feelings for her. She'd already known that, but it was suddenly very clear just how real they were. It hurt knowing she didn't feel the same, and that she was going to wreck his hopes. She didn't want to hurt him.

Time heals all things. That's how the saying goes, right? Well, it's wrong. There are things that time can't heal. Wounds that can't be mended. Hearts that cannot change. No matter how desperately a person wants it to be so.

She thought she wanted to give Cas a chance, and maybe she should, but it wasn't what her heart wanted. Every fiber of her being reached for him. He called to her, begging her gaze to melt against his. Her stomach twisted again, and she clutched a hand against it.

"Violet?" Cas asked, resting a hand on her shoulder. "Are you okay?"

"Violet?" Jax called over Cas' concerned words.

Shaking her head, Violet pushed out of their booth, crashing against a waitress with a platter full of food.

"Oh!" the waitress cried as the platter tipped.

Patrick was on his feet stabilizing the waitress and food order before Violet could turn to apologize.

"What reflexes!" the waitress exclaimed, winking at Patrick. "Thanks for the save, handsome."

Violet's stomach roiled as the room erupted into applause and she bolted for the bathrooms. As she neared them, a darkened door with a neon exit sign dangling over it beckoned to her.

She crashed through the door and sucked in the sharp, chilled night air. "I'm fine," she lied to herself and walked into the alley. "I just need a minute."

A minute passed.

And then another.

And another.

Violet paced back and forth. Her heart and mind were at war. Logic told her Patrick was unavailable. He would have a mate. Doc already told her it was unlikely that Violet ever would. The tiniest kiss ever had been a mistake to Patrick. It had been a shining beacon of hope for her. He would be beta. Beta's needed strong mates. Violet was the weakest in the clan.

And then there was Cas.

Available and interested. Sweet. Accepting of her friendship with Lexie even with barely knowing her. Wanting to make a place of his own and not ruled by old laws. Sure... Cas was great.

But as she thought about his brown eyes, they shifted to hazel. His hair turned curly and flopped into his eyes. His easy smile gave way to a hard earned one that lit up her world.

A groan filled the empty alley and she tilted her head back to stare at the night sky.

Patrick was rough around the edges. He could be brooding. And he could hurt her like no one else... but she'd peeled back those prickly facade layers before, and his warm, sweet interior captivated her. There was so much more to Patrick than most people realized.

The door opened and Violet startled.

"What are you doing?" Patrick asked while the door swung shut behind him and he jogged down the three steps into the alley.

Oh no. Having him be here did not help anything. She turned down the alley, toward the back of the building. "Leave me alone, Patrick."

"You can't just leave," Patrick chided... and followed after her.

"I wasn't leaving, I just..." Her hands curled into fists and she drew in a deep breath. "I can't do this. You need to go back inside."

He didn't. "I'm not going anywhere until I know what's going on."

"Nothing," Violet snapped. "I just needed some air." She turned the corner, but he was hot on her heels.

"Vi."

She really wished he wouldn't say her name like that.

"Violet!"

She turned and yelled, "What?"

Patrick froze in his tracks. For a moment, he just stared at her and she almost started walking away again, but his foot slid forward another step. Slowly, he reached toward her, then ran his hands up and down her arms. "You're freezing."

Was she? She hadn't noticed, but she'd left her jacket inside. The heat from his hands practically burned her skin. Pinching her eyes shut, she stepped into him and his arms wrapped around her back, enveloping her in his warmth.

"I thought I could do this, but I can't," she admitted quietly. "I want to go home."

Patrick's body deflated against her. "Then let's go."

Violet jerked back. "What? No. You're on a date. I can't ask you to do that." She shook her head and stepped away. "I'll figure it out. Or just..."

"Hey." His fingers wrapped around her shoulder and turned her back toward him. "You didn't ask."

Tears built in her eyes and she nibbled on her lower lip.

"Let's go home." Patrick nodded toward the exit of the alleyway and lightly tugged on her.

It didn't take much convincing on his part. Home was exactly what she wanted, but that didn't stop the pit of guilt that rolled dubiously in her stomach.

Patrick shrugged out of his jacket and draped it over her shoulders while they walked. The lingering heat from his body eased her tense muscles, offering a nice reprieve from the chilly spring night.

When they reached his truck, Patrick pulled open the passenger door for her. "I told Jax that I'm taking you home."

She climbed into the seat with a mumbled thank you, and he closed the door.

The drive wasn't long, but it was quiet, leaving her with her thoughts... which were pure torture.

"I must be the worst date in the world," Violet mumbled, breaking the silence as Patrick directed the truck through the clan gates.

Patrick snorted. "No. Robin easily takes the cake on that."

She swung her head around to stare at him as they were waved through the second gate. "Then why did you..." she held up a hand. "You know what, never mind. I don't want to know."

"Ask your question, Vi," Patrick practically whispered.

He pulled the truck into a parking spot while Violet sat shaking her head. "Thanks for the ride home," she said, then yanked on the door handle.

"Violet."

She slid out of his truck and shut the door.

"Violet, stop." Patrick rounded the bed of his truck. "We need to talk."

"No, we don't." She made it two steps before he skidded in front of her. "I don't want to talk."

A frustrated growl left him. "Then you can listen."

"I don't want to do that either."

"Tell me what's going on."

Gravel crunched beneath her shoes when she pushed around him. "I'm fine."

"Are you?"

She didn't answer.

"Vi—

"Just stop, okay!" she yelled, spinning toward him. She threw her arms out to her sides as a hurricane of emotions pressed against her chest and his over-sized jacket sleeves practically draped over her hands. "No! No, I'm not fine! I'm not okay! Too much has happened and it's all built up and it's just..." her words failed when that stupid, annoying, unbreakable mask had slipped over Patrick's face.

Violet knew it was a habit, but it annoyed her to no end. Even if she could still see the dismay swimming in his eyes. Suddenly she wished she'd never noticed how much his eyes betrayed his emotions.

"Talk to me," his voice was almost a plea.

It shattered her resolve.

"You want me to talk?" Her voice broke.

Patrick nodded.

"Fine." She nodded, then sniffled before continuing. "I'll talk. How about the fact that I'm still coming to terms with not having a wolf? Or the fact that Doc believes I will never have a mate? And I know how you feel about them, but I wanted one." She pressed her fingers against her sternum. Sorrow dripped through her words as she continued, "I wanted someone to love me despite my weaknesses. I wanted someone to be my perfect fated half."

He swallowed, but remained quiet.

"I'm still struggling, knowing that I will never hold an official place in the clan. And then there's the sickness that my mom has that no one wants to talk about." Anger surged through her veins, turning her voice hard. "Oh, and speaking of people not talking... what about the silent treatment I got when I was gone for *weeks,* and the only contact I had was my mom and updating Jax about my visions?"

Patrick flinched.

"And don't even get me started on those. I don't know what is happening with them or why I have them." She ran a cold hand down her heated face. "And the date... I don't even know where to begin with Jax and Jess. When did that become a thing? And then there's Cas..." Her arm dropped to her side. "I'm trying to move on since it's clear whatever was going on between us..." Violet moved her hand back and forth in the space dividing them. "... isn't working out. You took another girl to solstice after kissing me. You went on a date with that same girl tonight, no matter what you say about her being a bad date. And given the promise I made to Jax, we were never going to happen anyway!"

Patrick's expression pinched a fraction more.

"I've been trying to act normal all night in a situation that I was completely uncomfortable in, and be on a normal date when I don't even know what that means because Jax never let me date! But even with my lack of experience, I'm pretty sure you're not supposed to be thinking about the guy sitting across from you when your date can't keep his hands off you." She lifted her hands up. "And I know I have no claim over you, but I can't stand seeing you with Robin! And I don't know what to do about that either!" Violet's chest heaved.

The longer Patrick stared at her, the more time she had to process everything she'd just blurted... and if word-vomit was a thing... she'd just done it.

Mortification built in her eyes, disguised as hot tears, and she shook her head. "No, no, no, no... You were not supposed to know all of that." She bit her lower lip and the first tear fell.

"What promise did you make?" Patrick asked, keeping his voice low.

Violet covered her mouth and released a pained sigh into her palm, then said, "It doesn't matter."

"It does to me."

Violet turned to leave, but he stepped in front of her.

He closed the distance between them until they were nearly toe to toe. "What was the promise?" He asked in hushed tones and hesitantly brought his hand to her cheek. The pad of his thumb wiped at the tear that had fallen. His mask cracked beneath her gaze. Worry, anger, longing... even hope... shone through his softened expression.

And just like before, Violet's resolve wavered, and so did her voice. "A few weeks after you moved here I made a comment about your good looks. It was the first time I ever saw his wolf eyes. He threw me up against a wall and made me promise that I would never date you."

Patrick stepped back as if he'd been slapped, releasing a ragged breath. He raked a hand through his hair, then watched her with wide, unblinking eyes.

Dragging her bottom lip through her teeth, Violet nodded to herself. Now he knew everything. Even her tears had halted their fall, waiting to see what would happen next.

Nothing.

That's what happened.

Not trusting her voice, Violet nodded and stepped around him. She couldn't stay there another minute, not with her heart lying in the gravel of the clan's parking lot waiting to be trampled.

Large, gentle hands seized her arm and pulled her back.

She opened her mouth to plead with him to let her go, but he softly led her backward until her shoulder blades pressed against the side of his truck.

A small gasp filled her lungs and his hands landed on either side of her head while his gaze darted over every inch of her face as if trying to burn it into his memory.

Their chests rose and fell together, and a second heartbeat filled her ears, just as it had in the trial ring. The two stampeding beats raced each other.

Patrick swallowed hard, then his lips parted and his hand left the truck to trace the soft slope of her shoulder to her neck. Fingertips lifted her chin, angling her face toward his until their gazes collided.

Crimson circled his eyes, giving life to the fire she'd seen before.

"Patrick?" she breathed. If Alistair was playing some evil prank, she'd find a way to make him pay.

A charming, half-smirk lifted one corner of Patrick's mouth as golden-flecked hazel returned, drowning out the red. "I'm right here," he whispered.

His breath tickled her lips and she wet them in anticipation. She pulled her bottom lip through her teeth.

A low, smoky groan left him, making her blush, but her fingers had curled into his shirt all on their own, and she drew him closer. He responded willingly, until their lips brushed, and then he hesitated. Slowly, his mouth melted against hers, almost as if he were testing the waters. Or giving her the opportunity to back away.

Not a chance.

Violet pressed against him and his hand found her waist, tugging her closer while his other hand weaved into the hair at the base of her skull. A bolt of pleasure surged through her veins and her hands trembled against his chest. She sucked in a quick breath and he drew her lower lip into his mouth. The tip of a fang grazed her lip, and a shiver rolled down her spine.

Patrick froze, then whispered against her lips, "Is this okay?"

She breathed a laugh and nodded.

His sigh of relief filled her soul and then he took her mouth with his. This was nothing like the mistaken kiss days before or the tentative one moments ago. This kiss felt like a confession, raw and beautiful. A dam giving way to hopes and dreams of years past.

A perfect reflection of her own heart.

That second heartbeat thundered along with hers, and she smiled against his swollen lips. Her hands slipped up his chest, wanting to feel his heart racing with her own hands. A soft growl rumbled through him into her fingers as they trailed his neck and his quickened pulse that beat against her touch.

His hand cradled the back of her head, ever protecting her from harm as his lips strayed from her mouth, leaving a scorching trail down her jaw.

The hand at her waist dropped to her hip, pulling her against him... and then his head jerked back and he released her hip as though he'd been shocked. "Wait, wait, wait... slow down."

He lowered his head to rest his forehead against hers with his eyes shut tight while their chests rose and fell in rapid succession together.

A minute passed and Violet lowered her hand to his chest. "Patrick?"

"I'm so sorry." He groaned through his teeth, clenching his jaw. "This shouldn't—"

"Don't," Violet pleaded.

His eyes snapped open and he stood tall, shaking his head. A pained expression passed over his face. "I don't want to hurt you, Vi."

The sweltering haze that had settled over her evaporated. She pressed her hands against his chest and he easily stepped back. "If you say this was a mistake, that's exactly what you're going to do."

Anguish passed over Patrick's face. He traced the side of her face with his knuckles down to her chin and then let his hand fall to his side. "No, but being with me will only put a bigger target on you."

Violet opened her mouth to argue and he closed the space between them again.

"You know Blood Moon is after me. I can't put that kind of danger on you."

"That is *my* decision to make," Violet hissed. "You don't get to choose that for me!"

Patrick's throat bobbed.

She cupped his cheek with her palm and he leaned into her touch, closing his eyes briefly. "Blood Moon has made it clear they want more than just you. And besides..." A smirk tilted one corner of her mouth, leaking a hint of teasing into her words. "Who's gonna have your back when they come for you?"

A breathy laugh escaped him as he stared down at her.

"Jax is not going to like this," Violet groaned.

Another laugh left him, but it was warm and soothed the last aches of her heart. "Actually," he lifted her hand, slipped his sleeve up her arm, and kissed her knuckles. "He already approved this."

Violet's jaw dropped. "That two-faced little..."

Patrick captured her mouth with his.

She laughed against his lips. "You can't interrupt me while I'm ranting."

"Hmm." He pressed another quick kiss to her lips, then the tip of her nose, and finally her forehead. "I have a feeling I'm going to be interrupting you a lot."

Flames danced across her cheeks, and she buried her face against his chest.

A rumbling chuckle shook him.

"So Jax knows?" Violet finally asked, tilting her head back to meet Patrick's warm gaze.

"About this?" He shook his head. "He believes we left because you weren't feeling well. He assumed you'd had a vision that didn't sit well, and I didn't know what was going on, so I didn't correct him."

Violet groaned. "What about Robin and Cas?"

Patrick growled. "I really don't like his name on your lips."

There was nothing she could do to stop the smile that spread across her face, but then it slipped. "Why did you call that kiss on the mats a mistake? And why did you go out with Robin after that?"

A sigh dropped his shoulders. "I should have clarified, but I was caught off guard." He lowered his forehead to hers, and drew in a deep breath. "It was only a mistake because I had already agreed to take Robin to solstice."

"Why?"

His face pinched. "I've been fighting a losing battle trying to hide my feelings for you. Dating other people seemed to keep you at arm's length, so I played the part. Robin really drove a wedge, so... I kept pushing that."

"All for the sake of trying to keep Blood Moon away from me?"

Patrick shrugged a shoulder.

"You're a fool."

A goofy grin slipped over Patrick's lips, something she'd never seen before, and she squealed when he lifted her off the ground. His hands cradled the back of her legs, just below her butt as he said, "A fool for you."

It was cheesy, but it tugged a grin from her before he planted another kiss against her lips. When he set her back on the ground, she blinked at him, stunned by how affectionate he was being. As if he'd been holding back behind a wall for years, and now the wall had been obliterated.

Violet did not mind.

Not one. Single. Bit.

# Chapter 14
## Patrick

***Unease curled inside Patrick's stomach*** *as he walked Robin home.* Jax had announced when they returned to the base and that Robin had requested the escort. He figured it was the perfect time to tell her things were most definitely over between them, so he'd said goodnight to Violet, and met Robin halfway to her room.

Robin typically carried the conversation for the both of them, but apparently she'd had enough. She was quiet, and the silence hung heavily between them.

And then there was Alistair, who hadn't stopped yelling at him since Patrick agreed to walk Robin home. Patrick tried to tune out his angry wolf, but the effort made his head pound. Not to mention his skin felt like it was on fire. He could still feel Violet's skin beneath his hands and the taste of her lips against his.

Robin unlocked her door, snapping Patrick out of his spiraling thoughts, and leaned against the frame. She tilted her forehead against the wood while one of her legs rocked back and forth. "I was going to invite you in, but I don't think I'm the one who's on your mind." She gave a small smile. "Am I?"

Surprise widened Patrick's eyes.

"Don't insult me," Robin chuckled. "I've been following you around for weeks, but you've never shown any more interest than you did in that diner when I interrupted you and Violet." She pushed off the wall and shrugged. "I thought maybe I just needed to try a little harder. I must have been stupid to think I could turn your head away from her."

The sound of Violet's name sent pleasant chills over his body. "You knew? Yet you tried anyway?"

Robin smirked. "There's a reason Violet and I never became great friends."

"Aside from the fact that you two have nothing in common?" Patrick asked, crossing his arms.

Lifting her palms, Robin said, "Don't get defensive. I'm just stating a fact. Besides," She stepped farther into her room. "We had one thing in common. We both like you. I don't have anything against Violet. She's nice. She's strong. She cares deeply for everyone around her, but I was only her friend to get close to you."

Soft-boiled rage began to rise, prickling the back of Patrick's neck.

"Look, I knew this wasn't going to go anywhere. We've both been through the trials, so we know we aren't mates, but it was still fun." Robin smiled. "I have to ask though, if Violet wasn't here, would you want to be with me?"

Patrick slowly shook his head.

Robin's knuckles bleached while she gripped the doorknob, "Why not?"

"Because it's always been her," Patrick whispered. "And it always will be."

A frustrated sigh left Robin and she rolled her eyes. "Then why aren't you with her?"

He ran a hand through his hair. "Well, actually..."

"That's why you left, isn't it?" She snorted and her knuckles bleached as she clenched the doorknob. "She wasn't feeling sick, you left to hook up."

"No, she wasn't feeling well. That's why we left." Words failed him when he tried to explain more. Finally, he raised his shoulders. "We worked through some stuff when we got back here."

"So, you're breaking up with me?"

His brows pinched together. "We... weren't ever a couple. I just thought I should explain—"

Robin slammed the door in his face. The loud sound made him tense, and he stood, staring at the now-closed door for a few breaths before turning down the hallway. That conversation had been weird.

On the way out of the fourth commons building, Patrick found Jax whistling to himself as he stared into the night sky.

"That good, huh?" Patrick asked.

Jax smirked. "She's fun."

"I don't want to know." Patrick scuffed his foot against the ground and Jax sobered quickly.

"What's wrong? You and Violet have been acting weird all night."

Shaking his head, Patrick started toward his apartment in the first commons building. Sure, Jax had given the go-ahead, but the idea of telling his best friend he was dating his twin sister had been so foreign for so long.

"You're the reason she left, aren't you?"

Patrick stopped, then slowly turned toward Jax.

His arms were crossed tightly over his chest, and his eyes flickered between liquid gold and the purple he shared with Violet.

Wary of how his friend was going to react, Patrick drew in a deep breath and let it out slowly before answering, "Yes."

Jax had never moved so fast.

Pain lit up Patrick's jaw as his head snapped to the side.

"This is exactly why I keep guys away from her!" Jax nearly yelled at him, pulling his elbow back for another round.

Understanding, and a pinch of guilt, kept Patrick's fists at his side, but Alistair stirred in the back of his mind.

*"You're going to let him get away with that?"*

Ignoring his inner beast, Patrick said, "I'm not going to fight you."

"Good, 'cause I want to hit you again!" Jax's swing was sloppy with emotion and he swung wide.

It was easy to duck under.

"You told me you weren't holding me to my promise anymore," Patrick reminded him.

Jax's eyes flared gold. "Don't pin this on me! Did you see her face when she ran out of there? Whatever you did, tore her apart!"

"Jax."

Anger rolled off his friend when Patrick deflected another attack. "I take it back. I take everything I said back."

"No." Patrick withdrew a few steps, out of Jax's reach. "You need to listen."

"No, you do!" Jax growled. "I have trusted you with the safety of my sister from the moment you arrived. I've left you to protect her countless times. But the moment I give my blessing, you are the one to hurt her."

Guilt stabbed Patrick in the stomach, making him flinch. He *had* done that, but... "I was trying to protect her, Jax. That's all I've ever done!"

"You're protecting her by hurting her?" Jax snorted, his hands were still curled into fists, but he seemed less likely to strike again. "That doesn't make any sense."

Patrick's shoulders sank. "The Blood Moon clan is after me. If they found out she's my mate, they'd kill her."

All color drained from Jax's face. "She's what?"

Angry that he'd announced the secret he'd been keeping for months, Patrick lowered his chin and seethed. "Violet is my mate."

Heavy silence dangled between them.

"You're an idiot," Jax declared.

Patrick chuckled. "Violet called me a fool."

"Yeah, you're that too."

He lifted his gaze and found Jax watching him cautiously.

"You told me once that you were going to reject your mate."

"Yeah." Patrick shoved his hands into his jeans pockets. "That was before I knew it was Violet."

"Does she know?"

"No."

"I'm gonna hit you again."

Confusion bunched Patrick's face. "Why?"

An incredulous look swept over Jax's face before it was replaced with fury. He stomped toward Patrick. "You did all that, knowing she was your mate?"

"To protect her."

"You hurt her!"

"We're together!" Patrick yelled, surprising Jax into silence.

Both of their chests heaved with heavy breaths full of emotion, but Jax's mouth hung open. "What?"

"Violet and I are together. We settled things tonight after we left and made it back here."

Throwing his arms out to the sides, Jax shook his head. "So now you're okay putting her in danger?"

"No, but she kinda ripped into me for making that choice for her."

Jax watched him for a moment, looked off to the side and narrowed his gaze, then huffed a laugh. "Good. You deserved it."

Suspicion coiled Patrick's muscles. "That's it? You're not going to hit me?"

"Violet says you two are good," Jax told him and Patrick guessed the hesitation had been him reaching out to Violet through their twin-link.

"There's something else you need to know." Patrick started for his room again, not waiting to see if his friend would follow.

Jax quickly caught up and grumbled, "Now what?"

Lowering his voice, Patrick said, "Wait till we get inside."

He did, but he complained the whole time and the instant the door clicked shut, Jax expected answers.

"Do you want a drink or to sit?" Patrick asked, feeling uncomfortable with the information he was about to divulge. This was something he hadn't spoken about in years.

"Spit it out," Jax snapped, his rage barely contained.

Running a hand through his hair, Patrick moved to the couch but never made it into a sitting position. He froze, staring at the small coffee table in front of him.

"You already know I've killed."

"Obviously," Jax grumbled.

"What you don't know is that it wasn't one. It was three." Patrick swallowed the knot in his throat. "And one of them was a daughter of the Blood

Moon pack."

# Chapter 15

## Patrick

***Silence.***

*It was the weirdest thing.*

Three and a half years had passed since there had been complete silence in Patrick's mind.

It was unbearable.

Dwelling on his thoughts and feelings was agony. He'd much rather be fighting against Alistair. Which, he guessed, was exactly why his annoying darker half had suddenly adopted the silent treatment.

Last night, Jax hadn't taken the news of Patrick's victims well.

"Three?" He'd yelled. "THREE? And the Blood Moon pack? How do you know that? Are you sure?"

Nearly an hour passed in discomfort while Patrick explained what had happened that night three and a half years ago.

"It was stupid, but I felt like I needed a break from my clan. I'd been invited to a party for the teen wolven in surrounding clans, and..." He'd shaken his head. "Things got out of hand. Teenagers get stupid when they are left unsupervised, and some idiot decided to bring alcohol, not realizing it packs a much harder punch for us than it does for humans."

Jax had swiped his hand down his face and leaned back heavily in the armchair he'd claimed. "Were you drinking?"

"No." Patrick had answered sharply. "I tried to stop others too, but they didn't take me serious. They were all older than me. One of the three that I'd been hanging out with had drank way too much and she started talking about her mom and her red eyes. About how she was still like her mom just a little scarier."

Jax watched him with a pinched expression while he continued.

"When they decided they wanted to go home, none of them were in a position to drive, so I did."

"Patrick... you were fifteen."

"Fourteen," he corrected Jax. "I hadn't had my birthday yet. My dad had given me a few lessons, but nothing in the snow."

He clenched his jaw against the flood of memories. The crash killed five people. Two humans in the oncoming car that hit them and the three teen wolven in the car that Patrick had been driving. He was the only survivor. The police determined the other driver was at fault and didn't know Patrick had been driving.

But the goddess knew.

That was the night Alistair became a part of him. Despite having control over his bloodthirsty wolf, his father kicked him out of the clan, two days before his fifteenth birthday with nowhere to go.

"Patrick?"

He jerked his attention to Jax, then glanced across the dimly lit room. He'd forgotten where he was. Two other men sat on the opposite side of a thick, wooden table. Alpha Klaus of Stanislaus Clan and their future alpha, Talon Break.

Jax and Patrick had been sent to Stanislaus to discuss the change of title and power in Alpha Draven's stead. And, from everyone's expectant faces, he had missed something.

The elderly man sitting directly across from Patrick cleared his throat. "Was there a problem with that timing, future beta?"

*"What is going on with you?"* Jax snapped through the clan-link, his tone slightly clipped as it had been all day. *"They're talking about when to pass the alpha title to Talon. Ask when they're planning to do that because they haven't told us exactly when, yet."*

Patrick straightened himself in his chair. "No, sir. My apologies. I got lost in my thoughts for a minute. When exactly are you planning on transferring the title? You've danced around a date, but not offered it."

The young man sitting diagonal from him drew in a breath as he raised his thick, dark eyebrows. He nodded. "We were looking at the Summer Solstice."

Talon had grown since the last time Patrick had seen him. A full inch, maybe two, but he'd filled out, appearing more and more the alpha of Stanislaus Clan. If he kept up on his training, Patrick could see him as a significant threat one day—or a fantastic ally.

"... gives us plenty of time to prepare, and it's a wonderful time to welcome a new alpha," concluded Alpha Klaus. Wrinkles donned the older male's face, and smile lines showed he was generally a happy fellow... even if he hadn't stopped frowning since they arrived. He'd lived a long life, but never found his mate and never chose one either. And so, there was no heir.

Vikter had been the future alpha until paranoia had driven him mad. That's when Talon had stepped in and Vikter had turned to Blood Moon pack for revenge. The deranged teenager had killed Patrick's neighbors and delivered a chilling message.

"Talon." Jax cleared his throat, drawing Patrick from his thoughts. "If I remember correctly, you have an older brother, right?"

Stanislaus' future alpha clenched his jaw and his brows pulled downward. "He won't be a problem."

Nodding his head, Jax continued. "You've cleared this with him, then?"

"Is this something your father's asking? Or you?" Alpha Klaus asked.

Jax let an amused smile tilt one corner of his mouth. "My father wondered about the bloodline, and I second his concerns. Since I am here on his behalf and filling the position of acting alpha, I believe it is an area for concern."

A vein began to pulse in Talon's neck.

No one answered at first, but then the older man raised an age spotted hand. "If I may, Hunter now runs with the Blood Moon pack."

The sudden information made Patrick clutch the arms of his chair. It took everything in him to keep his face clear of any reaction, and he didn't dare look at Jax after last night. Talon, on the other hand, had enough reactions for the entire room.

Talon's eyes rounded, then he drew in a deep breath that flared his nostrils. "I understand why he did what he did." Talon sighed. His shoulders dropped, and he ran a hand down his suddenly weary face. "But the consequences…" His words trailed off as Alpha Klaus shot him a warning look.

"They aren't always fair," Patrick finished Talon's lingering thought, surprising the future alpha into looking at him.

"Exactly."

The alpha cleared his throat. "Regardless, Blood Moon wolves have no place in this clan, and we are grateful for the clear indicator of their red eyes that shows their true nature."

"That proves nothing," Patrick answered without thinking and internally groaned as all three males looked at him.

Talon leaned forward, his toasted almond skin catching the light from the desk lamp at his left, and placed his elbows on the table. "Please, explain." He ignored the direct glare from Alpha Klaus and continued, "I would like to understand your view better if we're going to work together in the future. Although, I've heard rumors that you won't be staying with Sentinel Clan."

"I have no plans to leave."

From the corner of his eye, he saw Jax's shoulders ease a fraction.

Talon nodded. "Good to hear."

"Talon," Alpha Klaus chided. "We do not encourage such blasphemy in our clan."

"Then you will be happy to have a reminder that Patrick is not part of this clan."

Tension rolled off the old alpha, but it was clear his influential aura had lost its effects on Talon long ago. The young man blinked casually as a vein appeared in the elder's forehead.

"Alpha," Jax interrupted the stare-down between old and future alphas. "If you would hear Patrick out, it might set your worries at ease."

With a grumble, Alpha Klaus leaned back in his seat. "I'm listening. Let's see if you can change an old man's mind."

*"Don't screw this up."* Jax's voice filled Patrick's mind, and a quiet, dark laugh echoed in the background. *"I actually like Talon. I can't say that for most of the future alpha's I've met."*

*"I'll do my best,"* Patrick admitted, then cleared his throat.

Talon waited on bated breath, his eyes focused solely on Patrick.

"Having red eyes doesn't mean you're a blood thirsty killer. I've seen the effects of taking another's life destroy people, and it changes something inside of their predatory half. It doesn't seem to matter if the death they caused was intentional or accidental. It's a mere indicator that they took the life of an innocent. It doesn't tell you if the act was malicious."

"That's all well said, young one," Alpha Klaus leveled Patrick with his steely blue eyes and the term "young one" made Patrick tense. "But you're beating around the fact that every single one of them turns vicious whether it was intentional or not."

Talon slammed his palms into the table, the sudden outburst made both Jax and Patrick jump. "Then maybe we should be searching for a way to fix that!"

"Talon, we've been over this before."

"And you always dismiss it."

"Going down this path only leads to death."

"But if we succeeded, think of all the people we could help. Think of my brother."

"*If* he is still alive."

The air thickened. Patrick wondered when it had gotten so hot.

And then, a far away blood curdling scream shattered the evening.

Patrick jumped out of his seat, while the other three watched him. He was at the window before any of them could speak. He pushed the curtains open just enough so he could see outside.

"What's wrong?" Talon asked.

Nothing. That's what Patrick could see.

A few people and wolves leisurely wandered around the cabin like structures of Stanislaus' Clan base, but there wasn't a single warrior in sight. No wolves running to and from shifts. It was calm and peaceful… too peaceful.

Forests were loud. Filled with the sound of the wind blowing through the leaves and branches, or animals scurrying about in the underbrush. The call of birds from the treetops. But it was eerily quiet. Like the forest was holding its breath in anticipation. Something was out there amongst the darkening trees.

*"Alistair, I need your eyes."*

Like waking from a long sleep, Alistair's presence was muddy and sluggish. *"Now you want my help? You refused to acknowledge the favor you already owe me."*

*"You can't call in the favor when it involves Violet or Jax."*

*"So you said, but that wasn't specified when we made the deal."*

*"I didn't think it needed to be,"* Patrick spat. *"Are you going to help me or not?"*

Alistair hemmed and hawed. *"What do I get out of it?"*

*"Why does there always have to..."* Dread filled Patrick, cutting off his thought.

It didn't matter that Alistair wanted to strike a deal. Rubies pin pricked the farthest reaches of his vision. "Jax, turn off the lights."

"What's going on?" Alpha Klaus asked, not bothering to lower his voice.

Darkness blanketed the room and Patrick turned away from the window to find Talon standing between him and the alpha. "Blood Moon is here," he answered in a hushed tone. "We need to get you out of here, sir."

With minimal light peeking above the window curtains, the four males could see just fine. As long as there was a light source, no matter how small, wolven could see as if it were only dimly lit.

Patrick started toward Alpha Klaus, but the older man held up a hand to stop him. "I've lived much longer than many wolven. I will only slow you down. Protect my protege. Help my people get out. We are not the fighters you Sentinels are."

Talon lowered his chin, and for a moment Patrick wondered if he was showing a deep sign of respect. Then, the future alpha's mouth started moving as though he was talking quickly.

"If you're telling the clan to get out," Patrick interrupted, drawing Talon's attention. "It may be too late. We don't know how many are out there."

Alpha Klaus leveled Patrick with a withering glare. "Exactly how do you know they're here?"

"Patrick has better eyesight and hearing than any wolven I've met," Jax announced. "You should believe him."

"Our clan can't stay here," the older man growled. The tone was quiet and frail.

Patrick shook his head. "If they try to leave, Blood Moon will pick them off one by one. Their only chance is to leave in groups, but even then they could run into trouble."

"You don't know our safety protocols." Talon explained. "I've told them to make their way to the tunnels without being spotted. If they can do that, they might have a chance."

Jax's head dipped to the side. "You guys have tunnels?"

"They were built for the alphas of old. Quick ways to get to the clan borders in case of a runaway breeder or a deserter." Alpha Klaus explained with a dismissive wave of his hand.

"Breeders?" Jax growled.

Patrick clenched his jaw. Breeders were enslaved females forced to have as many children as possible for a designated length of time before they were released from servitude. It was a despicable act that the kings and queens had abolished decades ago.

Talon cleared his throat when it was clear Alpha Klaus wasn't about to elaborate. "Stanislaus was one of the first to terminate the Breeder Act. The tunnels serve as reminders to never return to such horrific deeds, but they are also used as escape routes when necessary."

Relieved to hear the future alpha's explanation, Patrick's shoulders lowered a fraction. "Are you certain these tunnels are still safe?"

After nodding, Talon peeked out the window while he spoke, "They are patrolled regularly. Those on duty right now have already checked in." He pulled away from the window and looked at Patrick. "I've never known a wolven to have such amazing eye sight. The two warriors who have reported to me said the Blood Moon members just passed the border." When Patrick didn't responded, Talon added, "And those warriors are on opposite sides of our territory."

"So, we are surrounded." Alpha Klaus lowered himself into his chair. "Talon, I would like to perform the Alpha Rite. Now."

Jax shook his head. "We don't have time."

Talon's gaze softened as he looked at the elderly man. Sorrow poured off him in waves. "Nor do we have one of the kings or queens here."

"A lycan isn't needed to perform the rite," Patrick offered the information as he looked out the window again. Blood Moon was getting closer. "They are only needed to confirm and approve the transition, which can be done at a later date."

With that new information, Talon's jaw set, making the muscle pulse. "What do I need to do?"

"I can help," Jax told them. "Alpha Draven and I have been going over this frequently."

Both Stanislaus' current and future alphas nodded.

Jax turned toward Patrick. "Will you go outside and see if anyone needs help getting to their destinations? I'll meet up with you as soon as we're done."

"Be safe." Patrick demanded his best friend, who's mouth quirked into a quick smirk. One that often led to trouble. "Violet will murder us both if you get hurt."

Chuckling, Jax agreed while Patrick made his way toward the door. His hand clenched around the handle, but instead of leaving he found himself looking at Alpha Klaus. "I'm sorry. This is not the end you should've had."

The old man raised his chin, but surprised Patrick by offering the smallest of nods. "I've lived a long time. Dying for my clan is an honor."

Perhaps it was honorable, but it was unnecessary. The clans had been at peace for so long.

But peace is a fragile thing. The smallest crack can shatter the strongest fortress.

With a final, respectful bow of his head, Patrick left the room and Jax began the rite.

Five steps out the door, a chorus of screams sounded from somewhere to the right, but they were cut short.

A family hadn't made it to their designated escape route.

After a deep breath, Patrick ran in their direction. He couldn't save everyone, but if he could clear a path for some, it would be something.

The stench of blood made his stomach roll and moments later he caught the hint of a heartbeat. Then two. Then three.

He dipped his head and let his eyes shift to red.

*"Are you letting me out to play?"* Alistair practically purred... it was a creepy sound.

*"No."* Patrick growled his disgust to his other half as he slowed his pace and stalked toward the owners of those heartbeats. *"Just playing the part."*

"How many?" He demanded, trying to imitate the gravelly tone Alistair preferred.

The trio spun around, all bloody eyed and ready for a fight.

Until they saw his eyes.

Hesitantly, they stood from their crouched positions. The dark-haired male took one step toward him and said, "A family of five. They didn't even see us coming. Vikter's information was good."

Heat swelled in Patrick's core, leaking to his fingers which he clenched into fists. He sent a message to Jax, telling him of Vikter's betrayal before he said, "Good to know. Spotted any others?"

The second male shook his head. "Not yet. We aren't sure if anyone saw us, but this is more fun." A crooked smile pulled at his face, revealing a long scar that stretched from his chin to a small tear in his earlobe. "We think a lot more will be coming this way if you want to join the fun."

Unable to hide his disgust, Patrick snarled.

The two males shrunk away from him with narrowed eyes.

*"Easy Boy Scout. They're getting suspicious of you."*

*"I've got it covered."* Patrick growled at his darker half.

He tried to adjust his stance so he would look more offended than threatening as he said, "I have my own orders."

The third-party member, a female with moonlit paper white skin, stepped toward Patrick from her position in the back. "Oh, you're one of the loyal ones, eh?" She swung her hips with each step and reached toward him.

Warnings flared off in Patrick's system making the hairs on the back of his neck stand on end and his shoulders press down and back in anticipation of a fight.

She was only a foot away from touching his chest when she asked, "What'd the king offer you, eh? A place at his side?"

Seeing a way through his disgust, Patrick allowed a half smirk to raise one side of his mouth. He huffed a laughed and was about to respond when Alistair interrupted.

*"You aren't cut out for this game she's playing."*

*"I've got this."*

*"No, you don't. You're too loyal to your friends and Violet. They'll see it in an instant. Let me get us out of this alive."*

Patrick hesitated and took a good look at the three wolven around him. Even the female, who was attempting to distract him, was tense as she approached him. While she'd been calling his attention, the two males had moved almost to Patrick's sides. How had he missed that?

None of them trusted him. Which was smart, but it also made him wonder if any of the Blood Moon members fully trusted another. These three at least had reason not to trust Patrick. They didn't know him. He came out of nowhere. He'd just snarled at one of them, and insinuated that they were trying to make him fail his orders.

*"There are only three of them."* Patrick reminded Alistair. *"I can handle this."*

*"And while you're* handling *it, they will be signaling all the other Blood Moon members."*

They couldn't afford to draw more attention to this area. Getting as many people out as possible was the goal, not taking on all of Blood Moon single handedly. Imagining himself taking a step back, Patrick offered the lead to Alistair who snatched the position from him as fast as he could. Patrick's body moved, and surprise rolled through the female's face when Alistair leaned toward her. He kept the smirk Patrick had raised, but added a sinister edge.

Alistair lowered his voice, but Patrick knew the males would still be able to hear. "Maybe he offered you to me."

Disgust rolled in Patrick's stomach, but when the female snarled and stepped out of range, he had to admit that it'd worked.

The two males were clearly displeased by her treatment because they bared their teeth in a barbaric fashion as she moved to stand closer to them.

*"Patrick, where are you?"* Jax's voice was muddy through the clan-link. He tried to clear his mind to hear his friend better, but he wasn't the one in control right now.

While his darker half continued to converse with the Blood Moon members, Patrick tried to tune him out and answer Jax. *"I'm almost to one of the escape tunnels. I ran into some trouble."*

*"Need help?"*

*"No."* Patrick snapped and the link between him and Jax nearly severed. In a gentler tone, he added, *"Stay away. I let Alistair out in order to be more convincing. He's handling three of them right now."*

Jax didn't respond right away, and Patrick imagined his friend cursing his stupid decision. *"You're playing a dangerous game."*

Patrick sighed internally. *"I know."*

*"Hey! Would you quit with the chitchat?"* Alistair growled at him. *"It's distracting."*

"What did you say your name was again?" asked the female who was back to being sweet. Her mood swings could give a person whiplash. She swung around a nearby tree and smiled at him flirtatiously.

"Fenrir," Alistair answered without missing a beat, which surprised Patrick. His body shifted to one side and his arms folded. "You?"

The male with the crooked smile snickered. "Your parents must have a sense of humor."

A deep undertone growl filtered through Alistair's voice, issuing a warning even while he responded civilly. "Why's that?"

The male's smile disappeared. He looked everywhere he could that wasn't filled with Alistair's looming form—a sure sign that the warning had worked. The second sign was the slight tremble in each word. "Y-you kn-now, n-naming you after the s-son of L-Loki? The, uh, the mischief god?"

The dark chuckle that rolled out of Patrick's mouth sent chills down his metaphorical spine. It was a weird sensation because he didn't feel it down his actual spine. He wondered briefly if this was how Alistair experienced things.

"The giant wolf god." Alistair tilted his head to the side. "Perhaps they saw my future."

A snort sounded from the dark-haired male. He opened his mouth to speak, but the rustling of leaves in the distance and the hushed tones of a child admitting their fear to their mother drowned him out.

Patrick's pulse quickened.

The three Blood Moon members didn't seem to notice yet. Which meant they had a small window of opportunity.

Confusion passed over him. His heart rate gaining speed made sense if he was in charge, but he wasn't.

*"Alistair?"*

His wolf counterpart remained silent.

*"Alistair. What are you doing?"*

*"Shut up,"* Alistair snapped as the dark haired male's gaze flickered in the direction of the incoming family.

"You know," he said, making brief eye contact with the other two. "I don't think the four of us would play nicely together."

Casting a wicked smile Alistair's direction, the female nodded emphatically. "For sure, you should run along now."

"I told you already." Alistair softly snarled. The brilliance in the forest around them grew nearly to the light of day.

Patrick's terror was reflected in the widened eyes of the wolven before him. Their breathing quickened and became sporadic. He imagined his eyes resembled rubies with the sun passing through—a measurable degree brighter than the trio's red eyes.

"I have my orders," Alistair growled and Patrick's jaw ached.

*"Alistair, no!"* Patrick reached for control, but his darker half had learned a thing or two from being barricaded so long. A mental barrier separated Patrick from reaching Alistair, and he slammed his fists against it.

The trio hunkered down in response, baring their dull teeth briefly before Alistair launched his body toward the closest male. There was no hesitation, and with the power Alistair was using, there wasn't a moment for preparation either. He fell on the guy with the crooked smile like the angel of death, tearing his claws up the male's torso.

Gurgled screaming rent the air and crimson soaked through what was left of the guy's shirt. He staggered away as the dark-haired male attempted to rush Alistair from the side.

Pain seared across Patrick's brain with each attack he issued against the mental barrier.

*"We don't need to kill them!"* he screamed at Alistair who was dancing around the male, toying with him.

*"I disagree."* Alistair blocked a punch to the stomach then spread his claws and reached for the male's throat.

Like a hole being knocked through a wall, Patrick's fist broke through the barrier. He clenched his clawed hand at the last second and his knuckles collided with his opponent's throat.

The male choked. He covered his throat with his hand, struggling for air.

Patrick winced. If the guy was a quick healer, he would probably be okay, otherwise he'd condemned a man to suffocate to death.

Paralyzing pain tore through his side. His brows pulled together as he looked down to find a hilt, mostly hidden beneath the male's meaty hand, buried to the guard in his abdomen.

*"Guess I missed that one."* Alistair growled from the depths of Patrick's mind.

Dark satisfaction spread across his opponent's face, even as he struggled to breathe. Then he ripped the dagger free. Its serrated tip shredded more skin and muscle.

Patrick roared in pain and stepped away clutching his side. It didn't stop the bleeding. Red seeped through his shirt from beneath his hand and ran down his side.

Alistair sat cooly in the back of his mind. *"I told you I could get us out of this, but you don't want to do things my way."*

*"So, you let us get stabbed?"* disbelief coated Patrick's thoughts. *"Out of spite?"*

*"Wolven heal too quickly."* Alistair reminded him, making Patrick feel

like he was in a lecture instead of bleeding to death in an unfamiliar forest. *"Removing them from the equation is the only way to ensure that family's safety and the others to follow. Now you're dragging the fight on and they'd be stupid if they haven't signaled others already."*

Hatred seethed through Patrick's body. He knew his darker half was right.

The dagger wielding male sucked in a deep breath, smirked, then started toward Patrick for another strike.

Patrick blocked the attack.

Barely.

A sharp impact hit the back of his knee and his leg buckled.

High pitched laughter rang in his ears as his knee drove into the damp earth.

He'd forgotten about the female.

Shifting his body, Patrick moved so he could see both of his attackers. The other male, the one with the crooked smile that Alistair had nearly disemboweled, lay unmoving a few feet away.

The world tipped sideways and Patrick planted his forearm against his bent knee.

Panic struck a chord, making his hands shake as three more blurry pairs of blood-red eyes appeared in the forest. His fingertips tingled. His limbs were heavy. *"Alistair..."*

*"Oh, I know, Boy Scout."* Alistair pressed against their mind-link, not to take control, but the close proximity to Patrick's own thoughts felt like ants crawling across his brain. *"We've been poisoned."*

*"You're not going to let us die."* Patrick caught the male's foot when he attempted a kick to Patrick's chest.

A dark laugh rolled through his mind. *"Are you sure about that?"*

Patrick gave the male's foot a sharp twist and something snapped.

Agony tore from his mouth even before he hit the ground. Patrick could probably take these two out and manage to make it to Jax who'd been carrying around an antidote to the wolfsbane poison since they lost Aiden... but his odds grew a lot slimmer if he wanted to help the family.

Swinging a fist toward the female who kept glancing at the male with the now broken leg, Patrick groaned when she sidestepped him.

"You won't be able to hold out much longer," she withdrew a dagger from her boot. "Frankie's blade had a concentrated dose." Pointing the tip of her knife toward him, she sneered. "We weren't sure if it would change anything. Looks like good news for us."

Risking a glance at his side, Patrick tucked his fingers into his already torn shirt and ripped the material further. Black lines were already spreading from his stab wound toward his heart.

*"Alistair!"* Patrick snarled, but his darker half remained complacent. He rushed the female whose eyes rounded before she turned to bolt.

She didn't make it very far before Patrick, attempting to tackle her, collapsed against her back instead. She screamed. They hit the ground with a thud and Patrick's shoulder digging into her kidney.

His chest fell in short, rapid succession while he pushed off her to sit on his heels. She didn't move. He'd probably knocked the wind out of her.

Staring at the hazy ground, Patrick blinked. Blood seeped into the forest floor. Wondering briefly if he was bleeding that much, he looked at his wound. He was bleeding, but not enough to cause a puddle like that.

When the female still didn't move, Patrick crawled to her side. He winced when the movement pulled at his wound, then lightly shoved her shoulder. It was enough to make her hair shift, which exposed the tip of her dagger. Patrick quickly turned away, not needing to look closer to see where it had gone through. She wouldn't be getting up.

Alistair paced back and forth in his mind. *"How embarrassing. Death by accidentally falling on your own weapon."*

Patrick groaned and wished he could punch Alistair in the face... which only made his wolf half laugh.

The dark haired male snarled at him from his weakened position on the forest floor. "Who are you?"

Patrick breathed heavily, not bothering to answer, and managed to get his feet under him. Three non-defined figures appeared as his legs began to tremble. One gestured to him. Warbled orders were given.

Alistair was waiting.

*"Do what you must."* Despair spread through Patrick and he stepped into

the recesses of his mind. "P*romise me you'll save that family.*"

*"You're letting me free?"* Alistair asked suspiciously, filling the main consciousness of their body.

*"Yes, but my favor to you will be finished."*

The image of a deranged, toothy grin filled his mind. *"We'll talk about the details later, Boy Scout. I suggest you sleep now. You won't want to witness this."*

Patrick imagined himself turning away from Alistair, and it was like closing his eyes. Exhaustion and pain dragged him into the depths of sleep as a deeper, more gravelly version of his voice said, "This is going to be fun."

# Chapter 16

## Violet

***Grumbling to the moon goddess*** *about how big of a jerk Alpha Draven was* didn't ease as much of Violet's frustrations as she wished it would. The moon simply stared back at her, unphased by her wild emotions. The steady burn of the moon's brightness started to make Violet's tantrum feel childish.

When Jax had finally come home last night, his face was solemn, but he'd barely said a word to her. He wrapped her in a hug, said he was glad Patrick and her had worked things out, then went to bed. By the time she was up the next morning, he and Patrick were gone. Patrick hadn't woken her up for training, so she overslept. Evalyn had filled her in on their whereabouts—future alpha and beta duties in Whiskey and Stanislaus Clans.

Violet spent the day helping her mom with the day-to-day duties of the luna, helped organize a few things for the ruined clan house and talked about plans for a new one, and even shared a hot chocolate with Evalyn in the comfort of her room, curled up on her bed.

That is... until Alpha Draven interrupted.

Her father hadn't asked if she wanted more responsibility around the clan or if she had any other plans after graduating high school, but because she was the daughter of the alpha it was expected for her to take on more tasks to aid the clan. Fine. He could be a little nicer about it, though. Actually, he could be a lot nicer.

Yelling her name from the main floor and being mad at her for not sprinting down the stairs to answer his call was not okay. Being angry when she didn't answer immediately after he gave her surprising orders was also not okay. The fact that he was talking to her at all was surprising after the way they had left things weeks ago, but it was business related.

Nothing more.

Sorrow or worry or both darkened her mom's eyes while she watched their heated exchange, but there was nothing she could do, so she said nothing when Violet walked out of the house. It wasn't Evalyn's fault that Alpha Draven hated his own daughter.

The flashlight on Violet's phone exposed a rock in the dirt path, and she kicked at it as she trudged toward Lockup. With how happily the moon mocked her, she didn't necessarily need the extra light, but it was comforting to have.

Alpha Draven wouldn't have even sent Violet if either Patrick or Jax were around, but they were both off talking about the future with Stanislaus' current and future alpha. The future was looking bright between their two clans. Hope had been bleak in the midst of everything Blood Moon related. Having something to look forward to was a nice change.

On a happier note, though, she was about to see Mya and actually have time to talk. Solstice had been so crazy that she hadn't been allowed to visit since. It was easy to burst in there when she was worried about Mya, but checking in and relaying the message Alpha Draven ordered her to deliver was much more difficult.

Clearing her throat, Violet tried to think how to start things with Mya.

"Uh, hey, Mya. Long time no see." Violet slapped her forehead and ran her hand down her cheek. That was definitely as lame as it sounded. "Mya, hey! It's your friend who has been completely absent since you lost your mate." She flinched.

"Maybe don't lead with the most tragic thing she will ever face in her lifetime."

Startled, Violet jumped away from the soured lemon-scented male that had intruded on her private moment. Her foot slipped on the edge of the path, nearly sending her tumbling off the gentle cliff, but she was able to right herself through windmilling her arms, slightly bending her knees, and planting her feet.

Zander watched her with rounded blue eyes, arms partially extended, unsure how to help.

"Zander!" she hissed at him and stomped a foot, flashing her phone's light directly at his face.

He flinched away from the harsh light and mumbled, "Sorry." His arms fell uselessly to his sides. "How else was I supposed to announce myself though? You were so focused I'm pretty sure a mouse squeak would have scared you."

Violet stepped away from the edge of the path and folded her arms across her chest, which dropped the light to his torso. "What are you doing sneaking around in dark clothing in the middle of the night anyway? And on the path to Lockup?"

"I wasn't sneaking!" He scoffed and Violet almost believed his act of offense. "And I've been wearing this shirt all day. It just so happens to be dark gray."

Violet bunched her lips to the side and decided letting that argument go was for the best. He probably had been wearing the gray shirt and black jeans all day. For as long as she'd known him, he seemed to have an aversion to color.

"I saw you heading up the road and thought if I caught up we could chat, but then you started talking to yourself and well..." he grimaced. "That didn't seem to be going so well."

"Gee, thanks."

A boyish smile zipped across his face. "That's what friends are for, right?"

Guilt stabbed at her and she dropped her gaze to the stretch of dirt between their feet. "Zander, you're not supposed to be talking to me. And if Jax and Patrick knew you were seeking me out to chat, they would be livid."

"They aren't here, and besides they have no authority to come between—"

"Don't say it!" Violet snapped. Heat pulsed through her body, but when his jaw clamped shut, it disappeared. Shaking her head, Violet shifted her weight to one side. "Why can't you just drop it?"

Silver flared over blue. "You can't expect me to let you go at the drop of the hat. You are my mate."

Violet groaned. "If that were really true, you would have let me discover it on my own."

"Why wait? I knew we were perfect for each other even before my trial." He stepped toward her, and she backed away, keeping a few arms lengths between them. He clenched his jaw. "Violet..."

"How do you always seem to know when Jax and Patrick aren't around?" She interrupted and her brows pulled toward each other.

Zander shrugged. "How do you always know?"

"I'm Jax's twin." The light from her phone made a wide arc across the ground when she held her hands out to the sides in a gesture that said the answer was obvious. "Of course I would know."

A huff of humorless laughter left him. "I know for a fact there are things he doesn't tell you."

Violet paused with her mouth hanging slightly open. It was tempting to ask what those things were, but that was exactly what he wanted. Instead, she shook her head and brought the light back to his torso. "Answer my question, Zander."

Sighing, he shook his head. "I'm actually disappointed you think I wouldn't know. It's the only time I can talk to you. Of course I would make it my business to know when they aren't around."

"Not being able to talk to me when they are should be a hint. And, there have been plenty of times when they aren't around that you don't find me."

The corners of his mouth tilted up into a cocky smirk. "Miss me?"

"Zander."

He threw his head back and took a couple of agitated steps in a tight formation. "Come on, Violet, give me more credit than that." Staggering a step toward her, he gestured to himself. "Of course I'm not going to seek you out every time those goons are gone. If I did that, they would never leave." He swung his arm out and a large breath deflated his chest. When his gaze settled on her again, he clicked his tongue. Silver still dominated his eyes and they burned brighter as they roved over her body like she was a dessert he'd been waiting his entire life for. "And then I would never get these precious moments to cherish."

Unease wound knots in Violet's stomach. She pulled the sides of her red full-zip hoodie until they overlapped each other and rolled her shoulders forward. "Knock it off."

Slowly, the silver faded and his features softened. "You know I'd never do anything to hurt you, right?"

With that look and the gentle tone he was using, she would have believed him in a heartbeat if his past actions didn't speak louder than his words.

"I did." Violet shrugged a shoulder and swallowed the knot in her throat. "Now, I'm not so sure."

Silver pulsed in Zander's eyes, gone as fast as it arrived. "Your distrust hurts."

Violet's shoulders sagged. "Sorry." And, she was. Hurting Zander was never what she wanted. She missed the old Zander, but he'd been gone a long time. She took a backward step toward Lockup. "I really shou—"

*"We're pulling into the base right now."* Jax's urgent message flitted through her mind, laced with panic she hadn't heard in her brother's voice in a long time. *"Patrick's hurt pretty bad."*

Violet turned in the direction of the base parking lot, leaving Zander at her side with a confused look on his face. *"What? Why didn't you tell me sooner?"* She almost started running when another thought came to mind. *"Do I need to get Doc?"*

*"She already knows. Meet us there."*

"Violet?"

Zander's voice faded behind her as she sprinted toward the parking lot, her phone's flashlight moving in rhythm with her arms. It was a good thing she didn't need the light to know where she was going because it wasn't helping at all.

Headlights illuminated the dark when Violet made her way around the seven-foot hedges that stretched around the clan parking lot. She fluttered her eyes against the brightness burning them. And then, they faded, hovering at a dull yellow just a moment before blinking out.

Doc stepped up to the passenger door, syringe in hand, with two nurses flanking her. A stretcher rested on the ground behind them and Violet's breath caught in her lungs.

"How is he?" Doc's raspy voice asked when Jax jogged around the hood of Patrick's truck.

Shaking his head, Jax opened the passenger door. "I have no idea. He's been unconscious the whole way home."

"There's so much blood." One of the nurses whispered.

"Most of it isn't his." Jax informed them, stepping out of their way.

Doc reached into the truck. "You gave him your dose, correct?"

Jax nodded. "Yes."

"How deep was the wound?"

"The blade was about six inches. I don't know how far it went in."

"Let's assume it was all the way," she announced, and the uncapping of the syringe echoed in the quiet of the night.

Violet stepped forward on trembling legs, drawing Jax's attention.

"Violet." He headed toward her, allowing Doc to do her thing. His amethyst eyes, a mirror of her own, were wide with concern as he threw his arms around her shoulders. "He's alive," he whispered. "And he's home."

Burying her face against her twin's shoulder, she muttered. "So are you."

They squeezed each other tightly.

"I'm assuming his wound is still bleeding because the poison remains in his system." Doc called to them and they released each other to turn toward her. "We'll get him to the clinic and I'll be able to examine him better there."

Jax led her toward the small group gathered around the truck. "No. I told you we are taking him to Lockup."

"Jax—"

"As an order from your future alpha, you will take him to Lockup and examine him there."

Doc glanced at her nurses, then dipped her chin as she looked back at Jax. A silent conversation passed between them. Understanding rounded the doc's eyes a few moments later, and the firm set of her jaw relaxed. "You heard him. Let's get Patrick to Lockup. I need to check in on Mya, anyway."

The three of them moved to the passenger door, while the nurses retrieved the stretcher off the ground. Together, they managed to get Patrick's mountainous form out of the truck and one of the nurses swore when his dead weight hit the stretcher.

There wasn't a moment lost. The nurses started toward Lockup the second his body was settled and Jax fixed Patrick's legs while they walked. Doc took care of one arm and Violet started to do the same, but froze at the sight of claws protruding from Patrick's fingers. She brushed her thumb along the length of a long, curved, bone-like weapon of destruction marred with dried blood. What had made him be able to draw those? She thought only Lycan had the ability to partially shift their form. Then again, Tucker shouldn't have been able to shift, and yet they now had a fully compatible and connected seventeen year old wolven.

"Violet."

Doc's voice pulled her back to the present and she muttered an apology when she saw the doc waiting to drape a trauma blanket over Patrick. Violet carefully rested Patrick's arm over his stomach, then tripped over a rock in the road.

"Watch it," barked the lead nurse when Violet caught herself on the stretcher.

She mumbled an apology, which made the guy shake his head.

"Move," Jax ordered, then hastily added, "please."

She stepped to the side while Jax moved Patrick's arm and began strapping his wrist to the stretcher.

"What are you doing?" Violet asked, grabbing her brother's arm.

"It's just a precaution," Doc told her, letting Jax concentrate while he tied his friend down during their trek. "We don't know what state he will wake up in after what he's been through."

Jax helped lay the blanket over Patrick, tucking it under his sides, before letting out a sigh of relief. Risking his anger, Violet brushed her fingers against his. To her surprise, his hand wrapped around hers and gave a little squeeze as the group moved together.

"He's gonna be okay," he told her, but Violet wondered if he was telling himself that, too.

"Are you?" Violet asked, giving his hand a return squeeze.

His face was streaked with blood. The sweet, metallic scent covered both him and Patrick, nearly drowning out their scents. His jaw pulsed twice before his presence settled into her mind.

*"Things went from bad to worse tonight. I'm…"* Jax's hand tightened around hers.

For a second, she thought he was about to admit he was scared. And, maybe he was, but that wasn't like her brother, so she made it a little easier on him. *"It's okay to be scared, Jax."*

*"Good, because I am. I have no idea what the future holds, but I know without Patrick, we won't stand a chance."*

# Chapter 17

## Violet

***Violet tilted her head to the side*** *and gazed at her brother* through narrowed eyes. *"I thought you said he was going to be okay."*

*"He is."* He shook his head. *"That's not what I was talking about."* A heavy sigh left her brother, and he released her hand without any further explanation.

Lockup came into view, and the warriors on duty stepped toward them. The three in wolf form sunk their heads, pinned their ears back, and bared their teeth while the three in human form greeted Jax.

A familiar male voice rose above the wolves snarling. "Do you need anyone to stand guard outside his room?" The warrior in the middle took a few steps beyond where the others had stopped, and Tucker's blond hair captured the moonlight.

Jax shook his head. "No, thank you." He looked over the other five warriors and nodded. "Looks like you're settling right into your father's shoes."

Tucker bristled, his shoulders going rigid.

As they walked past, Jax patted one of the new lockup master's shoulders. "He would be proud."

Lowering his chin, Tucker stared at the ground. His father's body had been found amongst those killed during solstice, but the young man hadn't wasted a day. Taking his father's place as lockup master had always been the plan, and they'd been training for that time. No one expected it to be so soon, though.

No one expected Tucker to turn months before his birthday, either. Apparently, he was the only seventeen-year-old to do so in at least two hundred years. Doc was perplexed as well, but guessed it was the stress of the moment and the prospect of being killed that pulled Tucker's wolf out of the time constraint.

Once Jax had moved past, Tucker lifted his gaze to scrutinize everyone in the party. Including Violet, who offered him a sad smile, but no emotion crossed his blue eyes. She knew Tucker and his father had their disagreements, but they had been close. She remembered the salty scent of his tears when he'd told her he couldn't reach his dad.

Violet couldn't stop herself from staring at the place she'd seen the warrior with black veins covering his body propped up against the wall. They'd cleaned all the blood away. The dirt had been swept. But she remembered where each and every body had lain. Blood Moon and Sentinel alike.

Cells had been repaired, and a few were filled once again. Killing was always a last resort. Even after the last attack, it was still protocol to knock them out and lock them up.

A warrior patrolling the hall nodded to them as they passed, and Violet turned to watch as she walked the opposite direction of them. Lockup had never had warriors stationed *inside* the facility before. She wasn't the only one either. They passed five others on their way to the top floor; the level reserved for members of the clan who needed a little extra help and attention.

Maybe they should've thrown Zander in there.

Violet snorted at the thought and Jax shot her a curious glance.

They stepped into the hall that contained Mya's cell, and Violet waved her brother away. Now was not the time to bring up Zander's more than a little creepy stalker vibe.

Mya jumped up from her bed, making her chestnut coils bounce, and hurried to the plexiglass wall that separated them. "Is he okay?"

Placing her hand over the one Mya had pressed against the transparent wall, Violet shook her head and shrugged. "I don't know. I'm not sure we will until he wakes up."

Green eye's rounded with concern and Mya's chest rose and fell heavily with each breath. She wet her lips and nodded. "Okay. Where will he be?"

"Right next to you," Jax answered, punching in a code to the shared keypad between Mya's and Patrick's cells. "I hope you don't mind having a roommate for a bit."

Shaking her head, Mya left Violet and walked along the wall until she was as close to Jax as she could be. "Was he poisoned?"

Jax's gaze snapped to hers, and his lips parted. His purple eyes darted to Violet, and then back to Mya. "Yes."

Mya's shoulders caved in and she shrank away.

"He's going to be alright, Mya," Jax insisted and pressed his hand to the plexiglass. "I was carrying an antidote on me, and Doc gave him more when we arrived. He'll be okay."

"Jax, let me in there." Violet moved so she was in position to step through the doorway. Her friend needed a hug and someone to lean on.

"No," Doc's raspy voice called to them as she made her way from Patrick's cell to Mya's. "Just open the door. Mya isn't going anywhere, and I think being able to move around out of her cell would be good for her."

"Doc?" Jax's brows pinched together, uncertain of the order he'd just been given.

"You heard me correctly." Doc turned to smile at Violet. "I believe Violet was on her way here earlier to deliver some news."

Surprise widened Violet's eyes. "You want me to do that now?"

The plexiglass door to Mya's cell slid open.

Doc eyed Mya who had sat down on the edge of her bed. "Maybe not this second. Give her time to process what she's just heard." Then, a little louder, she added, "I'll be here for a while, Mya, if you want to come visit Patrick and say hi to everyone."

With that, the older woman shooed Violet and Jax into Patrick's cell where the nurses had moved the restraints from the stretcher to the bed.

"Have you never seen claws before?" Doc snorted, joining the nurses at Patrick's side.

One of them stood up a little straighter and purposefully did *not* look at the claws protruding from Patrick's fingers. With a sigh, the doc sent that nurse to retrieve a few personal items for Patrick, like fresh clothing and sheets, now that blood and dirt marred the bed he was laying on. The other nurse was sent to the clinic to retrieve all the supplies they needed.

"Violet and I will start cleaning what we can."

"We will?" Violet asked, her voice came out a little squeaky and the doc smirked at her. "I don't know anything about this stuff."

One of Doc's brows lifted as she pulled a pair of medical scissors from her pocket and began cutting away Patrick's shirt. "He told me that you helped clean him up after Blood Moon's first attack on the clan. When Jax's arm had been broken."

Jax groaned from his corner of the room, clearly not happy about the reminder.

Swallowing the lump in her throat, Violet took a step toward the doc. "Well, yeah, I did, but..." Her words failed when Dr. Penmann peeled Patrick's shirt away from his stab wound. A hushed tone filtered her words while she made her way to Patrick's side. "That was minor compared to this."

With a shake of her head, the doc told Violet to grab the small body cloth by the sink.

Violet did as she was told and wet the square of material before finding herself back at Patrick's bedside, gently removing the blood and dirt from his skin. The nurses returned with the items they'd been sent to retrieve, but were quickly dismissed yet again, after being told to take care of the clinic.

Once they were gone, Violet leaned closer to the doctor to whisper, "Why'd you send them away?"

"Because Alistair was in charge when I found Patrick," Jax answered instead of the doc as he leaned against the far wall. "That blasted wolf was still in control when he passed out."

Violet stared at her brother wide-eyed. "Did Patrick let him out? Or did he lose control?"

"Boy Scout let me out to play." A deeper, slightly gravelly voice jerked

Violet's attention to Patrick's face. His eyes fluttered open, and rubies stared at her. Alistair looked exhausted. "Hello, gorgeous."

Panic shook Violet's hands as she glanced at the Doc, but the older woman's narrowed silver gaze was intensely focused on Patrick's stab wound. Violet leaned down until she was inches from Patrick's face. "I told you not to call me that."

One corner of his mouth quirked up, then slowly fell again as if holding a smirk took too much energy. "Still not a fan of me, I see."

"You're putting him in danger," Violet whispered, afraid his crimson eye would give him away.

Alistair's red eyes narrowed. "I saved our life."

Worried, Violet tempted a look at the doc again.

"I'm a doctor, Violet." The older woman lifted her gaze and smiled at them both. "Do you really think I didn't know about my patient's unique circumstances? Why do you think I sent the nurses away?"

An airy chuckle, followed by a groan of pain left Alistair. "I like her."

"I suggest trying not to laugh, Alistair." Dr. Penmann ordered, then pointed the clamp in her hands at her patient. "And no sudden movements."

"No promises, doc." Alistair's eyes drifted shut.

Violet nibbled on her lip. Hesitantly, she reached out with a trembling hand and brushed Patrick's curls away from his face. His head turned into her hand and he drew in a deep breath, which made him wince.

"She told you no sudden movements."

"Breathing is not a sudden movement," Alistair argued, watching her through half-lidded eyes. "You smell good."

*"Be careful, Violet."* Jax's warning shot loudly through her mind, making her flinch. *"You can't trust him."*

Alistair growled. "Get out of her head, *future alpha*." He slowly raised his head to glare at Jax. "She's in no danger from me."

Contempt twisted Jax's features. He pushed off the wall, uncrossed his arms, and moved to adequately glare back at the male bound to the bed. "I don't trust you."

"The feeling's mutual," Alistair grumbled.

"Jax, back off," Violet warned, but tried to throw in a bit of an order as well. Her twin passed his glare to her. "I've got this."

A frustrated sigh left Jax, and he stormed back to his position against the wall.

Violet looked back at Alistair, who watched her with open curiosity. His features pinched suddenly and he narrowed his gaze at the doctor. "That hurt."

"At least you can still feel," Doc mumbled, continuing her stitches.

When his attention didn't immediately return to her, Violet gently said his name.

"Yeah, gorgeous?"

Her chest deflated with a breath, but she wasn't sure if she was annoyed or amused that he continued to call her that. "Is he okay?"

Alistair held her gaze for a long time before answering. "I kept us alive."

"That's not what I asked."

His gaze drifted shut.

"Alistair?"

A sigh sank his well-defined chest. "He's not going to be happy when he wakes up, but he will be fine."

"And you?" Violet bit her lip, unsure how her question would be answered.

Alistair's eyes slowly opened to stare at her. The red was dying out, looking dull and brownish.

She nibbled her lip nervously, then figuring he wasn't going to answer, leaned forward to wipe away more blood and dirt from the side of his neck. His face turned toward her hand again, and his lips brushed the inside of her wrist, sending a bolt of... something... up her arm and through her body. Whether it was pleasure, disgust, or just shock—she wasn't sure. She'd never admit it to anyone, but disgust was low on her list. If it was there at all.

Alistair was a creep and was always looking out for himself, but he was part of Patrick and that alone made Violet care for him.

"Tonight's taken a lot out of me, gorgeous. It's been too long since Patrick let me out."

Shocked that Alistair had used Patrick's real name, and the fact that he was being pleasingly conversational spurred her into saying, "He might do it more if he could trust you."

"He can trust me with you."

Violet drew in a sudden breath. Her gaze snapped to Doc, who had a slight smirk playing at her lips while she tied off another stitch, then to Jax, who looked like his ears might be on the verge of steaming.

Ignoring the hate pouring off her brother, Violet slowly brushed her fingers down the length of Patrick's arm and carefully wrapped them around his clawed hand. She swallowed the knot of nerves that built in her throat at the sight of the claws hovering above her skin. The last time she'd seen them, a piece of one had been left behind in her back.

As if sensing her thoughts, the claws shrank back, returning to normal human nails with an abundance of blood and dirt caked beneath them. Then, ever so gently, his hand curled around hers, nearly swallowing it whole.

"What do you think you're doing?" Jax hissed.

She turned to see Alistair's eyes had closed, and his chest had fallen into a deep, steady breathing rhythm. He was still holding her hand. Gently, but at the same time, she might have to pry her fingers out of his grasp to get away.

Returning her attention to her brother, she hissed back, "I'm being friendly. That's more than I can say about you."

"He can't be trusted, Violet."

"Alistair doesn't want to hurt me."

"No, he just wants to make you like him."

Violet stared at Jax with her jaw hanging open. "What is wrong with you?"

"He can't be trusted!" His whisper grew into a hushed yell as he thrust his hand in Alistair's direction. "He has killed people, Violet!"

Clamping her teeth together, Violet rolled her shoulders back. With a calm surety she didn't know she possessed, Violet said, "So has Patrick."

The anger drained from Jax's face, and his arm fell to his side. "That's different. He didn't mean to and took no pleasure in it."

"Alistair is part of Patrick." Violet shook her head. "You can't have one without the other."

"Patrick will take back control. You'll see. He's getting stronger every day while Alistair grows weaker."

Dr. Penmann cleared her throat. "If I might interrupt. Something you may not have considered, Jax, is that Violet kept the beast calm while I worked." She finished off the last stitch, put her utensils down, and turned her gaze on the future alpha. "Perhaps even allowing him to relax enough to sit back into the shadows so Patrick could return."

"You don't know that. We've never seen another wolven be able to resist the call of the hunt." Jax scratched at one of the wounds on his arm that had already healed to an angry pink. "Once the wolf gets a taste for blood, they can't seem to turn it off."

Nodding, the older woman turned to clean her area. Throwing away swabs of red and brown cotton, stained by blood and iodine. "You're right. We haven't seen this before. Which means we have no idea how this works." Her gray eyes fell on Violet. "Another mystery to be solved."

A small smile played at the corners of Violet's lips. At least she wasn't the only freak in the clan.

"What are you smiling at?" Jax snapped.

Shaking her head, Violet returned her attention to Patrick's sleeping form. He was still covered in grime and after a few tries, she was finally able to slip her hand from his. Jax kept a tense watch over them, ready for the unconscious Patrick to leap from his bed at any second, while the doc and Violet finished cleaning Patrick. It wasn't until the doc suggested changing his clothes, that Violet backed away.

She walked backward, lightly clamping her hands together and pointing at Dr. Penmann. "Maybe it would be good for me to peek in on Mya." Thick, cold plexiglass abruptly stopped her, and she spun, laughing at herself until she could see where the door was. "I'll just uh..."

"Get out!" Jax snapped, shooing her with his hands. "I'll tell you when he's decent again."

"'Kay, thanks! Bye!" She slipped out the door and practically sprinted into the next cell where Mya watched her with an amused eyebrow planted high on her forehead.

"Afraid of seeing one of the most eligible guys in the clan without his shirt?"

The teasing glint in Mya's emerald green eyes made a smile curl Violet's lips. "The shirt is not the problem. I am more than happy to see Patrick without a shirt."

"I heard that!" Jax called from the other cell.

Violet was about to retort when Mya's lips bunched like she was trying to hold back the words that blurted from her mouth a moment later.

"If you don't like it, then don't eavesdrop!"

She stared at her friend with amazement while Mya huffed and grumbled to herself.

Suddenly remembering she wasn't alone, the coil-haired young woman blushed. "Sorry."

Laughter bubbled up inside Violet and she launched herself at her friend who jerked back with rounded eyes. Her arms wrapped around Mya's shoulders while she said, "I've missed you."

A soft laugh rolled out of Mya and she hesitantly encircled Violet's waist. "I've missed you, too."

Mya was the first to pull away, placing her hands neatly in her lap, while Violet removed herself. She sat at polite distance, unsure how healed her friend actually was. And she'd already bombarded Mya's space without thinking. She didn't want to overwhelm her.

"So," Mya began, and her hands found their way into her coils, twisting one around her fingers. "What's kept you away?"

Guilt crushed Violet with the force of a tsunami. She sank into the spot she'd claimed on Mya's bed, then stared at the purple ruffled comforter. "I tried to come see you that night, but they wouldn't let me."

"Good."

The surety of her friend's answer snagged Violet's attention away from the pretty blanket. "What?"

"I'm glad they didn't let you come that night. I probably wouldn't have remembered it anyway, but I definitely would have tried to hurt you." Mya's features pinched into a frown. She scrunched her freckled nose, then shook her head. "No, it's better you stayed away. I wasn't right."

Violet smiled sadly. "I know, but that's why I wanted to be here. I wanted to help you."

"Maybe." Mya caught Violet's gaze and shrugged. "Or I could have tried to rip your throat out."

"If it's a fifty-fifty chance, I'd take that bet."

Mya chuckled and shook her head again.

"So, I was on my way here earlier, before everything with Patrick happened."

"Who'd he kill?"

"What?" Violet blinked at Mya, taken aback by the sudden question.

Mya watched her expectantly, but when Violet didn't answer she rolled her eyes. "I've known for a while that Patrick's wolf has red eyes, Violet. Remember when Jax elbowed you and gave you a concussion? I saw him trying to hide them."

"Why didn't you ask before now?"

Shrugging, Mya stood to tuck one of her feet under her, then sat back down. "It wasn't important, and I'd known him for a while already. It freaked me out at first, but then he kept acting like Patrick, so I figured you and Jax and probably Alpha and Luna already knew."

Violet's shoulders dropped. "I didn't know until his trial."

Mya's green eyes rounded. "Seriously? Oh, I've known longer than you, then."

"That's not helpful."

Mya laughed which made her nose scrunch and Violet smiled at the sight of her old friend coming back to life. "So, are you going to tell me?"

Shaking her head, Violet leaned back on one hand. Mya's lower lip stuck out in an adorable mock pout and Violet chuckled. "It's not my story to tell."

"Fine. I can admire that." Mya fiddled with one of her chestnut coils and then gestured to Violet. "So, what were you coming to see me for?"

Drawing in a deep breath, Violet sat up a little straighter. "Alpha Draven would like to offer you an official position and job."

Mya's hand froze in her hair. "No."

"You haven't even heard what it is."

"It doesn't matter, Violet." Her hands dropped to her lap and her fingers clenched. "I'm not ready."

"Mya—"

"I said no, Violet!"

Violet jerked back when her friend's eyes blazed silver. The old Mya had incredible control over her emotions. She could count the number of times she'd seen Mya's wolf eyes on one hand.

Slowly, Mya's eyes faded to green. Chest heaving with heavy breaths, she stood and moved across the room. "I'm sorry. I think you should leave. I don't want to hurt you."

Nodding, Violet made her way toward the door. "You can come see Patrick if you want. He's unconscious, but I'm sure he'd appreciate knowing you came to see him."

There was no response. Not in word or action. Mya had retreated to a shell of herself once more, avoiding Violet's gaze while she leaned against the little desk. With a sigh, Violet stepped out of her friend's cell to return to Patrick's side.

# Chapter 18

## Violet

***A bitter, antiseptic scent wafted*** *through Violet's room.* She scrunched her nose against the assaulting smell and rubbed her face against her pillow. Clean, but slightly stiff sheets made her freeze.

This was not her bed.

Straining her senses, Violet told herself not to react until she had a better understanding of the situation. Her forehead was primarily resting on her right forearm, but warmth blanketed her hand. Deep breathing settled her nerves, along with a slight snore behind her somewhere.

She was still in Patrick's cell.

Slowly, Violet sat up and stared at the red mark left behind on her forearm from the weight of her head. How long had she been out? Her gaze snagged on the hand covering hers. Utterly human and clean. Not a speck of grime had been left behind under Patrick's fingernails or the crevices in his knuckles.

It was then that Violet's tired brain connected the dots that she was holding Patrick's hand. Or rather, he was holding hers since his hand was on top.

When Violet had returned to Patrick's room after Mya had shut down and Jax gave his approval, she'd pulled a chair to the bedside. Jax finally gave in to her questions and told her a little of what happened.

Alpha Klaus was dead. He'd insisted on staying behind so he wouldn't slow them down, and ultimately went down with the ship.

Talon was also dead. He'd given his life protecting a young family from a larger group of Blood Moon members.

Stanislaus Clan was leaderless.

Not that there was a clan for anyone to return to now that Blood Moon had overrun the territory. Any refugees would make their way here or to another clan.

Jax spared her the gory details and hedged over a few that involved Patrick and Alistair. Maybe he didn't know or maybe he didn't want to frighten her, but he wouldn't tell her anything when she pushed further.

She didn't remember resting her head or even closing her eyes, but she must have at some point.

Tilting her head side to side relieved some of the pressure that had built up in her neck and offered her a view of Jax's whereabouts; he was sleeping soundly on a cot, lightly snoring, a few feet behind her.

Violet startled when her cell phone buzzed and Patrick's fingers tightened around hers briefly. Warmth spread through her as she stared at their hands, but it faded just as quickly. She looked at Patrick's face, peaceful in the depth of sleep, and wondered whose eyes she would see when they opened. Would golden-flecked, hazel eyes gaze warmly at her or would cold, calculating blood red dominate his stare?

Not knowing if Alistair was still in control or not, Violet needed to pull away, but her hand fit perfectly inside his, and she could easily look at her phone with one hand.

One message blazed across the screen.

`Lexie - Where are you?`

Confusion pulled Violet's brows together and she was about to respond when another message came through.

`Lexie - We're supposed to go birthday dress shopping, remember?`

A groan like the roar of a dragon left her, and she winced as both boys' sleep patterns halted. It really hadn't been that loud, but their hearing was epically good and Lockup was ridiculously quiet in the mornings.

When their patterns returned to normal, Patrick with his deep, soothing breaths and Jax with his light snore, Violet typed a reply to Lexie.

`Violet - I'm on my way. Just stopping in to check on Mya. Be right there.`

She didn't have to wait long for a reply.

`Lexie - Tell her I said hi and that I miss her freckled face.`

Violet grinned, then pocketed her cell.

Now, for the tricky part.

Patrick hadn't woken up all night, but from the way he was looking now, he seemed a lot better which increased his chance of waking. The dark circles had receded from his eyes. Color had returned to his slightly tanned skin. And his lips were no longer ashen, but full and soft and...

Violet shook her head. She was not going there! Yes, she loved Patrick, but she was not about to ogle him like a creeper.

*"Get it together, Violet,"* she told herself and began to maneuver her fingers out of Patrick's grip.

The pace was agony. If she moved too fast, his hand would clench, and she'd have to wait until he relaxed again so she could move. If she continued slipping away for too long, his hand would clench. If she breathed too heavily because she was concentrating too hard, his hand would clench.

Eventually, her fingers wiggled free, and she restrained the cheer that rose in her throat.

Instead, she stood, avoiding putting any weight on the bed, and turned toward the door.

But her feet didn't move.

She looked back at Patrick's sleeping form.

Why did all the movies make it seem like kissing someone in their sleep was okay? No matter how tempting Patrick's lips were, she wouldn't violate his trust like that.

That didn't mean she couldn't kiss his forehead.

That was always seen as a sweet gesture. Right?

Violet pulled the length of her dark chocolate ponytail to one side. Then, after a deep breath, she bent at the waist hesitating a breath away from his forehead. Closing her eyes, Violet feathered a kiss against his freshly cleaned head.

*"Thank you for coming home to me."*

Those words would never be spoken out loud, but her heart echoed them a hundred times over in the space of time she lingered there.

Then she stood, took a last look at Jax to make sure he was alright, and determined that his arm dangling off the cot would be just fine before she quietly left the cell.

"Morning," Mya's whisper startled Violet.

She was expecting to find her still sleeping like Patrick and Jax, but Violet was happy for the chance to apologize and say goodbye.

"Sleep well?" Violet whispered back, peeking her head through the door that had been left open.

Mya shrugged, then righted her green pajama cami. "Sleep is difficult for me, but it was as good as it has been since..." her calm demeanor cracked and her lips pulled into a frown.

"I know." Violet offered, hoping Mya didn't feel the pressure to talk about what happened. "I'm glad you got some rest. I'm sorry for last night."

Chestnut coils bounced as Mya shook her head. "You don't have anything to apologize for. You did nothing wrong."

"I could have been a bit more tactful."

"When has tact ever been your strong suit?"

A grin tugged at Violet's mouth. "That's fair." She glanced toward the cell the boys were sleeping in, then took one step into Mya's room. "The job would be here, in Lockup. You'd be helping keep the place going and hopefully make it a bit more hospitable."

Mya toyed with one of her curls. "That doesn't sound that bad."

Not wanting to interrupt, Violet waited for her to think it through.

After a moment, Mya lifted one shoulder. "I don't have an answer for you right now."

"That's okay." Violet insisted. "You don't have to. I was only told to offer it to you. You think about it, and if you want more details, reach out to any of us. Does that work?"

Green eyes blinked back at her blankly and Violet wondered if her friend was still present... then she gave a small smile. "That sounds doable."

Violet nodded. "Good." Her phone buzzed and another message from Lexie telling her to hurry up lit the screen. "Lexie says hi and that she misses your freckled face."

A soft chuckle reached her ears and she looked up to find Mya grinning. "I miss her too."

"You know..." Violet bit her lip, but wanted to offer even if Mya said no. "We're going dress shopping for my birthday. You could join us... if you want."

Sorrow stretched across Mya's face. Her light, laughing demeanor faded and she shook her head. "Thanks, but... I'm not ready."

Nodding, Violet leaned her shoulder lightly against the thin plexiglass door frame. "I figured, but I wanted you to know you were invited."

That brought back a smile. Or at least a half one. For a second.

"Thanks." Mya pulled her purple blanket up to her shoulder and waved Violet away. "Go have fun."

"I'll come tell you all about it when I get back, okay?"

Mya nodded, and Violet quickly made her way out of Lockup to meet up with her only human friend.

Spring had officially arrived.

Most people were elated that the colder weather was beginning its end and flowers were blooming. It truly was a pretty time of year, but the assaulting smells of pollen were hard on many clan members' noses. Even someone like Violet whose senses were not nearly as developed.

She was grateful the smelliest part of spring typically arrived after her and Jax's birthday. Suffering from wolf-sized allergies on your special day was never fun to deal with. The threat of a sneeze tickled her nose, and she quickly brushed her finger back and forth across it to stop from sneezing. As she walked around the last bend of towering trees, the sun feathered a kiss over her light, golden tan skin. Raising her face to its glorious caress, she sighed. Pity she'd agreed to spend the day shopping with Lexie because it would have been a wonderful day for a long run.

The luxurious morning faded instantly when Alpha House entered her view. Half-dressed men and women were coming and going, quickly shifting into or out of wolf form in a chaotic dance of fur, clothing, and flurried movements. Alpha Draven's booming voice echoed from the house as he shouted directions to anyone within earshot.

Instead of making her way around to the front door, Violet decided to slip through the commotion of the back door, nearly getting thrown out by a man tearing his shirt over his head as he began to shift forms. She stared wide eyed as his gray wolf form emerged, shredding his borrowed sweatpants, and bolted away like his tail was on fire.

"Violet!"

Alpha Draven's thunderclap of a voice made her jump, then a meaty hand was on her shoulder, dragging her out of the doorway and through the kitchen. "Did you manage to meet with Mya while you were fooling around last night?"

Violet's brows slammed down as she glared at her father who jabbed a finger at a paper another clan member held out for him.

"There!" he snapped and the young woman scurry away.

"I wasn't fooling around." Violet defended while he half listened, signing another paper someone held out for him. "I was helping take care of Patrick and making sure Jax, *your son*, was okay."

Alpha Draven's weird ombre blue eyes turned on her, swirling molten gold. He thrust the pen against the chest of the man holding the paper, who then backed away without another word. "Do not speak to me like that."

She didn't know what had gotten into her, but Violet crossed her arms over her chest and squared off with the towering man before her. "Then don't assume I'm not pulling my weight around here. I have met every task and challenge you have thrown at me since my graduation." She wished her mouth would have just stayed shut, but it seemed to have a mind of its own as she said, "And maybe you should be asking how your son and his future beta are doing after being ambushed."

A man took two steps through the back door before Alpha Draven turned his whole attention on Violet, and the guy turned right around and hurried out the door. The alpha's jaw clenched, and his fingers curled. A threatening, dominating aura washed over her, but as always... it had no effect. She stuck out her jaw and stared defiantly at her father.

"Violet!" Her mom stepped between her and the alpha, quickly planted a kiss on the alpha's cheek, then seized Violet's arm to pull her away. "Lexie and I have been waiting for you. What took you so long?"

The alpha was still seething when another clan member stepped up to him, and he shouted at everyone to get out. Lexie flinched when he chased everyone out of the house and then slammed the door shut.

"Well..." Evalyn's lips pressed into a thin line before she offered a tight smile to both Violet and Lexie. "That's a lot quieter, at least." She wrapped Violet in a tight squeeze, then pulled back to cast a reproachful look upon her. "I really wish you wouldn't taunt him like that."

"And I wish he would see me as a daughter and not a clump of dirt under his shoe." Violet snorted. "Shoot, that may even be too good for me in his eyes."

Evalyn sighed her daughter's name and shook her head, but didn't offer any other response. That particular long-fought argument never went anywhere. Her mom would insist that Alpha Draven loved her, and Violet would insist that he didn't. Round and round they would go until one of them gave in.

Scratching her head, Violet nodded toward the back door. "Was that craziness the result of last night?"

Lexie's gaze snapped away from the computer she'd been working on. "What happened last night?" She spun the chair until she was facing Violet. "Is that why they almost wouldn't let me through the gate?"

Violet eyed her friend, model tall and thin, with high cheekbones and shockingly natural white-blond hair. Between the two of them, Lexie looked much more wolven than Violet ever had. "What did they do?"

Lexie shook her head and leaned back in the chair. "Nothing. They just said I couldn't enter. So, I told them to check with your mom, and they opened the gate a minute later." She tilted her head to the side and gazed at Evalyn. "Actually, they were a lot nicer than usual."

Pride practically poured from Violet's mom as she smiled at Lexie. "You earned a lot of respect with your help during the solstice."

Violet smirked and shrugged a shoulder. "I already knew you were amazing. They're just late to the game."

A sheepish grin lifted the corners of Lexie's mouth. "Thanks."

Violet looked at the computer her friend had been working on. "What are you doing?"

Evalyn beckoned Violet toward the computer while Lexie turned her chair again. Her mom pointed at a spreadsheet sprawling across the screen as Lexie scrolled through the document. "Lexie is quite the genius, and has been teaching me some tricks."

"And people say you can't teach an old dog new tricks." Lexie turned with a grin beaming across her face, but the stoic expression on Evalyn's face made her grin falter. "Uh, sorry."

"For calling me old or a dog?"

Violet bit her lips together and failed to hide a small laugh.

"Um... both?"

One of Evalyn's delicate eyebrows arched.

Lexie cleared her throat and straightened in her seat. "Both."

Shaking her head, Evayln's stern expression gave way to her own small smile. "I'm teasing. I know the old human saying." She tapped Lexie on the shoulder when the young woman turned back toward the computer. "It still wasn't nice."

Lexie nodded. "It won't happen again." She clicked on the mouse and a different page consumed the screen. "Anyway, it's just a few things I learned at school that should make her work go a lot faster." She saved the document and then turned the chair toward them again. "So, what happened last night?"

Evalyn's smile slipped and her shoulders drooped. "One of the neighboring clans has been overrun by the Blood Moon pack."

All of the color drained from Lexie's face.

"And," Violet continued the explanation. "By the old laws, the land now classifies them as a clan."

"No." Evalyn waved her hand as if it were out of the question. "That's an ancient law that shouldn't hold any weight with the kings and queens."

Leaning her hip against the desk, Violet snorted. "Like they care about us. When was the last time you saw one of them around here?"

"Violet!" Evalyn's sharp tone caught Violet by surprise and she snapped her mouth shut. "They do care, but they have laws they must follow, as well."

Annoyance zipped through Violet's limbs—a useless emotion because all she could do with it was complain. "None of this would have happened if they'd stepped in sooner."

"That's what the Paladins are for, and they are kept very busy." Evalyn raised both hands and let out a long breath. "This is not something either of you needs to worry about today. If it helps, I have been in contact with one of the queens, and hopefully some good will come from that. For now, you two are going to have a normal teenage day and go shopping for a beautiful dress."

Lexie nodded. "Oh yeah, preferably one that will make Patrick wake up and smell the violets."

"Lexie!" Violet stared at her friend with wide eyes while Evalyn chuckled. "He may not even be there. He hasn't woken up yet and has a lot of recovering to do."

A creased line appeared between Lexie's brows. "What's wrong with Patrick?"

Violet bit her lip. "Oh, um... Patrick and Jax were visiting Stanislaus last night on business when Blood Moon attacked."

Lexie swallowed hard, and her lips pressed into a thin line.

"They helped a lot of people get out, but Patrick was stabbed and poisoned in the process." Her friend's blue eyes widened and she opened her mouth to speak, but Violet continued, "They're both okay. Or, at least they will be. I'm sure Jax is all healed by now."

The white-blond girl took a second to draw in a deep breath and Violet could imagine the wheels spinning in her mind as she compartmentalized all the information she'd just received. When she finally met Violet and Evalyn's gazes again, she softly asked, "Are you sure it's safe to go?"

Nodding her head, Evalyn grabbed the water bottle sitting beside the computer. "I thought about that, too. Especially without a bodyguard. Both Patrick and Jax are down, and we can't afford to let any of our warriors leave right now. But, you're driving out to Merced, right?" When both the young women nodded, Evalyn continued. "Blood Moon tends to avoid human-populated areas. They are bloodthirsty, but they aren't stupid. They also prefer to attack in the evening or at night. You'll be home long before that, since you need time to get ready for the party tonight. Four-o-clock should give you plenty of time to drive there, shop, and drive home."

Violet scoffed. "Oh, yeah, I bet we'll be home way before that."

"You have a very specific color we're looking for," Lexie reminded her. "Don't jump to conclusions."

Evalyn held up a hand to interrupt. She turned to Violet and placed her hands gently on her shoulders. "Go. Have fun. Keep your guard up. If anything is suspicious, get out and keep Lexie safe. And don't..."

"...talk to strangers," Lexie smirked, earning a quick, amused grin from the mother-daughter duo. "I learned that one in kindergarten."

Tension built beneath her mother's hands as Evalyn stared at her. "Don't forget your phone. If anything happens, and I mean anything, tell Jax and call me. We'll be there as fast as we can."

"Got it." Violet nodded, suddenly feeling a little nervous. "We're just going to the mall. A *very* human mall."

Lexie stood and took her hand. "Are you sure you want to go?"

Staring at her, Violet couldn't believe how lucky she was to have a best friend like Lexie. She knew, without a doubt, Lexie would be okay to give up their plans if Violet wasn't up for it. With a small shrug, Violet said, "It'll only be a few hours. I'm not much use sitting beside Patrick waiting for him to wake up, and Jax has already been tended to. He just needs sleep. I'm sure he'll tell me when he and Patrick wake up." She looked at her mom. "And if there's anything you need help with when we get back, I'm happy to do that."

"No. You are not helping with any setup. It's your birthday celebration. I will lock you in your room with Lexie and a bowl of candy if I have to." Her mom grinned like the Cheshire cat, making both young women laugh.

"If candy was involved, I guess I could stay put." Violet tucked a loose hair behind her ear before walking toward the stairs.

"You should have said cookies," Lexie loudly whispered.

Violet rolled her eyes and went back for her friend, tugged on her arm, and moved her in the direction of the stairs.

"That's her kryptonite."

Evalyn smirked. "If it were cookies, I wouldn't be able to get her out of her room for the party." She waved the girls away and they jogged up the stairs to Violet's room.

On her way to the closet, Violet ran her hand along the back of her chair where Patrick's shirt was resting and smiled. She was glad she hadn't given it back.

"So, if Patrick is unconscious, how exactly am I able to tear you from his side?" Lexie asked while closing Violet's door. "Geeze, why is your room still clean?"

Violet laughed as she pulled a clean shirt from her closet. "What are you talking about?" She closed the door and pointed at a small pile of clothes by her desk chair. "I've got clothes on my floor."

One side of Lexie's face bunched. "It's still weird. It's not enough. Can't you just empty out one of your drawers?"

"I'm not going to ruin the hard work I did to actually make it clean." Violet grabbed a pair of black leggings from her dresser. "And as far as tearing me from Patrick's side... he's unconscious. It's not going to do me any good to watch over him like some creepy girlfriend."

Lexie took a couple of steps back, knocked into the bedroom door, and placed a hand over her chest. "Did you just say girlfriend?"

A slow grin spread across Violet's face. She shrugged, and then laid the clean clothes on her bed. "I kinda forgot to mention that Patrick and I are together."

"Since when?"

"Since two nights ago."

Lexie stared at her wide-eyed.

"We went on a triple date. He was with Robin. I was with Cas. We ended up going home together because I couldn't handle anymore, and when we got back... we worked things out. And he did not call our kiss a mistake this time."

Her friend's shoulders relaxed. "Good, but what was his excuse for taking Robin to solstice and on the date?"

Violet sighed. "Trying to keep me away to protect me. I told him that he couldn't do that."

Nodding, Lexie moved to the desk chair and plopped into it. "Okay. So... You're together and everything is okay?"

Not wanting to stand anymore, Violet turned to sit on her bed, and then remembered her clothes weren't clean. Instead, she folded her arms and rested her weight to one side. "I mean, Blood Moon is making life crazy, but Patrick and I are good."

"Okay." Lexie took a second, then her brows pulled together. "Wait. You said triple date. Who was the third couple?"

"Oh, Jax and Jess."

Lexie's face fell. "The girl he had with him during solstice?"

Violet's head tilted to the side and she narrowed her gaze. "Yeees. Why does that matter?"

Alarm passed over Lexie's face, but it was quickly replaced by a giant smile. "It doesn't. I was just curious. Why would I care what your dog brother does?" She winked and then jumped up to head for the door. "Hurry and get changed. We have a big day of shopping, and we are going to find the perfect dress to make Patrick's jaw drop."

Laughter rolled out of Violet despite the feeling her friend had been lying to her. "Lexie, we're already together."

Lexie pulled the door open. "Yeah, so let's make him never want to look at Robin again."

"I don't need to worry about..."

"Change and meet me downstairs." Lexie closed the door and Violet grabbed the hem of her shirt. The door flew open again, making her jump, but it was just Lexie with a big smile on her face. "I know how slow you change, so I'm sweetening the deal. I'll pay for breakfast if you're down in five minutes."

# Chapter 19

## Violet

***Violet made it downstairs in three,*** *and Lexie did indeed buy breakfast for her.* The rest of the drive was filled with the sound of food munching and idle, friendly chatter.

When they finally made it to the mall in Merced, it quickly became clear that finding a sage green dress was not going to be an easy task.

"This is the one!" Lexie lifted a ridiculous lime green dress with frills for days high into the air. She pinched her lips together to keep from exploding as her body shook with glee.

Violet rolled her eyes, but a warm, easy smile slid over her face. "You're ridiculous."

Pent-up laughter burst from Lexie, and she returned the dress to the rack.

"Why is sage green such a hard color to find?" Violet moved around to the other side of the rack. "You'd think they'd have a bunch of it with it being spring."

Lexie snorted.

A familiar presence filled her mind, making her hands pause on a hideous pea-green sequin jumper. *"Where are you?"*

Violet dropped her head back and groaned.

Lexie peered over the rack. "Jax again?"

About an hour into their drive, Jax had messaged her to inform her that he was awake and fully healed, but Patrick was still unconscious. Now, hours later, the repeated question of "where are you" every twenty minutes was getting old.

Violet pressed her fingers to her temples as a low ache began to pulse against her skull. "He is being annoyingly persistent."

Hangers screeched across the metal bar, and she flinched against the harsh sound.

"Just tell him to back off." Lexie poked her head through the hanging clothes and winked.

Violet grinned, pushed her friend's face back through the clothing, and then closed her eyes to concentrate. Longer distances made it hard for Violet to reach him, but thankfully she only felt a small strain. *"Why do you keep asking that? You already know I'm with Lexie in Merced."*

*"Mom wanted me to check in, and I need to talk to you."*

*"You* are *talking to me."*

*"In person."*

*"I'm not going to be back for a few more hours,"* she reminded her twin. *"Even if we left right now, it would still be over an hour. So, either tell me now or wait and stop giving me a headache."*

Violet pulled her cell phone out of her back pocket. Her teeth nibbled on her lip as twenty worried text messages from her mom blazed across her screen. Guilt propelled her thumbs over the screen and she shot a message back.

Violet - Sorry. I forgot to turn my sound up. I'm fine. Just enjoying some normal girl time.

Jax hadn't updated her on Patrick since his first message... maybe she should ask... she debated half a second before rapidly firing another text.

Violet - How's Patrick?

The moment her phone showed the message had been read, three little bouncing dots danced in the bottom corner.

Mom - Patrick is awake and in control. It's good to hear from you. Have fun. Be back by 4.

Violet - Yes, ma'am.

She tacked on a thumbs-up emoji, then tucked her phone back in her pocket. A loud rumble rolled through her stomach, and her eyes bugged. "Hey, uh, we've been in this store for over an hour." She grimaced at the sight of a hot pink mini dress with ruching down the butt crack. "I don't think they have what I want, plus I am super hungry."

Lexie laughed. "You're always hungry, but I think the entire mall heard your stomach growl just now."

Grinning, Violet peeked her head around the rack and nodded toward the door. "Then let's go eat! The stores will be here when we're done. She held her arm out for Lexie to take when her friend came closer. "You lead. I have a bone to pick with Jax."

With a nod, Lexie held Violet's upper arm and became her seeing-eye human. Although Violet could see while she was speaking to Jax through their twin-link, the added level of concentration set her in a bit of a dazed state. And, she really didn't need to be crashing into a pillar, or a person, or a glass window.

*"Why didn't you tell me Patrick was awake?"*

It took a moment, but slowly a muddied aura settled in her mind and grew clearer with each of Jax's words. *"Would it have made you come home faster?"*

*"Jax! That's an important detail."* She imagined her shoulders dropping with a huff of air that she hoped he could feel.

*"No need to get huffy. He hasn't been awake very long. He was very confused when he woke up. Kept asking how we got back and where you were. Now it's taking everything I have to convince him not to hunt you down. He's mad we let you go without a bodyguard."*

*"Really?"* She couldn't stop her girlish feelings from leaking through, making her mental inflection spike higher than usual.

*"Violet..."*

She didn't need Jax to chide her for that because she was already kicking herself. *"Okay. Will it help set you all at ease if I send you a message every hour?"*

The caress of another presence brushed across her mind. A warm, chocolaty rich voice floated through her thoughts like a voice on the wind.

*"That's not good enough."*

Gasping, Violet's feet stopped moving as Patrick's aura faded away.

Lexie's wide eyes turned toward her. "Everything okay?"

After a quick nod, Violet tried to respond to Patrick, but whatever connection had been there was gone.

Disappointed, she sent a message to Jax instead, *"Tell him I'll try for every half hour, but no guarantees."*

Confusion trickled through her thoughts from Jax. *"How did you know he wasn't happy about the one-hour thing?"*

*"Actually, I heard him... As clearly as I hear you."*

*"What? Is that ne—no, never mind. Stay focused. Stay safe. Keep Lexie safe. We'll talk when you get home."*

Jax's voice faded away along with their connection and Violet looked at Lexie. She hadn't resumed their trek to the food court so Violet waved her to follow as she started walking.

"Patrick's awake, still healing, and apparently pushing out the door to come find us," Violet announced when Lexie fell into step with her.

"Is he going to?" Lexie pointed to the right and they headed toward an aroma of warm, welcoming food.

Violet shook her head. "I don't think so. But... I heard him speak."

"Seriously?" Lexie's eyes bugged and a smile crept up her face. "That's amazing!"

"It's progress, that's for sure!"

"See, you're just a late bloomer. You'll have a wol..." Lexie cleared her throat as a couple of people passed them. "A second half before you know it."

Violet barked a laugh. "That ship has sailed, and I definitely know it."

But Lexie's enthusiasm was contagious, and soon Violet found herself grinning like a madman... Especially once the warm, savory fragrance of soft pretzels wafted to her. She seized Lexie's arm and followed her nose, nearly dragging her friend along, while her mouth watered. "I'm definitely getting a pretzel.... Or three."

"Mmm, that sounds good," Lexie agreed as they hopped into the order line.

Three large pretzels and a few cheese dips later, Violet's stomach was satisfied, and her headache had settled.

Excitement bubbled out of Lexie in a giggle that nearly made Violet miss the trashcan. Her friend hopped sideways toward another shop showcasing beautiful prom dresses in the window.

"I have a good feeling about this one."

"Why do you love shopping so much?" Violet wondered, following after her.

Lexie's lips bunched to the side, then she shrugged. "I don't know. It's fun trying on new clothes and finding ones you love and then bringing them home! Plus, spending time with you is always a bonus."

Violet smirked. "Thanks. I agree with that last part, at least."

Scoffing, Lexie walked through the doors, beckoning her to follow.

A violent shiver rolled down Violet's spine. She spun around, searching the area frantically while her chest rose and fell in heavy, rapid succession. The few people who passed by gave her a wide berth and weird looks as they continued on their way.

Nothing was out of the ordinary.

Nothing was out of place.

"You okay?" Lexie asked, drawing her back to reality.

Violet's heart thundered against her ribs, but she turned toward her friend. "I guess so." She gave the area one last sweeping look before heading into the store.

Another hour, and two check-ins with Jax, went by roaming the racks before Violet lifted a dress high into the air. Lexie bounced over to her with all the excitement from before and shoved her into the changing rooms.

"You better show me!" Lexie yelled.

Violet chuckled as she wiggled out of her clothing and into the dress. The hem landed just above her knee, and it clung to her curves enough that even without straps, she didn't think it would be going anywhere.

Chewing on her lip, Violet opened the fitting room door. "What do you think?"

Lexie was gone.

Panic zipped through Violet's limbs and she bolted from the changing room. "Lexie?"

White-blond hair draped over Lexie's shoulder as she peered around the wall toward the department store doors.

"Lexie, you scared me!"

"Hmm?" Lexie turned her chin a fraction toward Violet but continued looking around.

Violet stepped toward her, and that same violent shiver from before rippled through her. "What's going on?"

"Nothing." Lexie shrugged. "Just some creeper I saw in one of the shops earlier. I was going to tell him off, but he walked right past the store." Lexie shook her head. She turned toward Violet and her eyes rounded. "Where have you been hiding that gorgeous little figure?"

"You don't think it's too much?" Violet worried, smoothing her hands down the lightly-ruched sides. At least it wasn't on the butt.

"You might give Patrick a heart attack," Lexie snickered. "But that's kind of what we're going for so, no, it's definitely not too much. Plus, it's sage green, like you wanted."

Violet's worries faded with a sigh. "You're right. And we've been here for hours. I doubt I would find another one."

"You don't like it?" Lexie walked in a circle around her.

"I love it! I'm just not used to this kind of stuff," Violet admitted. Her idea of clothing was oversized shirts and loose-cut jeans or athletic gear. A toothy grin crept up her face when she looked into the nearest mirror, and she nibbled her lip. With a confirming nod, she said, "I'm buying it."

"YES!" Lexie pushed her back into the changing room. "That gives us plenty of time to go find some dessert before we head back to the base. Remind me to thank your mom when we get back. I didn't think I'd get five minutes with you for your birthday, so this has been awesome."

Violet pulled her shirt on and flicked her long ponytail out from under the neckline. "I'm sure she would love to hear that."

"I wonder if I'll be invited to even more events after the last one." Lexie mused while Violet finished getting dressed and gathered the dress in her arms.

"Oh, so should I be worried that was all an act?" Violet teased and opened her changing room door.

Lexie quirked an eyebrow. "Absolutely not." A mischievous smile lit up her face as they made their way toward the cashier. "However, I have thought since then that it would be a fun perk."

"I wouldn't complain about having you around more." Violet laid her dress on the counter for the clerk to ring it up. "Jax might though."

"Hmm, even more reason to be around then."

Both girls chuckled, and Violet paid for the dress.

Terror rolled along her spine when they stepped out of the mall and headed for Lexie's car. She darted a look around, but once again, saw nothing.

"You need to stop looking so worried," Lexie advised, raising a hand to block out the harsher rays of the sun. "You just bought a gorgeous dress and have a super fun night planned. You don't have to worry about anything."

Violet nodded as they weaved their way through a couple of cars. "You're right. I've just had a weird feeling. I'm glad we found the dress when we did, or we may have had to leave. You heard what my mom said."

"Yeah." Lexie smirked. "It was meant to be, then!"

She tried to smile back, but her nerves were a little frayed, and her fingertips tingled. "Do you think I should reach out to Jax?"

"Didn't you just do that?"

Violet nodded, and a relieved sigh deflated her tense shoulders when Lexie's bright purplish-pink car came into view. "You're right," she made her way to the passenger's side and pulled on the door handle. "I'll update him while we're getting dessert. Which reminds me," she slid into the passenger's seat. "What are we getting for dessert? Something cold or..." She looked over to find an empty driver's seat. "Lexie?"

A quick look into the back seat showed her friend wasn't there either.

Violet smacked her shoulder on the door frame when she shot out of the car. The area instantly throbbed, and she rubbed the sore spot while peeking over the car. "Lexie?"

That same dreaded shiver rolled down her spine. She dropped into a low crouch, and cursed herself for not taking it more seriously. With muscles pulled tighter than a mouse trap, she crept around the back bumper.

Bright blue converse covered feet stuck out from the other side of the car.

Violet lurched around the car and knelt beside her friend, softly calling her name. Nothing appeared broken. She was breathing evenly. Gently, Violet rolled Lexie to her side. Blues and purples already darkened her jaw and minor scrapes marred her skin—probably from crashing to the ground.

Why had someone attacked Lexie? And why didn't Violet hear anything?

Violet mentally shook herself. Now was not the time to debate things. She tried to keep an ear out for any movement or sounds that weren't her own, while she shifted her hands underneath her friend. It took a bit, but she managed to move Lexie into a sitting position with her back pressed against the truck's back tire.

With a heavy huff of air, Violet opened the back door of Lexie's car, and after glancing around nervously to make sure no one was watching, she turned back to her friend. "Okay, let's get you into the back seat, so we can get out of here."

In the small space between Lexie's car and the giant truck at Violet's back, there wasn't a ton of space to maneuver. She had to be careful which way she was bending and moving Lexie, so she didn't accidentally injure her. If it weren't for her enhanced strength, Violet wouldn't have been able to lift her friend at all. The girl was much taller than Violet, and her dead weight made it feel like she weighed a ton. She was sure Jax would have been able to throw Lexie over his shoulder like a sack of potatoes. Even Mya would have been able to lift and move Lexie with ease, but neither of them were there, and she couldn't wait.

She lifted Lexie with a small groan, and used her knee to push her friend's hips back so she was sitting on the very edge of the backseat. "Good. We've got you up and—woah!"

The back of Lexie's head softly thudded against the door frame and then again on the seat. Violet tried to slow her fall. Maybe she had a little, but she'd been nearly pulled on top of Lexie in the process.

"Oh my gosh, I'm so sorry, Lexie." She yanked her arm out from under her unconscious friend and awkwardly backed out of the car.

Thankfully, the small space between the cars and the giant truck hid them pretty well from the public eye. Violet bit her lip and looked at the truck again.

It hid them from the public eye.

There had been a small green Geo in its place when they'd arrived. She faced the massive black vehicle and rose up on her tiptoes, but the inside was dark, and the windows were deeply tinted.

Violet grumbled at herself to keep moving. Lots of people drove trucks, and black cars, and almost every window was tinted these days. Looking for the attacker, and essentially looking for a fight, was not what she needed to be doing. She was alone. Responsible for the safety of a human. The best human in the world. Her best course of action was to get them out of there as quickly as possible.

Another dark shiver cascaded down her spine, and Violet nearly hit her head as she ducked into the back seat. "Okay, Lexie. Where are your keys?"

She popped open the small belt pouch on Lexie's hips, and fumbled around, knocking chapstick and a cardholder to the floor of the car. There were no keys. Violet's hands began trembling.

"Sorry," she muttered as she groped her friend's pockets.

Nothing.

Frustration burned the back of Violet's neck and the tips of her ears. She pushed herself out of the car to look along the ground. "Where are they?"

Beep. Beep.

Violet nearly jumped into the side of the truck when Lexie's car sounded. Panic flooded her veins with ice. Lexie was still unconscious.

Beep. Beep.

She flinched and then glanced around, trying to find who was toying with her. If it came to it, the small space between cars would work to her advantage. A larger opponent would have a much harder time maneuvering in the tight space.

Beep. Beep.

Violet softly shut the back door of Lexie's car to protect her friend, then crouched low and started feeling under the car. The spare key was around there somewhere. She'd seen Lexie have to grab it multiple times when she locked her keys in the car.

Beep. Beep.

A shadow formed in the corner of Violet's eye. She turned to see a large figure, draped in loose-fitting, dark clothing that gave nothing away. He lifted his gloved hand and dangled Lexie's keys in the air.

Beep. Beep.

"What do you want?" Violet snapped in a slightly breathy voice.

Years of training taught her to keep her body loose in the event of a fight, but those safe scenarios did not prepare her for this. Her muscles complained when she slowly made her way to her feet, and the hooded figure dipped his head to the side.

She had two options. Fight in close quarters and hope he didn't get a hit on her. Or run, leaving Lexie alone in the car with a psychopath who had her keys. It wasn't much of an option when she laid it out like that.

The shadow man swung his arm to the side and then dropped the keys, letting them clatter against the hood of the car. They screeched as they slid down the frame.

He stalked toward her.

The keys clattered to the ground.

Violet turned and bolted around the back of the giant truck.

A whispered curse met her ears, and loud footsteps thudded after her.

She grabbed the spoiler on the red car on the other side of the truck, turning herself quickly to the side, before she ducked down. Her heart thundered against her chest, and she willed her breathing to slow down.

Some wolven had the ability to hear even the shallowest breaths.

Violet seriously hoped this guy wasn't one of those.

The tell-tale crunch of his heavy footfalls filled the air.

She leaned back, resting her weight on her arms, and lifted one of her feet.

One well-aimed kick was all she needed.

His leg appeared and Violet grunted as she drove her heel against the side of his knee. Something snapped. His roar was a mix of rage and pain as he dropped to the ground, clutching his knee. Then his hand snaked out, clawing for her foot. His fingertips grazed her toes while she scrambled out of reach.

This was her chance.

He wouldn't be down long. His wolven healing would have him on his feet soon, but she'd already be gone.

Violet darted around the front of the cars back toward Lexie. Gravel dug into her fingers when she snagged the keys from the ground on her way to the driver's door. She almost face-planted when her toe caught, but she snared the mirror, and used it to right herself before wrenching the door open.

It was torn from her hands when a wrecking ball in the shape of the shadowed figure plowed into her side. The skin along her arm burned as she slid against the ground under his mighty weight. She cried out when his gloved hand shoved her other shoulder down, pinning her against the pavement.

He shifted over her, and she drove her knee skyward. One of the hands on her arms dropped between his legs while he squeaked a moan, freeing her hand to thrust the heel of her palm into his nose.

Bone cracked.

His tiny whimper turned into howling agony, and his gloved hands grabbed his face, freeing her in the process.

Violet rolled to her stomach and frantically clawed her way out from under him. She was fast. If she could get him far enough away from the car, she could run back and leave. That was the plan.

And it worked, too.

He'd underestimated her.

With his new injuries, it took him much longer to hobble after her, but it also told Violet that she was his intended target. Not Lexie. Or maybe he wasn't concerned about the human girl because she was unconscious. Either way, the hobbling man chased after her, falling farther and farther behind the more she weaved through the cars in the lot.

When she could no longer see or hear him, Violet sprinted back to the car. Lexie was still asleep in the backseat when she slid into the driver's side and jammed the key into the ignition.

"Let's go home, Lexie." Her voice trembled and her shaky hand grabbed the stick to put them in reverse.

Glass shattered as a fist went through her window. She threw a hand up to protect her face, but tiny shards cut her cheek while the majority blanketed her lap. She clutched the stick ready to drive off with the guy hanging out of the car when a cloth was pressed over her mouth and nose, slamming her head against the headrest.

A sickeningly sweet smell flooded her nose. Violet tore at the cloth and the hand pinning her head. Blood splattered on the door just inside the smashed window.

Violet opened her mind to her twin as her world went dark.

# Chapter 20
## Patrick

***After a lot of convincing***, *Patrick had finally managed to get both Jax* and the doc to allow him out of Lockup. He was still under strict orders to sit and rest and not do anything... fat chance of that happening. His achy, hot limbs twitched now and then as he sat in the living room of Alpha House under the watchful eye of Evalyn Draven, who looked up from her computer every few minutes, and Jax, who looked as if he had fallen asleep with his head tipped against the back of the sofa.

"I can feel you glaring at me," Jax mumbled.

"That would stop if you would let me leave."

Jax sighed. "We've been over this. The Doc says you are in no condition to go gallivanting off, and Violet and Lexie deserve some time to themse—" His eyes snapped open and he sat up.

"What's wrong?" Patrick leaned forward, then rested his elbows on his knees so he wouldn't fall off the armchair.

Jax's jaw clenched and his brows pulled together, then shook his head. His fingers touched his temple and he swayed ever so slightly in his seat on the sofa.

"Hey!" Patrick snapped at him, drawing his best friend back to the present. "What happened?"

Evalyn's gaze had left her work and she watched her son with wide eyes.

"Something's wrong," Jax whispered.

"With Violet?" If Patrick had more energy, he may have seized his friend's shirt to draw information from him quicker.

The alpha's office door opened and a few male voices chattered with glee.

Evalyn shoved out of her chair, knocking it into the wall behind her, and drawing the attention of the males exiting the office. Alpha Draven's eyes followed his mate as she rushed around the love seat to grasp Jax's shoulders. "Jax, focus. What's wrong with Violet?"

"What's going on?" The alpha stepped forward with Beta Paul close on his heels.

Patrick's hands curled into fists as the third male joined them.

Cas.

"Jax?" Evalyn lightly shook his shoulders.

"Violet opened our link, but then... nothing." Jax's pinched his brows together, his eyes growing hazy once again. He shook his head a second later. "There's nothing. I can't feel her."

Alpha Draven's gaze danced between them, but he remained silent.

Patrick pulled his phone from his pocket. "Call her cell."

"On it." Cas already had his phone in his hand and everyone had turned to look at him as he lifted the device to his ear.

Patrick wanted to snap 'not you' at the intruder, but he wasn't quite that thick-headed. At least someone else was on top of things, and they needed answers. "I'll send Lexie a text. I don't think she'll answer if I call her."

"Why?" Jax asked as he turned his attention back to Patrick.

"Because she doesn't know it's me."

"Didn't you message her before when Violet needed some cheering up?"

Patrick nodded as he tapped his message. "She didn't know it was me."

`Patrick - Lexie, this is Patrick. Are you guys okay?`

"I got her voice mail," Cas announced, then pocketed his phone.

Evalyn's face had gone pale. "I can call Lexie. We don't know when she will see that message." She stepped away to grab her phone from her desk.

Alpha Draven moved into the living room and Patrick shakily rose from his seat to meet him. "This wouldn't have happened if you had followed orders and left."

"With all due respect, sir." Patrick narrowed his gaze. "You did not give me an order."

The alpha clenched his jaw. "Would it have mattered if I had?"

"I did not disobey you. I've been making plans to leave, but not very many clans want me around. Besides, Violet and—"

"You should have left anyway."

"Dad!" Jax snapped. "He may have started out as Blood Moon's target, but I don't think that's what they're after anymore. They could have hit us hard and fast and gotten what they wanted, but they've taken their time coming down through the state and now have Stanislaus's territory." He pushed his way off the sofa to stand. "This is bigger than Patrick."

"Nothing." Evalyn's concerned, quiet tone bled through the tension surrounding the three males. "Noah…" Her light gray eyes swirled into a vortex of gold and silver with tendrils of bronze as she moved to her mate. "Noah, we have to find her."

Something akin to hatred passed over Alpha Draven's face even as he pulled his mate to his chest and kissed the top of her head. "Why didn't you send someone with them?"

Evalyn shoved out of the alpha's arms and glared at him. "Excuse me?"

"If you're so concerned with your daughter's safety, why didn't you send someone with them?"

"*Our* daughter." Evalyn snapped, her kaleidoscope eyes practically glowing. "And who was I supposed to send? Jax was still healing, Patrick was unconscious…"

Patrick flinched.

"And we can't spare any warriors right now in case Blood Moon decided to attack."

"You're willing to break the laws of nature to save your children. But you wouldn't send a warrior or two to protect her?"

Confusion, curiosity, and unease twisted the faces of the four males not included in this conversation. Patrick looked at Jax, who quirked a brow and shrugged, while Cas and Beta Paul both shifted their weight uneasily.

Evalyn lifted her chin defiantly. "You want to get into that now? Or should we focus on finding Violet?"

Silence fell over the room. The tension was palpable... and Patrick didn't have time for it.

He headed for the door. "I'm going."

"Going where?" Jax asked as he followed.

The doorknob was cold against Patrick's feverish skin, but when he yanked the door open, it was closed again by Jax shoving his shoulder against it.

"Move," Patrick growled through clenched teeth as rage spread through his body.

His friend shook his head and then whispered, "You need to calm down."

"I need to find Violet."

Cas's voice interrupted the growing stress of the room. "Do we know where the girls went?"

"The mall in Merced," Evalyn answered.

A low whistle sounded. "Why so far away?"

"They were looking for a dress for the party tonight."

Patrick didn't need to be part of this conversation. He could have already been at his truck.

"Jax, move," his voice pitched low and animalistic.

Instead of moving, Jax flattened himself against the door. "We don't even know where they are."

"I'll start at the mall and find a trail. You can message me if you get a hold of her."

Jax's jaw pushed to the side for a moment, then he nodded and moved away from the door. "I'm coming with you."

"You will remain here with your clan," Alpha Draven's voice rose above the din that had consumed the house.

Jax turned to stare wide-eyed at his father. "We've already discovered that you're not much of a match for me anymore. Should I demonstrate that again?"

"Jax." Evalyn hissed. She gazed between her mate and son, then stepped toward the latter with a frown. "He has a point."

Outrage cascaded over Jax's face.

She continued before he could respond. "I didn't send you with her earlier because you were still healing, but don't forget you are the future alpha. Like it or not we can't risk your safety for that of your sister."

Jax caught Patrick's eye, gave a subtle nod, and moved away from the door.

The moment his friend was out of the way, Patrick yanked the door open.

"Where are you going?" Alpha Draven snarled.

Fury boiled Patrick's blood. He rounded on the alpha as power washed over him and his vision flared red. "I am your best hope of finding her!"

"I don't care what you are at this point!" Alpha Draven stepped toward him as his lips curled back, challenging Patrick.

The power of the alpha pressed against Patrick, but it had no effect. He stood taller, looking down with his scarlet gaze on Alpha Draven's molten gold.

"I am the best tracker in the clan. I have a unique advantage." He tilted his head to the side, "And you can't stop me."

The alpha's aura slapped against Patrick like a child's fist hitting out of anger. His power may not have worked, but his words did. "Don't come back."

Something snapped inside Patrick's chest and he grunted in pain, curling in on himself ever so slightly.

Jax clamped a hand over his father's shoulder. "Stop. If you sever his connection with the clan and banish him, he won't be able to bring Violet home."

Breathing heavily, Patrick turned and took a step out the door. "It's already begun."

Breaking ties with your clan wasn't pleasant, Patrick knew from experience. While the pain didn't last long, it felt like a part of you was being torn from your soul only to be filled with a deep, aching hole of loneliness. They were pack animals—not meant to be alone.

"What did you do?" Jax growled.

"What I should have done a long time ago," the alpha answered. "It will continue to deteriorate, Patrick. But you already know that."

Patrick clenched his jaw and walked down the porch steps. He stopped, then turned to look back at the alpha who had graciously taken him in years ago. "You'll finish it when I return with Violet?"

Alpha Draven nodded, then turned into the house and disappeared from the doorway.

The disbelieving, sorrowful voice of Evalyn Draven drifted on the wind toward Patrick as she fought with her mate.

Jax stared at Patrick.

"I'll find her." Patrick promised, taking a step backward. "I'll bring her home."

He turned and jogged toward the parking lot.

Heavy footsteps raced after him. "I'm coming with you."

Patrick groaned as Cas matched his stride. "No."

"I care about her, too."

"Then stay here."

"Why?" Cas scoffed as they turned toward the parking lot. "Because you think you have this all under control?"

Patrick snarled and jumped in front of Cas, forcing the male to a skidding stop. "I don't trust you."

Surprise melted into derision and Cas folded his arms. "I'm not the one with the red eyes."

"That's exactly my point," Patrick growled, although really it was only a fraction of the distrust Patrick felt for the guy. "Who finds out a person has red eyes and then decides to tag along with them? No one reacts that well."

Cas shrugged a shoulder. "Guess I'm special."

"No," Patrick countered. "You're trouble."

"You expect me to let a known killer go find the girl I like?"

Patrick flinched. "You don't know me very well," his voice lost its threat and sank into a soft and vulnerable tone, "but I would never do anything to harm Violet."

"Your eyes say otherwise." Cas pointed at him. "They mark you as a killer. As someone who lost control."

"They tell nothing!" Patrick yelled, his chest heaved with emotion while Cas watched through narrowed eyes. "You can't tell if I killed on purpose, in a fit of rage or passion, if it was self-defense, or if it was an accident. All you know is I killed someone. What you really need to know is people died because of a decision I made, and there isn't a day that goes by that I don't wish I could change that. I fight *every day* against the monster in my head to make sure no more innocents are lost."

Cas' slightly annoyed and disrespectful look tightened to one of anger. The bridge of his nose bunched as his brows pulled together. He closed the distance between them, so they were nearly toe-to-toe. "Prove it. Let me go after her."

Snorting, Patrick headed toward the parking lot again.

"Prove you have the control you say you do!"

The parking lot hedges were just ahead, but Patrick spun and glared at Cas who had continued following him. "I'm not sending you after her because I am her best chance! That isn't me being petty or prideful, it's the truth. I've been guarding Violet for years. I know how she thinks and often how she feels. I've been charged with her protection since I came here. I'm not leaving her fate in the hands of someone she just met who has a crush on her."

"I'm just gonna follow you." Cas stomped after him when Patrick continued on his way.

"At least you won't be in my truck."

# Chapter 21

## Patrick

***Impatience rattled through Patrick,*** *making his leg bounce.* He clenched the steering wheel, and pushed his old truck to the limit. Cas had indeed followed him, and the black car behind him drew a low growl from his throat. He tried to remind himself that another set of eyes and ears would be good to have, but Patrick couldn't shake the feeling that he knew Cas from somewhere. That he was not to be trusted. That he was dangerous.

*"How's it going,"* Jax's voice interrupted his thoughts.

*"Exactly the same as five minutes ago,"* Patrick told him. *"Except we are almost at the mall now."*

*"Is Cas still with you?"*

Patrick glanced in his rearview mirror and glared at the black car tailing him. *"He's practically in my truck bed."*

*"Try to remember he's helping find Violet."*

*"I don't trust him, Jax."*

Jax's sigh filled his mind. *"You told me Violet is your mate. You have no reason to be jealous."*

*"It's not jealousy."* Patrick turned the truck into the mall parking lot and grunted. *"At least... that's not the only reason."*

*"Are you sure?"*

Patrick didn't answer. Admitting he was jealous felt like admitting defeat. Knowing Violet was his mate, and that she already had feelings for him, would make it pretty difficult for someone to come between them... but they'd only just admitted their feelings for one another and he'd been pushing her away for so long.

And soon he would be clan-less.

After driving around the mall for five minutes, Patrick growled as he pulled into the nearest open spot. Black dots peppered his vision when he stepped out of his truck, and he leaned back against the cool metal frame. The poison hadn't made its way completely out of his system yet. He needed to be careful.

"You alright?"

Cas' voice snatched Patrick's attention from the ground, and he narrowed his eyes. Was he imagining it or did Cas seem almost pleased that Patrick was struggling? The tiniest hint of a smirk lifted the corner of Cas' mouth, and a spark of glee glimmered in his eyes.

Setting his jaw, Patrick shoved off his truck and shut the door. "Just waiting on you," he snarked, and couldn't deny the satisfaction that spread through his chest when Cas' pleased expression cracked.

Cas crossed his arms and looked at the nearest mall entrance. "What's the plan?"

Patrick started toward the doors without answering. What was the plan? He wasn't sure. He was just annoyed that he was driving around in circles and needed to get out of the truck.

"You don't have a plan, do you?" Cas snorted when he caught up to Patrick. "Of course not."

"What's your problem?" Patrick turned his head to look at him.

Cas' face hardened. "I thought that was obvious." The lines in his jaw sharpened. His eyes narrowed into slits. A low growl rolled out of him as one side of his nose and mouth scrunched. "Do you have a plan or not?"

*"This cretin needs to back off or I'm gonna make that look on his face permanent."*

*"Alistair!"* Much to Patrick's dismay, relief washed over him at the sound of his wolf half's voice.

*"Miss me, Boy Scout?"*

*"You wish."*

A low, tired chuckle rumbled in his mind.

*"Where have you been?"*

*"I've been here the whole time. Tell the nitwit that we need to find Violet's scent."*

Doubt echoed in Patrick's thoughts. *"In a sea of human stench?"*

*"We can do it."*

"Patrick!" Cas snagged his arm, dragging him to a stop. "Do you have a plan or not?"

Unfortunately for the eager nuisance in front of him, Patrick had been playing a part for years. He'd learned how to craft a facade and make a lie believable. It was easier when there was a hint of truth behind the charade.

Patrick focused on Cas' hand, then slowly lifted his hardened gaze to the young man's eyes and pushed a bit of rage into his voice, "Do you really think I would have driven all the way out here and marched up to these doors if I didn't have a plan in mind?"

Cas released his arm as if it were a snake about to bite him. "Then what is it?"

"We need to catch Violet's scent. It will give us our first clue."

"You're joking right?" Cas' tone was a mix of incredulity and skepticism. "The human—" A group of girls passed them giving him wary glances. "Ladies." He nodded and flashed a toothy grin that made the girls giggle.

Patrick groaned.

The girls disappeared down through the doors and Cas' expression hardened again. "The human stench overpowers ours. Besides that, I can't find one scent among thousands."

It was Patrick's turn to flash a toothy grin and he did so with much pleasure. "I can."

Nearly an hour passed and Patrick still hadn't found even a whiff of Violet.

To be fair, neither did Cas, but the coffee-scented young man had already admitted that *he* couldn't locate Violet's scent. And he had no problem reminding Patrick of that.

"Really," Cas called around his last mouthful of soft pretzel. "There's no harm in admitting this was a horrible plan and going with mine instead."

"Your plan is stupid."

Cas licked his fingers. "Why? The police would find the car for us, and we could be on our way."

"To where?" Patrick asked while he practically stomped toward one of the mall's exits. "Hmm?"

Cas scowled.

It was a horrible plan. Not only would the cops swarm the parking lot, which would make it harder to leave, but after they found the car—if it was still there—they would block it off so no one could get near. Which defeated the purpose of trying to find it in the first place. And where would they go then?

"Finding the car isn't going to tell us where to go either," Cas grumbled, then dumped his soft pretzel container in the nearest garbage.

*"Let me try."* Alistair paced back and forth like a caged animal in Patrick's mind, but it was slower than usual. Less threatening.

*"The last time I let you out, you did horrible things."*

*"The longer you take, the farther away they could be."*

Patrick shoved out of the doors and breathed in the crisp spring air. It was a momentary reprieve before Cas' coffee-saturated stench filled his nostrils again. He coughed.

"It's no wonder I can't smell anything. Do you have any idea how badly you reek?"

Cas looked down at his clothes, then self-consciously smelled near his shoulder. He shrugged. "I smell like I always do."

Shaking his head, Patrick looked out at the cars and the darkening sky. They were taking too long. "Doesn't the coffee smell bother you?"

"It used to."

*"Boy Scout. Let me out."*

*"And when you're done? Will you hand back the controls or will I have to fight you?"*

Alistair gave a dry laugh. *"I don't have the energy to fight you right now, Boy Scout, but I'd be happy to take a rain check."*

Considering his options, it wasn't a bad plan. Alistair wasn't asking for anything. The desire to help seemed genuine and his dark half was weak right now... granted, so was Patrick.

*"Take it away."*

The feeling of Alistair refusing was strange. It gave Patrick an instant headache, and unease wound its way around his stomach.

*"I'll lend you the power."*

A solid surge of energy rolled through Patrick. He gasped, his knees nearly buckling under the force of it.

"You alright there, hot shot?"

Patrick smirked as the overwhelming sensation subsided. "I'm fantastic."

*"You still there, Alistair?"*

*"You can't get rid of me that easily."*

Patrick laughed in his mind. *"Just checking."*

The once-darkening sky now appeared as bright as noon. Patrick closed his eyes as the riotous noise of the city and the stench of humans—all artificial scents and overpowering—overwhelmed him.

*"Focus."* Alistair coached in a tone that bordered on uncaring and bored. *"You know what Violet smells like. Imagine that. Bring the memory forward and breathe in her scent."*

"We aren't going to catch her this way." Cas griped. "This area is too heavily trafficked."

"Not for us," Patrick answered softly, but Alistair had said it, too, which tipped his voice toward a growl.

It felt wrong to trust Alistair. To work as one. They had fought against each other for years... but they both loved Violet.

Patrick drew in a deep breath.

Then another.

And another.

He sifted through the different smells—only to come up empty.

*"Alistair..."*

*"Try the doors."*

Cas followed him as he moved, and they both grinned sheepishly when a group of gaggling young women shoved out the doors. The girls eyed them but continued on their way.

Patrick held back a groan when he found the same result as before.

*"Breathe in again,"* Alistair ordered. *"And this time savor each smell."*

Patrick grimaced. *"There are some smells here I really don't want to savor."*

*"You'll immediately recognize those and be able to move on to the next one. Close your eyes."*

Patrick followed Alistair's instructions.

*"Breathe deeply. Push each one away as it comes and goes. Hold on to the fainter smells. She was here hours ago, it won't be easy to pick up."*

*"If she even walked through these doors."*

*"Focus!"* his darker half snapped.

It wasn't quick, but Patrick's ability grew with each breath he took, until the smell of Christmas cookies, and the hint of cedar that followed, filled him with warmth. "I found you," he whispered.

"What?"

Cas' surprised tone would have been enough for Patrick to laugh, if the use of his abilities hadn't left him feeling more exhausted than before.

"You really found her?"

Patrick breathed again and another familiar smell hit him. He and Alistair growled as one, and he opened his eyes to find Cas warily watching him. "I really hope I'm wrong about this."

*"Unlikely."* Alistair muttered.

"What?"

Annoyance flickered through Patrick. This would be so much easier without the puppy following him around. He laughed to himself at the thought of calling Cas a puppy, considering the guy was older than Patrick, but it was fitting and satisfying.

"There's another scent with Violet's."

Cas shrugged and then followed Patrick when he began chasing after the scent. "Yeah, Lexie. We already know that."

Patrick shook his head. "I don't know Lexie's scent well enough to pick it out amongst all the others. It's too human. This is someone that should not have been here."

As Patrick followed the warm vanilla with hints of cinnamon and brown sugar, the tiniest tang of nutmeg curled within Patrick like a warm fire. He could lose himself in the smell, but the heady cedar perfume blended with rotting lemon tainted the beautiful aroma.

The farther he followed the atrocious combination, the fainter Violet's scent grew, nearly being overpowered by the other.

"There!" Cas called and rushed forward. "That's Lexie's car, right?"

Pinkish-purple called to them from behind a small gray Honda. Patrick picked up his pace, and stepped around the car to find Cas with his hands inside the window. "What are you doing?"

Cas' gaze snapped to his, then down at the car. "The window was busted in."

"I can see that," he sneered, marching toward the suspicious young man. "What were *you* doing?"

Slowly, Cas looked back at Patrick. His jaw clenched.

They stared at each other.

Then Cas backed away and motioned toward the door. "There's blood."

Patrick slowly stepped forward, eying Cas suspiciously, then looked at the door. Sure enough, a large drop of blood had splattered just inside the window and dripped down the frame. The overwhelming stench of decaying citrus was enough to make Patrick's eyes water. He shut down his heightened senses and coughed.

He clenched his teeth together and snarled, "Zander!"

"Who's Zander?" Cas asked, his confusion evident in his tone as he peered into the car.

"A dead man walking."

Careful of the glass, Patrick reached through the window and unlocked the door. He pried it open and stuck his head in, looking around the small space in the dusky evening light. Without using his abilities, his eyesight had diminished.

Cas copied Patrick and opened the back door to look around. Once his head was in, Cas glared at Patrick. "Easy there, *killer*."

Patrick glowered at him. "I'm not actually going to kill him."

"Your eyes say otherwise."

Silently cursing, Patrick tried to force a mask of calm over his threatening emotions. "How long have they been like that?"

"Since you caught Violet's scent." Cas gazed at him with curiosity. "You can't tell?"

Patrick felt under the seats and looked in the center console, but there wasn't anything there. "I usually can," he admitted. "Are they still red?"

Cas looked up from his examination of the floor, then shook his head. "I've never met a blood-eyed wolf with so much control."

"It's not always easy," Patrick murmured, then pulled the trunk lever and backed out of the car. "I'm not finding anything helpful. You?"

With a sigh, Cas joined him by the trunk. "No." He thrust his chin toward the back of the car. "You think we'll find anything in there?"

"I hope not." Patrick held his breath as he lifted the lid.

"Woah." Cas let out a low whistle as the two of them stared.

It was gloriously messy, like Violet's room usually was, but it was more of a Lexie rushing to clean her car before her best friend got in kind of mess. Clothing, shoes, old takeout containers and fast-food drinks. Apparently, Lexie had a thing for slurpees.

"This isn't helpful," Cas grumbled.

Patrick opened his mind to the clan-link and a stab of pain ricocheted off his skull. He clamped his hands over his head and groaned.

A huff of laughter left Cas. "Did you just try to use the clan-link after the alpha started to dismiss you? How stupid are you?"

"Excuse me if I take pride in the fact that I haven't traipsed around from clan to clan."

Cas' amusement vanished. "I don't traipse."

"Whatever." Patrick pulled his cell from his pocket and called Jax.

"This is weird." Jax answered, sounding confused. "I don't even know the last time you called me. If ever."

Patrick ran a hand through his curly hair and groaned. "Yeah, well, whatever Alpha did to me, it's affecting the clan-link too."

"Odd," Jax said. "It was fine before."

Alpha Draven's voice called from a distance. "His connection to our clan will grow weaker and weaker by the minute."

"Perfect." Patrick shut the trunk and moved to do the same with the driver's door. "I've got bad news."

Jax snorted. "Worse than Violet and Lexie going missing?"

"Zander was here."

The line went quiet. After a moment a low growl vibrated through the ear-piece. "I'm going to kill him."

"Get in line," Cas called from the other side of the car as he closed the back door.

"I thought he wa..."

Worry threaded through Patrick. "Jax?"

No response.

"Jax?"

"Violet just reached me, but I can't feel her. You need to try."

Patrick startled. "What?"

"You connected with her before. Maybe you can again."

Patrick threw his head back and stared at the starless sky. "I just told you my link to the clan has been severed."

"We both know your connection with Violet goes beyond the confines of the clan."

Breathing in a deep breath, he leaned against Lexie's car. "Okay."

"Great. I'll stay on the phone."

Clenching his jaw, Patrick closed his eyes and focused on Violet. Her Christmas cookie scent. Her radiant smile. The alluring way she bit her lip and had no clue how enticing it was. Her brilliant amethyst eyes. The crystal bell-like sound of her laughter. Strong, loyal friendship, and her sense of ri—

There, in the far reaches of whatever their connection was made out of, Patrick could feel her.

Or... a hazy version of her.

*"Violet,"* He called to her, and Alistair stirred in his mind, reaching for her as well. They worked together to seize her attention, and when her foggy outline grew a little more solid, Patrick tried again. *"Violet. Tell us everything. Help us find you. We're coming."*

"Patrick, what's going on?" Cas asked and Jax shh-ed him through the phone.

Minutes passed.

Cas began to pace.

"North." Jax breathed through the phone, and they all let out the collective breath they'd been holding.

"She got through to you?" Patrick asked as he and Cas hurried toward their cars.

"No. It was more like images of what she was seeing. Something's wrong with her."

Patrick's knuckles blanched when he clenched his fist. "I need to call the police about Lexie's car. I'll call right back. That way you can give us information as you receive it, so we can change course as needed."

"Okay." Jax agreed. "You're telling me about Lexie's car when you call back."

"Understood." Patrick nodded to Cas as they split up, and he hurried into his truck.

"Careful, Patrick." Jax warned. "Zander's not thinking straight."

Patrick twisted the key in the ignition. "He never was."

# Chapter 22

## Violet

***Coppery sweetness assaulted Violet's nose,*** *pulling her out of a deep, dark sleep.* The remnants of a strange dream clung to her waking mind, pleading with her to remember. But remember what? She searched the dark recesses of her subconscious as it slipped away.

*"We're coming."*

The achingly familiar timbre of Patrick's voice whispered to her. Faint, but clear.

Coming? Why were they coming?

Violet gasped as reality flooded back to her. They'd been attacked. She'd fought back, but it hadn't been enough. And Lexie...

Violet pried her unwilling eyes open, winced against the brilliant light, and shut them again. A deep throbbing beat against her skull. She groaned.

The heady scent of cedar wafted over her. "I thought I heard you."

She groaned again. Why was he there?

"I imagine you have quite the headache."

That was an understatement.

A few clicks sounded around the room, and the light faded behind her eyelids.

"It should be safe to open your eyes now."

Hesitantly, Violet opened her eyes again. At first, the shape standing at the foot of the bed was blurry. Then his light brown hair and blue eyes came into focus, and Violet glared, "Zander, what have you done?"

A wicked smirk lit his face. "How are you feeling?"

Threadbare, mud-brown drapes were pulled tight, making it impossible to guess the time. The popcorn ceiling above her head dated the room, and the brown-orange accents did nothing to make the place inviting. In fact...

Violet's stomach tumbled.

Zander raced to her side and shoved a trashcan under her face when she rolled to the side. Her shoulder cried as her arm was yanked back, but she continued to pull, aiming for the trashcan while her stomach revolted

"Not well, I take it?" He sighed. "An unavoidable side effect, I'm afraid."

Her stomach tossed once more, but there was nothing left. Trembling overtook her limbs, and she settled back on the bed. She tried to lift her arms, but they only made it a couple inches off the hard mattress.

Zander sighed again, and took a seat on the edge of the bed beside her. She shifted her legs away from him... or at least she would have, but they only moved a couple inches as well.

"Take a breath, Vi."

"Don't call me that." It was an automatic response, but the animosity she usually felt for him ebbed and slipped away. She pinched her brows, and lifted her head to look at her body. Black straps wrapped around her ankles and wrists holding her securely to the bed.

That was unfortunate.

"Let me clean you up." Zander reached for her, but she jerked away. He hesitated, smiled, then closed the inch she managed to put between them. The thin tissue scratched her skin while he wiped her mouth and chin. "That should feel better."

"Why am I tied to the bed? And why am I only a little upset with you?"

He settled a hand on her other side, causing him to lean over her. "That's probably the sedatives I gave you. They'll dampen your emotions, but I'm surprised you feel any anger at all."

Violet's brows lifted, but he was right. The annoyance she felt was a thin ribbon in her unnatural calm. "You drugged me?"

That would explain why she threw up.

"It was the only way to make sure you wouldn't try to break my nose or contact that overprotective twin of yours." He walked his fingers from her knee to her mid-thigh. "I didn't realize how compliant it would make you."

"I'm not compliant," Violet noted. "I just don't seem to really care."

Zander shrugged. "I can work with that."

"What's your plan, Zan?" Violet asked, tilting her head to the other side.

He quirked a brow, and amusement lit his blue eyes.

"Drug me, take me away, then what?"

Thump.

Violet jumped a little at the sudden sound and stared at the reddish-brown door on the inner wall.

Zander's pleasant expression hardened before he made his way toward the door. "I'll be back."

Something dark and heavy pressed against Violet's shoulders and chest, making it hard to breathe. "Where are you going?" she asked breathlessly.

"I have to take care of something."

"Zander, wait." Panic tinged her words.

Something was wrong. Very wrong. There should have been panic about being tied to a bed or anger over being drugged. An explosion of emotion would have been better than their casual appearance, but this...

A muffled moan cried from behind the door.

Violet jolted against the straps as the image of Lexie laying across the back seat of her car, a deep bruise forming along her jaw, emerged in her mind.

"What are you doing?" She yelled, startling Zander into removing his hand from the doorknob. "Where's Lexie?"

Blue eyes turned toward her. "I promise, I'll take care of everything." He opened the door a fraction, and a sob sounded from the other side.

Panic flooded her sedated state. "Zander."

"We can't have any witnesses." His eerily calm tone sent goosebumps over her flesh. "I'll make it quick."

Violet thrashed violently against her restraints, but whatever he had given her had affected her strength as well. "Zander!" She called his name over and over, but he disappeared behind the door, and it clicked closed.

Hot tears scorched her face. She threw all her weight to one side and nearly tipped the mattress over, but the straps stayed put. Stretching to one side and pulling her closest arm toward her face, she bit at the black contraptions… even though they were inches away from her mouth.

A frustrated roar tore from her throat.

THUMP.

Violet froze. Her stomach twisted.

"Lexie?"

Violet's breathing hitched. Tears slipped down her cheeks. Pain tore through her chest.

He'd killed her.

Zander had killed Lexie.

The door opened and the same sweet metallic taste from before consumed the air.

Glowing ruby eyes beamed at her as Zander stepped through the door. The grin tugging at his blood-splattered face was that of a monster. "How has Patrick denied this power?" His crazed laugh sent a chill up her spine. "If I had known this is what it felt like to be a member of the Blood Moon pack, I would have killed him long ago."

"You joined the people who are destroying our clan?" Violet stared at him wide-eyed.

"Well, no, not yet. My absence would have alerted your father that something was wrong." Zander shrugged a shoulder. "I had to remain mostly harmless until the opportune moment, but now that we're free from Sentinel Clan, and that good-for-nothing brother and useless bodyguard of yours, Blood Moon will welcome us with open arms. We'll have a respected place in their ranks once we deliver every ounce of information we have on Sentinel Clan and Patrick."

"Do you even hear yourself? Do you know how crazy you sound?" Violet asked, her voice breaking as she cried. "You killed Lexie! Do you even care that you took one of the most important people in my life away from me?"

Confusion twisted Zander's face, then he laughed—loud and boisterous. "I didn't kill Lexie. Why would I do something that would make you hate me? I'm trying to make you love me."

Violet blinked.

He didn't kill Lexie.

Zander did not kill Lexie.

Lexie was alive.

She ran that through her brain a couple hundred times, but she didn't understand. She shook her head. "Then who did you kill?"

Zander snorted. "One of the maids. She saw me carrying you over my shoulder into the room. I couldn't let her go." He looked down at his hands, caked in blood. "I'm glad I didn't. I've never felt more connected to Mirko."

"Mirko... Oh, your wolf."

A skewed grin lifted one corner of his mouth. "It's like he and I are now one. My wants are his wants. His needs are my needs. No more fighting. It feels amazing."

Disgust rattled through her and her limbs trembled. "You just killed someone, and you're talking about how amazing it feels."

"Hmm, sounds like your sedative is wearing off." Zander sneered, then moved to the backpack sitting on top of the dresser. The light from the lamp gleamed off the needle as he pulled a large syringe from the bag.

"No." She shook her head. "Zander, don't do this."

He stalked toward her. "We have to keep you compliant. Until you love us. Until you see we are your mate."

Violet tugged on the straps once again and the bed moaned. She pulled harder. Zander's hand clamped down on her arm, pinning it to the mattress. She snarled and tried to pull away, but the added strength given to him from taking another's life, and her weakened state from the drugs, made it impossible to throw him off.

Zander's voice dipped into an animal-like growl as he traced her cheekbone with his closed fist, the needle almost grazing her skin. "This will only sting for a moment."

Tears spilled over her eyes when the needle entered her arm.

Zander backed away while Violet shook with rage. "If you think I could love you after all of this, you're more delusional than I thought."

He capped the syringe. "The sedative will take effect soon, and you'll fall asleep. When you wake up, we'll be in your birthday hotel where we'll stay the night before heading to Blood Moon in the morning." Zander deposited the offending needle in his backpack. "You'll like it. It's much nicer than this dump, but I needed a spot to throw off your dogs."

No, no, no.

*"It's a trick!"* She screamed into the void of her foggy mind, not sure the message went anywhere.

He stood at the foot of her bed as her eyelids betrayed her and began to drift shut. "Oh, when you wake up, remember, I have no guilt over killing that maid. So, unless you want another person to die, I suggest you go along with my plan."

"Wake up."

Violet blinked her eyes open.

A blurry Zander smiled at her, but with the drugs still heavily in her system, Violet simply rolled her head to the other side. "I've been terribly rude. I haven't even wished you a happy birthday yet." His fingers snatched her chin and roughly turned her attention to the hotel in front of them. "Happy Birthday, my love. This is quite the upgrade from that awful motel, isn't it?"

"I don't care where you take me," Violet answered in a monotone voice. "Try not to kill the housekeeping this time."

Zander chuckled darkly. "No promises."

He stepped out of the car, and Violet pressed her head back. She closed her eyes and breathed through her nose, trying to settle the ocean of waves in her stomach. If it was possible, her headache was even worse than before. Even her eyes ached now.

Well, really everything was achy... and heavy.

She looked down at herself and found she wasn't tied to anything. A sliver of excitement made her heart race a fraction faster. Escape was possible.

Zander was busy checking in at the counter.

But by the time Violet managed to get her hand on the door handle, it opened for her and her arm fell helplessly at her side.

Red eyes blazed as Zander leaned toward her. "You wouldn't have been trying to sneak away, were you?"

"Of course I was."

He blinked. Then a low laugh rolled out of him. "I know you tend to be bluntly honest with me, but revealing your plan... that must be the drugs talking."

"You're the one who keeps giving them to me."

"Well, right now I need you to walk." He stretched an arm across her lap to unbuckle her, then hoisted her out of the car... er... truck... Violet stared at the giant black truck, then looked at Zander.

Her legs wobbled, then her knees buckled.

She crashed against his chest and his arms wrapped tightly around her waist. "To think, there was a time when you could take me in a fight." He nuzzled her hair and she pathetically tried to push away. "How times have changed."

The decaying citrus smell exuding from him twisted her stomach. "I think I'm gonna be sick."

"Again?" Zander turned her away from him.

Her mouth watered, but her stomach stayed put. There wasn't anything left to throw up anyway. She blinked at the truck. Oh, she was going to ask Zander about that. Keeping a train of thought was like trying to hold smoke in her hands.

"When did you get the truck?"

After closing the passenger door, Zander wiggled his arm around her waist and walked her toward the hotel doors. "It was a gift from Blood Moon."

Alarm bells sounded in her mind, but her heart remained steady. Stupid drugs. She had a much longer question, but the only word she managed to get out was, "Why?"

The arm around her waist tightened, crushing her to his side. His lips brushed the shell of her ear as he whispered, "For capturing the bait."

Bait?

For what?

Fish liked bait.

Why was she thinking about fish?

Violet groaned and mashed the heel of her hand against her eye. What had they been talking about?

"They promised me one night with you to celebrate your birthday."

Blood Moon. Bait. Violet gasped. Patrick. They were going to use her to lure Patrick.

"No!" Violet shoved against Zander's side, but his path toward the doors didn't alter. She clawed at the arm around her waist, but it tightened painfully, making it hard for her to breathe.

A quiet growl filled her ears and rumbled through her side that was smashed against his. "I suggest you stop making a scene, before I have to."

She tipped her face up to give a witty retort, but the words died on her tongue when crimson eyes glowered back.

"There's a young woman watching us, and she looks quite concerned. In fact..." he tipped his ear toward the girl he'd mentioned to his right. Her straw-colored braid swung over her shoulder as she turned to point at them. "She just told the guy she's with about us."

A young man joined the girl a second later, a severe look on his face. His brows pulled together when he caught sight of them. Then he turned to whisper in her ear.

"I suggest you make us believable as a couple, or you'll have two dead innocents on your hands."

"Stop trying to crush me then." Violet bit out, feeling a touch of her usual spark coming back.

Zander's eyes narrowed, but he finally relaxed his hold. The young man started toward them. Forcing a smile to her face, Violet wrapped an arm around Zander's waist, which would hopefully make his confining grip look more like a loving embrace, and then she tipped her head back. Watching other girls flirt with Patrick for years had apparently come in handy. The laugh that left her was full of false mirth, but it was believable enough to make the guy freeze in his approach.

He glanced back at his girl, shrugged, then continued to watch Violet and Zander.

A wide smile split Zander's face. His eyes returned to their normal blue and he nuzzled the top of her head. "Good girl. Keep it up."

Heat swarmed her cheeks as she played the girlfriend, laughing hysterically at something her boyfriend said instead of the girl who was drugged and kidnapped.

By the time they made it through the doors, the young man and woman had driven off, no longer suspecting foul play. Zander nodded at the woman behind the desk and then led Violet to the elevators.

It wasn't the nicest hotel ever, but it was multiple steps up from the one they'd been in before. However, there was an odd, slightly sour smell that wafted through the hall, mixed with the bleachy stench of an indoor chlorine pool. And a white patch of something marred the floor of the elevator... a stain?

Violet's stomach rolled as the elevator started moving.

Now was not the time to investigate whatever was on the floor.

The elevator jolted to a stop on the third floor, and Violet's knees buckled. Zander crushed her body against his. A nasty grin slipped across his face, which was way too close to hers.

"Wait till the room at least," he teased as the doors opened and a man in swim trunks and his towel-wrapped daughter waited to enter the elevator.

The man mumbled something to his daughter about ignoring them as Zander led Violet down the hall.

She could have run. A stairwell was close to the elevators, and she had always been a faster runner than Zander. There was a good chance she'd make it all the way down the stairs and out of the hotel... but then what? Anyone who saw her panic, or the fact that Zander was chasing her, because there was no way he would let her leave, could potentially lose their lives.

Fighting was always an option, but her limbs still felt like they were being tied down. Even lifting her arm to wrap it around Zander's waist had needed quite the amount of effort. She was weak. She was tired. She was *drugged*. He'd win.

Zander stopped in front of a door and pulled out a room key. An audible click sounded and he pushed the door open. "After you."

Even from the door, Violet could see there was only one bed. One large bed. With rose petals. She froze.

His arm left her waist to bruise her upper arm with his vice-like fingers. "Don't try it," he growled and his eyes flared red. "You know what will happen."

"Only if you catch me."

A dark laugh tipped Zander's head back. "Do you honestly believe I can't? From what I've heard, you've lost your fighting edge. Even Patrick said you were slower and weaker. Whereas, I've been going the opposite direction."

Violet jerked away, but his bruising hold never wavered. He dragged her over the door's threshold, and a small tremble entered her voice. "Please, don't do this."

Instead of softening his hold, Zander's eyes thinned to slits and he growled, "You didn't give me a choice." He yanked her toward him and into the room.

Using her opponent's strength against them was one of the first lessons Patrick had ever taught Violet. So, she did as she was taught. She lifted her arm as she was propelled forward and threw her fist out. Bone gave way under her knuckles and a sickening snap echoed in her ears. Zander reared back in rage and pain, holding his broken nose, as blood seeped through his fingers.

Breathing heavy, Violet bolted out the door and down the hall. The walls swayed as she ran, twisting her stomach. She misstepped, and her shoulder crashed against the wall.

Violet struggled to regain her step. Lead filled her legs, making them heavier and harder to lift with each stride.

Zander snagged a fistful of her shirt and tugged, careening her back. She choked down the scream that rose in her throat.

No one could hear them.

The fabric split, ripping her shirt along the side seam.

The elevator dinged.

Violet's heart sank.

No one could see them.

Zander snarled behind her, and goosebumps rose along her arms.

The elevator doors began to open. He seized her elbow, and the resounding thud of her back colliding with the wall rattled a nearby picture. Violet cried in outrage when Zander's body pressed against hers in an intimate imitation.

"Don't. Move," he snapped as the couple from the elevator approached them. "Or they die."

Whispers of inappropriate behavior made Violet's heart race. She opened her mouth to tell him to back off, but Zander's lips crashed against hers.

Violet's body tensed as she pinched her lips together and stared at him.

Rage circled behind the crimson in his gaze.

A door shut.

Zander lifted his head and ran a thumb along his bloody lip. "It's not how I imagined our first kiss, but it wasn't the worst either."

"Really?" Violet growled as he hauled her back toward the room. "Cause I can't think of anything worse."

"You'll change your mind soon." Zander opened the door and then tossed her through it.

Violet tripped and sprawled across the carpet. Unable to catch herself, her chin skidded over the rough surface, burning her skin. "Unlikely," she growled and rolled onto her back.

"Tonight's supposed to be a night to celebrate." Zander closed the door and secured the bolt at the top. "I even ordered champagne." He directed a hand toward a bottle resting on ice near the bed.

Violet swallowed the knot building in her throat. "I don't drink."

"Pity, I was hoping it would soften that sour tone of yours."

"I bet it will still work if you drink it."

Zander chuckled. "Nice try." He laid the backpack on the couch against the far wall and began unpacking things... like the stupid black restraints. "I won't be getting myself drunk so you can slip away again."

"Too bad," Violet said.

"By the way." Zander dug another bag out of the backpack and Violet's heart sank. "I found this in Lexie's car."

Violet's shopping bag dropped onto the floor beside her.

"Put it on."

Violet glared. "No."

Sighing, Zander squatted down and reached into the bag. Sage material cascaded over his fist as he lifted the dress. "You have two options. You can willingly change into this gorgeous little dress or…" Zander leaned toward her, and Violet pressed herself against the floor. "I'd be happy to help you into it."

Violet's breathing hitched. "You're disgusting."

"You won't think that for too much longer."

Violet yanked the dress out of his hands and rolled out from under him.

"Don't take too long," he called after her as she stepped into the bathroom.

She slammed the door shut, locked it, then threw the dress. It hit the beige shower wall helplessly, and then landed in a heap in the small tub. Her body trembled. She leaned back against the closed door and slowly slid to the cold tile.

She was feeling emotion and keeping a train of thought. Maybe she could get a message through to Jax or Patrick.

*"Jax?"* Violet prayed he could hear her. The void in her mind was vast and she couldn't feel even a hint of her twin. She imagined herself stretching out her hand for her brother. *"Jax, can you hear me?"*

The sweet scent of chocolate filled her senses and a warm voice filled her mind. *"He can hear you, Vi."* Her nickname said by Patrick's voice brought tears to her eyes. *"He just can't reach you. Keep talking. We'll find you."*

*"Patrick!"* She reached for his comforting presence, but it started slipping away the moment he stopped talking. Frustrated, she slammed her fists against her legs. After a few deep breaths, she tried to contact Jax again. *"I can't tell you much, but here's what I know…"*

She shared images she had seen, signs they had passed, people's faces she remembered, the details of the carpet and smells of the indoor pool. Any information she had gathered, she shouted into the void and hoped Jax could hear her.

*"Jax, tell Patrick to stay away. Send someone else! It's..."*

BANG! BANG! BANG!

Violet nearly jumped off the ground when the door rattled against her back under heavy assault.

"How long does it take to change into a dress?"

"I've been unconscious for hours! Excuse me if I needed to use the bathroom."

A growl sounded from the other side of the door. "If you're not out here in one minute, I'll break the door down."

"No, you won't." Violet scoffed. "That would make too much noise and you're trying not to draw attention."

"You overestimate how much I care anymore."

Violet sucked in a breath, then quietly made her way to her feet. She flushed the toilet to hide the fact that she hadn't been using it and quickly changed her clothes.

That sad truth was, he was right. She had been hoping he'd hold on to what was left of his sanity after killing that woman, but Zander was not Patrick. Zander killed on purpose. Zander kidnapped her. Zander drugged her. Zander was going to take her to Blood Moon...

He had no sanity left.

"Five. Four. Three."

"I'm almost done!" Violet snapped, the zipper stuck and she groaned. "You're the one who drugged me, you know. It's making everything more difficult." A wave of dizziness crashed over her and she gripped the counter to keep from falling over.

"I wouldn't have needed to take such drastic measures if I knew you would have come with me, but I know you, Violet." His voice turned airy. "I know you better than anyone. Even yourself."

Violet snorted and then muttered, "Yeah, right."

The zipper finally gave, and she glared into the mirror. Disgust wrinkled her nose. She'd been excited to wear the sage green dress tonight. The thought of Patrick's face when she joined the party had made her grin. It wasn't as though the dress was inappropriate, but it fit her as well as a dress could, accentuating her curves.

It was the last thing she wanted to wear in a secluded hotel room with the guy holding her captive.

"Violet!" Zander pounded against the door again.

"I'm struggling with the zipper," she lied. "I'll be out in a minute."

"I'd be happy to help with that."

Violet gagged, then wrenched the door open. "No thanks, I got it."

Frowning, Zander stepped out of her way so she could leave the bathroom. "Wow, you are—"

"Don't," Violet growled, trudging into the room. "I'm tired. I'm hungry. I've been drugged and kidnapped. I have cuts and bruises all over my body. I'm not what you're thinking and I don't want to hear you say it."

With a sigh, Zander made his way to the backpack. "It sounds like it's time for another dose. You're adapting faster each time. Much faster than I anticipated." He withdrew a syringe and a bottle as his face turned contemplative. "I guess I need to up the dosage, but I also want you awake for your birthday."

There was no way he was giving her another dose of whatever concoction he'd gotten his hands on. Violet crept up behind him thinking over her next move while he mumbled to himself. A kidney strike might give her time for another hit with the hopes of knocking him out. Once he was out, she'd tie him up using his own restraints. A bit of poetic justice. After that, she could figure out where they were and finish the plan.

Distress slowed her movements. What if Blood Moon was already there? She clenched her teeth. Then it was even more important that she found her own way out of there. Quickly.

She pulled her elbow back and—

Zander's log-like arm swung into her side, knocking her off balance. She stumbled over her feet only to trip. The desk cracked against the side of her head and black spots dotted her vision, making it difficult to catch herself as she fell. Even with her attempt, the ground welcomed her with a hard landing and she groaned.

"Why couldn't you just accept the fact that we're mates?" Zander's blue eyes gazed at her sorrowfully as he started toward her, the full syringe clutched in his fist. "Why couldn't you just accept me? Love me the way I am?"

The heels of Violet's hands dug into the carpet as she scooted backward. Whatever burst of energy she'd been given had drained from her with the blood now trickling down her hairline.

"Any chance I ever had of loving you disappeared the moment you killed that woman," she cried, tears falling down her cheeks.

His eyes flared red and the sorrow faded into fury, tightening his jaw and drawing his brows low. "You don't care that Patrick killed someone."

Her chin trembled when he knelt over her. "That was an accident."

Zander snagged her arm and she yelped. "It doesn't matter. You'll see. As soon as your birthday comes, you'll forget all about him." His bruising grip was a stark contrast against his other hand which lightly brushed her frizzy hair, the syringe handle grazing her skin. "You'll see. Soon we'll be happy together."

"Zander, don't!"

But it was too late. His strike was fast and true. The sedative was already in her by the time she'd finished. Hot tears burned her face, and he gathered her in his arms. She tried to shove him off, but the drugs worked quickly, and her limbs were weighed down. Heavy as an anvil, they hung limply at her sides as he laid her on the bed. Then they weighed nothing at all. She weighed nothing at all. For a brief moment, she worried she'd drift away, but then she wondered what she was worried about. Then she felt nothing.

# Chapter 23

## Violet

***Blurry, neon-red numbers glared*** *at Violet as she blinked the sleep from her eyes.*

11:49 pm

Slowly, she rolled her throbbing head, so she could stare at the ceiling. The room rocked as if she were on a boat, and her stomach flipped.

A groan left her, and she rolled onto her side before curling into a ball. Well, she would have if she could've moved her arms. Or legs.

Those blasted restraints were back. She shook her arm against one of them, but dropped it again when it was too heavy.

She needed someone strong.

Patrick was strong.

Man, that guy was hot.

Wait... what was she thinking about again?

A frustrated sigh left her, but then she wondered why she was sighing.

Muffled muttering sounded from across the room, "No. No, I don't wan... yes, I know that, but..."

Violet lifted her head to find Zander pacing across the far side of the room.

He curled a fist in his hair and then shook his head. "No. That's not what we..."

Crimson blazed in his eyes when he turned to look at her, but the room had gone all spinny so she clamped her eyes shut, dropping her head back on the pillow.

"It's almost time," Zander's voice evened out, sure and steady, and lower than she was used to.

The bed sank near her hips. Her eyes bugged when he brushed a hand along her side. Her vision was a little blurry, but only a blind man wouldn't be able to see that Zander had changed into a tux. Kinda an odd thing to wear when you weren't expecting to go anywhere.

She looked down at herself. Then again, he *had* made her change into the dress.

"Do you think anyone has noticed you're missing yet?"

A snort followed by some of the most awful laughter on the face of the planet left Violet. "Of course they know. I've been telling them where we were every chance I could."

Zander's face darkened and although his eyes stayed blue, there was a hardened, threatening edge. "What?"

"Granted, I haven't been able to tell them much. I have no idea what hotel we are in or what the last one was. I only saw a symbol and a couple of signs." She sighed. "That's not very helpful, is it?"

The deep, satisfied chuckle that rolled out of him sent goosebumps over her skin. "It's helpful to me."

"Well, I do love being helpful." She gave a toothy grin as a weird feeling of smugness settled over her, and she wobbled her head back and forth.

This time when Zander chuckled, the sound was lighthearted, almost sounding like her old friend. "You're a little out of it still, aren't you?"

His hand trailed down her jaw and throat. She knew she should be annoyed. And disgusted. Very disgusted. But she just rolled her eyes and looked at the clock.

11:56

"Thirty seconds," Zander whispered while caressing her arm.

Violet blinked at him, "Till what?"

He blinked back. "Uh… your birthday?"

"Really?" Violet looked at the clock again right as it flipped to 11:57.

She pulled her brows together and stared in confusion. "This isn't my birthday."

Zander's fingers curled into her chin, dragging her gaze back to him. "Yes, it is. Look at me. Don't you feel something?"

A small part of her wanted to bite his fingers for touching her, but that seemed like a lot of effort, so she just shrugged instead. "Nope."

The sound her lips made when she said the "p" sound made her giggle, then she did it a few more times.

"How could you not feel anything?" Zander growled, leaning away from her as his eyes burned red.

Violet shrugged again. "Because it's not my birthday."

Rage lit Zander's gaze. "You and Jax are twins!"

"Duh, but we weren't born the same minute."

His face softened a fraction. With a nod, he looked at the clock again. "When were you born then?"

"Why do you want to know?" She grinned. It was fun messing with him.

"You know why!" His voice dipped more wolf than human.

Violet nodded. "Right, you think you're my mate."

His eyes faded back to blue as they narrowed. "I don't think. I know."

"Mmm-hmm." She looked at the clock again.

Hey, her vision was getting clearer! The blocky red numbers weren't blurry anymore.

12:01 am

"Oh hey, my birthday is in one minute!"

"Really?" Zander asked, and even being drugged, she couldn't have missed the sarcasm in his tone.

Violet nodded, "Yup, I am officially eighteen riiiiiiiiiight..."

He leaned toward her.

"Now!" She looked up at him, and frowned. "Huh."

Zander shifted so he was practically leaning over her, "Huh what? You see that I was right, don't you?"

"I don't feel anything."

Zander jerked back. "What?"

"My arms and legs are heavy, but I don't really feel them."

He sighed and then traced his finger along her jawline. "That's a side effect of the sedative. It will wear off, I promise."

"I don't feel a rush of power. I don't feel connected to anything. I don't feel another presence."

As she listed things, Zander lowered his hand to rest beside her head. She turned to look at him, and her breathing hitched when his blue eyes met hers. The feeling of their old friendship washed over her, filling her with hope and warmth. An overwhelming scent of Cedar flooded her senses, but the moldy lemon that usually accompanied it was muted.

"No," she said softly when his presence filled her mind and she could sense his heartbeat.

A grin stretched across his face. "Yes. I told you. I've been telling you for months, Violet. We are mates." He straightened and extended his right hand upward. Two fingers in the shape of a V pointed at the white ceiling above then slowly crossed before he brought them to his lips. Sealing his next words with a kiss, he said, "I, Zander Silas Gladden..."

Violet shook her head.

"...under the light of the moon and with the goddess as my witness..."

"Zander, please don't."

"...accept thee, Violet Ayah Draven, as my mate."

A ripple of goosebumps ran across her skin from her head to her toes. The urge to take his vow and make it her own, as the bond demanded, pushed her to speak, but she bit her tongue to stop herself and give herself time to think.

He had been her friend once. They used to play chess together, and he could never win. They would train, and most of the time she would be the last one standing. Even though she was always beating him, he always had a smile on his face. Zander used to tell the best jokes. He had amazing hugs. He was the goofy kid everyone liked.

Even with all of that. Even with the mate bond pushing her to accept and reminding her of her old feelings for him... Violet knew what she had to do. She trembled as she whispered words of truth that would wreck him. "I don't feel anything for you, Zan."

Surprise swam in his vision. "What"

Tears filled her eyes. "The things I'm feeling are from the past, and you destroyed that version of yourself."

"No." He shook his head. "No, I'm still here."

"Zander..." she sighed. Pain and hatred lanced through her chest and she blinked at him. Those were not her emotions. She needed to end this before they grew even more connected. "I, Violet Ayah Draven, under the light of the moon and with the goddess as my witness, reject thee—"

"NO!"

His hand slammed into her throat, cutting off her words when he squeezed. "We'll give it time. You'll see. By the time the full moon comes around, you'll remember how good we are together."

A low simmer settled in her chest, and she wriggled under his hold. She coughed when he released her.

"You'll... cough... have to keep me... cough cough... sedated or gagged until then." She let out a raspy cough, and warning bells sounded in her mind when his eyes slowly swirled crimson. "I will reject you with my last breath if that's what it takes."

A low growl rumbled from Zander. "You don't mean that."

"Yes, I do," she promised. "I, Violet Ayah Draven, under the light of the moon—"

His hand fell over her mouth. "Violet, stop."

She held perfectly still until he sighed and moved away. "—and with the goddess as my witness—"

Zander's fingers clenched around her throat, cutting off her words and any air she might have breathed. Even with the sedative, panic spiked her veins, the simmer in her chest turned to a rumbling boil, and her limbs sprang to life. She flailed against the restraints, but Zander knew what he'd been doing. Beyond thrashing her shoulders about... she couldn't move.

"I told you." The growl of Mirko, Zander's wolf, startled her into freezing for a second. "She was never going to accept us."

Another wave of panic hit her, not her own.

Zander had lost control.

"She's either ours or no ones," Mirko snarled, tightening his fingers.

Little black dots danced in her vision.

*"I'm sorry, Violet!"* the boyish voice of young Zander cried in her mind.

A white-hot flash erupted from her chest, burning to the top of her head down to the tips of her toes. It built and burned until her head was knocked back and her body lurched off the bed.

Zander jumped away from her, screaming.

Violet sucked in enough oxygen to fill her lungs, then coughed. The dry, hoarse, rattly existence of what was left of her throat made her wince.

Screams of pain and terror vied for her attention and pulled her back to the present. She lifted her head as a blinding light slashed Zander's chest. His cry was cut short, and his body slumped to the ground.

Violet stared, wide-eyed as a wispy wolf turned away from him. Light blues, purples, and greens waved through the wolf's translucent fur. No blood marred its crystalline claws, but from the howls Zander made, he had been in severe pain.

The wolf, no bigger than an average, normal wolf, jumped onto the bed. The mattress didn't cave under its weight, and the blankets didn't shift.

Violet was beginning to wonder how much she was hallucinating, when the wolf laid down beside her, and its warmth poured over her like a brook over smooth river rock.

Violet's heavy breathing grew softer as she stared into molten gold, silver, and bronze kaleidoscope eyes. "What are you?" she rasped, and then coughed.

*"Rest, young one. You are safe."* The wolf's calm, warm feminine voice rolled through her mind like a summer breeze.

Violet cleared her throat as sleep tugged at her eyes. "Did you kill him?"

*"No, but he will be unconscious for some time."*

"Why doesn't he have any scratches?"

A very human sigh brushed through her thoughts. *"I can only attack the spirit, not the physical form."* She nodded to Violet's hands. *"Which is why I can't free you."*

The beautiful creature rested her head on Violet's stomach, but there was no weight to it. Only warmth. Warmth that fluttered through Violet, lulling her to sleep as she regained strength and feeling in her limbs.

"What are you?" Violet repeated sleepily in her raspy tone. "What's your name?"

*"Rest. You've over-exerted yourself. Sleep and heal."*

Violet's eyes shuttered.

*"Help is coming."*

# Chapter 24

## Jax

***By the time the day was over,*** *there was going to be a hole in the gray carpet* of Alpha House's gathering room from Jax's pacing. No one had heard from Violet in hours. The last time he'd spoken with Patrick, he was heading to a new hotel, one that seemed way too nice for Zander's style, but Jax trusted his friend's hunch.

Violet's messages had been cryptic and hard to decipher. It wasn't her fault. Jax was sure whatever Zander had done to her made any communication more difficult. The ones that bothered him were when she'd said it was a trick. It took them longer than it should have for them to realize they were heading the wrong direction. And telling Patrick to stay away. That didn't sound like Violet... but again... The goddess only knew what Violet was going through.

While he paced, Jax thought over the last few months and years, regretting every moment that he chose to push his sister away. Hating every command and order Alpha Draven gave him to do so. How could a father ask that of his kids?

When Patrick had first come to Sentinel Clan, Jax and Violet were nearly inseparable. Patrick became an easy third to their party, and they went everywhere together. He and Patrick were always protecting his little sister from everything... without her knowing, of course.

He still remembered the day he asked Patrick to keep her safe, no matter what. To make it his first priority.

Patrick hadn't hesitated. "Always."

He was an idiot for not seeing it then. For not seeing that his best friend was in love with his twin sister. Maybe he had and just didn't want to face it.

Jax tipped his head back and sighed at the ceiling, wishing he could reach Patrick... but Alpha Draven's banishment had taken a toll on their clan-link, and calling every five minutes was an intrusiom during a rescue operation.

He rubbed at the center of his chest, willing away the burn that had settled there.

*"It will stop soon,"* Dalim promised, Jax's wolf half was a comfort. Knowing he wasn't alone. Knowing someone else knew *exactly* how Jax felt... It was a huge relief. It also made him sad knowing Violet didn't have that.

*"She must feel so alone,"* he told his wolf.

*"To you, it would be strange to have me disappear, but to Violet."* Dalim sighed. *"Violet has never known the companionship of a wolf spirit. A quiet mind is what she's used to."*

*"I'm scared for her, Dalim."*

*"Do not forget how fierce our twin is."*

Jax smirked. The first time Dalim had called Violet his twin, Jax had argued with his wolf half. It took a while for him to understand that Dalim was just as much Violet's twin as he was.

The burn in his chest ignited into living flame, making him gasp, and searing his entire body. He trembled as raw, primal power stretched to the tips of his fingers and toes. It lifted the hairs on the back of his neck and poured goosebumps down his arms.

*"Happy birthday to us."*

Dalim's voice had never been clearer. Jax had felt like he heard his wolf spirit just fine, but this was as if Dalim was standing right beside him and speaking in his ear. And then, there were the other senses. The smell of the dirty dishes that had been left in the sink for merely an hour made Jax's nose scrunch. The scuffle of gravel and muted conversation outside from the wolven patrolling near the front door.

Warm vanilla filled his nose.

"Happy birthday, Jax."

Jax opened his eyes and barely resisted the urge to step away from his mother.

Distressed lines etched into her skin around her eyes, amplified by dark circles that hollowed out her face which was frailer than ever before. Her skin stretched over her knuckles as she reached for him and cupped his cheek with frigid fingertips.

Biting back his questions and worries, he offered a tight-lipped smile. "Thank you."

Her pale lips lifted into a smile. "And happy birthday to you too, Dalim."

"Thank you. It's a pleasure to officially meet you." Jax's mouth had moved, but it wasn't his words that came out. He shook his head and blinked as Dalim shrank back into his mind. "That was weird. Don't do that again."

Dalim laughed. *"You'll get used to it."*

Evalyn chuckled, but the sound had lost its comforting warmth that he'd heard every day of his life. It was breathy and weak. "Remember, you and Dalim are two sides of the same coin. You will work together as partners. He has as much right to speak as you do. You'll feel when he moves forward to speak and find that most of what he says falls right in line with how you feel."

*"We won't tell her that I'm a little more handsy with the ladies,"* Dalim whispered.

Jax coughed and bit his cheek. *"Those words will never be spoken again. Ever."*

Dalim laughed again.

The realization that his birth time had come and gone, pulled his attention to the clock. The numbers shifted to 12:02 am.

"Happy birthday, Violet," he breathed the words sadly, the gaping hole in his soul feeling for his twin. Working together, Jax and Dalim searched the recesses of their mind to find her... but it was dark and cold where her presence would normally reside. "I can't feel her. I thought for sure she would be stronger, but... Mom, what if we're too late?"

Evalyn wrung her aged hands and shook her head. "No. She's alive. I would know if she wasn't."

Jax's brows pulled low, and Dalim's curiosity matched his own. "How would you know?"

"The clan connection. Obviously."

Dalim growled. *"She's lying."*

*"I know."* Jax agreed as annoyance fluttered through him. Why would she think she could get away with a clumsy lie like that? "Violet can't connect to the clan."

Sucking in a slow breath, Evalyn shook her head. "I'm sorry. I... we should have kept you more informed about Violet's condition."

"Condition?" Jax stepped toward his mom. "Is Violet going to be okay?"

She held up a hand, signaling him to wait. "Have you ever met or heard of another set of wolven twins?"

Jax tipped his head to the side. "I know how rare Violet and I are, Mom."

"No, not rare." Evalyn grabbed one of his hands and held on like he was her lifeline. "Wolven twins are *impossible*."

He slammed his brows down. "What?"

*"Listen to her, Jax. She's trying to explain."*

Jax grumbled to him, but remained silent as his mom continued.

"Call it what you will; fate, survival of the fittest, moon blessed by a wolf spirit, or plain hormones... but only one child ever survives beyond the first twenty-four hours. People don't talk about their twins... if they even knew they existed."

Her words replayed in Jax's mind, and his breathing quickened as puzzle pieces fell into place. "What did you do to her?"

Evalyn shook her head, her dark brown hair, a mirror image of Violet's, swung around her shoulders. "Not to her. *For* her." She directed him to the couch and he hesitantly sat while she paced a step or two back and forth. "I knew you were the strong one. Strong and beautiful and perfect. I knew you would have the wolf." She dropped her hands to her sides and stared at the couch beside him. "But I couldn't lose her. She was my baby girl. So, I found a—"

She gasped, loud and sudden, making Jax jump off the couch. Her head tipped back, her mouth hanging agape, while her swirling wolf eyes faded to white. Her body shook uncontrollably, and then... it stopped. Her eyes shut, and Evalyn collapsed.

"Mom!" Jax shouted, catching her before she hit the floor.

Panic scorched his nerves as he laid his mother on the couch. Her pulse was weak, her skin paler than before, and if he thought she had been cold earlier, she was like ice now. One of her heels had fallen from her feet and he frantically grabbed it. He didn't know why it was so important for her to have her shoes on, but it was. It slid onto her foot while Jax called his dad through the link.

Only seconds passed, and Alpha Draven stormed into the room, eyes blazing molten gold as he took in the scene. His gaze fell to Evalyn, and his features softened, sorrow wetting his ombre blue eyes... and then, sorrow vanished, giving way to cut glass and hard, angry features.

"She collapsed. We need Dr..."

"No," growled Alpha Draven. His fingers curled into fists. "The doctor can't help with this."

Anger hammered through Jax's heart and Dalim snarled in his mind. "What? Mom needs help!"

"I said a doctor can't help!"

The power the alpha wielded pulsed through the room, making Jax's head drop immediately, but for the first time in his life, Jax fought to meet his father's gaze again. An unspoken challenge passed between father and son. A challenge Jax had never wanted to invoke before now.

Jax's nose wrinkled as he glared at Alpha Draven. Dalim pressed forward, and Jax stepped aside, allowing his wolf spirit the same control he had. His newfound power exuded from his being, and the alpha's shoulders trembled as they lowered a fraction.

Surprise softened the rage in Alpha Draven's eyes. His shoulders sagged.

They both knew what it meant if Jax could resist and press back against his father's command. His *alpha's* command. And although Alpha Draven had been raising Jax to take over one day, it was clear the alpha wasn't ready to relinquish his power just yet.

"She brought this on herself," the stranger of a man growled, before backing out of the room. It was the first time Jax had seen him refuse to turn his back on someone.

Confusion, rage, horror, and a bunch of other emotions tumbled through Jax as he watched his father walk away.

Ignoring Alpha Draven's words, Jax opened his mind to the clan and seized hold of Dr. Penmann's essence. *"Doc, I need you at Alpha House. Luna has collapsed."*

A hesitant presence entered Jax's mind and the doc's raspy voice filled his thoughts. *"I'm sorry, Jax. The alpha has told me I'm not to interfere."*

Fury shook Jax's hands. *"I am your future alpha and now have the ability to challenge my father. Your Luna needs you. Get here* now."

As if she had been waiting for the order, Dr. Penmann responded loud and clear, *"On my way, future alpha."*

Jax's phone rang, loud and awfully high-pitched. He flinched against the ringtone he'd once loved.

*"Yeah, that's obnoxious,"* Dalim announced.

*"I'll change it,"* he told his wolf as he checked the screen.

Patrick's name was all he saw before he had answered and shoved the device against his ear.

"Have you found her?"

"Yes." Patrick growled, low and quiet.

"Is she okay?"

"She better be," Patrick and Dalim answered at the same time.

*"If she's hurt, we will tear Zander apart, piece by piece."*

*"I think that's Patrick's right,"* Jax reminded Dalim.

A quiet beep echoed through the phone, and a small amount of disappointment rattled through Jax. "Did you just use a key card? Why not just break the door down?"

"Violet," Patrick said softly, ignoring Jax. "Violet, can you hear me?"

Jax held his breath, waiting for his friend to update him... waiting to hear his twin's voice.

A sigh filled the phone. "She's unconscious, but seems physically okay. For the most part."

Jax and Dalim growled as one. "Most part?"

"Don't worry, Jax. We've got her. She's safe."

Pushing down the fury, Jax allowed relief to settle in his bones, sinking his shoulders as he knelt on the ground beside his mom. "Thank you, Patrick."

"Always."

They said their goodbyes, and Jax dropped his head into his hands. He drew in a few shaky breaths then gathered his mom's cold hand in his. "He found her, Mom. Patrick found her. She's okay." He focused on his hearing, and her thready heartbeat made his pulse faster. His mouth ran dry. "You need to be okay, too."

# Chapter 25

## Violet

***I reject thee...*** *Reject thee... I reject...*

Violet moaned and rolled to her side. Her body ached. A low fever burned her from the inside out.

"Hang on, Vi." Patrick's comforting voice settled deep in her bones. "Let's get you home."

The comfort didn't last.

Violet's eyes fluttered open to light gray walls. The small desk and walled-off bathroom area clued her in that she was in Sentinel Clan's Lockup. She pinched her eyes shut again and curled in on herself as she groaned.

"Violet?"

Mya's worried tone called her from her wallowing state, and she slowly opened her eyes to a concerned green gaze.

"Hi." Her voice was still raspy and the one word made her cough.

Mya launched away from the bed, hurried to the desk, grabbed a small cup, and pushed it into Violet's hands after she sat up. "Doc said you would need to drink this when you woke up. The damage to your throat was pretty bad."

The liquid was warm and savory, with a hint of sweetness. She wasn't sure what she was drinking, but it eased the rawness of her throat, and that was good enough for her. If only it could help with the ache in her bones. "Where is everyone?"

Twisting a chestnut coil around her finger, Mya glanced at the door. "We've been taking shifts. You've been out for a couple days."

"Days?" Violet shrieked, which made her cough again. Once the fit passed, she tried again in a much quieter voice. "I've really been out for days?"

"Just two, but yeah." Mya pulled one knee toward her chest, bracing her heel on the chair she sat on. "Doc kept you under at first. You spiked a really high fever, were shaking uncontrollably and kept muttering things about spirit wolves." She cast her eyes down. "And... rejecting Zander."

Violet looked at her hands, resting in her lap. "Oh."

"So... he was right then? You were his mate?"

"Am." Violet corrected and hot tears gathered in her eyes. "I *am* his mate."

"But you were talking—"

"It didn't work." Violet lifted her gaze to Mya who was leaning forward in her chair now, both feet on the ground. "I tried to reject him. He kept stopping me. And then..." she softly brushed her hand over her throat. "Zander lost control and Mirko tried to kill me."

Mya bit her lips together and watched Violet with raised, pinched brows. After a tense minute of silence, she finally said, "That answers one question."

Tipping her head to the side, Violet waited for her friend to explain.

"You have some pretty nasty bruising on your neck." Mya indicated to her own throat for reference. "It was pretty obvious you were choked, we just didn't know why."

After a nod, Violet looked around the room. A cot was set up against the plexiglass wall, just as Jax had done when Patrick had been here. "Jax has been sleeping here?"

It was Mya's turn to nod, and her curls bounced a little as she did. "He hasn't left your side since you were brought back."

"And Patrick?"

Sorrow dragged Mya's face down. "He... didn't come back."

Violet blinked at her friend, thinking she had heard her wrong, but Mya didn't take it back. It wasn't a mistake. It wasn't a joke. Her heart began to race. "What?"

"I'll take it from here, Mya."

Violet whipped her head toward the open plexiglass wall to find Jax watching her with relieved, wide eyes. "Jax, where is Patrick?"

Her twin stepped into the room and claimed a seat at the foot of her bed. He seemed... older than before. His demeanor was calmer than it had been in months, and a sense of assurance, or maybe confidence, exuded from him. "Patrick's place in Sentinel Clan has been dissolved," Jax explained in a gentle, cautious tone. "Alpha Draven banished him right before he left to find you."

Violet shook her head. She had to still be dreaming. This was a nightmare. Her life had turned into a nightmare.

"Patrick didn't want to trespass or bring any more harm or threats to the clan, so he had Cas bring you home." Jax drew in a breath so deep that it lifted his shoulders. They sagged when he sighed. "I don't know where Patrick is. I can't reach him through the clan-link anymore, and he won't answer my calls."

Pain cracked in her chest. Violet wrapped her arms around herself and refused to let the tears burning her eyes fall. She would not cry over a decision her father made. "Do you think he'll come back?" she asked. "When you're alpha?"

Jax shook his head. "I don't know... but I'll have to find a new beta before then."

Violet bit her lip and nodded.

A surprised gasp left her when he lunged toward her and threw his arms around her shoulders. "I'm glad you're okay."

That did it. She wrapped her arms around his waist as tears rolled down her cheeks in heavy waves. Deep, bone-wracking sobs shook her body, and Jax's hold tightened.

"It's okay," he whispered. His hand rubbed up and down her back while she cried. "You're safe."

She didn't know how long they sat like that, but it was the best hug they'd shared in a long time. Years had passed in cold, distant, and aggressive comments. This was like that time had never happened. She had her twin back, and that was a huge blessing. Maybe it wouldn't last. Maybe he would start to push her away again, but in this moment it felt like a new beginning.

"Not to break up the happy reunion," the raspy voice of Dr. Penmann filled the quiet space. "But I need to check on Violet, and we have other news to share."

Jax cleared his throat, and Violet wasn't about to comment on the moisture gathering in his eyes when he pulled away from her. "By all means," he directed a hand from the doc to Violet. "Please make sure she's healing properly."

As the doc made her way to Violet's bed, Mya stood to offer her the chair. Together, Jax and Mya watched with anxious expressions as Dr. Penmann ran her vitals.

"Well, you're healing, and that's the most important part," the doc said, sitting back in her chair. "Without knowing exactly what Zander gave you, I've been playing a bit of a guessing game, but I think most of that should be out of your system."

"I didn't wake up dizzy or nauseous, so that's a good sign to me." Violet gave a thumbs up and a small smile tugged at everyone's mouth.

Doc's gaze dropped to Violet's throat. "Unfortunately, only time will tell how your voice will heal." She traced her fingers over the scar crossing her neck. "But I'm glad you're able to speak. I have a remedy for you to drink three times a day that should help."

Mya cleared her throat. "I gave it to her as soon as she woke up."

"Thank you." A weary sigh left the doc. It dropped her shoulders and she turned to look at Jax. "As for other news."

Sorrow crossed over Jax's eyes. "Right. There's something... Um..." His eyes swirled into molten gold and an air of assurance straightened his spine. "Jax's emotions are running a little high at the moment. I'll take over for now."

Violet's eyes widened. "Dalim?"

A soft smirk lifted one corner of Jax's mouth. "Hey, sis." He moved to her side and sat on the edge of the bed. "While you were gone, Mom's health took a turn for the worse."

Violet sucked in a sharp breath.

"She lost consciousness the night you were found and has been very weak sinse."

"Is she okay?" Violet looked at Dr. Penmann and then Jax... er... Dalim again. "I mean, I know she's been sick for a while, but..."

The doc nodded. "She's stable. Weak, but stable. She's been ordered to rest more than work, but I know where you get your stubbornness from, so I doubt she'll listen to me."

Violet huffed a laugh, but it sounded more like a sob. "Can I see her?"

"Of course." Dr. Penmann stood and shoved her hands in her lab coat pockets. "I think you're healed enough to get out of here. And sorry for the placement, but these rooms are better suited for long-term than my clinic rooms are." She looked around, then nodded. "Mya's been a huge help in taking care of you, as well."

"Thanks, Doc." Mya beamed.

"One more question," Violet called when the doc turned to leave. "I don't really know who to ask, so I'm just asking all of you. Did you find Lexie?"

Any happiness that had been in the room disappeared.

Worry crashed over Mya's features, dragging her smile down.

Dr. Penmann looked bone tired.

Dalim scowled, his eyes blazing so bright it cast small bits of golden light over his cheekbones. "No," he growled. "But we will."

# Chapter 26

## Violet

***"Are you sure you want** to come with me?" Violet asked Jax* for the fiftieth time as they stepped out of the car.

Jax walked around the hood, joining her on the sidewalk. "You're never going anywhere alone again. Besides..." He glanced at the house they were parked in front of. "We may not like each other very much, but Lexie's my friend too."

After leaving Lockup, Violet immediately found her mom, but Evalyn Draven had been sleeping, pale as a ghost, in her bed. Jax had convinced her to wait and assured her that their mom's heart was beating. With his new connection to Dalim, Jax could do a lot of things. Hearing heartbeats was one of those new abilities, but only if he concentrated pretty hard and there wasn't a lot of interference.

In the time that she was waiting, Violet knew she needed to see Lexie's parents.

"I don't think that's a good idea," Jax had told her. "You were just kidnapped. You shouldn't be leaving the base."

Violet sighed. "They know she was with me. I need to tell them what I can."

"And what can you tell them?" He waited for her to respond, but when she didn't, he continued, "They don't know about us, and they can't."

"I know." She started for the parking lot. "I'll figure it out, but I'm going. You can either throw me in Lockup or assign someone to go with me."

Red tinged Jax's face. "I'm going with you."

And that's how they ended up staring at Lexie's hunter-green family home. Violet crossed the stepping stones lining the right side of their driveway, and brushed her fingertips over the hip-height hedges on her right.

Only a few weeks had passed since Lexie had opened the front door, and in her pink llama pajamas, nearly tackled Violet. That was the morning she'd been attacked... She stopped walking.

Jax immediately turned toward her. "What's wrong?"

"Do you think Zander was the one who attacked me?

Concern pinched Jax's face and he rested a hand on her shoulder. "Violet, Zander *did* attack you... remember?"

Violet eyed him like he had three heads, but then shook her head. "What? No. I meant when I was staying with Lexie. The last morning I was here, some guy attacked me while I was out on my run."

"Oh, yeah, I remember you mentioning something like that." Jax sighed, and his hand fell back to his side. "I don't know. I don't think he's capable of doing that, but I didn't think he was capable of kidnapping either. Did you catch the guy's scent?"

Violet groaned. "The coffee shop we were next to drowned out everything. All I could smell was coffee."

"Okay." He shifted his weight, glanced at the house, then back to her. "Whether it was Zander or not, Lexie is missing." His gaze fell to the ground. "I don't understand what any wolven would want with a human. I don't know where she went or if she was taken."

"Lexie wouldn't have run away, Jax," Violet snapped.

Jax's attention shot to hers. Sorrow deepened the purple in his eyes and worry pulled at his features. "I know," he nearly whispered. "But Zander didn't take her. So, who did?"

Words came to her tongue and she opened her mouth to let them out, but they died before they could be said. She didn't know either. Tears gathered in her eyes, and she shook her head. "I don't know."

Sighing, Jax seized her shoulders, and hauled her into a bear hug. His chin rested atop her head, and she circled her arms around his waist. "I know Lexie and I fight like..."

"Like you'd die if you stopped?" Violet mumbled against his chest.

He huffed a laugh, making her head bounce. "I was going to say, like a..."

"An old married couple?"

"Very funny." Jax pushed her away until she was at arm's length. "I like her. She's a great friend to you. She's a good person." Another burst of laughter left him. "And I'd be lying if I said I didn't miss our fights."

Violet sobbed a laugh.

Pulling her in for another tight hug, Jax said, "We'll find her. We won't stop looking until we do."

Muffled barking dragged their attention toward the house.

"That's Thor."

Jax groaned. "You didn't tell me she had a dog."

Shooting a glare at him, Violet made her way toward the front door. "Be nice. Thor loves me."

"Yeah..." He heartily knocked on the wood. "We'll see how he feels about me."

A small smile tugged at Violet's mouth.

"You're sure you don't want to cover that?" Jax asked, indicating to her neck.

Self-consciously she touched the bruised flesh. She'd only had a quick glimpse, but it was still very dark with blues and purples. Only the outer edges had begun to lighten.

She didn't get the chance to tell him either way.

The door ripped open, exposing the two hopeful faces of Lexie's parents. Thor shoved passed their legs and planted his front paws on Violet's thighs, begging for attention.

"Violet!" Mrs. Davies lurched forward. Thor jumped out of the way as the older woman's arms banded around Violet. A bone-rattling sob shook Mrs. Davies' body.

Violet buried her face against Mrs. Davies' shoulder.

Mrs. Davies always wore a small amount of perfume, but for once Violet didn't mind. The strong scent of lilac didn't hide the familiar scent of Lexie's family. She hadn't been able to place it before, but it was warm and homey. Like snuggling up under a fuzzy blanket in front of a fireplace. Lexie's own scent was always a bit woodsier than her mom's or dad's.

Tears slipped down her cheeks, falling against Mrs. Davies' gray sweater.

"Thank goodness you're alright," Mrs. Davies spoke through her tears, then kissed the side of Violet's head, narrowly missing the cut across her cheekbone from smashing her head in the hotel. "We've been so worried."

"I'm so… so sorry." Violet rasped, her tears making the sound worse. "I couldn't protect her."

Mrs. Davies leaned back and gazed at her incredulously. "No. Don't you dare blame yourself for this." Her blue eyes lowered to Violet's neck and moisture pooled before spilling down her cheeks. "Oh, honey." She met Violet's gaze again and shook her head. "This is not your fault."

Hot, guilty tears cascaded from Violet's eyes. "I'm so worried about her."

"I know." Mrs. Davies nodded, gently stroking Violet's hair. "I know, but the police are looking for her. We've spread her picture, and others are doing the same. We'll find her."

Mr. Davies stepped out of the house. His expression was severe, but not unkind, just like his voice which was raw with emotion. "It's good to see you made it home." He rested a hand on his wife's shoulder. "It gives us hope that Lexie will make it home, too."

Thor jumped against her leg, and Violet shot him a quick look before patting his head. "Hi, boy. I missed you, too."

"And who is this young man you brought with you?"

Mr. Davies' voice pulled her attention away from the dog. "Oh, this is my twin."

A sly smirk tilted one corner of Mrs. Davies' lips, saddened as it was. "Jax, right? I've heard a lot about you."

"Uh oh," Jax muttered, drawing short laughter from the married couple. "Lexie and I had a way with words when we were around each other."

Mr. Davies nodded. "So, we heard." He wrapped an arm around his wife's shoulders. "There always happened to be a compliment somewhere in the mix of Lexie's raving though." A hint of a smile touched the corners of his mouth when his wife gazed at him. "It reminds us of another couple we know."

Jax shook his head. "Oh, no, I think..." His chest heaved heavily twice and then stopped. Lexie's parents looked at him with concern before he drew in a deep breath and tried again. "Lexie and I aren't a couple." He glanced at Violet, then looked at Lexie's dad. "She deserves better than me."

Understanding smoothed Mr. Davies' face and deep respect filled the older man's eyes. "I've come to understand that most of the young men who realize that are usually more worthy than they know."

"I..." Jax closed his mouth. His jaw tightened and then he nodded.

"Where are our manners?" Mrs. Davis wiped at her eyes and lightly smacked her husband's chest. "Do you want to come in?"

Violet looked at Jax who caught her gaze and raised his brows.

*"It's up to you,"* Jax told her through their twin-link. *"But Doc told me a minute ago that Mom is awake."*

"Thank you," Violet answered, her voice more gravelly than it had been when they arrived. "But we need to get back home. I just wanted to stop by and check in with y—." Her voice gave out, and she laid a hand over her throat.

Mrs. Davies' eyes tracked her movement, and fresh tears gathered in her eyes. "Thank you for coming. You know you're welcome anytime."

Violet nodded, then smiled her thanks.

Jax held out a hand toward Lexie's dad. "It was nice to meet you."

Mr. Davies grasped his hand and held it. "That invitation is extended to you too, Jax."

Jax's throat bobbed when he swallowed, then he gave a sharp nod. "Thank you."

Violet hugged Thor goodbye before she and Jax made their way back to his car. Lexie's parents stood on their front porch, arms wrapped around one another, watching until Jax had driven them out of sight.

"Jax?" Violet breathed her twin's name as they pulled onto the road that would take them into Yosemite National Forest toward Sentinel Dome. "Do you like Lexie?"

His knuckles bleached against the car's steering wheel. "Stop talking.

You'll make your voice worse. You need another dose of Doc's drink stuff."

Violet shot him an annoyed look and then opened their twin-link. *"Answer the question."*

A sigh eased the tension in Jax's shoulders. "I already told you I like Lexie. She's a good friend to you."

*"That's not what I meant and you know it."*

With a quick glance her way, he shook his head. "We just need to find her."

Avoiding the question would only work so long, but Violet didn't have the energy to argue, and instead settled into her seat. She missed the rumble of Patrick's old truck, and the blasting heat it would pummel against your face if you weren't careful where the vent was pointing. Closing her eyes, Violet longed for the bench seat he'd pulled her across to let her rest on his shoulder while he drove.

Violet clenched her jaw as tears welled behind her lids.

She would not cry.

There were ways he could contact her if he wanted. Patrick had her cell number. The fact that he hadn't told her he was cutting all ties... No matter what their kiss meant a few nights ago.

A stray tear deserted her resolve and splashed off her lashes. She quickly swiped it away, but not without being noticed.

Jax's warm hand landed on her arm. "I'm sorry," he breathed, the words caught in his throat.

"For what?" Violet croaked. Hopefully, more of Doc's magic drink would help ease her vocal cords again.

"I can feel it." His hand released her arm to press against his chest. "You're in pain."

More tears fell, and she angrily dragged her sleeves down her face. She was so sick of crying.

Jax rested his hand on the gear shift. "I'm sorry he's gone."

She froze with her sleeves partially covering her face, then she slowly returned her hands to her lap.

"I'm sorry Lexie's missing."

Violet looked at him in time to see his jaw tense. His eyes swirled with gold for a moment, but quickly returned to their shared amethyst hue.

"I'm sorry for the last few years. I promise I'll make it up to you... somehow." His eyes flooded with gold again and a slightly more gravelly version of his voice said, "*We* will make it up to you."

Hesitantly, Violet wrapped her fingers around Jax's hand. He lightly squeezed her fingers and then held on the rest of the drive. She didn't know what had changed, or why he was acting more like the brother he once was, but she was so glad for it.

They made their way to Alpha House as soon as they stepped out of the car. Violet made a beeline for her mom's room, and then froze in the doorway when Evalyn was folding laundry.

"Mom?" Violet rasped.

Evalyn's attention snapped to her daughter, and the laundry was forgotten. Her mom's arms were around her shoulders before the article of clothing she'd been working on dropped to the bed.

"Oh, my little miracle!" Evalyn cried against the top of Violet's head.

Violet slipped her arms around her mom's tiny waist and gingerly hugged her back. She'd never felt so fragile. Fear for her mom spiked, making her lean away until Evalyn finally released her.

"Are you okay? Doc said..." Her eyes fell to Violet's throat. A vortex of colors created a kaleidoscope in Evalyn's gaze. "Does it hurt?"

"Some," Violet admitted and clenched her fists at her sides so she wouldn't touch her neck. "Zander has a tight grip."

The kaleidoscope turned nearly luminescent. "If he ever shows his face again, I'll..."

Violet stepped back. "What?" She turned to look at Jax who had been standing silently behind her and now stared at the ground.

He shook his head. "He ran off as soon as Cas and Patrick arrived. Getting you home was the priority. If he ever tries to come back—"

"Tries to come back?" Violet's voice cracked. Pain pinched her brows together, and she fluttered a hand over her throat.

Jax's gaze tensed, then he nodded. "Doc is on her way with your remedy. We should have gone there first."

She shook her head. *"No. I wanted to see mom. Do we have any leads on*

*Zander?*"

Crestfallen, Jax leaned against the door frame. "No. We don't, but he won't ever come near you again."

"He has to," Violet whispered. "I need to reject him."

"Violet?" Evalyn touched her arm, drawing her attention yet again. "What are you talking about?"

There was no beating around the bush or trying to deny it. She had felt the wave of familiarity wash over her. The unwavering sense that somehow, they were more deeply connected. Even through her drugged state, she knew. He'd tried to tell her, but she'd refused to listen.

"Zander's my mate."

Her mom shook her head, and brought her fingertips to her mouth.

"That's not right," Jax said. "It can't be."

Angry that he didn't believe her, Violet spun around and glared. "Why not?"

"Because Patrick is your mate."

Violet swallowed the lump in her throat and then winced. "As much as I wish that were true, it's not."

Jax pressed away from the door frame. "It is. He told me himself right before our meeting with Stanislaus. And it's a good thing he did, because I punched him for hurting you and was about to do it again."

"You punched Patrick?" Evalyn asked at the same time Violet said, "He told you I'm his mate?"

Dr. Penmann appeared behind Jax and pointed at Violet. "You need to stop talking so much, or your voice will not heal as well as we are hoping."

Jax moved so she could walk into the room. Three eight-ounce water bottles rested in her hands and she handed one of them to Violet. Warmth seeped through her fingers as Violet held the bottle and unscrewed the cap.

"You need to drink one of these before bed and then another right after you wake up in the morning," Dr. Penmann explained while Violet drank. "Once you've done that, come find me, and I'll fill them up. They'll have a more soothing effect if they're warm, but cold works, too."

Instant relief crashed over her as the pain in her throat ebbed. "Tha—"

"Ah!" The doc held up a finger, silencing Violet. "No talking!"

A sheepish grin spread across Violet's mouth.

"But you're welcome." Dr. Penmann smiled at her and then turned to Evalyn. "You were told to rest."

Evalyn sighed. "I don't do well sitting still. You know that." She glanced at the laundry spread across her bed. "Besides, it's not like laundry takes that much energy to do."

The doc rubbed her temple and groaned. "Alphas, lunas, and their children. You all make horrible patients."

Jax, Violet, and Evalyn all grinned at each other. It was true.

"Fine. Finish the laundry and then get back in bed."

"But Viol—"

"No buts!" Dr. Penmann snapped, her permanently raspy voice cracking ever so slightly. "If you want to be with your daughter for the full moon tomorrow, then you will rest."

Adequately chastised, Evalyn nodded. "Understood."

Dr. Penmann made her way out of the room, sighing and shaking her head at all of them.

When she was gone, Violet looked at Jax. *"I totally forgot about the full moon tomorrow. Who is going with you?"*

"No one. I'll be going alone."

"Not completely," their mom corrected before Violet could snap at her twin. "He will have ten warriors with him, but he will be alone in the ring."

*"Are you sure you want to go alone?"*

Jax's throat bobbed as he swallowed, betraying his nerves. "I'll be okay. Dalim and I are ready for this." His eyes turned golden, and Dalim added, "Don't worry, sis. I'll take care of him."

A soft smile tipped the corners of Violet's mouth up. She felt it. A deep contentment settled into her bones. Jax and Dalim would be just fine.

# Chapter 27

## Patrick

***Anvils weighed down Patrick's limbs.***

*That was the only explanation for why his arms felt so heavy.*

His fingers tingled.

A dark chuckle rolled through the room. "... greater effect than..."

He knew that voice. Why was Vikter there?

The broken sentences of a second male said, "Didn't realize... the wolfsbane must..."

Decaying lemon assaulted his nose, and a low growl rippled out of him.

"Your beast is waking," said a female voice he didn't recognize. "If you want to keep him... too strong, otherwise."

Vikter's voice turned whiny. "Why do I..."

An annoyed snort sounded. "I got it."

Patrick's brows pulled together as he forced his eyes open. It was like they had been swollen shut. It was impossible to open them more than a crack, and it was useless. His vision was hazy. So hazy that only blobs of color were discernible.

"Back to sleep for you, Patrick." A cold hand clamped over his arm and felt a pinprick before fire raced through his veins. "We can't have you escaping or calling for help."

Not that he could anyway. His connection to the clan had been dissolved. He couldn't sense any member of Sentinel Clan. Not even Violet.

Patrick trembled with pain as he turned his head to glare at Zander... but the scent of moldy lemons must have been from somewhere else because the person at his arm was not Zander. His features were blurry, but Patrick recognized the scar running the length of his face and neck.

Violet called the lycan Scar Face. He and another Blood Moon member had attacked her and Lexie during the Clan Games. Scar Face had been in Lockup, until it was raided.

But Patrick had known him long before the scar had marred his face. "Topher."

"That's a name I haven't heard in a while. People here call me Dev." Fangs peaked through Topher's wicked grin. He yanked the syringe out of Patrick's arm. "I wondered if the prince remembered me. You put on a good show for your little friend."

Topher shoved Patrick's arm away, and it swung momentarily, suspended by chains from the ceiling and secured further by links extending from the wall. Two points for each arm to be secured. At least he was sitting, but the chair was metal, as well, and his feet were chained to the front legs. Even if he regained the strength to attempt an escape, it wouldn't be easy.

"I'm sure you miss her." Topher sneered.

Patrick let out a heavy, labored breath when the burning in his veins intensified. Black spots dotted his vision.

"Don't worry." Topher's voice sounded distant. "She'll be joining the two of you soon."

He pointed at something to Patrick's left, and his hearty laugh echoed in Patrick's ears.

Patrick turned his head and caught a glimpse of white-blond hair splayed across the ground before darkness fell over him.

# Chapter 28

## Violet

***"Will you be my anchor tonight?"***

*The memory of Patrick asking for her help swam in her head* as she watched Jax stuff his essentials into his car.

*"If anyone can help me get through this, it's you."*

Violet pinched her eyes shut.

*"Are you scared I'm going to say no?" she'd whispered.*

*Patrick's gaze had dropped to her mouth when she'd spoken, then he'd met her gaze again with creased brows. "Terrified."*

*"Do you really think I would?"*

*"With how mad you were, anything was possible."*

A smile grin tugged at a corner of her mouth. Yeah… she had been extremely mad at him. Her grin slipped. As mad as she was, Violet would have done anything for him.

"I think that's everything," Jax announced, drawing her back to the present.

Violet opened her eyes to find her twin backing out of his car to place his hands on his hips. He gave everything one more look, then nodded and closed the door.

"Are you sure you don't want to take someone with you?" Violet followed him around to the driver's door.

A loud snort left her twin, and he tossed a glance toward the two vans filled with Sentinel warriors ready to protect him with their lives. The driver nodded to him. They were ready to go when he was.

"I think I have a big enough entourage."

"I know, but Jax—"

"Hey." He spun toward her with a light, open expression on his face. "I know you're worried, but I'll be fine." His hands landed on her shoulders and gave a soft squeeze. "Dalim and I will ace this trial thing and be back before you know it."

Violet drew in a deep breath. Her chest fell when she exhaled, and Jax's light expression pinched a little. She rubbed her sternum where a weight had been pressing on her since she'd woken up. No vision, but she hadn't had them in a while. This was just an ominous feeling... and it didn't settle well.

"You didn't have a dream last night?" Jax asked for the umpteenth time since this morning.

Now they were staring down the barrel of a darkening sky and Violet wished she had more answers. Shaking her head, she sighed. "No, but that doesn't mean..." She shrugged. "I don't know what it means."

Jax nodded. "I'll be careful." He looked at the wolven warriors waiting for him. "And besides, they won't let anything happen to me."

"What if something happens while you're gone?"

"That's exactly why I argued mom down to only sending ten warriors with me."

A huff of laughter left her.

Jax pulled her in for a hearty hug and drew in a deep breath.

"Please come home safe," Violet whispered, squeezing her twin a little tighter.

"Of course I'm coming home. It's just the trial." Jax gently pulled away, his brows creasing in the center. "Are you okay?"

Violet fiddled with his jacket collar. "Aiden is dead. Lexie is missing. Patrick is gone. I can't lose anyone else."

Sorrow darkened his eyes. "I'm coming home, Violet. We're going to figure this out. We'll find Lexie. When the time is right, I'll take over the clan and bring Patrick home. I promise."

He pulled her in for one last hug, kissed the top of her head, then broke away to open the driver's door.

"You don't have any world-breaking secrets to get off your chest, do you?"

Jax looked at her from the driver's seat with a raised brow. "No?"

She smirked as the image of Patrick's eyes swirling blood red for the first time surfaced in her memories. "Good. I don't think I could take them right now."

He smiled, then shook his head. "I'll see you tomorrow morning."

The engine revved, and Violet stepped away from the car. With a final wave goodbye, Jax followed after the two warrior-filled vans to the trial ring. Violet wondered if he would undergo the same painful process that Patrick had, or if it would be easier since Dalim was already on his side. Patrick had been at war with Alistair from the moment they connected.

Violet made her way back toward Alpha House alone. The wooden streets were oddly void of people. She imagined most of the clan members were eating dinner somewhere, maybe nicely tucked away in their homes. A cold breeze lifted her ponytail from her shoulders, and she shivered. Wrapping her arms around her waist, she scolded herself for not wearing a jacket or even a sweatshirt.

The light of the moon hit her face when she rounded the final bend to Alpha House. It was up early tonight. Hopefully, Jax would have enough time to get to the ring and begin the process in safety.

Violet lifted her chin and basked in the cool light. She'd never really prayed to the moon goddess before, but now felt like as good a time as any to start. Not knowing how to do so, she opened her mind as if she were reaching for Jax through their twin-link, but this was to an open void.

*"Moon goddess above, please watch over Jax and help his trial be relatively smooth. I don't know how smooth a first shift can really be, but please make it as smooth as possible. Please protect him."*

"Praying to the goddess?"

Her mother's voice fell over her, and Violet lowered her chin. "I've never done it before. Not really. Just a thought here or there." She opened her eyes to find her mom standing beside her with a sweatshirt in hand. Offering a thank you, she took the warm material and pulled it over her head. "I'm not sure if she even hears us."

"I wish I had an answer for you." Evalyn wrapped an arm around Violet's shoulders. "I believe she watches over us, but I can't say if she hears us or not. I've defied her in my past, and I know I'll pay the price for it. But who's to say she's the one to do that, or if it simply comes down to restoring balance?"

Violet leaned away from her mom and gazed at her worriedly. "What do you mean, you defied her?"

Evalyn sighed. "I think it's time I tell you the story of your birth."

"Is this a happy story?" Violet asked, following after her mom who was walking past Alpha House.

"It depends on who you ask," Evalyn called over her shoulder as she walked up the road, then paused at the top of the hill where you could look over the clan base.

Violet made her way to her mom's side, then turned and followed her gaze.

"It's beautiful, isn't it?" Evalyn sighed, and leaned into Violet's side.

"Are you sure you should be out of bed, Mom?" Violet wrapped an arm around the older woman's waist to stabilize her.

Evalyn hadn't fully recovered from when she had lost consciousness, but continued to push her limits. Violet had been sure she'd inherited her stubbornness from Alpha Draven, but now she wasn't so sure.

With a smile, Evalyn gave Violet's shoulder a little squeeze. "I'm okay. Don't worry. Just admiring how much our clan has grown over the years."

"Do you want to sit down, at least?" Violet asked, eying the dirt road. Imagining her mother sitting on anything other than a chair was a weird thought, but at least it would exert less energy.

As if reading her thoughts, Evalyn laughed. "I'm a fully trained wolven, Violet. Do you really think I've never sat in the dirt before?"

Embarrassment fluttered warmth across Violet's face. "I just can't imagine it. I've never seen you train, and I can only ever remember you sitting on blankets when we were outside."

"Then allow me to aid your imagination." Evalyn lowered herself to the ground on the side of the road where she could still see the clan and Alpha House.

Violet blinked at her, then sat beside her. Her descent was less poised than her mother's, but the older woman didn't comment on her display. Tucking her knees close to her chest, Violet waited for her mom to continue with whatever story she was going to tell.

"You know that twins don't exist in our world. I believe Dr. Penmann has told you more than I wanted her to, but I know she did it out of the goodness of her heart."

"They do exist," Violet corrected. "But Jax and I are the only ones that have survived as a whole."

Evalyn bent her knees into a crisscross position and settled her hands in her lap. "Correct. Do you know why?"

Violet shook her head. "Some divine intervention I'm guessing."

Another chilly breeze rustled their twin ponytails and the two leaned against each other. "Not divine intervention, but something like it."

Annoyed with beating around the bush, Violet sighed. "Mom, what did you do?"

Evalyn reached over and clasped one of Violet's hands in her own. "Everything I did, I did for you. So you could live the life you deserved. With a wolf. With a mate."

The snort that escaped Violet couldn't have been stopped. "I hope you got your money back then, because I don't have a wolf."

"Violet, what did you do to Zander?"

She blinked. "What?"

"What did you do to Zander?" Evalyn repeated the question then lifted her gaze to meet Violet's. "Cas told us there were claw marks riddled across his chest."

Disbelief widened Violet's eyes. "What? No, I didn't do anything to him, and there weren't any marks on him anywhere. I was tied down."

"No scratches on him, anywhere?" Evalyn asked, sounding just as confused as Violet felt.

"No." Violet shook her head. "Mom, I *couldn't move*. But there was a wolf..."

Her words trailed off.

A beautiful, translucent wolf made up of light blues, purples, and greens. A wolf spirit with gold, silver, and bronze kaleidoscope eyes. Eyes that she'd only ever seen one other person with.

"Mom, show me your wolf eyes."

With a sad smile, Evalyn's eyes swirled into a vortex of gold, silver, and bronze.

Terror washed over Violet, making her breath come in quick gasps. "What did you do?"

"I ensured that my daughter would live," Evalyn answered. She lifted her chin defiantly as the sun slipped beneath the horizon. "I was not going to let my daughter die."

Violet jumped up from the ground and paced back and forth behind her mom. "So what? We... share a wolf? That doesn't work!"

No. It didn't. One wolf spirit per person.

Which was why...

She stared at her mom's back. "You're dying."

Evalyn's shoulders rose and fell with a large breath. "Wolven cannot survive without a wolf spirit. When you shift for the first time, Aurora will be yours."

"Then I won't ever shift!" Violet insisted, rushing to her mom's side. "I can't anyway, not without a wolf spirit to call that form forward."

"You've already started, Violet." Her mom ran an abnormally cold hand down Violet's heated face. "You call her when you fight or run. She came to your aid with Zander. I can feel her leaving me when you spar—"

"No." Violet shook her head. "Then I'll stop."

"Violet."

"I'll leave."

"Violet!"

"I'm not taking your wolf from you!"

"It's already done!" Evalyn yelled over her, shocking Violet into silence. "The deal was made before you drew your first breath."

Violet shook her head.

"And it cannot be undone."

Hot tears burned Violet's cheeks. "There has to be a way."

"Your father has searched since the moment I made the deal. There isn't one. A life for a life. At least I had the chance to watch you grow up."

"No wonder he hates me." Violet scoffed and turned to look at Alpha House. "I'm killing his mate."

A heavy sigh left Evalyn. Soon she stood beside Violet, threading her frigid fingers through her daughter's.

"Is that why you're here?" Violet breathed, her raspy voice cracking with the overload of emotion. "Is tonight the night?"

Evalyn gazed at her lovingly and shook her head. "No. I'm here to spend time with my daughter. I don't know when you'll have your first full shift, Violet. It could be tonight, it could be years from now. But it will come," She lifted her free hand to wipe at the tears drying on Violet's cheeks. "And when it does, it will be beautiful."

How could her mother call her death beautiful? How could Violet live with herself knowing her mother would have lived if she hadn't stolen the very essence keeping her alive? Agony clenched her chest, making it hard to breathe. How could she face Jax every day, knowing she was the reason their mother was dead?

No. There had to be another way.

Determination settled in her bones and she squeezed her mom's hand. "What if I—"

Both women jumped when a loud siren sounded, but it was cut short a moment later. Evalyn shoved Violet behind her.

"Mom, that was the breech siren," Violet hissed and batted her mom's arm out of the way. "We should get to the house."

"It's too late for that." The dark, maniacal laugh of Vikter Stravek chased a shiver down Violet's spine.

Instinctively, Violet jumped in front of her mom as the crazed red-eyed teen sauntered down the hill as if he had just come from Lockup. But he wasn't alone. A squadron of bloody-eyed wolven stalked behind him, eying the two women like they were their next meal.

"I told you, Violet." A sadistic, satisfied smile contorted his face. "I told you I'd get another chance at killing you."

A snarl that promised violence tore from Evalyn Draven as her eyes turned into that mesmerizing whirlpool of colors. "Stay away from my daughter!"

Vikter threw his head back and let out a hearty laugh. While his merriment continued, the other Blood Moon members stretched out around them.

"I've heard about you Mama Draven." He chuckled to himself and started pacing around them. "I've heard you've been having dizzy spells and headaches. Passing out as your time comes to an end. I've heard you're weak."

Violet growled and tried to place herself between her mom and Vikter, but even sick, Evalyn was still stronger.

"Stay back," her mom ordered as thunderous footfalls and paws bore down on their location.

Sentinel wolf and warriors collided with Blood Moon members, not bothering to slow down to assess the situation. Which meant their luna had summoned them. Alpha Draven would be there soon.

Vikter clicked his tongue as the chaos erupted around them, but he had little to no care for what was happening to his pack mates. A dark smile stretched across his face, and he hunkered down. "Shall we see who's stronger, Luna? Or do you want to hand over your daughter to me now?"

"Over my dead body," growled Luna, sinking low in front of Violet.

"That can be arranged."

A translucent aura wavered over Evalyn's skin.

Vikter hesitated. "Neat trick."

Violet's chest rose and fell rapidly as she watched Vikter stalk toward her mom. She knew his moves. She'd fought him before. Brute strength was his go-to. One hit and her mom would be done.

He wouldn't get the chance.

Using her mom's back and shoulders as a launching pad, Violet threw herself off of Evalyn, rolled across the ground, and popped up to her feet. Vikter was so taken aback by the surprise attack, that she managed to get a hit against his face and stomach, which he doubled over from, clutching his waist.

Her knuckles screamed at her when she beat them against his cheekbone, knocking his head to the side.

Dark laughter rolled out of him, and he caught her next punch in the palm of his hand. Panic settled over her. He didn't let go. Instead, he tipped his hand forward which forced hers back and eventually brought her to her knees.

"Violet!" Evalyn screamed, but she was facing off with her own opponents. Her split attention cost her a hit across the face, and she stumbled back from the impact.

Serenity settled over Violet. If she were no longer here, her mother would live. Evalyn would regain her full strength. She'd live a long, happy life. She would never have to give up her wolf.

"What are you waiting for, Vikter?" Violet snarled, the sound tearing through her still-healing throat, making it burn. "This is what you've always wanted, right?"

Hatred swam in Vikter's ruby eyes as he thought over her words.

"You said it yourself. I'm what would hurt Jax the most." She flinched when he cranked her hand back farther. "So what are you waiting for?"

There was a brief moment when Violet thought he might release her, but her taunting worked. His free hand jammed against her neck, stinging the bruised area, and cutting off her oxygen instantly.

Vikter dragged her toward him until their noses were almost touching, and she lightly clawed at his fingers. It was enough to fuel the fire within him, but not nearly enough to give her a fighting chance.

This was good. She told herself. If she died, her mom would live.

"Looks like Zander couldn't quite finish the job, huh?" Vikter sneered at her as her vision began to tunnel. "No one believed he would be able to bring you in, but he was so lost and helpless we thought we'd give him a chance." He sucked in a deep breath. "You know what I think?"

Violet curled her fingers and dragged her nails down the length of his face. He threw her into the ground then clutched his face as he howled in fury and pain. She gasped for air instinctively and scrambled away from him.

A heavy weight smashed into her lower leg, just above her ankle and something snapped. Pain ripped through her throat on the tail end of an ear-splitting scream. She rolled to her side, curled into a ball, and hovered her hands over the already purpling skin.

Deep, bloody gouges marred the side of Vikter's face as he seized her neck again and lifted her off the ground.

"Goodbye, Violet."

"NO!" Her mother's strangled scream.

Violet's gaze lifted to the moon, full and bright watching them from above. Blood tinged the air. Snarls and growls rent what should have been a peaceful night, but the sound of a clan war raged around her instead.

A sentinel warrior dropped to the ground, turning the dirt below him red. Another yelped in pain as she stumbled away from her opponent.

Violet's clan mates were in trouble. Her family was dying.

Her death wouldn't stop that.

Heat seeped through her body, starting in her chest and spreading through her limbs. An ache spread through her jaw and her ears itched. She clamped her hand around Vikter's wrist.

His eyes bugged before she clenched her fist. A startled bark of pain left him, and she fell to the ground, but instead of landing in a heap, her feet caught her in a crouch. The twinge of an old injury jarred her ankle that she was sure Vikter had snapped, but she found herself standing a moment later.

Stretching out the ache in her jaw, Violet ran her tongue over her teeth and froze. Four dagger-sharp fangs protruded where her normal canines had once been.

Vikter staggered back a step, and then rage drowned out his fear. "It's not possible!" He screamed as he rushed her. The glint of moonlight off a blade was her only warning before he slashed a knife at her gut.

She jumped back, narrowly avoiding what was sure to be a poisoned tip. He swiped the weapon at her again, and she caught his wrist before driving her elbow down onto his arm. The dagger clattered to the ground, but he was already going for his next attack. While she was distracted by one thing, he'd readied himself for a solid punch to her face. Lights danced in her vision when his knuckles collided with her cheekbone, barely missing her eye. Her head snapped back, and she released his arm.

A battle cry charged the air. The wind was knocked out of Violet when something slammed into her stomach, and she misstepped, sending her sprawling backward down the hill.

The body of another warrior stopped her careening. Black lines stretched across his skin from a stab wound in his chest. His eyes stared blankly at the moon above them.

Violet bit her lip, then flinched when her new fangs punctured her tender flesh. Sweet, metallic blood coated her mouth as she ran a hand over her clan mate's eyes. "May the goddess guide you."

Fury shook her hands while she made her way to her feet. The sun had set, but she could see as if it was only just beginning its descent. She started back up the hill where Vikter was waiting, a sneer contorting his face.

A female warrior to her right cried out when she was driven to her knee under the force of a downward strike. Her arms trembled trying to keep the knife her opponent wielded away from her face.

Violet launched herself at the Blood Moon member, tackling the surprised male to the ground. Before he could regain his faculties, Violet drove her fist against his jaw. His body went limp, and his weapon fell uselessly into the dirt.

The female Sentinel warrior stared at her wide-eyed, then nodded, and rushed off to help another. Violet rushed up the hill, pulling a ruby-eyed female off one of her clan mates and throwing her into another Blood Moon member. They rolled down the hill together, yowling in rage.

Up the hill she went, helping where she could.

When she was about twenty feet away from Vikter, he rushed her mom, who had her back to him.

"No!" Violet screamed and her legs jolted her forward.

But even her new heightened speed couldn't stop Vikter's dagger from driving into her mom's back.

Evalyn jerked in surprise, and forgot to block the weapon in front of her as it came down on her chest.

Anguish tore from Violet's throat, and a concussive blast of light blue, purple, and green erupted around her. A second and third aftershock struck, knocking everyone to the ground.

Silence answered her cry.

No one moved.

She stumbled forward on uneasy legs, then dropped to her knees beside her mom. "No, no, no," she repeated as tears poured from her eyes. A rotting stench wafted from Evalyn's stab wounds as the older woman lay on her side.

Her mom's bloodied hand trembled when she reached out to cup Violet's cheek. "My little miracle." She struggled with her words and red seeped into her mouth. "If I had known..." Evalyn's eyes drifted shut. "She was right."

"Mom. Mom look at me," Violet cried, leaning into her mom's shoulder as blood pooled into the dirt around them. "Please, open your eyes."

Evalyn's eyes fluttered open, a muted gold, silver, and bronze vortex, and for the first time in Violet's life, she felt her eyes change in response. "You are beautiful." Her mom smiled weakly. "You'll always have a piece of me with you."

Violet sobbed when her mom's smile faltered. "Mom, please, stay with me." The light faded from Evalyn's eyes, returning them to a dulled version of her usual gray. "No, mom. Don't leave me. Mom. Mom!"

Heat enveloped her body, and blinding light surrounded her as her torment rent the air.

# Chapter 29

## Jax

***The moon had reached its*** *peak in the sky, and Dalim worked with Jax* through the change in a matter of seconds, taking the pain for himself when it became too much for Jax to handle. Gray fur covered his body, and he trembled on all fours while Dalim promised it would be nearly painless next time.

He was right. Shifting back wasn't nearly as bad, but far from pleasant.

*"It will get easier each time,"* Dalim told him. *"Remember, your body had to figure out how to do what we were asking it to do. Now, it knows."*

They moved through the next stages together seamlessly, and Jax was grinning ear to ear as he walked toward his sleeping bag by the fire.

"That was amazing," he admitted out loud with a small laugh. His entire body tingled like it was brimming with power.

He bent to grab his water bottle, but gasped as pain lanced through him, driving him to his knees. Another wave propelled him forward, and he planted his fists against the soft material of his sleeping bag as images of his bloodied, lifeless clan mates flashed before his eyes.

"No," he whispered. Blinding light filled his vision before giving way to his mom, staring blankly at the sky with Violet huddled over her. "NO!" He yelled, and slammed his fists into the sleeping bag. The ground gave way beneath the force, creating two small craters that the bag sagged into.

Opening his mind, Jax felt for his mom... knowing she wasn't there.

*"Jax..."* Dalim called to him comfortingly.

"No. She was fine. Everything was fine," he insisted, then threw open the link that only he and Violet shared.

Darkness settled in the voice between their minds. He called for her, but felt her presence shy away from him. He drew back into his own mind.

"Something's wrong with Violet." He scooped up the sleeping bag and started shoving things into his backpack. "We have to get home."

*"We are supposed to remain here until sunrise."*

"Do we really need to? We've been through everything haven't we?" Jax asked, hesitating to add something else to his bag. "We are both on the same page. We want to work together. There is no quarrel here. Do we really need to stay?"

Dalim sighed into his thoughts. *"No. Let's go."*

Nodding to himself, Jax packed up as fast as he could.

When he walked from the ring, he stopped mid-step at the sight of all ten warriors on one knee. Their fists clenched over their hearts and their heads bowed.

"I assume this means you know what has happened?" Jax asked, his voice steady and sure even as his body trembled with barely contained rage and sorrow.

"Luna has passed away," came a quiet response from one of the females.

Jax swallowed the lump in his throat before adding, "It's worse than that. Our clan fell under attack while we've been here."

All ten pairs of eyes raised to meet his, waiting for his order.

"We cannot wait for sunrise to return."

They stood, almost moving as one entity.

"We are Sentinels!" Jax's power surged through him, and he saw it seep into the warriors around him. Each stood a little taller, their shoulders pulled back a little tighter, and pride for their clan flashed through their eyes as they shifted to silver and bronze. "And we will rise to defend our clan!"

A chorus of voices rose up with his. "We are Sentinels! We will rise!"

They ran as one through the forest, bypassing the vehicles for the faster speed of their wolves. Each shifted into their giant forms as they ran.

*"Dalim?"*

*"You don't even have to ask,"* answered his other half.

Jax leapt over a fallen log and gray fur rippled over his body as it expanded. Paws the size of dinner plates landed against the underbrush, propelling him through the trees alongside his companions.

Within minutes, they surged past Lockup and hurtled toward Alpha House. They moved as one unit into the blood-soaked air, then broke off, finding their own targets. Bodies were scattered in a wide circumference, and Jax padded toward the center allowing his warriors to handle any threat that might dare stand against them.

A white wolf, nearly his same size, stood over the lifeless form of Evalyn Draven, snarling at him as he approached. Jax's heart clenched. He whimpered, staring at his mom, bloodied beneath the ruby-tinted coat of the wolf standing vigil over her. He couldn't explain it, but he knew he was staring at his sister's wolf form.

*"Violet?"* Jax asked into the void between them.

The white wolf lowered her head and pinned her ears back as she bared her teeth.

*"Careful, Jax."* Dalim warned when Jax stepped toward her. *"She feels lost."*

*"I know,"* Jax answered sadly. *"I won't lose her too."*

He took another step and called to her again. *"Violet, come back."*

The white wolf thrashed her head side to side and snorted.

*"Please."*

A dark presence pressed against Jax's hind leg, and a groan made his ears swivel atop his head.

The white wolf snarled viciously, lowering herself protectively over Evalyn's body.

"Ugh, there are more of you?"

Jax's snarl matched Violet's, and he spun around. Vikter glared, and the crack of bone echoed through the air as his body began to shift.

"Have it your way then," Vikter growled as fur erupted over his skin.

Jax launched toward Vikter before his body really started shifting, spreading his jaw wide. His maw clamped down over Vikter's head and throat.

Silence filled his ears.

*"I figured you didn't need to hear that."* Dalim offered, before the sounds around them came crashing back.

Jax dropped Vikter's body, and then shook his head as he stumbled back, attempting to get the taste of blood out of his mouth. *"Was that cowardly?"* He asked Dalim when he saw the puncture wounds of his wolf teeth in Vikter's flesh.

*"No,"* Dalim answered firmly and directed their attention back to Violet's form which was now huddled in a tight ball beside their mom. *"He's done enough damage. We didn't need another fight with him."*

Jax looked around and found a young woman huddling nearby with a hand pressed over her other arm. *"Go gather clothing, and bring it back here so we can change."*

She nodded frantically and took off at lightning speed. It wasn't long before she returned and held up a pair of sweatpants for him. She turned her head away to offer some sort of privacy so Jax could shift.

The transition was practically painless, which he was grateful for. He snatched the sweatpants from her and quickly pulled them on. "Thank you. Could you please do the same for anyone else who would like to shift back?"

"Of course."

Jax eyed the wound on her arm. "What caused that?"

Her face paled. "Teeth."

"Good. That will heal. If you see anyone with a wound caused by blades," he pointed to a nearby body riddled with black lines. "Gather them in one place so they're easier to tend to."

With a nod, she headed off to follow his orders.

He sent a quick message to the doc, who was already gathering supplies, and would be there soon. Next was the alpha.

If he thought the void between him and Violet was dark, it was nothing like the hatred seeping through Alpha Draven. It grew stronger with each passing moment until Jax turned his head to see his father stalking toward them, making a beeline for his mate's body and the white wolf mourning beside her.

"Dad!" Jax jumped into his path, but the alpha didn't stop. "You're not thinking clearly. I know Mom's gone, but you can't lose yourself to this!" He pushed against Alpha Draven's shoulders then ducked under the hook his father threw blindly at him.

"She killed my mate."

Jax's eyes widened and he looked at Violet's white wolf, whimpering in her tightly curled ball. "No. Violet would never do that."

"She's the reason my Evalyn is dead!" The alpha screamed in his face. "And I'll kill her for it."

The mountain of a man lurched toward Violet, and Jax threw himself against his father's side. They crashed to the ground before both men bounced back to their feet.

"I can't let you do that."

"It's not your call to make!" Alpha Draven yelled, then beat his fist against his chest as his eyes pooled into a dull gold. "I'm the alpha of this clan!"

Unsteady glances passed between the Sentinel clan members around them. No one bowed beneath his aura.

Calm assurance settled over Jax, and he stood out of his defensive, crouched position. "I'm sorry, Dad, but not anymore."

Rage cast a haze over his father's eyes, and the older man let out a battle cry as he rushed Jax. In his blind frenzy, Noah Draven was easy to dodge. Dr. Penmann arrived with a bag full of tricks, and Jax restrained his father against his chest while she applied a heavy sedative.

Within seconds, the former alpha began to slouch in Jax's grasp. He called to a couple of warriors who hesitantly approached, eying Noah warily. "Please take him to Lockup. Stay with him. I'll be there when I'm done here."

They nodded and followed his orders.

Every Sentinel clan member he turned his attention on followed directions without a second thought. Soon, the battle-worn area was cleared of any living Blood Moon members—also taken to Lockup—and the wounded had been tended to.

Violet had not moved from her position beside their mother, and Dr. Penmann stood beside Jax as they watched her.

"She's beautiful," the doc finally said after a long stretch of silence. Her raspy tone was a soothing reprieve from his own thoughts. "I never imagined she would be able to shift."

"But she did." Jax scratched the back of his neck then folded his arms over his bare chest. "Now how do we get her back? Does this mean she has a wolf half?"

Dr. Penmann shrugged. "Your guess is as good as mine."

"I don't think she does," said a quiet, male voice and a young warrior, covered in blood, stepped toward them. "When she was fighting that guy," he pointed to Vikter's lifeless form and then continued, "she started to change. Her ears were pointy, and she had fangs and claws."

"But," the doc shook her head. "Those are lycan traits."

The young man shrugged. "If I'd been far away, I may have second-guessed what I saw, but she pulled the guy attacking me off and threw him like he weighed next to nothing."

Dr. Penmann lightly touched Jax's arm. "If he's right, then she won't have a wolf spirit. Lycan *are* the wolf."

"Okay, so how do we get her to change back?"

The doc shook her head again. "I don't know. It's a different process. It's more magic than what we do."

Sighing, Jax slowly made his way toward Violet's giant wolf form, and a small growl rolled out of her, but it turned into a whimper as she nosed their mom's arm. He held back the tears that threatened to fall. There would be a time for grieving his mom, but now was not it.

"Violet." Jax lowered himself to one knee and reached toward her. "I need you to turn back, so we can talk."

A sorrowful, low whine escaped her.

"I know this is painful." He looked down at their mom. "I know what you're feeling better than anyone. And..." Jax swallowed down the emotions rising in his throat. They made his voice crack, and it took a moment for him to collect himself again. "I need you, Violet. I can't go through this alone."

Violet's amethyst eyes settled on him, and her breathing slowed.

"Please." He held out a hand to her. "Don't make me do this alone."

If someone asked him what it was like to watch a lycan shift, he wouldn't have been able to tell them. There were no bones breaking, no fur erupting from the skin. She just... changed form. She reached for him with her massive paw, but her tiny human hand landed in his. Her clothes were intact, other than the signs of a fight.

Jax stared at her in awe as she trembled on the ground before him.

"She's gone," Violet cried and tears splashed down her cheeks, tugging at Jax's heart. "I tried to stop it. I did. I was going to give my life for hers, but they were dying! I couldn't save her!"

Jax pulled her into his arms, holding her tight as they fell apart together.

"I couldn't save her," Violet sobbed against him, her body going limp.

Pain that wasn't his own rose up in his chest to match the sorrow he felt. The difference was that guilt tormented his twin, twisting the emotions he gathered from her. He silently ordered warriors to take their mother's body and Dr. Penmann directed them where to go, leaving the twins alone while their world shattered out from under them.

That morning they had woken up as a normal wolven family. Dysfunctional sure, but what family wasn't? Now... their mother was gone. Their father may never be mentally stable again. Jax was the alpha. And Violet was a lycan.

# Chapter 30

## Cas

***Bodies littered the walk to*** *what was once Stanislaus Clan's great hall.* Members of the former clan who couldn't get out in time before the deranged Blood Moon pack invaded. Death permeated the air, and blood had become a permanent decoration with various colors of dried brown to fresh, vibrant red.

Cas' footsteps slowed when the body of a female warrior caught his eye. She had been at Sentinel Clan's gates the first time he'd arrived under the pretense that he wanted to join their clan. Multiple stab wounds made a mess of her stomach, and like so many others lying dead around him, her skin was riddled with bluish-black veins.

Rough, uneven breathing pulled his attention away from the Sentinel warrior, and he looked over his shoulder to find a couple of Blood Moon wolves watching him.

Hunger blazed in their ruby eyes. The thirst for blood and violence was all they cared about now.

Their lips curled back in snarls, some pinned their ears as well, when he turned toward them.

Cas felt the change in his own eyes, an answer to their threat, but his would never shine red.

"Don't you have a body to mutilate?" he growled at the pack of animals before him, then restarted his trek into the great hall.

They wouldn't touch him.

They needed him.

And as disgusted as it made Cas feel, he needed them as well.

He needed their numbers and raw brutality to ruin Patrick Cowen's life.

Riotous laughter reached his ears when he pulled open the great hall's doors, making him flinch. The acrid smell of wolfsbane burned his nose, and the stagnant air made it clear they needed to keep a window open or something.

Banners that had once hung proudly from the rafters were ripped in half or had been torn down to lay in shreds on the blood-splattered wood floor. Men and women lined the walls, their eyes blazing red, watching his every move as he stepped farther into the room. A multitude of small rectangular tables had been replaced by a single large table that filled the center. A giant map of California had been stretched over it, pinned down at each corner by daggers—no doubt laced with Blood Moon's favorite new weapon.

Aconitum Napellus.

Wolfsbane.

Even to humans, wolfsbane was considered highly toxic, especially the roots. It didn't take much for the bluish-purple flower to be considered lethal, but to wolven and lycan, death was imminent. Much to Blood Moon's dismay, Sentinel Clan's doctor had a cure if it was administered quickly enough.

Many had not been so lucky. Including one of Violet's close friends.

Fierce, hot anger boiled in Cas' chest at the thought of the tiny girl. The mate of his sworn enemy.

"You're back," acknowledged a mountain of a man at the head of the table. The sleeves of his shirt had been torn off to leave room for the massive amount of muscle bulging along his shoulders and arms.

A lithe woman with white dreadlocks tied behind her head was bent over a stone mortar and pestle, grinding its contents, as Cas took a few more steps into the room.

"I delivered the message."

"And the gift?" The giant man watched him with greedy, dark eyes.

Cas nodded. “Left in the bed of Patrick's truck, just inside their gates.”

The woman laughed maniacally and swiped a gloved hand over her leg, leaving a smear of white powder across her black pants before she scratched her head and continued her work.

“I have to admit.” The man smirked, and Cas’ wolf shifted uneasily in the back of his mind. “I prefer more blood and chaos, but you,” he pointed at Cas and laughed, the gravelly sound grated Cas’ ears. “You have a knack for revenge.”

“Vengeance is not the same as revenge.” Cas crossed his arms over his chest. “I am exacting retribution for a wrong that was committed.”

“And revenge is inflicting harm on someone for a wrong suffered at their hand,” answered the woman, lifting her chin just enough to watch Cas with large sea-green eyes. “We aren’t all brutes here, like Buer.” Her voice was like a lullaby wrapped in a silk blanket, and if it weren’t for the monster lurking beneath her softly tanned skin, Cas may have found himself attracted to her. Perhaps that’s why Buer didn’t so much as snarl at her for the comment... or the guy enjoyed being called a brute; that was a possibility. “Are you not seeking to cause harm?”

Cas ground his teeth. “It’s not the same thing.”

She laughed, and the crazed sound echoed off the walls. “Whatever helps you sleep at night, pet.”

When she bent over the mortar again, Buer leaned his hands over the map scrutinizing the writing and drawings that had been made on its surface.

A low groan rolled through the room.

Cas turned his head, keeping the two crazy wolven in his peripheral vision, and narrowed his eyes. “I thought the plan was to use him?”

The bane of Cas’ existence drooped in the far corner, dangling from chains that reached from the ceiling and the two walls. His curly hair was almost flat to his head, and his shirt had been removed to expose his muscled torso where a multitude of small cuts marred his flesh with tiny tendrils of black expanding from each of them.

A twinge of remorse for Violet nagged at Cas, and he beat it back down. He knew he shouldn’t have gotten so close to the little wolf, but she was different than he'd expected.

Which made his plan all the worse.

"We will," Buer answered. "Ivy wanted to experiment first."

"It's been very rewarding. Those little tentacles of perfection have been there for hours." A toothy grin spread across her face when she looked at Patrick's weakened state. "I've learned how to slow the toxin for longer periods of torture and pain. In doing so, I've also learned how to speed it up."

In the flash of an eye, Ivy smeared the pestle down Buer's arm, who leaped away from her, swiping at his arm.

Buer's eyes widened as blueish-black veins raced across his skin. "What have you done?" His words slurred. He looked around the room, but not a single person so much as twitched to come to his aid.

Ivy's grin melted into a sardonic smirk. "I've heard rumors that you've been plotting to overthrow me." Her smirk twisted into a scowl, and she seized the front of his sleeveless shirt with her free hand. "That ends now."

The dark veins stretched over Buer's chin, and he struggled for air. Ivy released his shirt, letting him crash to the ground as the convulsions started, but they only lasted a second. His dark eyes drained of color, and his body settled against the wooden floor.

With a disgusted snort, Ivy dropped the pestle into the mortar. She flicked a hand toward the mountainous body littering her floor. "Get him out of my sight."

Three ruby-eyed men stalked forward and dragged Buer's body from the great hall while Ivy made her way to the head of the room. A black throne had been brought in since the last time Cas had dared enter these walls, and she lowered herself onto its dark red cushions.

"You just murdered your best tactician," Cas noted.

Ivy shrugged a shoulder and leaned into the throne. "There are others just like him." She lifted a lazy hand and indicated the men and women lining the walls of the great hall. "Wolven who will break their backs to accomplish what I ask. Besides," she paused and a slow grin spread across her face, lighting her eyes with dark intent. "We have a pretty good hand in this game you're playing."

As if on cue, a soft feminine groan filled the room from the other side of the table.

The men and women along the wall shifted uncomfortably as Cas made his way around the large barrier.

A shock of white-blond hair spilled across the floor as a lengthy, thin body stirred. Sweat beaded her skin, and she began to tremble. Four gouges punctured the back of her neck, and two deep bites marred her forearms. Short, metallic chains practically pinned her to the floor by her wrists.

"What have you done?" Cas asked through clenched teeth as concern for the girl he'd saved with a napkin beat against his heart. "You said we would keep Lexie hostage until we had Patrick."

"And Violet," Ivy added, holding up one delicate finger. "Do not forget my prize of prizes."

Cas glared at the female dominating the room.

"Don't look so angry. It ruins that beautiful face of yours." Ivy gave a mock pout, jutting out her lower lip, then threw her head back and laughed. "All I did was grant her greatest wish—to be a wolf. Actually, I hardly did anything at all. Wolven can't turn humans." She turned her attention to the closest man in the room who had a scar running down the length of his face and neck. "Dev did the honor for me. I still have every intention of releasing her." She looked at Cas again, and a dark chuckle rolled out of her. "Well, if she survives."

The story continues in

Stars & Promise

Book 3 of the Sentinel Rising series

## NOTE FROM THE AUTHOR

Thank you for reading *Moon & Ruin*!
Please consider leaving an honest review on
Amazon and/or Goodreads!

# Acknowledgments

Moon & Ruin is only my second book, but I'm beginning to realize that the number of people I would like to thank will only continue to grow. My heart is too full for only a couple of short pages.

First and foremost, I want to thank my Heavenly Father for the wonder-ful gift he has given me. For worlds in my head and stories that never end. For giving me a love of the written word and a burning desire to share it. For not one, but two families that would love and support this dream.

An extra special thanks to my mom who gave me the tough love to keep writing this last year. You knew it was what I needed before I did. Thank you for being my alpha reader through your fight and constantly asking for more chapters! Knowing you were waiting drove me to write faster. And thank you for fighting! You are truly an inspiration to me and countless others.

And, of course, my wonderful husband, Richard. You shall forever be my anchor and I your wings. Thank you for cuddles, popcorn nights, butterbeer, and adventures. Nearly 15 years and we are still writing our own love story! Thank you for loving me through each crazy tale that pops into my head.

My kids – LW, ZABs, and KidO – I love you with all my heart. Thank you for thinking my being an author is the coolest thing in the world, for loving the silly reels I make on Instagram, and for believing I'm famous, hehe. You three are the best fan club anyone could ever ask for.

Trusting my own voice does not come naturally to me, but it has been one of the best pieces of advice I've ever received. I hold it dear to my heart and often hear those words while I'm writing and editing. Thank you, Tony, for being my big brother. Thank you for bear hugs, coffee smells, for helping me with my allergy to commas, and for making sure the boys in my stories act like boys – haha!

Every compliment I receive on my fight scenes goes to my dad. Every training, sparring, or fighting sequence is enhanced by your love of Shoto-kan.

To my siblings. My friends by choice. Thank you for always being excited about this journey! Thank you for being part of it. Thank you for your support and for spreading your love of these books with those around you.

I'd also like to thank my writing group – the Dust Jackets. Sitting beside fellow authors, writing, discussing books, geeking out over new ideas, or epically good sentences wouldn't be nearly as fun without you. Our lives make it hard to get together as often as we used to, but every time is a good time!

Oh, my beta readers! Thank you from the bottom of my heart. Thank you for making time in your busy schedules to read this book and help it become what it is today. Debby Barry, Tony Newell, Denise Nelson, Kim-berly Frost, Juli Mortensen, Heather Frost, Angel Call, Peaches - You're amazing!!!

A huge shoutout to Irlen Institute for helping me and my family. Thank you for opening the doors of possibility and helping me realize a love for reading and storytelling.

And finally, thank YOU! Thank you for diving into this story with me. I appreciate you so much.

# About the Author

Crystal Frost resides in the snow-capped mountains of Utah. She spends most of her nonwriting time being a mom to three rambunctious kids, a fur mom to Merlin the Poodle, and geeking out with her husband. Obsessing over Harry Potter and Zelda may play a part in her life as well.

As a dyslexic author, she is thrilled to be beating the odds and living her dream writing stories. She's a sucker for action-packed fiction, complex characters, and breathtaking slow-burn romances. She hopes to write exactly that and leave imprints on her reader's hearts.

Learn more about Crystal at frostcrystal.com

www.ingramcontent.com/pod-product-compliance
Lightning Source LLC
Chambersburg PA
CBHW030547310726
48979CB00010B/2060/J

* 9 7 8 1 9 5 7 0 5 1 0 3 1 *